Family Baggage

Monica McInerney grew up in a family of seven children in the Clare Valley of South Australia, where her father was a railway stationmaster. She is the author of four bestselling novels, *The Alphabet Sisters*, *Spin the Bottle*, *Upside Down Inside Out* and *A Taste for It*. She now lives in Dublin with her husband.

Praise for *The Alphabet Sisters*

'You'll be laughing out loud one minute
and crying the next' *Cosmopolitan*

'Ayone who has sisters will lap this one up'
Irish Examiner

'If you love Maeve Binchy this book will most
certainly appeal to you. This story has everything,
romance, humour, travel and adventure, making
it the perfect choice for holiday reading'
Woman's Way, Ireland, 'Book of the Week'

'McInerney is a dab hand at getting her
characters exactly right. They are utterly believable,
often lovable and familiar' *West Australian*

'A gentle and life-affirming story.
We come away feeling better about the world,
and, maybe, just a little more tender towards
those close to us' *Sydney Morning Herald*

Also by Monica McInerney

The Alphabet Sisters
Spin the Bottle
Upside Down Inside Out
A Taste for It

MONICA McINERNEY

Family Baggage

PAN BOOKS

First published 2005 by Penguin Australia

This edition published 2005 by Pan Books
an imprint of Pan Macmillan Ltd
Pan Macmillan, 20 New Wharf Road, London N1 9RR
Basingstoke and Oxford
Associated companies throughout the world
www.panmacmillan.com

ISBN 0 330 42743 1

1 3 5 7 9 8 6 4 2

A CIP catalogue record for this book is available
from the British Library.

Typeset by IntypeLibra London Ltd
Printed and bound in Great Britain by
Mackays of Chatham plc, Chatham, Kent

For Maura and her buachaillín Xavier

CHAPTER ONE

It was all coming back to her, Harriet Turner realised. The key to being a successful tour guide was to think of herself as a duck. A mother duck, to be precise. A thirty-two-year-old mother duck in charge of twelve elderly excited ducklings.

She glanced back over her shoulder, doing a quick headcount of her tour group. Good, all twelve were still in sight, obviously tired but upright, at least. They'd followed her obediently as she led the way off the plane, through passport control and here into the baggage collection area of Bristol Airport. Ten grey-haired women, two balding men, none of them under sixty-five years of age, all in comfortable clothes and sensible shoes. Each sported a large 'Turner Travel: Tours Tailored Just for You' nametag on one shoulder and a homemade 'I'm on the *Willoughby* Tour!' badge on the other. Some looked bedraggled from the long journey, but more than half were still smiling. The excitement of arriving in England had obviously lifted their spirits. Harriet was glad to see it.

Her protective feelings towards them had grown with each step of the journey. She'd arrived at Melbourne Airport two hours early so she could greet each of them personally. On the plane she'd regularly checked whether they were too warm or too cool and if they needed anything to eat or drink. During their overnight stopover in Malaysia, she'd kept a close eye when they crossed roads, walked across bridges or ate anything that might have bones in it. All the simple rules of being in charge of a group had come flooding back. Of course she could do this, she told herself for the hundredth time since her brother's surprise phone call. The tour would be a success. She'd do everything she could to make it a success.

They were among the first passengers from their flight to arrive at the baggage carousel. Harriet found a prime position, near the start of the conveyor belt and close to the exit. She was taken aback when the group clustered in a circle around her, looking up with big smiles and expectant expressions. It took her a moment to realise what they were waiting for. The customary Turner Travel welcome speech. James, her eldest brother, had begun the tradition, marking the start of each group tour with a little poem or funny speech beside the baggage carousel. He was usually so organised he had copies printed to hand out to the group members as souvenirs. Harriet's mind went blank. She had been brought on to this tour at such short notice she'd hardly had time to learn the itinerary let alone write a funny ditty.

She looked around at them again. Twelve faces looked back. Pushing embarrassment to one side, she smoothed down her official Turner Travel uniform, gave a big smile and threw open her arms.

'Welcome to England!' she cried.

It wasn't enough. They needed much more than that. She could see it in their eager expressions. She tried to ignore the curious looks from the other passengers coming into the baggage area and racked her brains. A rhyming game she used to play as a child with James and her other brother Austin sprang to mind. She'd have to give that a try. She threw out her arms again, hoping she looked confident and theatrical rather than weird and scarecrow-ish, and said the first lines she could think of:

'Here we all are on the Willoughby *tour*
Through Devon and Cornwall, across several moors
I hope you'll all have a wonderful time
And quickly forget this very bad rhyme!'

She cringed inside even as they rewarded her with a burst of laughter and applause. 'She's definitely James's sister,' she heard one of them whisper. She was saved from attempting an even worse second verse by the sound of the conveyor belt starting up with a metallic groan. Everyone sprang to attention, their eyes fixed on the emerging luggage.

As the first bags trundled past, Harriet felt a tug at her sleeve. She looked down. It was Miss Talbot. At seventy-three, she was the oldest member of the tour party. At four foot eleven, she was also the tiniest.

Her soft wrinkled face was all smiles. 'That was a lovely poem, Harriet. You hit the nail right on the head.'

'Oh, thank you, Miss Talbot,' Harriet said, smiling back. She had known Miss Talbot for as long as she could remember and was very fond of her. The little white-haired woman not only ran the Country Women's Association craft shop in Harriet's home town of Merryn Bay but also knitted most of the contents. She specialised in yellow matinee jackets and small knitted penguins with crocheted orange beaks. She was also well-known in the town for buying her clothes from children's wear shops. Harriet glanced again at Miss Talbot's travelling outfit of pink tracksuit and matching shoes, trying not to look too obviously at the Groovy Chick logo embroidered on the front. 'How are you feeling? Not too tired, I hope?'

'Oh no, Harriet. I snoozed like a bug in a rug the whole flight. And those little meals on trays were just delicious, thank you so much.'

'You're very welcome, I'm glad you liked them.' No matter how many times she'd tried to explain, Miss Talbot remained convinced that Harriet was responsible for every single thing that happened on the trip, the meals included.

Miss Talbot gave another happy sigh. 'I just can't believe we're here at last. All these years of seeing Willoughby on TV and tomorrow we're actually going to meet him. I know I'm old enough to be his grandmother, but it really is so exciting. He's such a dreamboat.'

Harriet grinned at the old-fashioned term, fighting an urge to pick up Miss Talbot and give her a cuddle. She wasn't actually sure whether Willoughby was a dreamboat or not. She could never admit it to Miss Talbot – or any of the others in the group – but she only had a dim recollection of the *Willoughby* TV series on which their entire trip-of-a-lifetime was based. All she knew was it featured a dark-haired detective disguised as a postman solving crimes in beautiful seaside villages in Cornwall.

Her brother James, lying in his hospital bed, had tried to assure her it wouldn't matter.

'You'll never know the series as well as the tour group, anyway. You know where the word fan comes from, don't you? Short for fanatics. And that's what the *Willoughby* fan club members are.' He'd lowered his voice. 'More *Willoughby* weirdos than fans, some of them, if you ask me.'

A bright blue suitcase decorated with a gaudy yellow ribbon came trundling past. 'That's mine, that's mine,' one of the tour group called. Harriet leaned across and retrieved it. In the pre-travel information pack, each member of the group had been advised to attach a distinctive ribbon as well as the Turner Travel label to their suitcases so they would be easy to spot on the carousel. They had certainly taken up the challenge, Harriet saw, as more of their bags appeared. They were decorated with everything from tartan bows to shiny red ribbons and chiffon scarves. It looked like they'd been on holiday in a haberdashery.

Another suitcase came towards them, decorated with the Turner Travel label and a bright pink pompom. It belonged to Mrs Dorothy Lamerton, the official president of the *Willoughby* fan club. English-born, wealthy, polished, a widow, she thought of herself as the social Queen Bee of Merryn Bay. Harriet thought of her as the High Queen of the *Willoughby* weirdos. She had a matching pompom around her wrist. Harriet leaned forward and lifted her suitcase off the carousel too.

Mrs Lamerton gave an imperious wave. 'Thank you, Harriet. Those conveyor belts go by far too quickly, if you ask me.'

A simple thing like collecting their clients' luggage off the carousel was just part of the Turner Travel personalised service, but Harriet still got a little glow inside at the thanks. Harriet's late parents, Neil and Penny Turner, had prided themselves on delivering personal touches. They had started the business thirty years previously in the small coastal town of Merryn Bay, two hours from Melbourne, after emigrating from England as part of the 'Ten Pound Pom' assisted passage scheme. The business had started slowly but grown successfully, with its emphasis on tailored tours and, latterly, themed tours like this one for the *Willoughby* fan club members. Harriet didn't have to try hard to be able to picture the handwritten list of Turner Travel official rules her father had pinned to the wall of the staffroom:

* *Always be punctual.*

* *Help our clients in any way you can.*

* *Check passports and tickets twice.*

* *Confirm everything and then confirm it again.*

* *Be sure to memorise everyone's names.*

Neil Turner had once drawn up an unofficial list, too, only half in jest, one Friday night when they were all sharing a bottle of wine after work.

* *Remember the quietest ones are often the most trouble.*

* *Beware the domino effect – repair all problems as quickly as possible before they cause more.*

* *All bus drivers are peculiar, the only difference will be in what way.*

* *Drink and jetlag never mix – for guides or clients.*

The most important rule, her father had always insisted, was the simplest one to remember.

* *Expect the unexpected.*

Even as it came to mind, the conveyor belt gave a jerk and came to a halt. A voice over the PA announced a slight delay with the rest of the luggage. Harriet took the opportunity to check the itinerary one more time. She flicked over the cover page showing the new brightly coloured logo of a suitcase with wings and their slogan – Turner Travel: Tours Tailored Just for You. She turned past page two: *Welcome Aboard the* Willoughby *Tour. Follow in the footsteps of one of TV's best-loved detectives in this special*

Turner Travel tailored tour of Devon and Cornwall! She stopped at page three, where the real business of the tour began. *Day 1. Arrive at Bristol Airport. We'll be greeted by Lara Robinson, our on-site guide, and then travel by bus to our hotel for the night!*

There it was in black and white. *We'll be greeted by Lara Robinson.* James had hastily had it added to the revised itinerary. That's what was supposed to happen. They were supposed to walk out into the arrivals area any minute now and be greeted by Lara, who would then lead them to a waiting bus and get them to their hotel, so they could all be tucked up asleep in their beds before eleven o'clock.

So if Lara was waiting for them just metres away on the other side of the baggage area wall, why wasn't she answering her mobile? Why hadn't she been answering it for the past four hours, in fact?

Harriet had rung her first from the airport in Paris, when she'd heard there'd been a delay with their connecting flight to Bristol. She'd got her voicemail and left a brief message. 'Lara, it's Harriet. Just to say if you're not already at the airport, there's no rush. Fog in Paris, so we'll be a bit late.' Businesslike. To the point. The only way they spoke to each other these days.

She had overheard several members of the group talking about Lara during the flight from Paris. Some of them were Merryn Bay locals and had taken Turner Travel theme tours before. They were cheerfully filling in the details for the others. Harriet heard every word. It was one of the advantages of travelling with people with hearing problems. What they thought were whispers were often almost shouts.

Mrs Lamerton in particular was holding court. As well as being the head of the *Willoughby* fan club, she had also appointed herself the Turner Travel and Lara expert. Harriet tried not to listen as her family's private business was shouted across the cabin. '. . . Yes, it's one of the last family-owned travel companies in the state. Started by the children's parents, Penny and Neil Turner, may their souls rest in peace. Marvellous people, emigrated to Australia to start a new life and just took the bull by the horns and started their own business . . . Actually, the *Willoughby* tour was my idea, well, mine and Lara Robinson's . . . Yes, she's meeting us at Bristol, she's at the end of a three-month study program at a tourism college in Bath . . . Yes, part of an international travel industry exchange program, she told me all about it . . .'

One of the other women managed to interrupt her. 'Is Lara married?'

'No, and nor is Harriet, for that matter.' Mrs Lamerton lowered her voice, but only slightly. 'They're both in their early thirties, too. One of the drawbacks of living and working in a small town like Merryn Bay, I suppose. Not a big catchment area for eligible males. They'd want to start getting a move on.'

Harriet had to force herself not to lean over the seat and explain that in fact she had been living with a man until quite recently and that Lara had also had several serious relationships over the years.

The other woman hadn't pursued that subject anyway. 'So why is Lara's surname Robinson not Turner? I thought you said all the Turner Travel tour guides were family members?'

Mrs Lamerton sounded almost triumphant with her knowledge. 'Lara grew up with them, and she's always worked with them, but she's not a real Turner. The Turners took her in when her own parents were killed in a car crash. She was only eight years old.'

'Oh, how tragic. So she's not related to them at all?'

'No, I understand both families emigrated from England to Australia at the same time. They all met on the ship, I believe.'

'So what do we call her? Harriet's foster-sister or stepsister or —?'

A PA announcement from the captain had drowned out their voices after that. Harriet wondered what Mrs Lamerton's answer would have been. Lara's title had always been a bit confusing, for all of them. Not a stepsister, or foster-sister, or even half-sister. An almost-sister, perhaps? Harriet remembered her brother Austin asking Lara once what she wanted them to call her. The four of them had been down on the Merryn Bay beach together, trying to sail a homemade raft Austin and James had built. It was about five months after Lara had come to live with them permanently. James was seventeen, Austin was fifteen, Harriet and Lara had recently turned nine. It had been a hot day. They were all dressed in shorts and T-shirts, sweating under their sunhats.

Austin had brought the subject out into the open. 'It's up to you, Lara. If you want me to call you my sister, I will.'

'I don't mind.' She'd said the same thing to Harriet when she asked.

'In that case, I'll choose a name for you myself.' Austin thought about it. 'Got it. I'm going to call you my blister, rather than my sister.'

'Blister?'

'Blister. Because you arrived suddenly but you've grown on me.'

Lara had given her sudden sweet smile. 'In that case, I'll call you my bother, instead of brother. Because you're almost my brother but you drive me a bit mad, so you're a bother.'

Harriet had always wished she'd thought of that. She'd often felt a few steps behind Austin and Lara, especially once the two of them started firing off each other.

She thought about phoning her brothers now, just in case Lara had been in touch with them to say she'd been delayed. No, the timing was bad. It was too early in the morning for James in Australia. Austin was at least in the same hemisphere, but he was probably on stage right at this moment. A percussionist with an opera company, he was currently in Germany midway through a European tour. She wondered if he had been told she'd taken over the *Willoughby* tour. It had all happened so quickly, so possibly not. She was still finding it difficult to believe herself.

It had started with a panicked phone call just four days before from James. He'd been calling on his mobile phone from an ambulance on the way to hospital, with a suspected broken leg. He'd fallen off a ladder while cleaning gutters at home. He got straight to the point. 'Harriet, I'm in trouble. I need you to take over my *Willoughby* tour.'

'The fan club tour? The one to England? The one that's leaving tomorrow?' Her voice rose in pitch with each question.

'I know it's short notice. And I know you haven't toured for ages. But please, Harriet, you know how important it is. And how much they've been looking forward to it. I'm begging you.'

Her heart started beating faster. Was she up to it? After nearly a year of saying no to even the smallest of the company tours? After everything that had happened the last time she led a group? She opened her mouth to automatically say no, of course she couldn't do it, when something stopped her. A split screen image appeared in her mind – one side showing the old her, out on the road, getting to know all the group members, loving the excitement of travelling; the other side showing herself recently: deskbound, suffocated by paperwork and unspoken pity, feeling more trapped each day. It was like being at a crossroads. The longing to be her old self again was overwhelming. There was a moment's pause and then she heard herself answer decisively, strongly.

'Of course I can do it, James. No problem.'

'Really?'

'Really.'

He'd given a loud whoop. The painkillers had obviously just kicked in. 'Harriet, you're a bloody saviour.'

She'd driven up to the Geelong hospital from Merryn Bay that night, feeling the excitement rise throughout the hour-long trip, almost cancelling out the doubts and fear. She was going back on the road. And not next month, or next year, but the next day!

James had been pale, but pain free, tucked up in a bed, his red hair and freckled skin vivid against the white of the sheets and the pillows. He was nearly forty years old, eight years older than her, but he still looked boyish. Harriet had heard her other brother, Austin, once describe James as looking like a ventriloquist's dummy, and the awful thing was she had been able to see the likeness for herself. She loved both her brothers but was the first to admit that James had missed out in the looks department. Austin had got the good looks in the family. His height, fine features and glossy black hair gave him a dashing appearance, like a pirate, Harriet had always thought.

She was neither pirate queen nor ventriloquist's dummy, but something in between the two. Her short black hair was a less dramatic version of Austin's dark locks – her hairdresser had breathlessly called his latest cut 'my own twist on the Audrey Hepburn elfin look'. Her skin was pale but without James's freckles. She was taller than average for a woman, nearly five foot seven, but still small beside her brothers. Their taste in clothes was different too. When he wasn't wearing his Turner Travel corporate suit, James unfortunately favoured check shirts and baggy jeans, adding to the ventriloquist-dummy look. Harriet preferred simple, unfussy clothes – jeans or cotton skirts; coloured T-shirts, usually in bright shades of reds, blues and greens, worn with one or two pieces of jewellery: the opal bracelet she always wore and perhaps a striking necklace or eye-catching earrings. Austin was the real follower of fashion, his lean frame the perfect clotheshorse for linen shirts and designer suits. He liked handmade leather shoes, too, when he could afford them. The only thing all three really had in common was their large dark brown eyes. Their mother's eyes.

Harriet kissed James on the forehead. She gave him a large supply of cricket magazines, grapes, crossword puzzles and chocolates, adding them to the pile his wife Melissa and daughter Molly had delivered earlier that day. At his invitation, she lifted up the cotton sheet and peeked in at the large wire cage protecting his plaster-covered leg.

'Wow, look at all that room. You could keep a few rabbits in there.'

'If they give me any more morphine I'll be seeing rabbits.' He got down to business, wincing as he leaned across the bed to pass her the itinerary and information folder. She could see extra hand-written notes on some of the pages. He'd been busy since he rang her. 'Harriet, you're a lifesaver, you know that? These international theme tours are going to be the future of the company. It would have been a disaster if we'd had to call this one off.'

She knew how deeply James cared about the family business. Since their parents had died and he and Melissa had taken over, he had thrown himself completely into making it as big a success as possible, working long hours, extending their range of tours into themed trips like this *Willoughby* one. The work was paying off. Turner Travel had nearly doubled its profits in the past year. Melissa hadn't let any of them forget it.

The *Willoughby* tour would be very straightforward, he assured her. Melbourne to Malaysia to Paris then on to Bristol. They'd have one night in a hotel and then drive the next day to their base in St Ives, where they'd meet up with their special guest, the English actor who had played Willoughby in the program. They'd spend the next five days visiting locations from the TV program. After that she was to escort the group to Bath for a handover to another company for two of their themed tours, an *All Creatures Great and Small*-flavoured visit to Yorkshire, followed by a *Monarch of the Glen* tour of Scotland.

'No need to completely reinvent the wheel,' James explained. 'We've set up a good working relationship with some of the UK companies. We link in with some of their tours, and they'll send people over for our *Neighbours* and *Thorn Birds* tours down the track. And that's it. You collect the group in Bath on their return and then bring them home safely. You'll be away two weeks all up.'

She'd been scribbling page after page of notes as he spoke. She looked up to find him studying her with a look of concern and affection.

'I'm throwing you in the deep end, Harriet, but you'll be okay, I know it. You were a great guide before all that stuff happened and you will be again.'

She was surprised at how much his words meant. James rarely spoke about personal things like that. She was about to thank him, when he leaned back against the pillow.

'And you won't be on your own with them once you get to

England,' he said. 'I've asked Lara to meet you at Bristol Airport and travel with you for the first couple of days. Just until you really find your feet again.'

'Lara?'

James didn't notice her tone of voice change. 'Don't you think it's a brainwave? The tourism college she's doing that course at is in Bath, practically down the road from Bristol. And the *Willoughby* tour's her baby really. She knows it all inside out. Better than me, even. She said it was no problem, she could take a few days off from her course to give you a hand. I rang her as soon as you said yes.'

'But you just said you knew I could handle it.'

'I do, but Lara's so close, it makes sense for her to help you out. It's all organised. She'll meet you at the airport, stay with you in the hotel nearby the first night, and then travel down in the tour bus to St Ives with you the next day.' He gave her a smile. 'The two of you will just have to toss a coin to see who gets the guide seat and the microphone.'

Harriet gave a half-smile back, trying hard not to let her feelings show. The excitement at the thought of going back on the road had abruptly faded. She twisted the bracelet she wore on her left wrist. It was a new habit. She'd only started doing it in the past few months. It hadn't occurred to her that she would be meeting up with Lara, let alone travelling with her. What could she have said to James, though? 'I'm sorry, James, but I'm not sure I can do the tour for you after all. I don't think Lara and I can work together any more.'

What would he have said in return? 'But why not? I always thought you were the greatest of friends. What's happened? Something you did? Something she did?'

Something Lara had done. But James hadn't noticed her reaction or given her time to explain to him how she felt. He'd finished his briefing, she'd driven back to her flat in Merryn Bay, hurriedly packed and now here she was, less than seventy-two hours later, in England, in charge of a group, just minutes away from meeting Lara again.

Mrs Lamerton came up beside her at the baggage carousel. 'The hotel's not far from the airport, I hope, Harriet, is it? We're all very tired.'

Harriet glanced at her watch. It was getting late. 'It's just down the motorway, Mrs Lamerton. I'll have you there as soon as I can, I promise.'

She stepped back out of Mrs Lamerton's earshot and surreptitiously tried Lara's mobile again. Still no answer. Where was she? Had she had an accident on the way to the airport? Or was it something as simple as losing her mobile? And if she wasn't there, should Harriet wait? Or get her poor tired group to their hotel as quickly as possible and then worry about Lara?

She felt a slow rising of anxiety and tried to ignore it. Another of her father's travel rules came to mind, also a duck metaphor, she realised. *A good tour guide is like a duck on a pond – serene on the surface and paddling like mad underneath.* He was right. Her job was to keep calm and show leadership, to stay serene in the face of all difficulties. She tried to imagine herself gliding across a pond but the only creature that came to mind was an agitated cat, eyes dilated, back arched, fur bristling. She imagined the group's reactions if they were to turn and see their tour guide down on all fours, hair standing on end, hissing and spitting beside their suitcases. She tried some deep breathing instead.

The conveyor belt started again and the last pieces of their luggage came past. She added them to the trolley and did a quick count. It was all there. Another step of the tour successfully completed. She decided it was a sign. Of course Lara was waiting for them outside. She would be friendly and Harriet would be just as friendly back. And yes, the next few days together would be difficult – very difficult – but they would work through it. They had to work through it. It was what her parents would have wanted . . .

Gathering her twelve ducklings around her, pushing a laden trolley in front of her, Harriet took another deep breath and stepped through the door into the arrivals area.

In Berlin at that moment, Austin Turner stood poised, watchful. He was dressed in a formal black suit and immaculate white shirt, with his dark hair slicked back. The music swirled around him, building to a crescendo. On the stage to his right the heavily made-up woman was kneeling, face wretched, voice pure, as she mourned the loss of her husband, only seconds from seizing a knife and plunging it into her own body.

Austin felt the wood of the hammers in his hands, running his thumbs along the smooth surface as the music surged. He watched the conductor, waiting. The sound of the violins and cellos was building, quickening, as the drama reached its height on the stage. The soprano's voice and the orchestra's music intertwined, rising and falling. Austin didn't need to look out into the audience to know that every person was sitting still, their eyes wide, caught in the story, seduced by the sounds. He focused on the conductor, waiting. The nod came, at last. Austin hit the hammer against the cymbal, the noise like a thunderclap, sharp, sudden. Again. Again. He kept one eye on the conductor, almost sensing the movement of the knife in the soprano's hand in the corner of his vision, matching his sounds to her actions. Again. Then his two hands a blur, rolling and hitting against the sides of the drum, the echoes of sound layered with the other instruments, a cacophony of swirling and building up and then —

Silence.

A faint panting from the soprano.

And then like a wave of sound, the applause, rushing at them. Austin bowed his head. Ten years of study, no money, constant travel, waiting for what seemed like hours every night for his short time in the limelight, when the only sounds filling the hall were the ones he was making. It was worth it, every time.

There was one curtain call. Then a second. As he was turning to the audience for the third bow the mobile phone in his pocket vibrated. Just as well he'd put it on mute before he'd come into the pit. The bassoon player had been bawled out in front of the whole orchestra at rehearsals last week when his mobile went off midway through the tower scene. It hadn't helped that he'd answered it, of course. Strictly speaking they were all banned from keeping their mobiles on them. But they all disobeyed. The violinists couldn't get away with it, under the nose of the conductor, but it was easy enough for Austin, tucked away to the side, surrounded by kettle drums and percussion instruments. Sometimes entire scenes went by and he didn't have a thing to do. He'd taught himself to text without looking, which filled some of the time. The messages were often even more misspelt than usual, but that was the whole fun of texting anyway. And he needed something to occupy his time. He'd become bored enough of the opera storyline by the fiftieth time he'd seen it.

He waited until the conductor had left the stage and the other musicians had filed past him before he checked the new message. It was from Harriet. One word.

HELP!

CHAPTER TWO

Harriet's bedside digital clock clicked over to midnight. Outside her door, the hotel corridor was quiet. Fifteen minutes had passed since she'd last heard the nearby lift being used. She knew the tour group members were safely in their hotel bedrooms, probably fast asleep already. Most had been so tired they'd started to fall asleep in the bus on the way from the airport. They'd only needed to be guided gently up to their rooms, although Mr Fidock, one of the two men, had insisted on being guided gently into the bar.

'Watch him, Harriet, won't you?' James had warned her. 'Mr Fidock treats these tours like lonely hearts club outings. He had poor old Mrs Kowalski in tears at the end of the *Man from Snowy River* tour two years ago. She fell for him, hook, line and sinker.'

'Mr Fidock? The short bald man? But he's more than seventy years old.'

'And so is Sean Connery, as Mr Fidock will tell you over and over again.'

Harriet was still wide awake. She'd changed out of her Turner Travel uniform into soft brushed-cotton pyjamas and her favourite red socks. She was now sitting cross-legged on top of the bed, facing the TV in the corner of the bedroom. Before she got started she took off her glasses, polished the lenses and put them back on again. She'd taken her contact lenses out after she'd spoken to

Austin, finding the routine task oddly soothing.

He'd replied to her text message within ten minutes, phoning as soon as he got off the stage, but it had taken a while to get him to take her seriously. It was often hard to get Austin to take anything seriously.

'Lara's gone missing?' he'd said. 'That's taking the *Willoughby* plot theme a bit far, isn't it? She's run off with some Cornish smugglers, has she? She's hiding in sea caves as we speak, drinking rum with pirates?'

'Austin, please, listen to me.'

Harriet ran through all that had happened: the unanswered mobile phone calls; Lara's non-appearance at the arrivals gate; the waiting for another half-hour before she decided to get the group to the hotel, trying Lara's numbers all the while. Once in her own hotel room she had tried Lara's flat in Bath yet again, and finally got an answer. Not from Lara, but from her flatmate, Nina. Harriet had texted Austin as soon as she'd hung up from her.

Austin's light-hearted mood changed as Harriet filled him in on the conversation.

'According to Nina, Lara's gone away for a while and it's nothing to do with the *Willoughby* tour. She seemed surprised I didn't know anything about it. She said Lara packed a suitcase and left this afternoon.'

'But left for where? She's supposed to be with you.'

'That's what I said. But Nina was positive that's what Lara told her. Lara handed her a month's rent in advance, asked her not to let out her room and then left.'

'Nina didn't misunderstand? She's sure Lara wasn't on her way to meet you?'

'Absolutely sure. Nina said she actually asked Lara what had happened with the *Willoughby* tour. She'd obviously been talking about it. Lara told her there'd been a change of plan and she wouldn't be doing it after all. That she had some other family business to take care of.'

'What family business? We're her family business.' Austin started firing more questions at her. Yes, Harriet had also checked with the local police and hospitals and no, there hadn't been any reports of accidents. No, Lara hadn't left any messages for her, either. She'd checked at the airport information desk, at the hotel, under her name, James's name, Turner Travel, everyone. Nothing.

'Did Nina say Lara seemed upset? Different in any way?'

'She said she was as calm as she always is. Focused was the word she used.'

Austin was quiet for a moment. 'It's weird. Really weird,' he finally said. 'This isn't about a man, is it? She hasn't mentioned meeting anyone to you?'

'No, she hasn't.' That wasn't surprising. In the few times they had spoken on the phone since Lara had left for England they had barely talked about the weather, let alone their social lives. 'What do you think I should do, Aust? Do I call the police? Go and look for her?'

'What could you say to the police? That she's left voluntarily? People do that all the time. The police will just laugh. And you can't go looking for her, can you? Not with a tour group trailing behind you. You can still go ahead with the tour, can't you, even if she's not there?'

'I think so. I mean, of course I can. I have to. They're so excited, there's no way I'd call it off.'

'Where did you tell them Lara was tonight?'

She knew he was thinking of another of their father's rules.

Never tell clients anything they don't need to know. 'I said she'd been unavoidably delayed. I'll think of something for tomorrow. Sudden study commitments perhaps. They've already had one change of tour guide, I don't want to unsettle them any more.' Her mind was racing now. 'And I'll just have to try and answer their questions about *Willoughby* as best I can. Change the subject as quickly as I can.'

'Change the subject? When the whole subject of the tour is *Willoughby*?'

'It'll be fine,' she said, hoping he couldn't hear the uncertainty in her voice. 'I'll just have to bluff it.'

'Aren't you forgetting something?'

'What?'

'Willoughby himself? Isn't the actor joining the tour too? He's the one they'll be asking questions of, not you, surely?'

'Oh my God, the actor!' Harriet laughed with relief. 'Austin, I love you. I'd completely forgotten about him. Let me check he's where he should be. Can I call you right back?'

She quickly dialled their hotel in St Ives, two hundred miles down the north Cornwall coast. If all had gone to plan the actor was in his hotel room at this moment, waiting for their arrival tomorrow afternoon. Yes, the young receptionist reported, Mr Patrick Shawcross had arrived safely that evening. Yes, the welcome basket of fruit had been delivered to his room. He had asked not to be disturbed but if it was urgent . . .

'No, no, that's fine, I just wanted to check he was there. Thanks very much.' She called Austin back and reported the good news.

'There you are. That'll take some of the pressure off you at least,' Austin said. 'Did you ever see any of the *Willoughby* programs? I'm not much help, I remember the theme tune after the news every Sunday night, but those slow motion shots of the actor always put me off.'

'I've got the videos with me. I didn't get the chance to watch them before I left.'

'Can you have a quick look at them tonight? Fast-forward through a couple of them if you have to. If nothing else they might put you to sleep. And in the meantime, leave Lara to me. I'll start making some phone calls. See if I can find out what's going on.'

'Are you sure? Have you got time?'

'I did have a date with one of my adoring fans tonight, but she'll just have to wait. Treat 'em mean, keep 'em keen, as the saying goes.'

'Austin, stop it,' she said, automatically. It worried her how cavalier Austin was about women sometimes. He always said he was too young to settle down or that he travelled too much to be a good catch.

'Relax, Harold,' he said, slipping into his childhood nickname for her. 'I respect my female fans. They adore me. It's a win-win situation. Have you told James what's happened, by the way?'

'Not yet, I didn't want to wake him. You're the first person I've rung.'

'I do have you well trained. No problem, I'll call him in a little while. It'll do him good to wake up early.'

'You know he's in hospital?'

'I do. My basket of grapes must have gone missing in the post.'

'He's a nice man, Austin.'

'He is. It's not his fault he's married to a she-devil. I'll ring him and then we'll get onto Lara, too, keep trying her mobile until we find out what's happened. We'll worry about her, you just worry about the tour group. Promise me.'

'I promise. And thanks, Aust.'

'Any time. And Harriet, I mean it, relax. It'll be fine. You'll be fine. You know and I know James wouldn't have let you within a hundred yards of one of his precious tours if he didn't think you were up to it. He's been trying to get you back on the road for months, hasn't he?'

'How did you know that?' The last she knew, Austin had told Melissa he didn't want to receive any updates or monthly reports about Turner Travel. He'd been extremely forceful about it. Something about Melissa sticking her overbearing, patronising, self-aggrandising reports somewhere the sun doesn't shine, if Harriet's memory was accurate.

'I pay Glorious to spy for me.' Glorious was his nickname for Gloria Hillman, Turner Travel's long-time office manager and a close family friend. 'Someone has to keep an eye on my inheritance. Now seriously, relax, little sister. Repeat after me: "I will be fine. I can handle this if I just take it step by step." Better than handle it. You'll do it really well.'

Behind his joking tone, she knew he really was serious. Austin knew better than anyone how important this tour was to her. He was the one who'd come to her rescue nine months earlier after that last disastrous trip. She smiled into the phone. 'You're actually very nice underneath everything, aren't you?'

'Talented and handsome too. It's a devastating combination.'

He'd cheered her up, as always. Calmed her down too. And despite the light-hearted tone, his advice had been good. Just the matter-of-factness of going down to the reception desk to ask about the use of a video player had helped. The receptionist, hair tied back so tightly she nearly looked plastic, had hardly blinked at the request. A video viewing at this time of night? 'No problem at all, madam. I'll have the equipment delivered to your room. Would you like tea and sandwiches delivered while you work?'

Harriet thanked her stars they were staying in a business-oriented airport hotel for their first night in England, and not a homely B&B. Within half an hour she had been set up, the stack of *Willoughby* tapes on the bed beside her. She also had a cup of tea in one hand, a remote control in the other, a round of sandwiches on a plate by her elbow and the tour itinerary on her lap. She forced herself to put the troubling thoughts about Lara to one side and pressed play, willing her brain to take in every detail of the program.

The screen flickered into life to a soundtrack of faint music and the barking of a dog. A man appeared on screen, walking across a very green field. He looked to be in his early thirties, tall, his dark curly hair ruffled in the wind. He wore a duffle jacket over black jeans. His face was craggily good-looking, interesting rather than handsome, his eyes dark, shadowed. As he kept walking, the blue of the sea became visible behind him. The music grew louder, a cross between folk music and something orchestral. The shot widened to include a farmhouse, beyond it a jutting cliff, further still a lighthouse. Lettering appeared.

PATRICK SHAWCROSS
as
Willoughby

More barking filtered in through the music. The man stopped, turned. A black and white dog came running towards him. The two kept walking along a cliff path, a spectacular bay in the background, all soaring cliffs and blue water. The shot changed to an aerial view of a red post-office van making its way down narrow tree-lined roads. A montage of shots followed, as other cast members appeared on screen against a backdrop of harbours, old churches, farms and moorland. Harriet pointed the remote control at the television, pressing the fast-forward button. There wasn't time to watch the opening credits. What she really needed was *Willoughby* in pill form.

She watched most of the first episode, pressing fast-forward again whenever the action slowed. The plot involved the arrival of Willoughby in the town of St Ives under mysterious circumstances, shots of several curious villagers watching him unpack his few belongings from a battered old Rover, and then a dramatic shot of him standing looking out over a cliff, talking to himself. It quickly moved on to the theft of some valuable paintings from a country-house hotel clinging to the hillside of a picturesque village nearby. The setting was magnificent, with spectacular views across the sea. Harriet remembered it was one of the first stops on their tour.

She flicked through the itinerary on her lap and read the activity description James had written. '*Let's go walking in Willoughby's footsteps in beautiful Lynton on the north Devon coast, better known to the true fan as Ecclesea! We'll also visit the very hotel that played host to the action in several episodes, including "The Case of the Stolen Sketchbooks" and "The Case of the Mournful Model".*'

She leafed through the other notes James had given her, feeling like she was cramming for a 'Trends in TV Light Entertainment' exam. *Willoughby* was like a cross between the Agatha Christie *Miss Marple* series and *All Creatures Great and Small,* she decided.

She'd already gathered that Willoughby – it was never explained if that was his first or last name – was a postman with a mysterious past, possibly involving a career with Scotland Yard and a nervous breakdown, now living on the north Cornwall coast, delivering mail to farms and villages and managing to solve crimes along the way.

Among the press clippings James had given her she found a serious magazine article from several years previously, trying to explain the show's continuing popularity in Australia. It had lasted for only two runs on the BBC, but in Australia it was repeated year after year, tucked cosily in its Sunday evening slot, after the news, alternating between reruns of *Fawlty Towers* and *To the Manor Born*. English migrants loved it, the magazine noted, and so did plenty of Australians not of English descent or origin, happy to be reassured by its safe, comforting messages.

'Emigrants look back at their homeland through increasingly rose-coloured glasses. For some, the sentimental outlook is supplied by music. For others, TV programs. *Willoughby* has managed to combine the two with its snapshot or capsule form of English life.

All the elements are there – the mysterious man with a past and a handy penchant for sleuthing, the job as postman a convenient cover, allowing him to travel the length and breadth of south-west England. His co-stars, a simple but wise farmer, a member of the upper class and the ordinary postmasters and mistresses at surrounding rural post offices, supply additional colour.

The glorious Cornish countryside plays a role too, with scenes of fishing villages, wild coastline and chocolate-box farms featuring prominently. Even a dog – so beloved in English society – has a part to play.

The plots might be predictable, the crimes old-fashioned, the acting uneven, but it somehow feeds right into the heart of a nostalgic viewing population.'

The whole tour had actually been sparked by another magazine article, Harriet remembered. They had all been at their desks late one morning when Mrs Lamerton swept in. Mrs Lamerton did a lot of sweeping in to shops in Merryn Bay. Settling herself in the waiting area until Melissa was free to take her to lunch, she had started leafing through the pile of magazines. On the top was a collection of old English magazines that Lara had found in a junk shop. She'd added them to the pile for novelty value.

Harriet had been working at her computer, updating the monthly newsletter they sent out to each of their clients. The job had been given to her when it became clear she wouldn't be able to go back on the road again for a while. Perhaps Melissa had been trying to put it to her nicely, but it had come out all wrong. 'We're hoping it's a nice simple job for you, Harriet. But if it gets too stressful at any stage, if you feel that little problem of yours coming on, you just let me know and we'll put you onto something else in a whisker.'

'Oh good heavens!'

They'd all turned at the gasp from Mrs Lamerton in the waiting area.

She was waving one of the English magazines at them. 'Where did you get this from? I used to get this magazine every single week. In fact, I remember this very issue. I read everything about *Willoughby* I could get my hands on.'

Mrs Lamerton sighed as Lara and James came over to her. 'We were still living in England when they showed the first episode. I'll never forget it. It was the night we decided to emigrate. We were so thrilled when we arrived here to see it on Australian TV too. It's still my favourite program, you know.'

Lara had looked at the magazine article while Mrs Lamerton gave James a detailed commentary, explaining that the series was set in fictional villages along the north Cornwall coast but in reality had used different aspects of a number of real towns and locations in Devon and Cornwall: the cobbled streets and long beaches of St Ives; the wild Bodmin Moor scenery; the village green of Widecombe-in-the-Moor; the harbour at Port Isaac; cliffside country hotels in Lynton. The magazine had full-colour photos and poetic descriptions of each setting.

'And would all these places still be there?' Lara asked, glancing up from the magazine.

Mrs Lamerton made a tchy sound. 'They've stood the test of time for hundreds of years, Lara. Of course they'd still be there. You have to remember, Australia hadn't even been discovered when these places were celebrating their sesquicentenaries.'

Harriet tried not to smile. Mrs Lamerton always had the unfortunate habit of talking about Australia as if it were a misbehaving toddler.

'I'm ashamed to say I've never been to Cornwall,' Mrs Lamerton continued. 'It's one of the few parts of England Timothy and I didn't visit.' Timothy was her late husband. He had died ten years previously, three months after he and Mrs Lamerton had retired to Merryn Bay. He had been something in the army, or the navy, no one had ever found out exactly what. It was often hard to get a word in around Mrs Lamerton. 'Though of course I feel I know it like the back of my hand from watching *Willoughby*. Such a beautiful place. And of course having a handsome young man like Willoughby stride through it gave it extra appeal too.' She gave a surprisingly girlish giggle.

Nothing was said at the time, but over the next few days Harriet noticed Lara looking up English websites. A guide to Devon and Cornwall appeared on her desk. So did photocopies of the

Willoughby magazine article. She revealed it all at the next planning meeting, standing up to make her presentation. Her uniform was so crisp it could have been freshly ironed, her shoulder-length blonde hair shining, her make-up flawless. Across the table Harriet wished she'd thought to redo her lipstick before the meeting, too. She bit her lips so much while she was working her lipstick was usually eaten off before morning tea.

It was a very impressive presentation. Lara had put together a full itinerary for a *Willoughby* tour of Devon and Cornwall, taking in all the locations from the TV series. She'd discovered that there were dozens of *Willoughby* fans in the Merryn Bay area. She'd put the word around and already had firm interest from eight people. She knew there would be no problem getting that up to twelve. She'd done costings, timetables and market research. It was extremely viable.

'Lara, you are a gem,' Melissa said, beaming. 'I couldn't have done it better myself. Absolutely full steam ahead with it, I say. Well done. Now Harriet, what about you? Any ideas for new tours?'

Harriet stammered an answer. 'No, I'm sorry, nothing concrete yet.' She'd felt unable to think about a shopping trip to Melbourne at that time, let alone plan an international tour.

'No? Never mind.' Melissa looked like she did mind. 'But you're happy enough with your workload? Not too much for you?'

'It's fine, thanks,' Harriet said as brightly as she could. It wasn't fine. It was hard and scary and suffocating, all at once. She sometimes felt that she had no right to still have a job there, that all the others were carrying her. Lara especially. It was like they were on a seesaw, she realised. Lara flying high, Harriet falling lower and lower.

Over the next few months, Lara methodically set about organising the *Willoughby* tour. The clincher had been the discovery that Patrick Shawcross, the English actor who had played Willoughby, was alive and well and living in Boston. It had taken Lara some time to discover the fact, sending emails and faxes to the ABC in Sydney, the BBC in London and to actors' agencies in the UK before she was given a contact number for a large American agency in New York. She'd sent two emails without reply and finally decided to phone them, coming in early one morning to make the call.

Lara had told the story over morning tea, twisting her blonde hair as she spoke, her habit when she was amused about something. 'I said I was hoping to speak to someone about one of their clients, a Mr Patrick Shawcross. And the receptionist said, "I'm sorry, his name again? Parma Shorkle, did you say?"' Lara was laughing now. 'I ended up spelling it three times. I had to tell her that he'd starred in a program on English TV called *Willoughby*. I heard a click of keys again and then she said, "I'm sorry, ma'am, we don't represent anyone called Willoughby, either."'

She had been passed from person to person until she had found someone who thought she knew who he was.

'I think she was on work experience from their French office. "You want him to do what? Why?"' Lara had explained they had seen the article about *Willoughby* in the magazine and wanted to base a tour around it. ' "When? And you would pay his expenses? And a fee?"' Lara did an excellent impersonation of a French accent. 'It was surprisingly reasonable. It sounds like he doesn't do much work with them any more so she was probably quoting from the last job he did. But I think we have him. I faxed over the magazine article to her and the dates we'd need him in Cornwall, and she said she'd come back to me as soon as she'd been in touch with him. If he says yes, I send all the flight details and a fee to her, they take their commission and we have our tour.'

Less than a week later, a fax had arrived from the agency. It was good news. They'd all gathered to hear Lara make the call.

'Mrs Lamerton, I'm calling about the *Willoughby* trip. What would you say if I was to tell you that not only is a tour to all the locations from the series possible, but our special guest would be Patrick Shawcross, the actor who played Willoughby himself?'

They had all heard the squawk of delight.

Harriet remembered James's words the night of the handover in the hospital. He was right. The tour really had been Lara's baby. Which made it even stranger that she would abandon it like this. Simply announce to her flatmate there had been a change of plan. Just up and leave . . .

Another episode ended and the closing credits played. Harriet sped through the opening credits of the next episode, then paused while she checked James's itinerary notes again. He had become very fond of exclamation marks in the past year, she noticed. '*Here in Marazion near Penzance is the dramatically stunning island castle of St Michael's Mount, used as the setting for those calamitous wedding scenes in "The Case of the Titled Temptress"! En route to Marazion keep a look out for the police station, scene of the hilarious confrontation between Willoughby and Sergeant Carling in episode eight, "The Case of the Hunted Hounds". The sergeant certainly met his match in our Willoughby, didn't he?!!*'

Harriet pressed fast forward again and Willoughby sped around the town in his red mail van, hopping in and out with amazing dexterity, before driving down a tree-lined lane and through some tall gates. She released the button and let it play normally again, as he pulled into the driveway of a large mansion, the gravel sounding under the wheels of the car. He climbed out and stood, broodily good-looking, against the van. The front door opened and a well-groomed blonde woman came down the steps and slowly made her way towards him. She was wearing a trim, pale-blue suit, high heels and a lot of jewellery for that time of the day.

'*Willoughby*,' she drawled.

'*Lady Garvan*,' he said. The shots were now full close-up. '*You know why I'm here?*'

She moved forward and stroked his cheek. '*I know why I hope you are here.*'

He didn't react. The camera pulled even closer and Harriet pressed pause. The actor certainly looked the part of a man with a mysterious past, with his dark hair and dark eyes. Would he have aged well? Fifteen years had passed. She leafed through the information pack but there were no photos of what Patrick Shawcross looked like these days. According to the brief biography, he had been living in America since the series ended, 'pursuing his acting career and other interests', whatever they might be.

She fast-forwarded again. As always the crime was solved and analysed in a scene between Willoughby and his best friend, George the farmer, sitting in their favourite pub in St Ives, enjoying a pint of bitter and shaking their heads.

'*That's people for you, George.*'

'*Aye, Willoughby, so it is.*'

Mr Douglas and Mr Fidock, the only two men in the tour party, had acted out that same scene at the airport. And on the plane. And in the hotel lobby. They were surprisingly good mimics, Harriet saw now. They had the Cornish accent with its rolling r's just right. She sped through the opening credits of the next episode as well, nearly laughing out loud as the black and white collie went

tearing across the fields. Had Lara and James thought about tracking down Patch the dog as well, Harriet wondered. She pictured
a sort of old pets' home, full of ageing animals from different TV
series, sitting around in their luxury, pastel-painted kennels and
hutches, reminiscing about their favourite scenes. The rabbits from
Watership Down. The cat from the opening credits of *Coronation
Street*. The pigs from *Babe* . . . She blinked hard, forcing herself to
concentrate.

An hour later she had fast-forwarded through all of the episodes
and felt slightly more familiar with the show. As long as everyone
in Cornwall did everything at twenty times the normal pace she
would be perfectly fine. She stood up and stretched, first one arm,
then the other, her bracelet sliding down her arm as she lifted her
left hand into the air. She had worn it every day for the past year.
It had belonged to her mother, a present from Harriet's father the
year they arrived in Australia. It was made of ten opals, each gem
a swirl of blue and red fiery colour embedded in gold rectangles,
simple but striking. As a child, Harriet had loved to sit on the
Merryn Bay beach beside her mother and move her wrist up and
down so the blue of the opal was lined up against the blue of the
sky. 'That's it, Mum. Leave your hand there. It's exactly the same
colour as the sky, isn't it?'

Harriet had a flash of wanting to be on that Merryn Bay beach
right now. A longing to be taking an early morning swim, with the
sea to herself. She and her niece Molly used to laugh about the fact
that Molly did all her swimming in the chlorinated swimming pool,
while Harriet stuck to the sea.

She decided on fresh air in the absence of water and went over to
her hotel window. It opened only a little way, looking out over the
car park, to darkness beyond. Her face was reflected back at her, her

skin pale, her hair a black cap, spiky in places from where she had been running her fingers through it. She didn't have to look closely to know there would be an anxious expression on her face.

The five days stretched out ahead of her. She thought of the daily trips to the different *Willoughby* locations, the problems that might crop up with traffic delays, bad weather. There were bound to be personality problems, too. There always were on these group tours. The only variable was how quickly they happened and how she reacted. *Expect the unexpected.*

As the list of possible black spots grew longer in her mind, she felt a shimmer of the frightening feeling inside her. No, she nearly said aloud. Not here. Not now. Think positive. Look on the bright side. She shut her eyes and did the breathing exercises she'd been taught. Talk to yourself, Harriet, she said as she breathed. It won't happen again. You will be fine. You are fine. Breathe in, breathe out. Centre yourself.

Slowly, gradually, the panic subsided. Don't be afraid of the feeling, her doctor had said. Understand it and where it comes from. The more you know, the less you'll fear it.

That was the trouble. She knew more about it than she wanted to. She could pinpoint exactly when her panic attacks had started and she also knew exactly what had caused them. She was reminded of it every day. Their empty chairs in the office, their voices missing from conversations, the daily task of explaining to people ringing Turner Travel asking to speak to Penny or Neil Turner. The knowledge that her parents no longer lived just metres away in the house that adjoined the Turner Travel office, her childhood home. Reminder after reminder. Even after the tour went wrong, after she had got out of hospital and come back to work, the deep sadness, the desperation had stayed with her.

She remembered her first week back at work, when it had all seemed so hopeless and overwhelming. Lara had come in early and left a little vase of jonquils on her desk, Harriet's favourite flower.

'Harriet, if I can help, will you just ask?'

She'd been very moved, as she had easily been at that time. She'd looked up and smiled gratefully. 'Thanks, Lara.'

'I mean it. With the tours, or any itineraries.'

'Thank you.' Even through her sadness, Harriet had noticed Lara's self-assurance, her elegance. Her clothes were immaculate, her hair tied back in a stylish ponytail. Even her nails were manicured. How did she manage it, Harriet had wondered. She felt like she was falling apart, inside and outside.

In the background, Melissa answered the phone. 'Oh, I'm sorry, you can't have heard the news,' she said as loudly as ever. 'Mr and Mrs Turner passed away earlier this year. Yes, both of them. No, not together, one after the other. Yes, it was tragic. Very hard on the children. They were with them, thank God. Well, all except Harriet.'

She and Lara were looking at each other as Melissa spoke. Harriet had replayed that moment many times in the past three months. She had seen the grief and the hurt in Lara's eyes, as she knew Lara would have been able to see it in hers. But what else had she seen in Lara's eyes? A flicker of guilt? Or had she imagined that afterwards? Wanted to see it?

'Yes, it's very tragic,' Melissa had said again. 'We miss them every day.'

Every day, every hour. Harriet hadn't needed Melissa's words to remind her how she felt. Every detail was only ever moments away from being recalled. It was like having something on loop tape, always on her mind, there for her to review, replay, time and again, wishing for a different ending, wanting to make it different, wishing with all her heart that it could be. Even standing here, in a motorway hotel in England, it was the same. All the memories, as clear as if it had happened the day before, not the year before.

CHAPTER THREE

Harriet called into the travel agency just before closing time the day her father would die. Her parents always worked the half-day on Saturday, insisting the children had the weekends off. She and her boyfriend Simon were on their way to Melbourne for the day on a shopping trip. He'd lost his mobile phone and was going to buy a new one, while Harriet wanted to browse in the bookshops. She had a cup of tea with her mother and collected measurements for some curtain material she wanted Harriet to buy from a department store in the shopping centre they were visiting.

She didn't see her father. He'd finished up early in the office to get ready for golf. She poked her head through the door that joined the travel agency to the house and called out loudly. 'See you later, Dad.'

His voice came down the hallway. 'See you, love. Drive safely.'

Three hours later she had a bag of new books and was walking around the department store, carrying the curtain material, hoping she'd chosen the right pattern. She didn't know where Simon was. They had arranged to meet at five o'clock, in two hours time. If they still felt like it, they were going to see a film. 'Don't be late, Harriet,' he'd said. 'If I don't find the mobile phone I want, I won't be able to ring you to remind you, remember.'

'I won't be late, I promise.'

'Harriet, you're nearly always late. You'll come dashing up, saying you couldn't help it, you got talking to someone who told you the most amazing story about being stopped in the street by a man in a giraffe suit —'

She didn't like it when he talked to her like that. 'I've never met anyone who said that.'

'I bet you will one day. So I'll see you at five o'clock. Will I write it on your hand?'

She softened and smiled. 'I'll shock you one day by turning up on time.'

'Yes, you will.'

She decided she'd shock him today. She was determined to be waiting there when he arrived. She'd be twenty minutes early, to make doubly sure. She checked her watch. Not even three o'clock. She had plenty of time yet.

When her mobile phone rang she thought it would be him on his new phone. She checked the display screen as she kept walking. No, it was Austin.

'Hi, Austie,' she said brightly.

'Harriet, it's Dad. He's had a heart attack on the golf course.'

She stopped in the middle of the shopping centre. Two people nearly ran into her.

'He's in hospital. You'd better get back as quick as you can.'

'He's alive? He's all right?'

'Get back as quick as you can.'

She couldn't get back. Simon had the keys to the car. There was only one bus a day to Merryn Bay and the bus station was miles away. 'Aust, I can't get there.'

He misunderstood. 'Harriet, I think you'd better. It's serious. Hurry. I have to go, I'm trying to get James and Lara as well. I'll call you back as soon as I can. Hurry up and get here.'

She ran from one side of the shopping centre to the other looking for Simon, trying to spot his sandy blond hair, the striped shirt he'd been wearing. Was it a striped shirt? Or had he been wearing a T-shirt? She suddenly couldn't remember. There was no sign of him in the mobile phone shop. What else had he said he was looking for? Sports shoes? There seemed to be twenty sports shops. She ran up escalators. She called his name into shops. She went back to the car park, in the vain hope he had got bored and was sitting in the car. He wasn't anywhere. She tried all the coffee shops and cafes. Where could he be? Where else could she look? She was getting desperate. She stumbled on the information desk. It hadn't occurred to her, but of course, she could get them to make an announcement.

The woman behind the counter made the call in a smooth, clear voice. 'Would Mr Simon Baxter, Mr Simon Baxter please come to the information desk as soon as possible. Mr Simon Baxter.'

Harriet waited. Nothing. There was no sign of him. She looked at every man his size and his age in the centre, but none was Simon. None of them was headed towards her. The woman was keeping an eye on her. She guessed before Harriet had a chance to ask. 'Shall I try again? The music is loud in some of the shops. Perhaps he didn't hear the first time.'

One more time. Again. Harriet couldn't stand still. 'If he does come, can you ask him to wait. Or to ring me?'

'Of course.'

'Where else would a man in his thirties shop in here?'

The woman answered as smoothly as if Harriet had asked for directions to the ladies toilets. 'Menswear on levels two and three; sportswear, videos, DVDs and CDs on levels five and six.'

'Thank you.'

As she ran down the side of the escalator, dodging people, her mobile phone rang. Austin. 'Harriet, where are you?'

'I can't find Simon. I don't know how to get there.' Her panic was rising. She was trying not to cry. 'Aust, how is he?'

'We're all here, at the hospital. Mum's in the room with him. He's had another heart attack, Harriet. Since they brought him in.'

She was more than two hours drive away. 'I'm getting a taxi.'

It would be several hundred dollars but Austin wouldn't have told her to hurry if he didn't mean it.

The first driver turned her down. He was nearly at the end of his shift. So did the second. 'You're only paying me one way. Who's going to want a fare back to Melbourne?' She hadn't been able to find the words to convince him. The third one hardly reacted, just nodded. She got into the back seat. He slowly put on his seatbelt, slowly put the car into gear, slowly indicated.

She leaned forward. 'You've got to hurry. Please. You have to do everything faster.'

'What?'

'My father is dying.' Her voice was shaky. 'He's in hospital. Please, can you hurry.'

He did his best. He shot her glances now and then as they made their way out of the city into the countryside. She stared at her mobile phone. If it didn't ring, it meant her father was all right.

'Black spot here, love. No signal for the next twenty miles or so.'

She didn't take her eyes off the phone, willing Austin to call with good news. Of course her dad was all right. He was in intensive care but he was all right. She'd arrive and he'd be sitting up, looking weak, a few tubes coming out of him and he'd be wearing one of those white gowns, of course, but he'd be all right. 'I hope you didn't rush,' he'd say. 'Didn't I tell you this morning to drive safely?'

The phone rang. It was Austin. 'Harriet?'

'Don't tell me.'

'Harriet.'

She knew before he said it. 'Don't tell me.'

'He's gone.'

'No, Austin.' They were still more than an hour away.

'They tried everything. We were all with him. Lara, James, Mum.'

But they hadn't all been with him. She hadn't been with him. She couldn't talk any more. She said goodbye. She said she'd be there as soon as she could. She cried, stopped crying, started crying again. The taxi driver kept driving.

They had just arrived at the hospital when the phone rang again. She stared at it. She didn't recognise the number. It kept ringing.

'You'd better get that, love.'

She pressed the connection.

'Hello.'

'It's half past five, Harriet. A joke is a bloody joke. Where are you?'

It was Simon. She couldn't answer him. She passed the phone to the taxi driver as she climbed out.

Simon arrived at the hospital at nine o'clock that night, coming in to the room, pale faced, where they were all gathered. Harriet's mother was inconsolable. She kept saying the same things, over and over. 'But he was healthy.' 'He exercised every day.' 'He was only sixty-three.'

He had been dead for one hour and thirty-three minutes by the time Harriet saw him. She'd walked into the hospital and been met by Austin.

'Harriet, I'm sorry. I'm so sorry.'

She moved into his arms, tears flowing down her cheeks. 'Where is he, Austie? I need to see him.'

It hadn't been her dad. It had been his face, his body. She had been right about the hospital gown. But there had been no sign of the smile, the soft accent, the teasing look in his eyes. She spoke to him. She touched his hand. She was overwhelmed by emotion, barely able to stand. Her dad was dead and she hadn't been able to say goodbye to him.

Austin was beside her. His hand was on her back. She turned to him. 'Austie, did he know I wasn't here? Did he know I was trying to get here as quickly as I could? Did he know?'

'Harriet —'

There was a noise at the door behind them. They turned. It was their mother. Lara was on one side of her, James on the other. They were both holding her tightly.

'Mum . . .'

'Oh, Harriet. Harriet.'

She needed her mother to come over and hold her, to make it all right, to make it better, but she stayed with Lara and James. Austin had moved over to them too. The four of them were holding on to each other.

Harriet looked at them. 'Were you all here? Was I the only one who wasn't?'

'Harriet, it was so quick,' Austin said. 'You couldn't have known.'

She didn't answer him. She needed to know exactly what had happened. 'Where were you when you heard, Lara?'

'I was in the office.'

'On a Saturday? Only Mum and Dad work on a Saturday.'

'I was working on that new tour.'

'Where were you, James?'

'At home. With Melissa and Molly.'

Austin came over and touched her arm. 'Harriet, stop it. It doesn't matter.'

'Yes, it does. It does matter.'

'Harriet? Come here, love.'

She turned. Her mother opened her arms. Harriet moved into them and cried until it hurt.

They closed the travel agency for two days. Gloria volunteered to keep it going, but they wanted her with them. Having her in their midst made it easier, held them together, stopped the shock from completely overwhelming them. She and Melissa quietly and methodically organised what needed to be done. Their mother was too distraught. The rest of them were too shocked.

Simon kept apologising, over and over again. It was his fault she had been in Melbourne. His fault for losing his mobile phone so she hadn't been able to ring him. She was calm with him. 'I wanted to go. It's not your fault.'

Gloria noticed something was wrong. She seemed to guess it was to do with Harriet not being there when her father died. 'I know it's hard, Harriet. But would it have been better if none of you were with him? If he had died on his own on the golf course? Would that have made you feel better?'

'No, of course it wouldn't.' But *why did it have to be me who was missing?* She didn't say that out loud. She felt so guilty, so terrible even thinking it, but it came from somewhere deep inside her. *She should have been there.*

Gloria moved closer, taking Harriet's hands in hers, squeezing them. 'Harriet, you can't change it. That's the way it was. That's what happened. It would hurt no matter how and when your dad died, or who was with him. It's awful, but it's the truth.'

They all wanted to speak at his funeral service. Austin and James went first. They spoke simply, briefly. They had loved their father very much. Harriet was supposed to be next, but she wasn't ready. Austin touched Lara on the arm. She glanced at Harriet, as if seeking permission. Harriet watched through her tears as Lara walked from the pew to the altar, adjusted the microphone, so calm, so collected. Her speech was brief. 'Neil welcomed me into his home as if I was his own daughter. I loved him for that, and I loved him for his kindness and his humour, and for all the parts of him that were special. I loved him dearly and I will miss him so much.' She cried then, but she managed to finish her sentence.

Harriet wasn't able to get past her first line. She had been up until two a.m. trying to write her tribute. Trying to put into words what her dad had meant to her. Trying to reduce thirty-one years of being loved and cared for and encouraged into three minutes. 'I loved my dad.' It was the past tense that got her. When he was alive she had been able to say to him 'I love you, Dad.' Now he was dead. Now he was in that coffin, in the middle of that aisle, and all she could say was that she had loved him. Because she hadn't been able to say 'I love you, Dad, please, Dad, get better. Please, Dad, don't die,' like the others had in the hospital room. If she had been there, would it have made the tiniest bit of difference that his spirit might have needed?

She started crying and she couldn't stop. Her mother didn't speak either. She broke down on her way to the altar.

Two months later, unbelievably, horribly, it happened again. They had all gone back to work, still numb with the hurt and grief, their father's empty desk a reminder every day of their loss, yet none of them wanting to sit there or move it out.

It had been a normal day: the phones ringing, customers calling in to book holidays or to show photos from a previous tour. A new set of company brochures arrived from the printers on the outskirts of Melbourne, two hours away. Harriet was the first to notice there was a problem with the photographs on the front page. The colours were out of alignment. Normally, that was something her father would have sorted out, quickly and easily. He'd have jumped in his car and driven there, and been back within the afternoon.

It was as if all their reactions had slowed when he died. Harriet knew her mother was still dazed. Time after time she had looked up and seen her staring out the window, not hearing phones ring, not realising someone had asked her a question. She had aged in just a few weeks, as if the spirit had gone out of her. Harriet noticed it again that day. Her mother was staring at the brochures as if she didn't know what they were.

Harriet needed to help. She desperately needed to try and make things better. 'Mum, do you want me to take them back to the printers?'

Her mother's smile was childlike in its relief. 'Oh, Harriet, would you?'

'Of course. Do you want to come with me? For a drive?'

Gloria looked up. 'Penny, you've got that lunch today, do you remember? Out at the golf club? And then Austin's arriving after lunch?'

'Oh yes, I'd forgotten. I'd better be here when he arrives too.

Harriet, thank you anyway. I would have liked that. We'll do it another time.'

Harriet was about to ask if there was anything else she wanted her to do while she was there, when the memory returned of asking about the curtains the day their father died. Instead, she picked up the brochures and her car keys. 'I'll be back as soon as I can.'

She planted a quick kiss on her mother's head. Her mother briefly touched her arm. 'Thank you, Harriet. I don't know what I'd do without you.'

Afterwards, the words had swum round and round Harriet's head. Is that what she'd said? Without you or without you all?

She had driven the two hours to the printing plant and spent nearly an hour with the production manager, trying to sort out the problem. She'd stayed calm, not even getting annoyed when he took a personal phone call on his mobile midway through, laughing for five minutes while he set up a football outing with a friend. How could that bother her? Her father had died. What could be worse than that? She was walking out of the printworks when her mobile phone rang. James.

Afterwards she couldn't remember whether she had said hello or whether James had started speaking first. She vaguely remembered getting into the car, turning it around, ignoring the angry blast of someone's horn and then driving back to Merryn Bay. She needed to stop for petrol halfway. She got out of the car, filled the petrol tank, went in and paid, like a robot. The whole time James's voice replayed in her mind.

'Harriet, thank God I got you. Mum's in hospital. Quick, get back as soon as you can.'

She drove straight to the hospital. She was too late. At the bedside she listened, staring at her mother's lifeless face, as James,

Austin and Lara told her what had happened, over and over, needing to give her the details, as if they could make sense of it that way themselves. Lara had been driving back from dropping train tickets to an elderly client outside the town when she found their mother slumped at the wheel of her car beside the road to the golf course, the car engine still running. The ambulance had been called. She'd had a second stroke soon after she was admitted to hospital. A fatal one.

Her funeral was held in the same church. She was buried next to their father. His grave was still a mound of earth. They hadn't been able to face organising his headstone yet. The wake was held in the same hall.

The whole family was devastated. The aftermath was as traumatic: the changes in the company, James and Melissa and their daughter Molly moving into the family home, the shifting and changing as the family came to terms with what it all meant, personally, professionally.

Everyone had felt the hurt and the grief. Harriet knew that. But underlying everything for her was one desperate, unassuageable fact. She was the only one who hadn't been able to say goodbye to her parents. The only one who hadn't been there with them when they died. Not just once, but twice.

The grief, the hurt and the shock at their deaths twisted into anxious feelings deep inside her, a constant watchfulness that something like that could happen again with someone else, without warning, without the chance to prepare or say farewell.

It began as a constant nagging unease. Over the following days and weeks it grew into something as pervasive as a migraine or a toothache, an anxiety, dark and encompassing, deep inside her mind, seeping into every part of her life.

She began to worry from the time she woke up until she went to bed. About small things at first. Checking and then having to double-check if she had enough petrol or if the brakes in her car were working. Having to go back home in case she'd left the iron on, left a tap running or the front door ajar. She started worrying about other people, especially people travelling anywhere by car. She kept imagining burst tyres, rogue truck drivers changing lanes without warning, faulty railway crossings. She started insisting her family, Simon and her friends phone her when they arrived at their destination so she would know they had got there safely.

The anxiety spilled into her working life. When she was typing up tour itineraries, she couldn't stop imagining catastrophic events. Bus drivers having heart attacks and crashing off the road. Viewing platforms on the edges of canyons or cliffs collapsing, taking groups down with them. Planes crashing. Trains derailing. Food poisoning outbreaks. She decided it was an omen of some sort, that she had to make doubly sure to check all the tours were properly organised, and that every possible safety measure was in place.

Everyone started to notice. James insisted she take some time off. She protested. Gloria was drafted in to take her home and put her to bed. She couldn't sleep. The worry turned from work to her personal life. She sat up, three nights in a row, thinking about Simon. He was away on a week-long conference. They had been together for four years, and had lived together in his rented flat for the past twelve months. They had started to talk about getting married, buying a house together. She inspected their relationship from every angle, made lists, went over every moment of their time together, paced the house. She didn't answer the door, or any phone calls. She was clear in her head when she rang him at the conference at six o'clock in the morning to tell him she was very sorry, but she had realised there was no future between them and she had decided it was best if they split up. She was as kind as she could be to him. She felt genuinely sad but she knew she couldn't give him any hope for a future reconciliation. He was extremely upset. Her family were shocked. Despite the anxiety, she knew it was the right thing. She moved out of the flat they shared, found a small house for sale four streets back from the beach on the opposite side of Merryn Bay, put down a deposit, all in the space of a few weeks. She ignored any advice that she was moving too quickly, acting irrationally. There was an urgency, she realised. She had to move quickly before anything else bad happened. She had to try and keep one step ahead of it.

She worked longer hours so she didn't need to go home to her empty house. She volunteered to do any extra tours going. She worked weekends. She did anything she could to try to block the anxious thoughts crowding into her brain.

Two weeks before she was due to take a group on a five-day tour of the Flinders Ranges in outback South Australia James took her aside.

'Harriet, are you sure you're up to this? I can take over, or Lara can, if you're not.'

'I'll be fine. Why? Who said I wouldn't be?'

'No one said anything. It's just you've checked all the arrangements at least six times already. The hotel in the Flinders Ranges rang me. They're worried we don't think they're up to scratch.'

'I was making sure of everything, the way we're supposed to, the way Mum and Dad taught us to.'

'Harriet, we've been staying in that hotel for more than ten years. You know they're good.' He paused. 'The helicopter company rang too. They said you've been querying their safety record.'

'I have to do my job. I can't take people up on a sightseeing flight if I don't have faith in the company.'

'Harriet, you've rung them every day this week too. I think you might be taking this all too seriously. Maybe it would be better if —'

'No.'

'Just this once. Maybe you need a break. You've been working flat out since Mum and Dad died and maybe —'

'No, James. We're all in this together. We're all sad. We've all been working hard.'

'Yes, but not all of us have ended a relationship and moved house in the past two months too.'

'Everything's under control, James.'

'Look, if you're sure. But if you change your mind, if you want to be taken off the tour . . .'

'I can do it.'

'Okay.'

It had gone wrong from the start. The group was a party of middle-aged car yard managers and their wives. They wanted the back-to-the-bush experience, and had asked Turner Travel to put together a tailored tour, combining luxury travel with some outback adventure. Harriet had organised short bushwalks through Wilpena Pound, the crater-like mountain visible on the desert horizon for hundreds of miles. She'd arranged for meals of emu pâté and kangaroo steaks in a luxurious pub at the end of a long dirt road. A scenic helicopter flight. One night of camping in luxury tents, the rest in an authentic bush hotel. Authentically renovated, anyway, to a four-star standard.

The bus driver was a sixty-year-old called Des. They'd used him several times before. He was brusque, but fine. Taciturn – they couldn't rely on him to add any local information or colour – but he knew the roads.

For the week before the trip Harriet had trouble sleeping. She was in her new house on her own, so at least she didn't have to worry about Simon making comments all night long. 'Come back to bed, Harriet.' 'What are you doing up, Harriet?' 'Can't you forget about work for a minute?' She would try to sleep but each time she lay her head on the pillow a detail would come to mind that she hadn't checked off. What if there was a vegetarian on the trip? What if Des got sick and they were out in the desert? Would she be able to drive the bus? Should she check if any of the group had heavy-vehicle licences, just in case?

The group met at the airstrip near Wilpena Pound and drove to the hotel for the first night. She had to go back to the airstrip twice to check they'd picked up all the luggage. The first time Des didn't mind. The second time he was cranky. 'I counted the bags, I told you. They counted them, too. It's their luggage, why couldn't you believe them?'

'I had an idea I'd left something behind.'

She worried about the seating arrangements on the bus and kept trying to move them around. They told her to relax. 'Harriet, we're old friends, we don't care where we sit.'

She was up all night, checking the map Des was using against an older one she'd found in the hotel reception area. She knew outback roads were often washed out by sudden rain storms. It wasn't the wet season but flash floods happened out of nowhere. Everyone knew horror stories of people camping in dry creek beds and being woken in terror by a ten-foot wall of water sweeping them away in the middle of the night. She woke Des at five the next morning to see if he would think about changing their route, just in case.

'No.'

'I'm worried about flash flooding.'

'No way, if that first no wasn't clear enough. You've got problems, missus.' He shut the door in her face.

She'd hammered on the wood until he answered. 'I'm worried about the wellbeing of the group. About something happening to them.'

'If anything happens to them it'll be because you woke me up too early. I'm going back to bed.'

She became fearful of hygiene problems and started checking the kitchen before and after each meal. The chef complained, and suggested if she wasn't happy she should move somewhere else.

She cancelled the helicopter ride, upsetting the group.

'But that was going to be the highlight,' one of the men said. 'It's a perfect day.' It was, too. Clear, blue. They would have been able to see for miles.

'I had a dream that it crashed.'

'You had a dream?' The man was incredulous. 'You cancelled our thousand-dollar flight because of a dream? Then you'd better have another dream that the helicopter takes off.'

He rang James. James rang the helicopter company. Then he rang Harriet.

'Harriet, what's going on? You can't cancel things like that. What's this nonsense about a dream?' She started to explain how real it had seemed. She'd seen the helicopter fall from the sky, crash and burst into flames. She'd heard the screams. She had woken up drenched with sweat, terrified. James spoke over her. 'Look, it was a dream, okay. It's not going to crash. That flight is the high point of their trip and it's going ahead, Harriet. This afternoon. Promise me.'

'I can't go, James. I won't be able to watch.'

'Are you getting enough sleep? Sounds like you were up all night with those nightmares.' When she admitted she was sleeping badly, his tone changed. 'Harriet, take the afternoon off. Go to bed. I'll get Des to take the group to the helicopter pad by himself. You take it easy and you'll be right as rain tonight.'

The group returned later that day, exhilarated from the helicopter flight. They talked about seeing hundreds of miles of red earth, deep gorges and dry river beds; wedge-tailed eagles, kangaroos, emus and camels; Wilpena Pound looking like an ancient bowl. None of it eased her worries. She managed to have dinner with them, hear all the stories, even put up with the teasing. 'See, Harriet, we survived.' But she was barely able to eat, and didn't join them in the bar afterwards. She couldn't sit there, talking and laughing. The feeling of dread had multiplied, except now she didn't know where the horror was going to come from.

She paced the room all night. They were supposed to be going camping the next night and all she could think of were flash floods, spiders, snakes. Her clients writhing in agony. Des sick at the wheel of the bus, shouting that she'd have to take over. Two of the men doubled over in pain, brushing away spiders. A woman screaming that a snake had crawled into her sleeping bag, that Harriet had to come, quickly. And what if the camp fire wasn't put out properly? A flicker of flame would spark on to a dry gum branch nearby, smouldering, sending out tendrils of low fire across the desert floor, towards their tents . . . Something bad was going to happen, and there was nothing she was going to be able to do about it.

She didn't come out to breakfast the next day. The group assumed she was in her room, or in the office making phone calls. They met Des at the minibus outside the hotel at nine o'clock, as arranged, but there was no sign of her. It was Des who came to her room.

The door was locked. She was inside, in the corner, the quilts and pillows bundled all around her. She had pulled the curtains across and locked the door, now so frightened she couldn't bear any light or the thought of someone being able to come in. His knocking sounded like bellows, shouts. 'Harriet? Are you in there?'

After a while he went away. She curled up tighter, trying to slow her heartbeat, feeling her nails pressing into her palms. She'd be all right, they'd be all right, she just had to be sure they didn't camp near any rivers, and check for spiders and snakes and . . . The waves of terror took her again. She couldn't help it. She screamed when the knock came at the door again. Des, and someone else with him. She saw the door handle turn. They were trying to get in.

'Harriet? Harriet?' It felt like they were screaming her name. She managed to crawl across the floor, still bundled in the quilt, and push a chair under the door handle to keep them out that way. She checked the bolt. Please, please, please let it be strong enough. She knew the window was already locked. She'd done that in the middle of the night. She'd locked the bathroom window too. She put another chair against the bathroom door, but it didn't make her feel any safer.

She heard a female voice and for one moment thought it was her mother, but it was one of the women in the group. More knocking. 'Harriet, are you all right? Please, answer us.'

She curled up tighter, as tightly as she could. If she spoke softly to herself, if she kept up a sort of murmuring, she discovered she couldn't hear their voices. She tried counting, repeating numbers over and over again, in order first and then at random, trying to fix them in her mind, something solid and normal like numbers . . .

It took the local policeman nearly half an hour to break down the door. By the time they got inside, she was so terrified she was screaming the numbers. They called the doctor. Austin flew up that night. She was taken to a clinic outside Melbourne. An anxiety state was diagnosed. A nervous breakdown. A severe grief reaction. She was given different names for what had felt like a boiling mass of fear and hurt and deep, endless sadness.

She'd discharged herself from the hospital after three weeks of treatment, rest and medication, and returned to work. She'd thought she was okay. But then James asked her if she would be able to lead a three-day tour to the Riverland. The idea terrified her. Lara had taken it instead. She was offered another one two weeks later. Again, she'd turned it down. Then another. James stopped asking her. It went without saying that she wasn't up to it. She was moved into the administration side of the business, while James and Lara spent nearly all their time out on the road with the tour groups. Yes, she was fine again, she told people. Yes, absolutely. No, she was perfectly happy being in the office. It was a nice change, not to have to do all that packing and unpacking. Oh, she'd go back on the road again, one day, just not quite yet, she said as brightly as she could. She'd been trying to convince herself as much as them.

Harriet turned away from the hotel window and the darkness outside. It was quiet now, barely any noise from the motorway. It could be anywhere out there – England, Australia. She knew the same thoughts would have been in her mind wherever she was. She'd learnt that from all her years of travelling. You didn't leave your memories, your worries, your problems behind when you got on the plane. They came with you, whether you wanted them to or not.

It was the slow aftermath of her parents' deaths that still shocked her. There had been the initial grief, the everyday wallop of feeling, when she would realise over and over that they were gone and that she wouldn't ever be able to see them or speak to them again. That rawness had faded, changed in shape, but something else was emerging. The sharpening picture of how life would be now.

It wasn't only the physical details that were painful: her parents' absence in the office, at family gatherings, in Merryn Bay, or the fact that James, Melissa and Molly now lived in the house where they had once lived. It hurt in her heart and mind, too. She had never realised how often every day she naturally thought of her mother and father, wanting to tell them something, remembering something one or the other had said, a flash of childhood memory, an idea, or the beautiful comfort of a memory of conversations with someone she loved and who she knew loved her. Thoughts like that which had once brought warm feelings now produced a sharp little stab of grief.

It was as if all the safety nets she had never even known existed around her had been snatched away, leaving nothing to buffer her from what could be so frightening about life. Pain, grief, shock, sadness – she found it hard to believe she had made it to the age of thirty-one without truly knowing how any of those emotions felt. Her childhood seemed idyllic now, bathed in a glowing light of safety and familiarity. Even Lara's arrival all those years ago had started fading into that golden state of memory, as if she had simply imagined that things were tricky at the start. It felt like she'd had two lives: the one before her parents' deaths, when the world seemed full of promise and good things; and then afterwards, when it felt as if the ground beneath her feet was unsteady, prone to sudden chasms and gaping holes.

As she started preparing for bed, washing her face and brushing her teeth, Harriet made herself focus on the present, on the tour. She talked herself through all the positives of the situation. She had tomorrow morning to do some final checking before the bus arrived to take them to St Ives. Out of consideration for the age of most of the group and the long journey, James had scheduled a late start. Once they got to St Ives she could sit down with Patrick Shawcross and talk through the itinerary, before his first official meeting with the tour group, an informal cocktail party at the hotel itself. All straightforward. All manageable. All of it under control.

All except for Lara's disappearance.

'I'll do what I can from here to track her down,' Austin had repeated before he hung up. 'I'll ring James for you as well. He can get Melissa and Gloria on the job. Between all of us we'll find out what's going on with her. It'll be something simple, you wait and see. So don't worry about her. Your job is to worry about the tour.'

She knew what he was trying to do, and she loved him for it, but what he was asking was impossible. Did he truly think she could block Lara out of her mind? Simply switch off the part of her brain that had worried about Lara for as long as she could remember? She had spent twenty-four years wondering if Lara was okay, if she was happy, and just as long being puzzled and confused by Lara's behaviour in return. It had become second nature to her.

Except this time it felt different. Since she had come out into the airport and there had been no sign of Lara, she had gone through a whole range of reactions. Worry. Concern. Confusion after she'd spoken to Nina, Lara's flatmate. But if she was honest with herself now – in a way she never could be with Austin, or even Gloria – the more she was admitting to a strange kind of relief.

Perhaps Lara was feeling the same way, wherever she was. Perhaps that's why she had gone away, not only to England in the first place, but away this afternoon, abandoning the tour. She'd realised what she had done to Harriet was so inexplicable that she couldn't face her again either.

The thoughts went round her head, as they had been doing for three months, ever since the night she had learned the truth from Lara. Harriet was still no closer to understanding it. She climbed between the white cotton sheets, turned off the bedside lamp and tried to sleep. Don't worry about Lara, Austin had said. It was so much easier said than done.

CHAPTER FOUR

On the other side of the world, Gloria Hillman moved across the bedroom of her Merryn Bay cottage, carrying a tray and listening to the rattle of the cup in the saucer. It always woke her husband up much better than any alarm clock could. 'Morning, darling.'

'Hello, my sweet.' Kevin sat up in the queen-sized bed. He'd greeted Gloria that way each morning for the past thirty-five years. She placed the cup in the same spot on the bedside table she used every day, then perched on the end of the bed watching, but not helping, as Kevin reached and felt for the saucer. He was sixty-three years old, a bit older than her, but still fit-looking. Tanned, too, from all the outdoor work he'd done as a roofer over the years. He even had a full head of hair still, even if it was more grey than brown these days. He took a long sip. 'Thanks, love. Did you sleep well?'

'Like a dream.'

'Any big news?'

'Nothing earth-shattering.' Gloria always delivered the seven o'clock news headlines with the morning cup of tea. 'Industrial action on the ports. Election campaign due to begin next week. And two goats from Melbourne Zoo seen making a run for it down Flemington Road.'

'Good for them. And the weather?'

'Blue. Sunny. Twenty-eight degrees, if you can believe a word any of them say.'

Gloria stood and pulled back the curtains. Their house was set back from the road, but if she leaned in a certain way she could get a glimpse of the sea through the pine trees, and a good view of the sky. It was cloudless so far. April was her favourite time of year. All the summer crowds had left and they had the small town back to themselves. Merryn Bay's normal population of five thousand swelled to nearly twelve thousand for a few months, the holiday shacks and caravan park down the end of the beach crammed to bursting point. People were drawn to the simple beauty of the town, with its curving bay, secluded beach, little wooden jetty and the view across the water to bare hills and other small towns, invisible in the day, twinkling lights at night.

Strolling around at lunchtime in the summer, down the only shopping street in the town, she'd often overhear conversations between holidaymakers from Melbourne, remarking on how well set up the town was, with its banks, hairdressers, clothes shops, supermarket, 'Look, even a travel agent,' one would usually say. 'Let's sell up and move down here. It's a big enough town, and we'd be beside the sea all the time.'

She was always surprised at how protective she felt, as if it all belonged to her – the changing colours of the water, the long beach path lined with imported pines, the big sky, blue and hazy in the summer, dramatic in winter. She didn't want it teeming with crowds all year round. She liked it the way it was.

'Any clouds, love?'

She turned back to her husband. 'Not that I can see. Blue skies ahead. Do you want the radio on? Your book, or anything, while I get ready?'

He shook his head. 'I'm fine. You look after yourself.' As she left the room, she watched as Kevin reached confidently to the back of the bedside table and switched on the radio. A Beatles song filled the room, too loud. Without hesitation, Kevin found the right knob and turned the volume down.

He smiled. 'Sorry. Bit early for a disco.'

'Just a bit,' she said. That was one of the advantages of it having been a slow decline in his sight. There had been time for him to prepare, to make almost a mental imprint of not only appliances like the radio and the CD player, but also the arrangement of the house. He'd been able to learn his way around before his sight went completely. The girl from the Institute for the Blind in Melbourne had been wonderful. They would never have thought of doing the things she'd suggested.

'The mind is amazing, it can remember more than you think possible,' she'd said. 'If you practise things before your sight goes, Kevin, it won't be as frightening when it happens.' She'd given some examples. The teacup and radio on the bedside table. The position of his knife and fork and glass of wine at meal time. 'You never know. You might find this opens up far more experiences than you thought possible, once you get over the shock.'

She'd been so honest about it. It was going to happen so they may as well be practical about it. Other people gave them false hope or avoided the subject altogether. She had helped Kevin, and Gloria and their three sons, come to terms with it in many ways.

Honesty was always the best policy, in Gloria's opinion. She remembered arguing with Penny Turner about it. Penny had been shocked at the way Gloria spoke so openly about it when Kevin was first diagnosed. The words had sounded so ominous: macular degeneration blindness. The lay term – the slow erosion of the retina – had sounded even worse.

Penny had been just as shocked to overhear a conversation between Gloria and one of their more tactless customers. The woman had asked after Gloria's health before leaning forward and lowering her voice, 'And how is that poor husband of yours?'

Gloria hadn't skipped a beat. 'Like a pig in muck. He has me running around after him from dawn to dusk. Says he should have gone blind years ago.'

'He's very courageous,' the woman said, unabashed. 'And so are you. It can't be much fun caring for an invalid in your home like that.'

'Oh, we have lots of fun,' Gloria had said cheerfully. 'We play hide and seek most nights. It's great. I always win.'

One evening, over their usual end of the working day cup of tea in the back room of Turner Travel, Penny had brought up the subject. 'Gloria, I think you're wrong to talk about this so bluntly. Kevin might get better and you're talking as though his sight has already gone. If you don't have hope, what's left?'

'Confusion,' Gloria had said. 'Disappointment when the inevitable happens. He is going to go blind, Penny. Kevin knows that, I know that, we talk about it, so his mind is already adjusting to the idea even before it happens.'

Penny had never liked facing up to the nasty side of life. If she didn't like something, she'd either pretend it wasn't happening or gloss over it. She called it being sensitive. Gloria called it being blinkered. It was the one thing they had always argued about, in all their years of friendship. Gloria and Kevin had often spoken about it too. 'Think about it, Kev. It must have had an impact on the kids. Penny did it with Lara's arrival, never wanting to acknowledge that there might be some repercussions on the others, especially Harriet. She chose not to see that Austin spent all his spare time teasing James. Is it any wonder James found a fierce woman like Melissa to protect himself with?' Penny had done it in another way, too. Trying to protect Lara from something. The one thing in thirty-five years of marriage that Gloria had never been able to speak to Kevin about.

In the early lean months with the travel agency, though, when anyone else might have given up or decided they had made a mistake, Gloria had been forced to admit it was Penny's attitude that had kept them all so cheerful. 'Our time will come. I know it will. We just have to stick at it.' She had been right. The terrible shame was that Penny wasn't there to see the agency these days, when it was doing better than they could ever have imagined.

'You know, I think I'm missing Penny and Neil more as time passes, not less,' Gloria said to Kevin now, as she came back into the bedroom to pick up her work jacket – her uniform, as she had to learn to call it – and do a final check of her hair and make-up in the wardrobe mirror. Not that she bothered too much with that side of getting ready. A quick brush of her now greying curls, perhaps a dab of lipstick, and she was done. Her sixty-year-old skin had seen too much sunshine over the years to be saved by any make-up now. Besides, she knew practically everyone who came into the travel agency and they'd get a shock if she started dolling herself up. 'I've been thinking about them so much lately for some reason. It would be great to have one more of those nights of good conversation with them, wouldn't it?'

'Good conversation? Good arguments, you mean.'

'No, not arguments. Spirited discussions. Remember that's what Penny always called them?' She glanced at her watch. 'Quarter to eight. I'll be late.'

'Run, Gloria, run. You'd better be careful or Melissa will sack you.'

'An old piece of the furniture like me? She wouldn't dare.'

'No, of course she wouldn't. That place would crumble if you left.'

'Once upon a time, perhaps. Not under this new regime.'

'Melissa's still on the warpath?'

'She was born on the warpath. But it's Melissa they have to thank for things turning around, as I keep telling Austin. If she hadn't come on the scene they would be bankrupt by now, whether Penny and Neil were still alive or not.'

'To which Austin replied, if my memory serves me right, it would have been better to be bankrupt than bullied to hell and back by the Evil One.'

Gloria laughed. 'He really is far too wishy-washy about her, isn't he?' She finished her tea, and leaned and kissed Kevin goodbye. 'I'll see you at lunchtime, love.'

'Good, because I won't see you.'

It made her laugh every day. Even better, it made him laugh. Picking up her bag and sunglasses from the bench beside the sink, she pulled the door shut behind her and walked down the path to the front gate.

At her desk in the Turner Travel office, showered, made up and in the full Turner Travel uniform, Melissa Turner hung up, cursing the nurse in the Geelong hospital. How dare she refuse to go and wake James up, especially after Melissa had stressed how important it was.

'Yes, Mrs Turner,' the nurse had replied in an infuriatingly calm voice. 'You said that last night as well. And the night before. It's not good for your husband to be woken in the middle of the night, you know.'

'But it's nearly eight, not the middle of the night. And I should know, I've been awake since five a.m. It's an important family matter.'

'Family? Close family?'

Melissa thought for a split second about inventing a problem with Molly, their fifteen-year-old daughter, before changing her mind. She had heard Molly come in from swimming training already and the adjoining wall between the office and the house carried sound so well there was every chance Molly would hear her and protest. Melissa told the truth. 'It's about his sister. His foster-sister, at least. Lara.'

'Has she been in an accident?'

'Well, no —'

'So it's not a life and death situation?'

'No, but —'

'Then I'm sure it can wait until after your husband's had his breakfast.'

Melissa had hung up, loudly. Perhaps it was a shame she had called so late the night before, pretending it was a family emergency. One of the nurses had obviously reported her. It had been important, though. She'd had an idea for revamping their coach tours to the Gold Coast. James told her he hadn't minded at all. He was always understanding about being woken in the middle of the night. She often had her best ideas then. And as he said many times, it was her middle-of-the-night ideas that had got the company back on track.

She'd been in a terrible state since Austin called two hours before with his bombshell about Lara not turning up to meet Harriet and the *Willoughby* group. He'd made it clear he'd only rung her because he hadn't been able to get past the ward gatekeepers to James either. They'd had a terse conversation – she and Austin had never got on and even an emergency such as this wasn't enough to forge bonds between them. She was desperate to talk to someone about it, to start putting a rescue plan into action. Thank God Gloria would be in soon. She could share the burden with her.

Melissa tried Lara's mobile number again, making sure she was dialling the correct international codes. It had been working perfectly two days ago, the last time she and Lara had spoken. A quick call, to confirm that the hotel in St Ives had a lift. Lara had sounded fine, businesslike as ever.

She tensed as Lara's recorded voice filtered down the line. She knew from Austin that Harriet had left several messages. She decided to leave another. Just in case.

'Lara, it's Melissa. We need to talk. I don't know what's going on, but I hope you're not in any trouble. Ring me, please. Or send an email. We'll sort it all out, all right?' She thought perhaps that she sounded too cross and hastened to make up for it before the space for messages was filled. 'I mean it, that I hope you're okay. So call us, will you?'

It was so odd. What could have got into her? Had she met someone and fled to a love nest? Discovered she was pregnant and run away to do something about it? No, that wasn't Lara's style. Not organised, under-control Lara. Organised, under-control Lara who had just left nervy, basket-case Harriet in charge of a group of twelve people. Melissa felt her temper rise. She should have known something like this would happen. Hadn't she told James it was a mistake sending Harriet back on the road? She should never have let him talk her into it. He'd sat there going on and on about

Harriet needing her confidence built up again, that she was much better again, she had been one of their most popular guides, all the groups had loved travelling with her, Melissa only had to read the comments book, they all said how kind and sweet and fun she was, blah blah blah, on and on until Melissa had eventually pleaded a headache and given in.

Not for the first time Melissa wished James had several other sisters, preferably six or seven, each with business and tourism management degrees, instead of just Harriet and Lara. Not that Lara was strictly his sister, of course, and one had to make allowances for Harriet since her breakdown, but it really did sometimes feel as though she, Melissa, was the only one keeping the business on an even keel.

What she found hardest about working with the Turner family was the ripple effect, she decided. Something happened to one, and it affected all the others. Like when Neil and then Penny had died. Of course it was sad, but that was the natural order of things, wasn't it? Parents died, children took over. You got on with it. Not that she was that close to her own parents, in fact she rarely saw them these days, but they were happy enough in the old folks' home, she knew. And she would only unsettle them unduly if she was to start calling in each Sunday the way some people's relatives did. The monthly visits worked well for them all. If they were to die, of course she'd be sad, but she would get on with it. Not like the Turners. James had gone so serious. Austin had become even more impossible. Harriet had fallen to pieces. Even Lara had gone strange, announcing out of the blue she was going to study in England. How were they supposed to work productively together in these kind of circumstances?

She checked the time on the airplane-shaped wall clock above the front door. Ten to eight. She'd have to pop her head in to the house soon and make sure Molly was ready for school and had remembered to have her breakfast. At least she was still eating properly, and doing her homework, and behaving normally, not like some other fifteen-year-olds around town she'd heard about, getting up to no good, going off the rails. And Gloria would be in any moment, too. Thanks heavens for one non-family employee, even if she possibly should have retired years before.

Melissa turned to her computer. She'd try and distract herself with work while she was waiting for Gloria. Beside her was a pile of books on the archaeological settlements of Sweden. Axel Dortmund, the owner of one of the guesthouses on the Merryn Bay beach, had come into the travel agency a month ago, offering to lead a study tour to Viking settlements in his native country. An early listing on the Turner Travel website calling for expressions of interest had yielded an encouraging number of inquiries.

There was no accounting for taste in travel, Melissa thought for the hundredth time since she and James had taken over the running of Turner Travel. And thank heavens for that.

CHAPTER FIVE

In her bedroom at the back of the house adjoining the travel agency, Molly Turner was nearly ready for school. She'd been up since six-thirty. She had crept out of the house and cycled, half-asleep, to the pool, barely spoken to the other members of her swimming club, swum her usual twenty laps and been back home and showered by seven-thirty.

Sometimes her dad was up when she got back, making coffee or sitting at the table reading the paper, but not this morning. Poor old Dad, stuck in hospital, she thought. Silly old Dad, falling off the ladder. She hoped he was missing them, stuck in Geelong. She and her mum had been to see him at the weekend and were hopefully going again this evening, after she'd finished her afternoon swimming training. He'd looked funny in the bed, with his leg all plastered up, a cage under the covers making him look five times bigger. He'd been as lovely as ever, though. Some of her friends complained about their dads, and she did her best to join in, but the truth was she really liked her dad. It was her mum she had problems with . . .

She went out into the backyard and slung her towel, bathers and damp tracksuit over the clothesline, pegging them haphazardly. It was a beautiful autumn day, the sky blue and clear even this early in the morning. She picked a late plum off the tree by the back door as she came in and bit into it, the juice already warm from the morning sun. Passing through the kitchen, this time she noticed the signs of life, the toaster out, the dishes drying in the rack. Her mum must have gone into work early. Gloria wouldn't like that, Molly thought. She'd heard her say many times how much she liked that quiet morning time in the office on her own.

Molly went into her room to dress. She was still wearing her summer school uniform, a knee-length blue cotton dress, but once the winds started up in May they would all switch to the longer blue winter skirt and jumper. She tied her still damp strawberry blonde hair back into its usual long thick plait, adding a glittery hair slide for that touch of glamour, as her friend Hailey called it. She rubbed moisturiser into her bare brown legs and applied the barest minimum of tinted moisturiser to her face. Proper foundation was banned, but she and her friends had discovered this was the next best thing. She found her lip gloss and put it in her pocket. That was also banned but they all still wore it anyway. She'd apply that on her way to school. Next, her earrings – simple gold studs, anything showier was also banned. Finally, she strapped her watch on, a small oval face and a blue leather strap. The school even had strict guidelines about what sort of style the band could be. Nothing too showy that might cause envy, apparently. It was stupid, she thought. All these rules and regulations, piled one on top of the other. If the teachers only knew what the kids got up to. Which reminded her . . .

She put her hand under the mattress, rummaged inside the little hole she had made in the stuffing and pulled out the packet. She pressed out the pill, swallowed it and hid the packet again. It was the only hiding place she'd been able to think of. Her mother still tidied her room and put her clothes in her drawers, even though

Molly had tried to make her understand she was happy enough to do it herself.

'You're still my little girl,' her mother had said, ignoring that at five foot five Molly was now nearly a head taller than her. 'I don't mind doing it one bit.'

Molly's friends couldn't understand why she complained. Their mothers insisted they clean their own rooms and do their share of the housework. Jacinta and Hailey even had to do their share of the washing – and so did their brothers.

'When does your mother get time to do this housework, Molly?' Jacinta's mother had asked, after overhearing the conversation in the car one afternoon. 'She works full-time, doesn't she?'

'She gets up early,' Molly said. 'And she does some of it at lunchtime.' It had got worse since they moved into her grandma and grandpa's house. At least in the old house, a couple of miles away from the main street, her mother hadn't been able to nip in and out during the day. Now there was only a door dividing the travel agency from the house. Molly couldn't leave anything lying around in the morning. She never knew when her mum might be popping in and out of her room, doing a spot of tidying, as she put it.

'So when does she relax?' Jacinta's mother had asked.

'She doesn't.'

Mrs Symons had laughed, but Molly hadn't. It was true. Her mother didn't relax. Not even when they went on holidays together. She would be checking out the hotel or the caravan park, or all the local tourist attractions. Molly always had to try out all the attractions for children, too, and give full reports.

'It was okay,' she'd say, in answer to her mum's questions after she climbed off a funfair ride or came out of a museum.

'What do you mean it was okay?' her mum would say, pulling out her notebook.

Molly hated those questions. 'It was just okay.'

She'd mentioned it once to Lara, the day before they were going away on another research holiday, even though she felt a bit guilty complaining about her mum. Lara had got it immediately. She worked with her mum every day, Molly supposed, so she knew what she was like. She'd given her some good advice. 'Okay isn't that descriptive a word, Mollusc. Think about it as if you were telling one of your friends what a place was like and use that word. Your mum wants to know what it will be like for kids, so that would be really helpful. One good, juicy word should do the trick.'

Lara had been right. Molly had described the next set of attractions as awesome, scary, wild. Her mum had been really happy and had got off her back. Molly had texted Lara straight away. It workd. U r genius. She'd got one back minutes later. No, u r. L xxx

Molly checked her mobile phone now, where it was recharging by the chest of drawers. She'd been keeping half an ear alert for it all night, hoping to get the reply text from Lara. Usually she came back to her quickly, as soon as she got one of Molly's messages, even if it was to say Stop Txting & Get Bk 2 Work! There were no messages, though. There hadn't been any for nearly two days now. It was a bit weird.

Maybe her latest message hadn't got through, she thought, even though she knew it had. She had waited and watched for the Sent sign to flash. But maybe it had gone astray on the way. It was a long way for a few words to travel, from Australia to England. It wouldn't hurt to send it once more.

She had to type it all out again. She hadn't dared to leave the

message in her outbox. Her mother had started occasionally picking up her mobile phone and reading her saved messages and Molly
had already had to explain a potentially embarrassing text she had
sent to one of the boys in her class. Luckily her mum hadn't known
what some of the abbreviations were, but she'd been suspicious.
'Your mobile phone is for communication not for flirting, Molly,
remember that please.'

She had to be joking. They all used their mobiles to flirt. She tapped
on the keys. L, Nd sm advce. Boy stuff. Cn u cll me? Lol M xxxxx

She pressed Send. Waited. Message sent appeared. She crossed
her fingers Lara would call her back soon.

Molly had thought it would be fine, Lara being away for these
three months. She'd been excited for her, too, getting the chance
to study in England. She'd gone to the airport to see Lara off, and
they'd been texting and phoning each other while she'd been away.
But she still really missed her. Things weren't the same when Lara
wasn't around. She knew some people thought Lara was a bit
stuck-up, but she really wasn't. She was quiet and calm, but underneath she was really good fun and she always seemed to understand
how Molly was feeling about things.

She was great with fashion tips too. Molly really liked Lara's
clothes and the way she wore her hair. Lara was always really
happy to let her borrow anything, too, or to show her different
ways to style her own hair, like in plaits or French twists, or once
even using chopsticks in a sort of bun. She'd even spent a whole
afternoon helping Molly get ready for a school dance, when she
was going in fancy dress as a pop star, helping her tease her hair
and put on loads of make-up until she looked exactly like someone
on MTV. It had been great fun, a real laugh, like being with a really
cool older friend or big sister rather than an aunt.

Molly had gone out a couple of times with her other aunt Harriet since Lara had gone away, once to see a film, the other time to do some shopping, and it had been good but they just didn't have the same kind of friendship as Molly had with Lara. Harriet had changed so much. She used to be great fun, always ready to mess around and have a laugh, but then all that stuff had happened on that tour, and for ages after she'd seemed to be really quiet. Molly's dad had taken her aside one day, asked her to be extra kind to Harriet, that she was finding life tough, ever since her mum and dad had died. That was fair enough, Molly thought. It had been awful, especially when it had been one after the other like that, but how come everyone else hadn't fallen to pieces the same way? She'd asked her mum once, really casually, but she'd been no help. So she'd asked Gloria. Molly was actually a bit scared of Gloria, the way she sometimes seemed to know what you were thinking before you knew it yourself, and the way she would speak her mind. But at least she always told you the truth.

Gloria had thought about it for a little while and then said she thought it had been extra hard for Harriet because she hadn't been able to say goodbye to her parents, the way Austin and James and Lara had.

Molly found that a bit hard to understand. 'She was at their funerals, though. She said goodbye then. Everyone did.' The church had been packed both times.

'I meant when they died, Moll. Harriet was the only one of the kids who wasn't with them when they died.'

Molly still didn't really understand why that would have made Harriet go funny. It wouldn't have changed things even if she had been there, would it? Her grandpa would still have died of the heart attack and her grandma would never have recovered from the stroke. She'd heard lots of people say it at her funeral. That it was better she had died, that she might have been paralysed if she'd lived, in a wheelchair or in hospital all the time.

She still wondered if that's what Lara and Harriet had been talking about that night out in the garden, the night of Lara's farewell drinks party. It had definitely been about Grandma but she hadn't heard enough to know exactly what. It hadn't been a big party, mostly their clients, friends of Lara's and Harriet's, people they knew from around Merryn Bay, friends of the whole family. Even Austin had come down for it, even though it was just a few weeks before he was going on that big tour of Europe and probably catching up with Lara anyway.

Molly had enjoyed it. She got to be waitress at these family or Turner Travel parties, which meant getting to move around as much as she liked and not getting stuck in boring conversations with clients like that scary lady Mrs Lamerton, who lectured all the time about how things had been in her day. Molly had run out of clean glasses and her mum had asked her to go and get some more from the boxes outside. She'd gone out and nearly jumped out of her skin when she heard voices in the garden, until she realised it was Lara and Harriet. She was about to go over to them when something stopped her. They weren't talking. They were fighting. But in a strange way. She'd never heard Harriet speak in a voice like that, either before or since. She wasn't shouting. Neither of them was. That's what Molly thought about afterwards. How quiet they had both been, but how strange Harriet had sounded. Lara had been standing still, not reacting at all. Harriet had been asking her something. 'Lara? Is that true? I have to know, can't you see that?' Molly hadn't been able to hear the rest of it or what Lara said in reply. She'd heard a murmur, and then Harriet's voice again, soft at first, then louder, sounding like she was really upset but trying not to cry. 'I can't understand. How could you have done it?'

They hadn't seen or heard her, Molly was sure of it. She slipped back inside as quickly as she could. Not long after, Lara came in, looking really strange, and then Harriet ages after, all strange-looking too, pale like she always was but like she was in shock. What had they been talking about? What had Lara done or not done?

Molly spent a lot of time in the office after school, folding brochures and helping out with filing and she hadn't once heard Harriet have a proper phone conversation with Lara in England since that night. Lara phoned fairly often but Harriet barely talked to her, just transferred the call or took a message as if it was a stranger, not Lara, practically her sister. Lara didn't ever ask to speak to Harriet, either, any time Molly answered.

One day, when Molly was talking to Lara on the phone, she asked her about it, out of the blue. 'Have you had a big fight with Harriet?' Lara reacted really funny, too, she thought. 'Why?' That was all she'd said. Molly had murmured something vague about just wondering and quickly changed the subject.

She'd nearly, *nearly* said something about it when her mum told her that Harriet was going to be travelling with Lara on this *Willoughby* thing now instead of her dad. But there'd have been a big fuss, she knew. 'What do you mean they had a fight? What about? What did they say?' And Lara didn't like fusses, Molly knew that. No, better to keep quiet.

'Good morning, darling!' A voice sounded outside. Her mother, poking her head through the adjoining door from the office. 'Come on, Molly, breakfast please. You'll be late.'

Five minutes later, she was rinsing out her cereal bowl and about to go and clean her teeth when her mobile phone beeped to say she had a new text message. 'Let it be Lara, let it be Lara,' she said under her breath. It wasn't. It was her friend Hailey asking her to remember to bring in the magazines she had loaned her last week.

NW, she texted back. It was short for 'no worries'.

She checked the time. Three minutes to eight. She'd have to hurry. She brushed her teeth then called out a goodbye to her mum through the door. 'See you later, Mum.'

'Bye, darling. Do you want to come and see your dad tonight?' her mum called out.

'Yes, please.'

'Leaving at six.'

'Okay. See you.'

Her phone beeped again as she was a little way down the street, letting her know another new text message had arrived. Perfect timing. She didn't like being home when this text came in. It was too special to read at the kitchen table. She stopped and checked. Not from Lara, she knew. Even better than Lara. And right on time, as always. His message came every day at eight a.m., on the dot. I l u. I love you.

She wrote the message she sent back every day. I l u 2. Then hitching her backpack on to her shoulders, she walked on to school.

Gloria picked up their mail from the post office and then stopped at the deli two doors from Turner Travel, taking a carton of milk from the still-to-be-unpacked delivery by the front door. The verandas on each shop in the main street gave plenty of shade, and kept the milk cool, which was especially fortunate in the hot summer months. Gloria had collected the Turner Travel milk from this step every morning for the past thirty years, paying for it at lunchtime. She looked across the road and saw Molly on her way to school. They waved to each other, as they also did every morning. Molly was getting so tall, Gloria thought. Almost a woman not a schoolgirl these days. And getting quite beautiful, in that long-limbed teenage way.

As she reached the Turner Travel glass front door she noticed the lights were already on inside. She could see them through the edge of the blind she had pulled down the night before. She felt a flicker of alarm. Had she forgotten to turn them off last night? Or, oh God, not burglars. She was trying to decide whether she should call the police when she saw Melissa emerge from the staffroom, with a large pot of coffee in her hand.

Gloria unlocked the door and pulled the blind up with a snap. 'You're up bright and early. You nearly frightened the life out of me.'

'I've hardly slept. Thank goodness you're in early.'

'I'm always in early,' she said, put out to see Melissa. She treasured the early-morning peace in the office, straightening all the brochures in their racks, dusting all the framed travel posters on the walls and then writing up her travel fact on the blackboard they placed on the footpath outside. It had been her job since the agency opened. She already knew what today's was going to be. *Did you know it took 1400 men eight years to build the Sydney Harbour Bridge? (Great bus/rail packages and guided tours to Sydney available now.)* Afterwards she would enjoy a slow cup of tea while she sorted the mail, sometimes even playing some opera or listening to the news programs on the office radio. Not today . . .

Melissa paid no attention to the tone in her voice. 'You know I'm not one to exaggerate, Gloria, but we've got a disaster on our hands. I've made you a coffee, here. Please, take a seat.'

Ten minutes later Melissa had filled her in on Austin's phone call and the situation with Lara, Harriet and the *Willoughby* tour. She put her cup down with a bang on the table. 'Which brings us to the serious question of our next step. How to rescue the situation. I don't suppose you could go?'

'Go where? To England?'

'Yes, to England.'

'Why would you want me to go? Or anyone to go for that matter?' Gloria was genuinely puzzled.

Melissa gave an impatient laugh. 'To stop the tour turning into a complete disaster, of course. You don't think Harriet's going to be able to cope on her own, do you?'

'Of course. Why wouldn't she?'

'You know why. The first sign of trouble, the littlest hitch, and it'll all be too much for her. It'll be harder to come to her rescue when she's on the other side of the world. At least she was only a few hours away last time.'

'Harriet will be fine. That was nearly a year ago. It's time you forgot about it.'

'It's taken nearly a year for me to get those people back travelling with us again. I've put a lot of work into it, regaining their trust.'

'I'm sure they coped.' Gloria noticed it was about the work Melissa had put into it, not how hard Harriet had worked to overcome her problem.

'I'm serious, Gloria. Would you be able to go there? Would Kevin be able to cope on his own?'

Gloria sat upright. 'Sorry, Melissa, let me get this straight. Quite apart from you knowing I hate long-haul flights, you're asking would my blind husband be able to cope on his own while I flew to the other side of the world to rescue Harriet from a situation that she doesn't need any rescuing from? In fact, a situation that might be just what she needs to build her confidence up?'

Melissa had the grace to colour. 'Look, I know you're fond of Harriet —'

'It's got nothing to do with me being fond of Harriet or not.' Gloria was surprised how angry she was. Perhaps it was the extra cup of coffee this early in the morning, but for a second she felt as though she was channelling Penny Turner, defending her daughter. 'Harriet has a great deal of ability. She has a lovely warm way with people. She gets things done, sometimes in her own unique roundabout way, but she still gets them done. All she needs is the confidence and the feeling that people believe she can do it. You are not to think for a minute about sending someone over to rescue her.'

'But it's one of our international theme tours. It's important to the company, to our future direction.'

'So was the *Lord of the Rings* tour of New Zealand that James ran last year. The one that got flooded out for two days. Did you send in anyone to rescue him?'

'No, but that was James. He's done dozens of these tours. And besides, the clients loved it. They were talking about it for days. Some of them were even on the TV news.'

'And the disastrous *Mutiny on the Bounty* trip to Norfolk Island? The one you were leading?'

'I wasn't to know there would be a pilots' strike.'

'No, but between us all we managed to organise other transport, didn't we? And your clients were fine. Leave Harriet alone, Melissa. You bully her enough as it is.'

A gasp. 'I do not bully her.'

Gloria suddenly didn't care what she said. 'No? What do you call it then?'

'I help her. And my number one priority is always the clients, Gloria. Which is how it should be in any business.'

'It's a family business. Family plus me. It should be us first, and then our clients.'

Melissa didn't have anything to say to that. Gloria knew it was her part shares in Turner Travel, the ones that Penny and Neil Turner had left her in their wills, that infuriated Melissa. She knew that Melissa, and to a lesser degree James, disliked having to come to her to float ideas, to pass any expansion plans. She had been as surprised as the rest of the family when the will was read out, but she had been able to imagine a conversation with Penny about her reasoning behind it.

'Will you keep an eye on all of them for us, Gloria? Not just the three children and Lara, but Melissa as well? Just to stop them fighting?' Penny had been asking her to do that since the early days. And she would have said yes, she knew.

She kept control of the conversation. 'Surely the tour is the least of our worries, in any case. The main worry is Lara. Where she is. How she is.'

'Yes, of course it is.'

Gloria suspected Melissa had completely forgotten about Lara. 'Have you got any idea why she might have done this? Has she seemed different to you? Worried about anything?'

'Not that I noticed.' Melissa was sulking now. 'But Lara isn't one to spill her secrets in any case, is she? I've always found her secretive, if anything.' She paused. 'Perhaps we should ring Austin back. He might have some ideas. And at least he's on the right side of the world.'

Perhaps *we* should ring Austin back? Chance would be a fine thing, Gloria thought. She knew perfectly well that the last thing Melissa would do was ring Austin again. The devil got into her, though. 'That's a good idea. You won't mind talking to him again?'

Melissa's chin lifted. 'I've never minded talking to him. It's Austin who doesn't like talking to me. He's got this idea in his head about me and James and the business, and he refuses to see or hear sense.'

Gloria had to bite her tongue again. Austin's idea that Melissa was putting ideas into action without checking with the rest of the family. Not so outlandish really.

'I'll ask James to phone him,' Melissa said, busying herself with a pile of papers and not looking at Gloria.

Gloria softened. This was about Harriet and Lara, not Melissa, after all. 'Would you like me to ring him? It might be difficult for James in the hospital.'

'Would you mind? I've got a lot more on than you today, so that would be helpful.'

Gloria only just kept her temper again. Fighting an inclination to pour what was left of her cup of coffee over Melissa's head, she checked her watch and did a quick calculation of the time difference. Morning in Australia meant it was after midnight the night before in Europe, a good time to ring Austin. She knew from his tales of past tours that the members of the orchestra didn't go to bed until at least two a.m. after any performance. He'd said in his last email that the orchestra was performing every night this week. 'No problem, I'll do it now.'

'Thanks, Gloria. I appreciate it.' Melissa didn't look at Gloria as she spoke. She'd already turned to her computer and was scrolling through the morning's emails.

CHAPTER SIX

Gloria decided to call Austin from the phone in the staffroom, preferring to be out of Melissa's earshot. She dialled his mobile phone number and was disappointed when it went straight to his voicemail. She left a brief message. 'Austin, it's me. Can you call me back as soon as you can? I think you know what it's about.'

She took the opportunity to make a pot of tea, hoping that would dilute some of the effects of the morning's coffee. As the kettle boiled, she gazed around the room. A stranger would assume the pattern on the walls was old faded wallpaper – rows and rows of little multicoloured suitcases, apt for the staffroom of a travel agency. In fact, each suitcase had been stamped individually, over the thirty years Turner Travel had been in business.

It had been Gloria's idea, a way of marking their bookings in the early days, when things had been slow and they needed all the encouragement they could get. She'd presented Neil and Penny with a custom-made stamp in the design of a suitcase, and different coloured inkpads, suggesting they stamp the wall each time they got a booking. In the first few months there hadn't been much stamping. Ten a week if they were lucky. That had gradually changed. The proof of it was on the walls now, hundreds and hundreds, thousands even, of tiny suitcases, thirty years worth. The rows of suitcases were in different coloured inks, each colour representing a new year. The one colour that hadn't changed was the green for group tours. There were hundreds of those, sprinkled all over the walls.

'Imagine all the stories each of those suitcases would hold,' Penny had enthused one afternoon, just two years ago, when they were all sitting in the staffroom. It had been either Lara or Harriet's birthday, Gloria remembered. They were both in May, so her memories of their parties sometimes got confused. There had been cake, anyway, and a bottle of champagne. It had been a happy afternoon, she remembered. Lots of talk, teasing, laughter. And a lot of reminiscing, too, of the early days, when the staffroom wall had been more paint than suitcase stamps. Neil had started to count the suitcases and quickly given up, not even reaching the first thousand.

'What about the suitcases that went missing en route?' Austin asked. He had been home for a few days, not working but hanging around getting under everyone's feet. 'All the lost luggage? Should we paint over some of the stamps in memory of them?'

'Turner Travel lose clients' luggage? Never!' Penny had said. 'I couldn't live with myself if that happened.'

That day Penny and Neil had started talking about the trips they'd like to take, if and when they ever retired. Harriet, or perhaps it had been Lara, had leapt up, gone into the office and returned with a big bundle of brochures about great cruise journeys of the world. There was a lot of discussion about which would suit their parents best. Harriet chose the one around the Mediterranean. James preferred the more adventurous one to the Antarctic. Lara argued enthusiastically for two weeks in the Caribbean.

'You're all just trying to get rid of us,' Neil said.

'No, of course we're not,' Harriet said quickly. 'You don't have to go anywhere. You know we don't want you to. You're the ones who mentioned retiring. If it was up to me you'd work here forever.'

Penny laughed, pink-cheeked from the champagne. 'It's all right, my pet, we're in no hurry to go anywhere, are we, Neil?'

'Of course not. How could we leave Turner Travel in the children's hands? Austin would have it sold and be off to Bermuda on the profits before the others knew what had hit them.'

Austin rolled his eyes, pretending to sigh heavily. 'Thanks, Dad. You gave the game away. Surprise was my number one weapon.'

'So you're not thinking about retirement yet?'

Gloria could still remember Melissa asking the question. She wondered was it only her who had thought the question was being asked in great seriousness. In any case, Penny hadn't noticed any undercurrent.

'No, not yet.' She'd gazed around the room, up at the walls. The champagne had made her sentimental. 'Not until the day we've stamped ten thousand suitcases. Then we'll think about calling it quits.'

Gloria picked up her cup and took it over to the sink. They'd all had such optimism back then, such a naïve belief that it was all in their control, that they had a choice about what happened. But they hadn't, had they? Neil had died suddenly a year later and Penny just two months after that. Everything had been different since then. Melissa – with James in the background – had somehow taken charge. The suitcase stamping had virtually stopped. Only Gloria thought to do it now, once a week, and she wasn't sure how accurate her numbers were, not now when so many of their bookings were made on computer and spoken of in terms like PAX and Clientele or Groups A, B or C, rather than customer names. Melissa had never been interested in the idea of the stamps, in any case, Gloria knew. She looked at balance sheets, not stamps on a wall, to measure their success. Things had changed in so many ways since Penny and Neil died. The new regime had taken over, as Austin had put it. There was no time for frivolous things like stamps. No time for enjoyment. It was a serious business these days. Even the monthly meetings, which had once been good fun, were now regimented to the last minute.

Gloria thought of the last one Austin had attended. Melissa had been in top form, making pronouncements, producing flowcharts and pie-charts as though they were discussing a major economy, not a travel agency. She had reported on new tours, travel trends and where Turner Travel was placed in the market. She also announced a new company rule. There had been no discussion about it. All clients, both in the office and on tour, were to be referred to as Mrs, Mr or Miss, or, in extreme cases, Ms. She'd quoted from a recent study that good manners in business dealings had a greater impact on customer relations that any other aspect of communication.

Gloria had decided to herself she'd be having no part of it. Most of their clients were Merryn Bay locals and there was no way Gloria was going to start calling a woman she had known since she was five years old by a formal title. She said nothing, though. She'd already learnt the art of passive protest.

Melissa stood at the top of the table, tapping her hand on a pile of paper in front of her. 'I think our older clients – the greater part of our business as I don't need to tell any of you – will find formal titles particularly respectful.'

'That's a fantastic idea, Melissa,' Austin declared, falsely bright. 'Let's start with me. From now on, I'd like all of you to call me Lord Austin.'

'Don't be ridiculous, Austin, please.' Melissa was barely able to hide her impatience.

'Why not? Have you got the monopoly on ridiculous behaviour? Actually, now I think about it, it seems you have.'

'Austin, give it a rest, would you?' James snapped, his face flushed red.

Austin fell quiet and left the meeting soon after, as Melissa finished presenting the quarterly figures. He hadn't spoken, simply stood up, gathered his papers and headed for the door. 'Austin?' James was the first to speak. 'Where are you going?'

He stopped, and gave them all a long look. 'Do you know, I'm not sure. Somewhere a long way from here.'

Harriet tried to stop him. 'But you need to be here. It's a family meeting.'

'She's right,' James said. 'Sit down, would you?'

'It's not a meeting. A meeting is a discussion of ideas, shared thoughts. This is a dictatorship and your charming wife,' Austin bowed at Melissa then, who was growing as red-faced as her husband, 'our self-appointed dictator. I don't recall that part of Mum and Dad's will, do you, James? Harriet? Lara? My understanding was they wanted us to carry on as a family business. With you as well, Gloria, of course.' He nodded courteously in her direction.

Harriet coloured. Lara went still. James straightened in his chair. 'Melissa is family, Austin. She's my wife. We come as a package and I think you are being bloody arrogant not to listen to her ideas. It's all right for you, sailing around the world, playing your drums, breezing in and out as it suits you.'

Gloria winced inwardly. Austin didn't just 'play drums'. He was the lead percussionist in one of Australia's best-known orchestras.

James kept going. 'What would you prefer, that we'd have shut up shop after Mum and Dad died? That we'd go on as we had for years, the same tours, the same profits, year after year? Well?' He looked around for support. 'What about you, Harriet? What do you think?'

Harriet hesitated for too long. Gloria knew what would be going through her mind. They had talked about it often enough. She thought that both her brothers were right, that was the difficult part of it. Melissa and James had practically taken over, but if they hadn't been there after their father and then their mother had died, who knew what would have happened. 'I think it's worth listening to what everyone thinks,' she'd finally offered.

Across the table Lara spoke. The three Turners were pink-cheeked, their dark brown eyes flashing. Harriet's hair was in tufty spikes from where she had been anxiously pulling at it during the meeting. Lara had looked as serene as usual, her blonde hair smooth, her blue eyes clear, no spots of angry colour on her olive skin. 'Aust, come back, please,' she'd said, quietly, firmly. 'James is right. I think Melissa's got some great ideas. Let's at least talk about them.'

He'd refused. He hadn't attended a meeting since.

The phone rang. Gloria snatched it up. 'Turner Travel, Gloria Hillman speaking.'

'Glorious, hello.' It was Austin. 'You've heard about Lara then?'

'First thing this morning. What's happened, Aust?'

'I haven't a clue. I told Melissa everything I knew. Harriet arrived with the group and there was no sign of Lara. She rang her flatmate and was told that Lara had announced there'd been a change of plan and she wouldn't be doing the tour after all.'

'That's it?'

'That's it.'

'How did Harriet sound to you?'

'Thrown at first, of course, but no more than anyone would be if they got to an airport and the person they'd expected to meet them hadn't turned up.'

Gloria leaned forward and checked through the half-open door whether Melissa had left her computer. No, she was on the phone herself. 'You didn't get any sense that Harriet was going to —'

'Fall to pieces on us again? No, if anything, I think she wants to prove something to everyone. She only texted me for help after she'd got the group to the hotel and sorted out their rooms. She's worried, but I think she's got it under control.'

'Of course she has. Melissa however has just asked me if I would like to pop over to Cornwall and help her out.'

Austin gave a short laugh. 'Dear, thoughtful Melissa. What did she suggest you do with Kevin? Drop him off at a Holiday Home for the Blind for a few days?'

'Thank you, Austin. I knew I could rely on you to say the unsayable.'

'Melissa seems to bring out the best in me. So what do you think's going on with Lara? I played it down as much as I could with Harriet, in case she got too worried about her, but it's weird, isn't it?'

'Completely. Lara sounded fine last time we talked. It was a quick call, mind you. She wanted me to fax over some information for a project she was doing at college.'

'I spoke to her last week. I've got a few days off next month and we were seeing whether there was any chance of meeting up, either in Bath or somewhere else. And she rang me quickly the day James had his accident. It was just a quick call but she sounded fine then too.'

'You're in touch with her a lot?'

'We ring a bit, and text. She nags me about my wild life, asks me when I'm going to settle down; I nag her about her perfect life, ask her when she's going to loosen up. No change there.'

Gloria slipped into their usual banter without even thinking. 'She's got a point, Austin. God knows, time's marching on. Late-thirties, still no sign of settling down . . .'

'If God wanted me to settle down he wouldn't keep putting all these beautiful women in my path, would he? What am I supposed to do, Gloria, pretend I can't see them? Ignore their pleas to be asked out? Ignore their shining, hopeful eyes?'

Another time Gloria would have kept up the teasing. But something had just occurred to her. When she first heard that Lara was going to England, she'd anxiously waited for Lara to come to her, to ask if she knew anything about her parents, to ask if Penny and Neil had given her any more details about them. It would have been the most natural thing in the world, surely, for her to go looking for her parents' homeplaces in England while she was in the same country. And perhaps also the most natural thing in the world to want to visit where they had died. But she hadn't asked Gloria anything. There had been no mention of them in any of her emails or postcards either. She'd sent weekly reports from the tourism college, enthusiastic about how much she was learning. She mentioned Penny and Neil, as she did often and naturally, but not her own parents. Gloria had found it strange, but also a relief. The closer Lara came to the end of her studies, the better she'd felt, too.

She hesitated and then made herself ask him. 'Austin, has Lara ever mentioned anything to you about her mother and father? Whether she was going to go and visit the towns they were from, anything like that. Go to where it happened . . .'

'No. No, she didn't. It actually puzzled me that she didn't. I would have, in her position. But you know Lara, she wouldn't necessarily tell me even if that was what she was thinking of doing. She might already have done all of that, tracked them down, without telling us about it.'

Gloria had an uneasy feeling.

Austin continued. 'Look, I've been thinking about this since Harriet rang. Maybe I should fly over to England this weekend. See how Harriet is doing in Cornwall. Then go across to Bath and have a chat with Lara's flatmate. Just in case there's more to it. Because something's odd. This isn't like Lara, is it?'

It was as if he had read her mind. She'd been about to ask him if there was any way he could do exactly that. 'There won't be a problem with the orchestra?'

'No, not once I explain what's happened. Anyway, we've got a break from the public performances after tonight. It might get me out of a very dull embassy event and two school workshops. I should be thanking Lara and Harriet.'

They had a quick exchange of business, checking he had enough money for the air fares – he did; checking that he had Lara's address in Bath – yes; that he knew where Harriet and the tour group were staying in St Ives – he hadn't known, but took down the details. 'And you're okay to sort out the flights yourself?' Gloria asked, finally.

'You're talking to the son of a pair of travel moguls, remember? I think a bit of it might have rubbed off.'

'Sorry, I'm getting forgetful in my old age. I'll leave you to it, then.' She hesitated. 'But will you tell her we love her when you see her?'

'Tell who? Lara or Harriet?'

'Both of them. But especially Lara.'

'Why do you say that?'

'I don't know. In case she's feeling . . . Just in case.'

'I will.'

'And everything's okay with you, Austie? The opera tour's going well?'

'No. It's a disaster. Every time I hit a cymbal a woman on the stage plunges a knife into herself. Do you think I should take it personally?'

'Good heavens, yes. Your drumming's always had that effect on me, too.'

She hung up and came into the office to report back to Melissa. The other woman was in her glass office, still on the phone, facing the wall. Gloria guessed she was talking to James.

'. . . I can't believe it. How could Lara do this to me? She knows how busy I am, and then she leaves us in the lurch like this . . . No, please don't go on about Harriet again, she's going to have to handle it, isn't she, whether she can or not . . . Yes, she's here, she knows, she's talking to Austin at the moment.'

Gloria suspected she'd be called in to give James a full report on her conversation with Austin any moment. While she waited she took the opportunity to finish her morning tidying, straightening the photo pinboard that had hung on the side wall since the early days. Under a handwritten sign 'Turner Travel: We go further for you!' were dozens of photos of the Turners and Lara with groups in front of landmarks all around Australia and, recently, some overseas ones as well. It was out of place in Melissa's newly painted and remodelled office, but even she hadn't dared to take it down.

A recently arrived photo caught Gloria's eye. Lara, with a group of fellow students from the tourism college, the Royal Crescent in Bath behind them, grey English skies above them. Lara stood out, even in a group shot like this one. She'd always had a certain presence, even in a photo.

Gloria had tried to describe Lara and Harriet to Kevin once. He had a memory of them as children and teenagers but not as adults, as they were now. Gloria had tried to use words that would give Kevin more of a picture. He already knew that Harriet had dark hair and those big brown eyes that all the Turner children had, and that Lara was blonde, with eyes halfway between blue and grey. She'd thought about it for a moment.

'Harriet's still all movement, you know, she laughs easily and she uses her hands when she speaks, and she's eager. Do you remember the way she was as a child, wanting to be helpful and look after people? But still ready for mischief at the same time? And the way she would follow Austin around, like a little sorcerer's apprentice?'

Kevin smiled. 'That's right, so she did. Lara did too, didn't she? He had a harem even back then. And what about Lara now? What's she like?'

That had taken more thought. Gloria started hesitantly. 'Lara is . . . she's like a gum tree.' She laughed at her own description. 'That's flattering for her, isn't it?'

'There are hundreds of different species of gum trees, aren't there? Which one do you mean?'

'Oh, aren't you the expert. She's like a particular type of gum tree. Do you remember out on the north road, Kev, the Melbourne road? There was that old farmhouse with a group of trees planted to the side of it, a whole collection of them, and there was that one on its own?'

Kevin was nodding.

'She's like one of those gum trees. Those slender grey ones that just sway in the wind, even when it's blowing a gale. That stand out, even in the middle of other trees. That's what Lara is like.'

Gloria looked at Lara's photo again and invoked Penny, as she had often done since she had died. She hadn't heard any answer yet, but it was still a comfort to talk to her old friend. She missed Penny and Neil very much. She missed the old days of Turner Travel too. Penny had joked one day that the agency was like a hippy commune, with the three Turners and Lara in and out from the adjoining house every day, and Gloria's three boys calling in after school until hanging around an office lost out against surfing and playing football. All three of Gloria's sons now lived in Melbourne, married with families of their own, but they still felt comfortable enough to call in, help themselves to tea or coffee, sit behind one of the desks, as if it was their family business as well. Penny had known all about Gloria's three boys in the same way Gloria knew all there was to know about Penny and Neil's family. More than she had wanted to know sometimes . . .

'Is it about her parents, Penny?' she said softly. 'Is that where she's gone?'

Still no answer.

'Gloria?' Melissa's loud voice cut into her thoughts. Gloria winced. If only it was possible to turn down her volume sometimes. If only it was possible to make her disappear sometimes. If only it had been possible for James to have met someone else he wanted to marry . . .

'Gloria? I've got James on the line. He wants you to fill him in.' The voice, even louder. 'Gloria?'

'Coming.' She turned from the photo board and walked out into the main office again.

CHAPTER SEVEN

The noise of planes coming in to land at the nearby airport woke Harriet before seven o'clock. She'd slept fitfully, but enough to set her up for the day, she hoped. She threw open the curtain and got her first daylight glimpse of England. The hotel was for business or international travellers like themselves, not far from the airport, on the edge of a village. Harriet was looking out over green fields, all so neat, with trimmed hedgerows on each boundary. There was a smattering of daffodils here and there. The sky was blue, but a watery, soft blue. She'd left autumn leaves and changeable skies behind her in Australia.

She fiddled with the window lever and pushed it open as far as it would go. There was the smell of bacon frying. She must be near the kitchen vents. She could hear traffic sounds from the nearby motorway. But she could also hear birds, snatches of conversation and surely that was the sound of a lamb or sheep? She heard an Australian accent and leaned forward. Yes, it was two of the group, chatting as they took a pre-breakfast stroll. It was a good sign that they were up so early.

An image of Lara came into her mind. She'd been her first thought on waking. Where was she at that moment? Waking up in a hotel somewhere else? With someone? On her own? Happy? Unhappy? If Lara had been at the airport as planned, what would the two of them have been doing now? Would they have been sitting here in Harriet's room, going through the itinerary together, as James had imagined? Laughing? Would they have swapped stories of tours they'd been on, the way they used to do? Once upon a time, perhaps. Not now. Harriet knew they wouldn't have been able to. There would have been too much wariness. Too much tension humming between them.

She heard Austin's voice in her mind, telling her to leave Lara to him, to concentrate on the tour. He was right. Her job this week was to make sure the tour group and Patrick Shawcross had everything they needed, wanted, or thought they needed or wanted.

She checked her watch. Time to get dressed and then go to the breakfast room and greet the tour party. She opened the closet and took out her uniform, glad to see any creases had fallen out overnight. She could hear Melissa's voice, extolling the fabric's virtues. She had produced samples at one of the meetings, passing them around the table. 'It'll make a difference for all of us,' she said. 'It's not only convenient to have a uniform, but time-saving too. I'm assured the material is virtually uncreasable and uncrushable.'

'Not to mention unspeakable,' Austin had muttered.

Harriet dressed quickly, pulling on the stockings, skirt, shirt, jacket and the scarf, which was patterned with dozens of tiny versions of the Turner Travel winged suitcase logo. Melissa insisted they added a jaunty yet feminine touch. She looked at herself in the mirror for the briefest possible time, cursing Melissa yet again for her choice of colour, fabric and style. Harriet was slim from all the swimming she did, but the design couldn't have been less flattering. Even Lara looked awful in this outfit. The only person it suited was, astonishingly, Melissa. She had the right trim little body, blonde hair and brown skin that the style and colour needed.

The day she produced the uniforms, Melissa had made a speech about how proud Mr and Mrs Turner would have been of them all, for keeping things going, for making the Turner Travel name live on. Harriet had wanted to stand up to her, to make her admit that all of these expansion plans were nothing to do with her memories of Mr and Mrs Turner and everything to do with Melissa's own ambitions. But she'd said nothing. It had been too hard to put up a fight against Melissa's bulldozer tactics when she felt as fragile as a paper doll, as if one tiny puff of aggression, argument, even a strong opinion from Melissa, from anybody, would send her spiralling, fluttering into the sky, never to be seen again.

But not any more. She turned away from the mirror. That was the old her. She had to try and forget about that uncertain Harriet, and find the Harriet who had loved being on tour, who had faced any problems, dealt with difficult groups, managed anything that was thrown at her. She knew exactly what she needed to help her confidence. She reached for her bag, opened her purse and took out a small envelope. Even holding it in her hand helped her feel better.

Gloria had given it to her. She had come into the Turner Travel office late one night, a month after Harriet had discharged herself from hospital. She'd found Harriet at her desk, not working, just staring at the screen, her eyes filled with tears. Gloria had said nothing at first, just come over and taken her in her arms, holding her tight.

'What is it, lovie?' she'd asked. 'Tell me.'

'I can't do it, Gloria. James asked me again if I could lead one of the tours and I told him I'd think about it, but I know I can't do it. I'm going to have to tell him tomorrow. I'll have to leave. Resign. It's not fair on everyone else – him, Melissa, Lara, you.'

'It's a family business, lovie. I don't think you can resign from your family.'

'You know what I mean. I can't keep asking everyone to carry me like this.'

'Why can't you? If your family can't carry you when things are tough, then who can?'

'We're not a normal family.'

Gloria smiled. 'No, I'll grant you that.'

'We're a business family, I mean. That changes everything.'

'You're a family before you're a business. That will never change.' Gloria glanced at the itinerary on the desk in front of her. 'This is the one James has asked you to consider?'

Harriet nodded.

Gloria read through it quickly. 'It's one you've done before. Only two nights away, only ten in the group.'

'But I wouldn't be able to look after them properly, Gloria, I know I wouldn't. All I keep seeing is things going wrong and people dying and bad things happening to everyone.'

'Then it's too soon for you and you shouldn't go. It's as simple as that, Harriet. There's no rush, is there? James just asked you if you were ready, didn't he? He didn't put any pressure on you?' She looked closely. 'Don't tell me. Melissa is putting pressure on you.'

'Melissa's thinking about the business, I know. And she is trying to be kind . . .'

'Kind? Perhaps, though I'm not sure she knows what the word means.'

'But she's right. I have got ground to make up. I know I ruined that group's holiday. Embarrassed the company —'

'You did not embarrass the company. And Melissa is out of line telling you you ruined that group's holiday.' She held up her hand.

'No, perhaps she didn't say it in so many words, but I know what she's inferred. I've got a large pair of flapping ears, remember. Harriet, you probably made those people's holiday. Think of the stories they've been able to tell. It's not every day a tour guide —'

'Cracks up?'

'Has a breakdown. Don't make it sound worse than it was. You had anxiety attacks and then you had a breakdown. Harriet, you have to be more gentle on yourself. You have been through a bad time. Losing one parent is hard; losing both within weeks of each other is even more traumatic, especially the way it happened for you. Of course you had to react to it.'

Just the mention of it . . . 'I miss them so much, Gloria. Everywhere I look, everything I think about —'

'I know you do, lovie. We all do. But that's all right, we're allowed to. You loved them very much. Of course you should miss them.'

'But James and Austin loved them and miss them and they didn't crack up, did they? They lost their parents too. Lara lost them. Molly lost her grandparents. You lost your oldest friends. You all miss them as much as I do.'

'But there's no rule book saying we all have to react in the same way. We've all been affected too. I talk to your mother the whole time, did you know that? First sign of madness, but it helps me. James has thrown himself completely into work. Austin has been touring non-stop, taking any job going, hardly been home. Lara only applied for that overseas study course after Penny and Neil died. She never even mentioned going to England before that. That's how everyone else is coping. In their own way.'

Harriet sat silently.

Gloria squeezed her hand. 'Harriet, what happened to you is

completely understandable. And it doesn't matter whether it happened in public with a tour group or alone; what you felt was what you felt. No wonder you feel scared. No wonder your world feels unsteady and scary and uncertain. But it will change, I promise.'

'It won't, though, will it? It can't.'

'No, your parents won't come back but you won't always feel as bad as you do now. And all the solid things you had, and all the things you were able to face before this happened won't have changed. You are still you, underneath the fear and the panic attacks. You just need to believe in yourself again.'

'I'm too scared of everything, Gloria. I feel like I'll never be able to manage anything again.'

'But you will, Harriet. Not yet but one day. I've known you since you were just a little girl. I've seen for myself all the things you know how to do. Do you want me to remind you? No, tell you what, you remind me instead.'

'What do you mean?'

'Tell me some things you can do. Can you drive a car, for example?'

That brought a faint smile. 'You don't remember teaching me? After Mum and Dad gave up?' They'd tried to teach her and Lara the year they turned seventeen but the combination of a parent sitting beside her and a constantly stalling or kangaroo-hopping car had left Harriet helpless with giggles during each lesson. Eventually Gloria had stepped in. Harriet and Lara had managed to pass their tests on the same day.

'How could I forget? The day I got my first grey hair.' Gloria reached over the desk for a pen and paper and passed them to her. 'Come on now. Remind me of some other things you've done. Write them down so you can't forget.'

Harriet's mind seemed blank. 'I can't think of anything else.'

'Well, that's nonsense for a start. You got dressed this morning by the looks of things. Unless you've started sleeping in the beautiful uniform Melissa chose for us, have you?'

Harriet smiled properly that time. 'No, wearing it for eight hours a day is bad enough.'

'Write it down, then. *I can dress myself*. No, not good enough? Will I help you remember some better things?'

Harriet looked up at Gloria's so-familiar face, her sun-worn skin, her clever eyes, her mop of grey hair. She couldn't remember a time without Gloria. She'd come to Gloria for years, bringing news, asking questions, seeking comfort, liking being around her and her husband Kevin almost as much as her own parents. 'You're my extra mother, aren't you, Gloria?' she'd said to her once as a child. The thought sent a ripple of that grief through her again. And guilt, for calling on Gloria again. Time after time. 'Gloria, I shouldn't be keeping you. Kev will be worrying where you are.'

'Kev knows very well that if I'm not home responding to his every whim and at his beck and call then I am here in the office. He'll cope. Absence makes the heart grow fonder. Now, don't change the subject. Tell me something else you've done or know how to do.'

Slowly Gloria coaxed a list of things out of her, with difficulty at first, and then eventually even through some laughter. They were written in no particular order, here and there over the page.

I have worked and supported myself for more than fifteen years. I am buying my own house. I have travelled all around Australia. I have led hundreds of tour groups. I can touch type. I know how to cook Thai food, Italian food and Malaysian food, make jam, chutney, and tomato sauce. I have grown my own tomatoes, sweet corn, parsley, coriander and pumpkins. I once made dinner for ten people on a camp fire. I can drive a car and a tractor and, in an emergency, a minibus. I know how to replace a fanbelt, change a tyre and put up tents. I can row a boat. I once killed a snake. I can almost surf. I can swim thirty metres underwater. I taught my niece Molly to swim thirty metres underwater. I can say hello and how are you in German, French, Spanish, Japanese, Italian and Dutch.

'Now we're getting somewhere,' Gloria said. 'More please. What else have you done?'

'I lived with Simon for four years. Is that an achievement?'

Gloria's lip twitched. 'Depends on what you thought of Simon, I suppose. I liked him. So did Lara, I think.'

'Then you were the only ones who did. Mum and Dad were only polite to him, I know. James barely noticed him and Austin hated him.'

'Your parents thought he was a fine young man who should have asked you to marry him, not live with him. James has barely noticed anyone since he barricaded himself behind Melissa and Molly. And of course Austin hated Simon. He's always guarded you like a hawk. You and Lara, actually. In any case, Simon was too ordinary for Austin. Too ordinary for you, too, I always thought.'

'Too ordinary?'

Gloria nodded. 'I'm not putting him down. But he wanted less out of life than you do. And he'll be much happier with that new girlfriend of his. You know the word is they're about to get engaged?'

Harriet nodded. She'd heard. All she'd felt was glad that Simon was happy again. She hadn't had any pangs at all.

'In fact, Harriet, difficult as it was for you, I'm glad you broke up with him.'

'You never said that before.'

'It wasn't my place. I'm the faithful old family servant. Silent and loyal.'

'Silent?'

Gloria winked. 'Don't change the subject. Go on, add Simon to the list. He's part of your life. I want you to write down all the big things you've done. In fact, let me remind you of another big one. You welcomed Lara into your family. You made another little girl feel wanted when she was probably feeling the way you are feeling now, scared and alone. That was a very important thing to have done and you did it. Not only shared your bedroom and your friends with her, but also shared your parents and your brothers. I was very proud of the way you did that.'

Harriet opened her mouth as if she was about to say something and then shut it again.

Gloria kept talking, leaning over and taking back the list. 'I'll write it for you. *I welcomed Lara into the family*. There. And that's just for starters, Harriet. All true, and none of it has changed. You've done all those things. You will be able to do those things and more again.'

Harriet tried to make light of it, embarrassed now. 'I'd rather not kill a snake again, if it's all the same to you. It was a bit messy.'

Gloria smiled at her. 'That's fine. No snakes.'

'And I don't know if I'll ever live with anyone again.'

'No, I'd say you'll end up on the shelf. Poor Harriet, condemned to a life as Austin's housekeeper.' Gloria folded the piece of paper, reached over for a small envelope and put it inside. 'Stop that nonsense as well. You'll meet a man when you're good and ready and when he's the right man for you. Now, keep that list. Use that as a reminder if you ever feel an attack coming on. It might help.'

Harriet leaned across and gave Gloria a hug. 'Thank you, silent and faithful family servant.'

'You're welcome, sweetheart.'

'How have you put up with us all these years? Don't you ever get Turner overload?'

'Not yet. I'll let you know if I do. You're like a spare family to me, you see. When my own three boys used to drive me crazy I pretended you lot were mine. You've actually been quite a comfort over the years.'

Harriet had come in the next day with the biggest bunch of flowers she could get from the Merryn Bay florist. She hadn't made a fuss, simply got a vase and put them on Gloria's desk.

'What's this about?' Melissa had said, sounding a little put out that she hadn't been informed. 'It's not her birthday, is it?'

'No, it's National Thank Her for Everything Day,' Harriet had said.

Gloria had just smiled. 'Any time, lovie,' she whispered.

Harriet read the list again now. It didn't always work, but most of the time it did. It was like a voice of reason when everything threatened to overwhelm her. She could almost hear Gloria's voice. 'One more thing to add, Harriet. Go on. *I led the tour group from Melbourne to Bristol via Malaysia*. You did it and nothing went wrong.' She'd rung Gloria the night James had asked her to take on the tour. She had been just as calm then. 'Of course you can do it, Harriet. You're more than ready.' Gloria was right. Austin was right. She could do this tour. Nothing would go wrong. She was going to manage. All she had to do was remember all the things she'd done before: driven a bus, killed a snake, cooked over a camp fire, changed a tyre . . . She stopped there, and actually laughed out loud. No need to get too carried away. She was here to be a tour guide not a stuntwoman, after all.

She put the list back into her bag and did as she had been taught to do every morning – took a chair by the window, sat herself neatly, straight backed, feet together on the floor, arms by her side, not clenched in front of her. Eyes shut, breathing slowly, deeply . . .

Her eyes snapped open once, as she realised she still had to confirm the tour bus. She forced herself to close her eyes again. Back to the breathing. Keep the mind clear. Five minutes later she was ready. Only then did she ring the tour bus company. It was too early to ring the office, so she rang the emergency mobile number listed. A weary-sounding woman answered. Yes, she said, the bus was booked. Yes, the driver knew which hotel to collect them from. Yes, he was one of their most experienced drivers, Mr Clive Tillon, who had done many group tours over the years. Everything was under control. She'd just hung up when she remembered another question. She dialled the bus company again. Yes, the woman confirmed, now sounding more cranky than weary, the bus was fully equipped with a microphone, guide's seat and video player.

A news jingle played from the radio beside the bed, followed by a deep-voiced man announcing the news headlines from the BBC. Harriet checked her watch was telling the right time. Turner Travel rule number seven. Yes, eight-thirty. A good time to ring Patrick Shawcross in St Ives and welcome him to Cornwall. She was about to ring his hotel when she remembered she hadn't checked the number of seats on their tour bus. She dialled the bus company's mobile number again, confirming quickly that the bus that would be arriving shortly was a sixteen-seater. She hung up and rang the St Ives hotel next, introducing herself and asking to be put through to Mr Patrick Shawcross's room.

'Of course, Ms Turner. We're looking forward to welcoming you and your party here later today. One moment please.' There was silence, then the soft burr of the dial tone, over and over, until the call switched back to reception.

'I'm sorry, there doesn't seem to be any answer. Can I take a message?'

'Yes, please. If you could just say I called, and that we'll be on our way to him shortly?'

'Of course, oh, excuse me,' Harriet waited as she heard the receptionist have a brief conversation. 'Ms Turner, my colleague spoke to him briefly this morning. She said he was on his way down to the beach. Are you sure I can't get him to call you when he comes back?'

'No, that's fine,' she said. 'If you could tell him everything's fine and I'm looking forward to meeting him this afternoon.'

Harriet didn't think her first conversation with him should be over a mobile phone on the bus. She had a bit of explaining to do. James had told her they would fax the actor's agency with the change of details, explaining that it would be Harriet Turner and Lara Robinson he would be travelling with, but now that had changed as well. It wasn't a conversation she wanted to have with him in front of the group. Not when there was every chance Mrs Lamerton would snatch the phone out of her hands and pass it around to everyone.

She had overheard them in the minibus from the airport the evening before. They were a-twitter, there was no other word for it, at the idea of meeting Patrick Shawcross. Mrs Lamerton was making it clear she considered him her property. It had been her idea for the *Willoughby* tour, after all. Harriet half-expected Mrs Lamerton to have that line tattooed on her forehead or made into a T-shirt slogan. It would save her repeating it over and over again. 'As I mentioned to Lara when I first mooted the idea of this *Willoughby* tour.' 'When we first started planning this *Willoughby* tour . . .' She reeled off facts about Patrick Shawcross like a *Mastermind* contestant. 'Born in Penzance, you know. The only son of Irish parents. That would explain those Celtic good looks,' she'd gushed. 'Originally wanted to be a dentist – a dentist!' Mrs Lamerton had trilled. 'Imagine the queues to get into that surgery!' He'd been talent spotted in a college amateur dramatics society staging of *Macbeth*. Appeared in three episodes of *Doctor Who*. Brief marriage to Caitlin Moore, a Welsh actress, no children. Second marriage to Alicia de Vries, one stepson. He'd played the part in *Willoughby* for the two series before the show was axed. None of the women in the group seemed too up-to-date with him after that. They didn't seem to care much, either. Their attention had turned to other favourite TV programs.

'I always liked that Richard Briers,' Mrs Pollard said. 'Something kind-faced about him. He'd bring you a cup of tea in bed each morning, I bet.'

'No, too easy to boss around if you ask me,' Mrs Hart said. 'I liked the one in *Yes, Minister*, what was his name? Geoffrey someone? Or was it Nigel?'

'Sir Humphrey, do you mean? No, too sarcastic. And you'd never see him, all those long hours he'd have to work. Wasn't he in another program too? You know, the one set in that hobby farm?'

'No, that was Richard Briers as well, wasn't it? With that blonde lady with the sweet voice? Felicity Kendal?'

'She was voted Rear of the Year, you know.' Mr Fidock interjected.

Mrs Lamerton ignored him. 'Aren't you thinking of *To the Manor Born*? That was Penelope Keith, wasn't it?'

'No, that was *The Good Life*. What about that pretty American waitress in that one about the hotel? The one with John Cleese and Prunella Scales?'

'Fawlty Towers, you mean? Harriet, will we be able to see the hotel in Torquay from *Fawlty Towers*? St Ives isn't that far from Torquay, is it?'

She'd done her best to explain that as far as she knew the hotel didn't actually exist, but certainly, if it turned out they had time, she'd see what they could do.

She made sure she was downstairs in time to greet the party and do a headcount as they came into the breakfast room. Several years before, James had done a count of one of his parties – a sixteen-strong group, average age seventy, exploring the sights of Sydney – and realised one was missing. After checking the foyer, the car park and the lounge room of the hotel they were staying in, he'd finally asked at reception for a spare key to check the room. The missing man had been found in his bed. Dead, unfortunately. Natural causes, the doctor had declared. Since then, all the Turners had been very particular about their morning headcounts. Harriet was pleased to see all her twelve had survived the night. They were, in fact, looking quite bright-eyed this morning. She moved quickly from table to table, hearing a complaint or two about lumpy pillows, and assuring them the pillows in the St Ives hotel would be far superior and if they weren't she'd do her best to get first-class replacements.

Three times in five minutes she was asked if she was absolutely sure Mr Shawcross would be waiting for them in St Ives. They had obviously been more shaken up by Lara's non-appearance the evening before than she had realised. 'Yes, I've called the hotel and he arrived safely last night,' she told them. 'He's there waiting for us right now.'

'And how is he?' Mrs Lamerton asked, practically elbowing her way across the room to Harriet. 'Did he sound excited about the tour?'

She didn't think it right to tell them she hadn't spoken to him in person. She nodded and smiled, hoping that wasn't quite a lie, then moved purposefully out into the foyer before they had an opportunity to ask any more difficult questions. A bus pulled up in front of the glass double doors. Renwick Hire. Their bus.

The driver's door swung open and a small, tanned man jumped out, wearing a khaki shirt, khaki shorts, long white socks up to his knees and very white shoes. He strolled in, blew a kiss to the receptionist then turned in Harriet's direction. As he came closer, she guessed he was probably in his mid-fifties. Not much more than five foot four in height. She stepped forward and held out her hand. 'Clive Tillon? Hello, I'm Harriet, from Turner Travel.'

He shook it. His grip was tight. 'You're the nervy one who's been ringing the office all morning?'

Her voice faltered. 'That's right.'

'Leave it to me, now, love. There's nothing I don't know about the roads around here, or buses, so if anyone is to do any worrying, it's me. So fill me in. What have we got here? How many and what for?'

'I beg your pardon?'

'It's a tour group, isn't it? We do dozens of them, everything from walkers to TV fans. What's our poison this time?' He peered past her shoulder, into the area of the foyer where her group was assembling. 'That your lot? The oldies? It'll be a nostalgia trip then, I suppose? A trip down memory lane before a trip to the cemetery?' He gave a monkeyish laugh, showing a row of very white teeth.

Harriet wasn't used to bus drivers taking an interest in the tours.

On the ones she'd run in Australia, the driver usually started yawning when he met the group, yawned all the way through, dozed at the wheel while they did any sightseeing, and yet somehow still managed to form an alliance with at least one of the women on the trip, often two. It was a travel industry phenomenon, Gloria had remarked once. Bus drivers were notorious lady-killers. She was convinced it had something to do with the uniform.

Clive barely reached her shoulder and his uniform was for a man a size or two bigger, so she wondered would it work its magic this time. She tried to imagine Mrs Lamerton clutching him to her breast ('Clive. Oh, my Clive') and failed. He was still waiting for an explanation of the trip.

'We're a tour group from Australia,' she said. 'We're visiting the locations of a TV series called *Willoughby*.'

He frowned. 'That one about the postman? Solving crimes? From years ago?'

'That's right. Are you a fan yourself?' She brightened. It would be a real help if the driver knew some of the episodes.

He made a snorting sound. 'Biggest load of rubbish I ever saw. All the actors were terrible, none of the plots made sense and when's a postman going to find the time to solve crimes? There's a lot more to delivering mail than pushing bundles of letters into slots, you know. It's all systems, organisation. My brother worked as a postman for a while, and the stories he used to tell. I didn't know the half of it until he told me. It's a science, dividing up the regions, the way they place the bundles in the bag, so they're in the right order geographically. Think about it – what did you say your name was?'

'Harriet.'

'Think about it, Harriet. You post a letter in, let's say here in

Bristol, and it has to be in London by the next day, and somehow it is. It gets there. In pristine condition, too. That's a science.' He stopped. 'What's with the gear by the way? You in fancy dress?'

They both looked down at her clothes. Her bright yellow skirt and shirt. Her bright yellow stockings. Her yellow scarf. Every single inch of it was a glaring shade of the colour. Melissa's idea again. She'd read a study that it would stand out best against all other colours in an airport. She was right. Harriet had a feeling it would be visible from the moon. 'It's the Turner Travel uniform.'

'You look like Big Bird.'

He was right, she realised in horror.

He must have seen something in her expression. He gave her several hard pats on her yellow-sleeved arm. 'Don't take it as an insult, love, will you? That's just my way. I say it as I see it. Now then, let's get this show on the road and have a look at all of this.' As he spoke he started rifling through the notes in the folder he was holding. 'Are you it from the tour company? I thought there was going to be two of you?'

She nodded. 'There was. But there's been —' What? 'A change of plan. I'm in charge on my own for now.'

He whistled between his teeth. 'That's a shame. Easier on everyone if you can share the burden and believe me, I know what I'm talking about. I've done dozens of these elderly group tours. By the time the fights start, and the moaners start moaning away, you'll wish you could swap places with me, at the wheel, my own boss. That's not even taking into account the possibility of one of them dropping dead, or having a heart attack. I said all that to your colleague, what's her name, Lara? When she rang last week to check a few details. Some story about your brother falling off a roof and you coming instead, was that it? I thought she was bad enough, until we got all your calls this morning. You two need to relax.'

'You spoke to Lara last week? On the phone?'

'No, love, via morse code. Of course on the phone.'

She ignored his sarcasm. 'And how did she sound?'

He shrugged. 'Like an Australian girl sounds on the phone. Why? Who should she have sounded like? Gina Lollobrigida?' He made the snickery monkey-laugh sound again.

Harriet was conscious that Mrs Lamerton was approaching again. She lowered her voice. 'She didn't sound worried about anything?'

'No? Why, what did she have to be worried about?'

'Harriet, good morning again.' The imperious voice, right behind her.

Harriet turned. 'Hello again, Mrs Lamerton.'

Mrs Lamerton was wearing a flowered dress that fitted a little too snugly over her matronly frame. She favoured bright nylon dresses, generally decorated with bold patterns of flowers, and underpinned by what she must surely have called foundation garments. Her bosom was remarkable, there was no other word to describe it, though Austin had suggested one or two rude alternatives over the years. She was also wearing one of her brooches. She had a wide selection of them, most of which depicted large insects, such as grasshoppers or ladybirds, their colours picked out in glass stones. Today there was a gold spider with emerald eyes and a matching emerald stone at the end of each of its eight legs pinned to her left shoulder. It made quite a contrast to the poppies decorating the fabric of her dress.

'Still no sign of Lara, I see.' As she spoke, Mrs Lamerton was fingering the corners of her mouth, checking for lipstick residue.

Harriet wondered if she should tell her there was a mark of her too-red lipstick on her front teeth. She decided against it. 'I'm afraid not.'

Clive ignored Mrs Lamerton and spoke directly to Harriet. 'She's looking for her too? Who is this Lara? Lord Lucan's daughter?' Another cackle and another flash of the white teeth.

Mrs Lamerton gave Clive a haughty glare, before Harriet hurriedly introduced them. Mrs Lamerton's manner defrosted. The uniform working its magic again, Harriet realised. 'Lara and I formulated the *Willoughby* tour together and I am greatly puzzled, and still unsatisfied, as to why she isn't here. In fact, it's a disappointment. I thought she would have put the tour first, before any other commitments that may have arisen.'

'That's a good point. So where is she then?' Clive looked back and forth between the two of them.

Harriet felt like glaring at him. With his brown skin and brown eyes he suddenly reminded her of a monkey. A nosy monkey. 'She unfortunately couldn't make it. Something else came up. At the last minute.' She couldn't say they didn't know where she'd gone or what had happened. 'I think it had something to do with the tourism course she's doing in Bath.'

'Bath's only a couple of hours from St Ives,' Clive said. 'She could nip over and join us when she's finished, couldn't she?'

Now the pair of them were staring her down. Harriet tried to stand her ground. 'That might be unlikely. She asked me to apologise on her behalf.'

'So you've spoken to her?' Mrs Lamerton leapt at the news.

'Not exactly. She left a message.'

That tchy sound again.

'Well, it all sounds queer to me,' Clive said cheerfully. 'Come on then, Mrs Lamerton. First here, first served, let me help you on to the bus.'

'I'm sure I can manage.'

'Of course you can. I'm just looking for an excuse to put my arm around you.'

Once again, Mrs Lamerton surprised Harriet with a girlish giggle. Perhaps her fantasy of Mrs Lamerton clutching Clive to her chest wasn't that far-fetched, she thought, as she watched them head for the pile of luggage.

CHAPTER EIGHT

By one o'clock the tour party was only halfway along the coast road from Bristol to St Ives.

It had taken Harriet nearly an hour to get everyone onto the bus. Mrs Lamerton had been first, settling herself into the front seat with a loud sigh. Harriet had been reminded of a large cruise ship docking. Mrs Pollard had been next. It had taken two people, one in front pulling and one behind giving her a gentle push, to get her up the steep steps. As she said loudly several times, it wasn't that she was overweight, it was more her problems with the arthritis. Mr and Mrs Douglas – the only couple on the tour, and keen world travellers – insisted on trying out every seat on the bus before settling on a pair right in the middle, the first ones they'd tried. In the Turner Travel office, Mr Douglas was known as Mr Been – as in Been There Done That. He had a fund of stories and they had all heard most of them, several times over. It was Gloria who had first noticed his habit of getting his words mixed up. Since then, an unofficial competition had been underway for the best Mr Douglas-ism. Harriet's personal favourite had been his account of a safari trip to Kruger National Park in South Africa.

'There we were,' he'd told them as he leaned over the office counter, 'sitting on a rocky outcrust, looking at the wilmerbees.'

As she listened now, she heard him and his wife talking to Mr Fidock in the seat behind them.

'You've got a bit of a cold, love, haven't you?' Mr Douglas was saying, patting his wife on the arm. 'She often picks up a cold on these long-haul flights, don't you, pet? We'll have to stop off at a chemist, get a few of those euthanasia tablets for you.'

'Echinacea, dear,' Mrs Douglas absently corrected.

Harriet smiled a welcome at the last few members of the group as they made their way onto the bus. Miss Talbot, dressed in denim, carrying a bag in the shape of a heart. Mrs Biggins, who'd undertaken five conquer-your-fear-of-flying courses in the past two months so she could come on the tour. Mrs Pennefeather and her twin sister Mrs Hart, both widows. They did two Turner Travel tours together every year. They also did a lot of whispering and giggling. Mrs Kempton – married to one of Mrs Lamerton's cousins, and another long-time fan of the *Willoughby* series – came aboard next, followed by Mrs Randall. She smiled shyly at Harriet as she took her seat. All the Turners knew her, too. She was famously quiet. Austin called her Rowdy Randall.

The last to arrive was Miss Boyd. She had read about the *Willoughby* tour in the local paper six months previously and had phoned Turner Travel almost daily since. She was on and settled within moments, practically swinging herself on board and then proceeding to start sucking noisily on a barley sugar to stop herself getting 'travel-motion sickness' as she called it. The noise reminded Mrs Kempton that she had an awful feeling she had left her supply of anti-travel sickness tablets on the cupboard beside her bed upstairs.

'Or perhaps I packed them, Harriet, do you think? Would I be able to check in my luggage?'

Harriet had already seen Clive load the last of the luggage into the compartment, heaving Mr Fidock's bag on top of the large pile. She just knew that Mrs Kempton's case would be right at the back. There really wasn't time to unload and check, not if they wanted to keep to their schedule.

'Could I offer you one of my anti-nausea tablets, Mrs Kempton?' she asked. James had insisted she take the company's large first-aid kit with her. He'd phoned through a detailed tour of the contents the morning she left. If the plane had crashed on a desert island Harriet had enough knowledge and supplies to open a small hospital. 'I'm told they're the best on the market. I'm sure they'll do the trick if you do start to feel queasy.'

'No, mine are a special brand,' Mrs Kempton said, looking teary. 'From a Chinese doctor.'

Behind her, Clive was hefting himself up into the bus and caught the last few words. 'Not into that herbal medicine business, are you? A man I know did that, spent all his time boiling up bags of sticks and leaves. The house stunk of it.'

Harriet shot him a look. 'That's fine, Clive, thanks. I'm sure Mrs Kempton is happy with her doctor and her tablets.'

'Could I please check in my bag, Harriet?' Mrs Kempton asked. 'Or could someone check upstairs for me? Just in case I left them behind. I've been getting forgetful of late.'

Clive was watching with interest, arms folded, leaning against the driver's seat. 'One tablet is like another, you know. It's probably a placebo, or whatever the Chinese word for that is. Made from sugar or something. Not that sugar helps motion sickness. It just gives you something to do with your mouth, rather than think about getting sick. I read a study last year that —'

'Clive, please.'

'Just trying to help.'

Harriet herself had gone back into the hotel, explained the situation, been given the key to Mrs Kempton's room and, to her great relief, found her Chinese pills on the bedside table. She also found a pair of spectacles in the bathroom, a raincoat in her wardrobe, her book (a James Herriot novel) on the floor, and an umbrella on the hook on the back of the door.

Back on board, Harriet took the microphone and, after one false start with the on switch, welcomed everyone, urging them to settle back and enjoy the scenery or doze, whatever they liked. James had made a handwritten suggestion in brackets on her itinerary (*You could sing 'We're All Going on a Summer Holiday' to get everyone in the mood.*) Yes, or she could just smile and sit down as quickly as possible. A bad poem at the airport was one thing. She didn't want to break the bus windows with her singing. She switched off the microphone.

The itinerary for the first day was deliberately light, with brief stops at just two of the *Willoughby* locations en route to St Ives. Harriet knew there had been a lot of discussion in the Turner Travel office about how to plan the trip, taking into account the age of the group. The number one concern of elderly travellers was getting enough to eat and drink, and their number one pet hate was packing and unpacking every day or two. She remembered Lara suggesting they base themselves in St Ives, which was not just beautiful but also where Willoughby had lived in the series.

'We can do day trips from there, all over Cornwall,' she'd suggested during her presentation. 'The distances aren't great, and that way our clients won't get too exhausted.'

Harriet felt a tap on her shoulder. It was Mrs Lamerton, sitting squatly in the first seat again, with her bags piled on the seat beside her.

'Harriet, have you decided yet where Mr Shawcross will be sitting each day? When we're doing our bus tours?'

She realised then why Mrs Lamerton was sitting in that seat and also why the seat beside her was piled high with bags and scarves. 'I don't really know yet, Mrs Lamerton. I suppose I thought I'd leave it up to him.'

Miss Talbot leaned over from the adjoining row. 'But he will move around, won't he? He won't sit in the same seat each day?'

Mrs Pollard leaned forward too. 'Yes, we'll all get a go at sitting next to him, won't we?'

'Are you ladies fighting over that actor? A bit young for you all, isn't he?' It was Clive, loud from the driver's seat. He turned back, taking advantage of the fact they were stopped at a red light. 'If you're looking for a bit of action, I'm right here. Much fitter than I look, too. You wouldn't mind, Big Bird, would you? All part of the service, heh heh heh.'

Miss Talbot gasped. Miss Boyd gave a giggle. Harriet realised she had to put her foot down. 'Thank you for that, Clive. Perhaps you could concentrate on the road and keep your comments to yourself?' She winced inside at her prim school-mistress tone.

He shrugged. 'Who is this Shawcross bloke anyway? A local fella, is he?'

He couldn't have asked a more welcome question. As a chorus of voices sent information to the front of the bus about his birth in Penzance, his Irish parents, his plans for dentistry, Harriet took the opportunity to put down the itinerary and take in the scenery instead.

Beyond the traffic and the motorway, the fields were very green, with neat, trimmed hedges around them, cows and sheep grazing, daffodils in clusters underneath trees. April was a good time to be here. The sky was blue, the air crisp. The light was softer than she was used to in Australia.

They passed a house called Owl Cottage; farm shops selling cider, vegetables, strawberries and clotted cream; signposts for villages called Chapel Allerton, Bradley Green, Wootton Courtenay. Everything looked so English. As they drove further down the coast towards Cornwall the scenery was becoming wilder, higher cliffs and sweeping bays instead of the neat fields and small farms of Devon. Harriet was waiting for some rush of recognition, some feeling that she was in her ancestral homeland, but so far it hadn't come. Not that her parents were from this side of the country. Her father had been born in Manchester, her mother in Leeds, with both their families coincidentally moving to Watford when they were children. They had been childhood sweethearts. They'd gone to school there, married there, and had James and Austin there, before making the decision to emigrate to Australia, where Harriet had been born.

She had addresses if she wanted to see where her parents had lived back then. She wasn't sure how she felt about that yet. The previous year James and Melissa had made a trip to the UK, and James had visited all the family places. He'd been planning on doing it again at the end of the *Willoughby* tour, as well, when he had a few spare days. It was different for him, though. He had childhood memories of Watford, even one or two schoolfriends that he'd looked up. Harriet tried to imagine standing outside the house where her parents had lived. It would be one more reminder that they were gone from her life, a reminder of all the gaps in her knowledge of them, as well. It had been a whole new hurt, a new layer to her grief, when she realised there were things about them, about her own history, that she would now never know. All those years she could have asked them about their early years in England, or why they had emigrated, or the early days in the migrant hostel, and she had never thought of it. Now they were gone, she would have given anything to ask them thousands of questions, to hear every tiny detail of their lives. She had taken the addresses from James, murmured something about thinking about it and then pushed them to the bottom of her bag.

She wondered if Lara had made any plans to return to her own parents' home places. Harriet didn't know a great deal about Lara's mother and father. She'd only met them once, when she was little. She remembered overhearing discussions about them over the years, and the yearly memorial day her mother had instigated to help Lara get over losing them so tragically like that, but it was all shadowy. She knew a few vague facts, that Mr and Mrs Robinson had left for Australia from Watford under that same 'Ten Pound Poms' scheme, emigrating on the same ship as her own parents, which was how they had met. She thought Lara's father was also from Watford, but she knew Lara's mother had been born in Ireland, then grown up in England. It meant Lara had three homelands in a way: Australia, Ireland and England . . .

'— and she said, "Over my dead body, Colonel!" '

Harriet registered too late that Clive had turned on his microphone and was treating everyone to a selection of bawdy jokes. The two men in the group laughed, two of the women tittered, the others looked scandalised. Harriet managed to interrupt him just as he introduced another one about a barmaid, a bishop and a monkey.

'Clive, please!'

'Just sharing some of that famous English humour,' he said, still speaking into the microphone. 'We're going to be together for the next five days, ladies and gentlemen, so no point standing on ceremony. Any of you have any jokes at any stage, hold up your hand and I'll get Big Bird here to pass back the microphone and we'll have a good old laugh together, all right?'

She needed to lay down some ground rules, Harriet realised. Her chance came an hour later, at their first scheduled stop for the day, the cliffside village of Lynton, home to the hotel featured in several early episodes. Clive announced he was going to stay in the bus and read his newspaper. Once Harriet had led the group safely inside to the tearoom and left them exclaiming over menu descriptions of piping hot tea, warm-from-the-oven scones, homemade strawberry jam and thick clotted cream, she seized the opportunity and went back out to the bus.

'Clive?'

He was reading a newspaper, opened on a page showing a topless young woman. He didn't look up. 'Mmm?'

She cleared her throat. 'Clive, I don't like to cause problems between us, but I am having a few difficulties with your manner.'

'What manner?'

That was it. He didn't have any manner. 'I think you're being a bit informal. Interrupting. And some of your comments have been a little blue.'

'The others like it. That bald fellow didn't stop laughing. You're too formal, that's your problem.'

'I'm in charge of the tour, I have responsibility for everyone in the group and your comments aren't helping me.'

'Just trying to lighten the load.'

'Really? By singing the theme from *Sesame Street* each time I stand up?'

'Not loudly.'

'It's a small bus. And you used the microphone.'

'But you do look like Big Bird. Not that you're big.' He looked her up and down. 'You've got a very nice figure, in fact. Pretty face, too. It's the yellow. The yellow legs especially.'

Harriet was going to kill Melissa as soon as she got home. And she was definitely going to stop wearing the yellow stockings. Melissa would never know.

He swung his legs around the seat and gave her his full attention. 'Do you change colour with each season? It being spring, you go for yellow. Do you go orange in autumn?'

'No, I'm yellow all year round. Clive, please don't change the subject. I'm serious.'

'I know. As I said before, that's half your problem. You're the most tense person I've ever met. And I've met a lot of Australians. Lived out there myself for nearly fifteen years.'

She thought she'd detected the trace of an Australian accent in his voice. 'You did? Where?'

'In the mines, in Western Australia. Worked as a driver in a place called Pannawonica. Picked it because the name made me laugh. Made a fortune but nearly went mad with the loneliness. And the heat. How the hell do you all stick it out?'

'It's not that hot where we live. It's a seaside place.'

'I'd have given my left ba—,' he stopped himself just in time, flashing her his monkey smile. 'Sorry, thought I was back in the mines for a minute there. I'd have given anything for a day by the beach back then. It was the homesickness that got me in the end. That and the minor matter of a family left back here.' He made that snickering sound again.

'You're married?'

'Yep, for my sins. One wife, two grown sons, four grandchildren.

Don't know how the missus puts up with me. She runs a B&B back in Bristol nowadays. Good company for her, I'm on the road most of the time.' As he was talking he was wriggling around in his seat. 'Do you know there was a study done once into whether bus drivers had fertility problems on account of all the sitting we do. No one asked me any questions, I could have told them a thing or two, though. Sheepskin is the key.'

'I'm sorry?'

He lifted himself up off the seat and she saw the sheepskin cover under his bottom. 'Keeps me cool in summer, warm in winter and lets plenty of air circulate. Now then, you wanted to say something?'

'Yes, Clive, before the others come back, I do need to clarify that —'

'Yes, yes, that you're in charge. Of course you are. But it's like that nanny business, really. The hand that rocks the cradle rules the world. The hands that drive the bus rule the tour. Har, har!' His laugh was like a motorbike starting up.

She wondered whether the best thing to do would be to ring the bus company and ask for a different driver. It was as if he read her mind. 'You're lucky you got anyone to drive this bus, you know. The most awful dose of gastro has been doing the rounds of our drivers the past few weeks. One of the drivers had it without realising. Before he knew it, he'd passed it on to the entire tour group. Imagine those pit stops!'

That answered that, then. What would James or Lara do in this situation? It was best not to think that way. It had to be her decision. She decided to give in for the time being. Sometimes that was the best option. 'The poor things. And you're feeling all right?'

'Couldn't be better.'

She swallowed again. 'Well, I'm glad we had this chat. And if you could help me a little more, Clive.'

'I'll do my best, BB, I'll do my best.'

She smiled weakly and went back inside to pay for the scones.

It was nearly three by the time they reached the second stop, the seaside town of Bude, over the Devon border into Cornwall. As they drove into the town, Harriet read from James's prepared script: '*Here in Bude is the grand hotel dating back to the 1790s that was used as the setting for the ballroom scene in episode two, "The Case of the Titled Temptress". That ball was, of course, also where our dashing hero Willoughby first met the beautiful yet wily Lady Garvan, who was to prove more than his match in subsequent episodes!*'

James's writing was getting more colourful as it went along. He'd either been getting further into the swing of it or further into a bottle of wine. It gave her a glimpse of a different James. If he hadn't been so responsible, so obliging, so barricaded behind Melissa and her ambitions, he might have chosen a different career, she suspected. He'd always loved writing, she knew. As a teenager, when he wasn't watching cricket, she remembered him scribbling away in notebooks, coming up with ideas for his own comedy skits or writing funny poems. But he'd been so loyal to his parents; there had never been any talk of him going to work anywhere but the travel agency. He'd been one of their hardest working guides and he worked even harder now as the general manager.

Perhaps that was the downside of a family business, Harriet thought. It brought a guaranteed income and a job for life, but it wasn't necessarily the job you would have chosen for yourself. Writing the notes for the itineraries was probably James's only creative outlet these days, she realised. It explained a lot. It also helped her forgive his more colourful phrases. She read on, much more cheerfully.

'*An extra five minutes with Patrick Shawcross to anyone who can remember what Lady Garvan was wearing the night of the ball!*'

The subsequent discussion – it came down to a choice between an off-the-shoulder green taffeta dress or a silver sheath with long white lace gloves – kept the group occupied throughout the twenty-minute stroll through the town.

They arrived in St Ives right on schedule. The whole bus – even Clive – fell silent as they drove down the coast road, past rows of terraced houses and hotels, tantalised by quick glimpses of blue water now and then.

The view suddenly opened in front of them. It was a glorious sweep of bay, beaches and sea, edged by a jumble of hilly streets crammed with whitewashed and stone-fronted buildings. The late afternoon sun shone down on the long curving stretches of sand, creating sparkling spots of golden light on the blue sea. They couldn't have timed their arrival better. There were white sails against the blue water, and along the shore line, families playing on the sand.

Clive leaned over to her. He'd been almost well behaved since their chat, having told only one vaguely ribald joke about a goose and a nun. 'The roads are clear enough. Do you want me to take a quick run along the seafront before we go to the hotel?'

'That would be great, thanks.'

Clive slowed the bus almost to a crawl, and they peered up cobblestoned laneways at the vivid splashes of colour from window boxes and pots of geraniums. There were art galleries, cafes, sweet shops, fish restaurants and old-fashioned seaside shops with buckets and spades, umbrellas, beach chairs and jaunty sunhats hanging outside. A sign by the road pointed to the Tate St Ives and the Barbara Hepworth Sculpture Museum.

Harriet turned on the microphone and read from the script, editing out James's more breathless passages as she went along. *'Over the years many famous artists have made St Ives their home, drawn by the natural beauty and the unusual quality of the light. We'll have plenty of time to explore over the next few days and to visit not just the cottage whose exterior was used as Willoughby's home, but also the lighthouse featured in episodes three, ten and fifteen and the post office featured in episode six.'*

'Episode seven,' Mrs Lamerton interrupted. ' "The Case of the Mislaid Mail".'

'Sorry, episode seven.' She had misread it. They'd definitely be keeping her on her toes. *'But now let's go to the hotel, check in and then all meet for cocktails with our special guest, Mr —'*

'Patrick Shawcross!' Three of them finished her sentence for her. Someone – was it Mrs Lamerton or Miss Talbot? – even gave a cheer.

CHAPTER NINE

'It's so homely,' Harriet heard Miss Boyd say as they all filed into the hotel foyer.

'My grandmother had that very same wallpaper,' Mrs Pollard remarked.

'It reminds me of that guesthouse we stayed at in Canada, Doris, do you remember it?' Mr Douglas asked his wife. 'It was so beautiful, with such wonderful views. The bay was still as a milkpond.'

'Millpond, dear,' she said wearily.

The hotel was in a perfect position, right on the cliff, looking down over Porthminster Beach and across to the lighthouse. The décor was a bit old-fashioned – overly patterned carpets, a mixture of chintzy and flock wallpaper, and big baskets of artificial flowers – but the tour members were delighted.

Mr Fidock came in from his exploring, rubbing his hands together. 'There's even a seaview bar, ladies and gents. Bring on happy hour!'

The hotel staff ferried bags up and down the stairs, leaving the old gated lift free for the tour party. Harriet made sure everyone was settled in their rooms, for the time being, at least. She knew there would probably be the usual complaints about itchy bedding, dirty windows, faulty bathroom lights and/or slow-boiling kettles over the next few days, but for now everyone seemed happy. She darted up to her own room. It was one of the smaller ones at the back of the hotel, in the same corridor as Mrs Lamerton, Miss Talbot and Mrs Kempton, but looking out over the road and several other hotels rather than the beach. It was the usual arrangement – she and Clive would have the equivalent of servants' quarters, leaving the good rooms for the tour guests.

There'd been an awkward moment at reception, when the woman in charge asked in Mrs Lamerton's hearing whether Lara would be checking in later.

Harriet had lowered her voice. 'I'll come back to you on that, if that's okay?'

'So she might be turning up?' Mrs Lamerton had still managed to eavesdrop.

'I'm still hopeful,' she'd said, before taking refuge in a pretend call on her mobile phone. She'd also slipped back to reception after Mrs Lamerton had gone upstairs, and asked if there was any chance of getting a TV and video machine installed in her room. It would be no problem at all, she was told. She'd have it within the hour.

Now, in her room, she called reception again and asked to be put through to Patrick Shawcross's room. She listened to the soft burr of the dial tone, her mind drifting as it went on and on. She jumped when it was finally answered.

'Good afternoon!'

It was an American man. A cheery American. Harriet was taken by surprise. 'I'm sorry, I must have the wrong room.' She hung up and dialled reception again.

'Hello, this is Harriet Turner again. Could you put me through to Mr Shawcross's room?'

'I'm sorry, Ms Turner, I thought I just did. Let me try again.'

The phone was answered quickly. 'Good afternoon again. And let me check, yes, it's still a beautiful afternoon.' It was the same man.

'Mr Shawcross?'

'That's right.'

'Oh, Mr Shawcross, hello. This is Harriet Turner. I'm so sorry for hanging up on you before.' Harriet had been expecting a Cornish accent, her head so full of *Willoughby* episodes she was imagining a Patrick Shawcross of fifteen years ago. He'd been living in Boston for years, of course he would have picked up a bit of an American accent. Had Lara mentioned that? Then she remembered Lara hadn't spoken to him while setting up the tour. Everything had been arranged via the French assistant in the talent agency in America, mostly by fax and email.

'Hello, Harriet. That's no problem.'

She tried to sound as businesslike as possible. 'I hope your room is fine, and that you had no difficulties getting here? And that you got my messages?'

'I did, thank you. Everything is fine. And your basket of fruit couldn't have been more welcoming, so thank you for that as well.'

'Oh, good.' He sounded so friendly. So normal. She took a breath and started delivering the explanatory speech she had been rehearsing all day. 'Mr Shawcross, I need to fill you in on one or two things. There's been a slight change in arrangements. We did fax your agents with this news, but you may have been en route already and not heard all of it. You were originally going to be travelling with my brother James, but unfortunately he had an accident, so I've taken over his role. My apologies also that neither Lara nor myself were able to phone and greet you last night as we expected. I'm afraid our flight was delayed, and then unfortunately Lara was unable to meet us . . .' she trailed off. He didn't need to know everything immediately, did he?

'It's a real family affair by the sound of things. No problem at all. I'm sure you and I will get on just as well.'

He sounded completely relaxed about it. Perhaps that came from the acting background. Presumably film sets and TV studios were unpredictable workplaces. Harriet gave a relieved laugh. 'Thanks so much. We've had a few unexpected ups and downs so I wanted to be sure that was all fine with you.'

'It's absolutely fine.'

'Perhaps we could meet for coffee before we go and have a cocktail? Have a general chat about the tour before we get started?'

'That's an excellent idea. Will I meet you downstairs? I'll carry a newspaper so you know me. Either the *Times* or the *Guardian*, I'm still trying to work out which political camp I'm in now I'm back in Britain.'

'You won't need to bother with the newspaper. I've been watching the videos of your show for the past while, so I'm sure I'll know you.' She was warming to him more and more. 'So how long is it since you've been home?'

'Home?'

'Here, in Cornwall.'

'I come back to England quite regularly, but, oh, I haven't been in Cornwall since we filmed the series. So it's nearly fifteen years.'

The more they spoke, the more she could hear his English accent coming through. Mrs Lamerton and Mrs Pollard had been particularly keen on hearing that voice of his in real life. She'd heard them talking about it the night before. They'd been competing to see who could describe it the best. Like warm treacle, Mrs Lamerton had said. No, deep and rich, like toffee, Mrs Pollard had insisted. They were both right. It was a warm, deep voice.

'And have you still got relatives in Penzance?' He might like to call in to them while they were so near.

'In Penzance? No, not that I know of.'

'Really? Oh, I thought you were born there. Your biography said —'

'You were given the Penzance biography? I'm sorry, please don't believe a word of it. My first agent and I made that up one night over a bottle of whiskey. I was actually born in London. Stoke Newington, to be precise. But my agent thought Penzance sounded far more romantic.'

'But your parents are Irish?'

'No, English. From London, too, though they're living in Spain these days. I've just come from visiting them, in fact.'

The image she had of him was crumbling away piece by piece. 'So you weren't ever planning on becoming a dentist, either? Before you were talent spotted?'

'It says that too? We really did get carried away. I'm sorry about that. No, I'd always wanted to try acting.'

Harriet mentally ran through the facts. He wasn't born in Penzance. His parents weren't Irish. His path to acting wasn't a romantic one . . . *Expect the unexpected*, she thought warily. What else would be different about him? An image of a prematurely old, wrinkled grey-haired man flashed into her mind. Quite a few years had passed, after all. She had to ask. She had to know before she saw him, so she had time to prepare herself if the news wasn't good. 'Mr Shawcross, getting back to what we were talking about a few moments ago . . . just so I'm sure I recognise you when we meet downstairs . . . ' How did she put this? She decided to try the roundabout approach. 'Would you say you've changed much in appearance since the *Willoughby* days?'

'Have I changed much?' She heard something in his voice, but she wasn't sure if it was amusement or annoyance. 'Well, now, there's a question. Tell me, do you look anything like you did fifteen years ago?'

'I hope not,' she said emphatically. Fifteen years ago she'd had braces on her teeth, puppy fat and a peculiar pair of spectacles that Austin and Lara had picked out for her. They'd insisted they were very cool. It was only years later, after she'd switched to contact lenses, that they'd admitted they'd picked the awful ones as a joke.

'It was that bad?'

'It was that bad.' She was kicking herself. Why couldn't she have waited until she saw him to find out for herself? 'I'm sorry, it's fine, I'm sure I'll recognise you —'

'No, you're right, it's a perfectly reasonable question. Fifteen long years have passed since then. Lots of water under the bridge. Lots of hair loss, too, unfortunately.'

'Hair loss?' Was this why there hadn't been a photo of him in the notes?

'Bald as a badger, I'm afraid. Oddly enough, I'm also finding it takes me longer to get around these days. My old legs seem to tire so quickly. Will we be able to stop now and again for a cup of tea and a bun, do you think?'

Another mental picture appeared, with more detail this time. An elderly bald man limping across green fields, a flask of tea in hand, an elderly lame dog limping behind him. She blinked it away. 'Yes, of course we can.'

'And I hope you don't mind but I decided to ask my doctor to travel with me, too. There'll be no problem with the expenses, will there? I've booked him into the room next to mine.'

'Your doctor?'

'I've had a couple of angina scares lately, so I thought it better to be safe than sorry.'

'Oh. Well, no, of course that's fine. I'm sure we can make room for him.'

He laughed then, a warm sound. 'Harriet, it's all right. I'm teasing you.'

'Pardon me?'

'I'm teasing you. You were being so diplomatic I couldn't resist it. It was only fifteen years ago, not fifty. I promise you I haven't changed that much since the series. And I promise my doctor isn't with me, either.'

She sat down, a mixture of embarrassed and relieved. 'Mr Shawcross —'

'Please, call me Patrick. We're going to be travelling together, we can't be standing on ceremony. Let's just enjoy ourselves. Isn't it a matter of us driving around beautiful Cornwall for a few days together? A few photo sessions? Interviews over dinner each night?'

'Interviews?'

'You're right, that's too formal. Let's call them conversations. We could probably have had it all done in a day, but that's neither here nor there now, I suppose. The two of us can take it easy.'

'The two of us?' It was her turn to be amused. 'You mean the fourteen of us.'

'Sorry?'

'There's fourteen of us on this trip, remember. Fifteen if I include the bus driver. And he's a handful, I don't mind warning you.'

'Very funny.'

'I wish I was being funny.'

'And don't tell me, the other twelve people are a handful as well?'

'Yes, I think they might be.'

'All right, Harriet, I think we're even.'

'Even?'

'I teased you and you teased me. So, to get back to this article . . .'

'Article?'

'The magazine article you're writing about me.'

'But I'm not writing an article about you. I'm leading a travel group. That's what I meant about the group of fourteen people. There are twelve in the tour party, plus you and me.' Things had turned very odd. 'This is the actor Patrick Shawcross I'm talking to, isn't it? The one who played Willoughby?'

'Yes, but we are talking about the same trip, aren't we? The trip down the *Willoughby* memory lane? Organised from Australia?'

'Yes, but Mr Shawcross, I'm not from a magazine. I work for Turner Travel. It's my family's travel business based in Merryn Bay, just outside of Melbourne. We specialise in leading themed tour groups, like this *Willoughby* one.'

'You're with a tour group?' His amused tone had now completely disappeared. 'But I was told this whole trip was for an Australian magazine article, one of those "where-are-they-now" features. Your colleague Laura —'

The back of her neck was prickling. 'Lara.'

'Lara faxed over a copy of a magazine feature I did here in England years ago. Sophie at the agency said it was all going to be based on that.'

'It is. That was the starting point for the whole tour. But we only faxed the article to give your agent an idea of the places we'd be visiting. Didn't you get the itinerary? The one we faxed last month? With all the notes about the tour?' Harriet had seen James fax it to the agency himself.

'No, I've been travelling in Spain the past few weeks, visiting my family. The only itinerary I saw was a list of dates and places, months ago, when I first got the invitation. I have it here.' There was a pause and then he returned. 'It's from a Lara Robinson to Sophie in the agency. "Dear Sophie, As discussed, the following is the suggested itinerary for Patrick Shawcross's trip." And then a list of placenames and suggested dates, St Ives, Boscastle etc., etc. "I look forward to hearing from you. Lara." Sophie sent it to me when she first got the invitation; I said it all looked fine. That's all I knew until I collected the tickets and details of this hotel at the airport.'

Harriet knew the fax he had mentioned. It was the interim one Lara had prepared. And he was right, there hadn't been any mention of a tour party on it. She was now extremely worried. 'What about the one we asked the hotel to deliver with your fruit basket?'

She heard him take a look. 'There's a card, but no itinerary.'

She tried to keep the alarm out of her voice. 'Mr Shawcross, I'm so sorry about this. We really need to talk, as soon as we can.'

'Of course we can talk about it. But Lara —'

'It's Harriet.'

'Sorry, Harriet. As I'm sure you don't need me to tell you, a tour group is a different kettle of fish to a magazine article. I'm not sure I can —'

'*No!*' She couldn't let him say it. She couldn't even let him think about pulling out. 'I mean, please, Mr Shawcross, don't make any hasty decisions. Not until we've spoken face-to-face.' She knew she sounded desperate. She was desperate. She could feel the colour rising in her cheeks. 'Could you tell me your room number?'

'Thirty-nine. On the third floor.'

She knew it was one of the rooms with a seaview balcony, but on a separate floor from the tour party. 'I'll be there as soon as I can.'

She quickly ran to the bathroom to splash some water on her face. As she turned on the old-style tap, a gush of water splashed out of the sink, all over her shirt and skirt. She swore out loud. She couldn't go up and see him like this, or wait for it to dry.

Within three minutes she had thrown off her uniform, opened her case and changed into the first outfit she could find – jeans and a simple red T-shirt. She pulled them both on and glanced in the mirror. Both a bit casual, but stylish enough. Jewellery would help, perhaps. She was already wearing her blue opal bracelet and added a pendant around her neck, a simple resin circle in a striking darker blue. She quickly took out her make-up bag and reapplied some red lipstick, mascara, a smudge of golden brown eyeshadow and a touch of blush, all in record time.

She was nearly out the door when she caught sight of her feet. She'd put on her Turner Travel court shoes again without thinking. It was a very bad look. Another scrabble in her case for some high-heeled boots. They were on in seconds. She checked from all angles that they looked okay and that the jeans hadn't got tucked up in the boots like jodhpurs. They had. She quickly fixed them up. There was only time for the quickest restyle of her hair – a matter of running her fingers through the short black strands and perking up the fringe – and a check that her lipstick was still in place. It would have to do. And at least her own clothes gave her more confidence than the Big Bird outfit. She gave herself one last glance in the mirror and then she was out the door, her heart pounding.

CHAPTER TEN

He answered at her first knock. It was definitely the man from the *Willoughby* videos. The same dark curly hair. The dark eyes. He was taller than she'd expected though. At least six foot. But apart from that he could have stepped straight off the set. It was a huge relief. She beamed up at him. 'Oh thank God. You look just like Patrick Shawcross.'

His lips twitched. 'Well, yes. That's because I am Patrick Shawcross. You must be Harriet.'

'Yes, I am. Hello, Mr Shawcross.' She couldn't take her eyes off him. It was like Dorian Gray. It was remarkable how little he'd aged. It had to be plastic surgery.

'No, actually it's not.'

Her hand flew to her mouth. She'd said it out loud. How rude. She blamed the jetlag, even though she'd been denying to herself she had any. 'I'm so sorry. You look much younger than I expected, that's all.'

'Oh, well done. Wrap an insult up in a compliment like that and you'll go straight to the heart of any actor, lapsed or otherwise.' He smiled then. 'You really do have quite a thing about age, don't you?'

'Not usually, no.' She was very embarrassed. 'I somehow got it into my head that you were in your seventies, grey-haired, one foot in the grave.'

'Not quite. I've just turned forty-five and I'm fit as a fiddle. I have my passport here if you'd like to check my birth date?' His face was serious but there was a definite sparkle in his eye.

'No, I believe you, I promise.'

'Then we're off to a good start.' He smiled at her again. Very nicely. 'Please, come in.' It was a suite, twice the size of hers. A lounge area with a table and chairs, leading on to a full length balcony with a stunning view over the beaches. Through a door she could see a double bed. She was pleased to see the large fruit basket on the side table.

As she followed him across the room, she got the scent of his aftershave. She loved the smell of aftershave. His was distinctive, something lemony, with musk or something deeper underneath.

'Can I offer you tea?' he asked. 'Coffee?'

'No, neither thanks. I thought it might be better if we got straight down to —'

'Business? Absolutely. Let me take a look at the itinerary and we'll see if we can get to the bottom of this.'

They had just sat down when a mobile phone on the table between them rang. He checked the number. 'Harriet, I'm sorry, but I've been expecting this call all day. Would you mind?'

'Of course not. Would you like me to wait outside?'

'No, please don't. I won't be long, I promise.'

He answered the phone, moving over to the open balcony door as he spoke. He was obviously pleased to hear from the caller. She heard a snatch or two, the talk punctuated with low laughter, his English accent coming through more obviously the longer she heard his voice. 'That's great news, well done. Fill me in . . . Four weeks worth? . . . No, I'll check the script when I'm back . . .' It sounded like he was lining up work.

As he leaned against the balcony rail looking out over the water, she took the opportunity to study him even more closely. It was odd to see him in the flesh after spending so long looking at him on the videos. He really had changed very little. It was like looking at Willoughby's older brother, she decided – his just as good-looking older brother. He was dressed in dark jeans and a white shirt, the sleeves folded up over his brown arms. A tan from his time in Spain, she presumed. He somehow didn't look the type to go for sunbeds. He was a solid build, but fit-looking. He turned back towards her then, saying his goodbyes. As he came closer, she noticed more details. There were traces of grey in his hair, at the temples. And perhaps a few more lines, especially around his eyes. She saw them again now as he sat down and smiled at her.

'I'm sorry about that. I'm all yours now. You're sure I can't get you coffee? Tea?'

'No, thanks, I'm fine.' There wasn't time. The cocktail party was due to start in less than two hours. They needed to get this sorted out quickly. She passed him the itinerary. 'Please, take a look.'

She watched his face as he read the cover page. Then he turned to the next page. Today's program. He started reading it aloud. If she wasn't feeling sick to her stomach she would have quite liked listening to his voice.

'*The tour really starts tonight with your first opportunity to meet and mingle with our SPECIAL GUEST! Patrick Shawcross, yes, Willoughby himself! Have you got your questions ready??! And go on, try an exotic cocktail, while also enjoying a buffet selection of the finest local produce in the comfortable setting of the hotel. The bolder ones among you might even like to kick on afterwards with a nightcap in the stunning seaview bar and lounge! But don't forget our early start tomorrow, now, will you??*'

He looked up at her. She saw his eyes weren't dark brown but in fact a dark blue. 'Did you write this?'

'No. No, I didn't.' She had a feeling that was just as well.

He turned the page and read aloud again. '*A day of* Willoughby *treats is in store for all of us today! We're off in the bus to the harbour villages of Boscastle and Port Isaac, the settings for episodes nine, twelve and fifteen, passing some of Cornwall's most spectacular coastal scenery en route. There'll be ample opportunities for photographs and, even better, plenty of chances to hear Patrick Shawcross's reminiscences of his* Willoughby *filming days. There's sure to be a few surprises!!*' He turned the pages and read some more. Kept turning. She watched his face. No reaction. Finally he turned to the last page, then closed the folder. He was silent, slowly patting it against his hand. Harriet was reminded of the flicking tail of a lion. An unhappy lion.

'I wish Sophie had shown me this.'

Harriet swallowed. 'Yes, so do I.'

'I'd have turned it down.' He gave it back to her. 'Harriet, I'm sorry, but I can't possibly do it.'

She couldn't hear him say that. She wouldn't let him say it. She tried to keep her voice calm. 'I can certainly see why you might think that. But Mr Shawcross, you're here now. We're all here. Surely the easiest thing would be to go ahead?'

'I can't. Harriet, that *Willoughby* series was fifteen years ago. I can barely remember it. What I agreed to do – what I thought I had agreed to do – was a simple "where-are-you-now" magazine feature, photos of me at all the different locations, you know, standing next to the church at Widecombe-in-the-Moor, recreating the scene from the opening credits —'

'Widemouth Bay.'

'They've moved the church to the Bay?'

'No, the opening credits started with you at Widemouth Bay and then went to the Widecombe-in-the-Moor church.'

'That's right, so they did. I'm sorry, but you must understand that being interviewed for a magazine article is a long way from being paraded from one part of Cornwall to the other like a prized pet.'

'We've called you our special guest, not a prized pet.'

'I'd feel like a prized pet.'

'But we thought you'd jumped at it. Sophie told Lara that you accepted immediately.'

'I did. I knew I'd be on holiday this month so the timing was good. I liked the idea of seeing Cornwall again.' He smiled. 'I also thought I'd better get in quickly, before you tracked down someone from *Poldark*.'

She gave a guilty smile. 'That isn't quite as popular in Australia as *Willoughby*.'

'It really is still a hit there?'

Harriet nodded.

'Amazing. I've had fan mail from Australia occasionally, passed on months after it's been sent, usually. I don't do much work with that agency any more, so I'm small fry to them these days, I suppose.' He sounded surprisingly relaxed about it. 'We didn't ever expect *Willoughby* to take off at all, you know. My suspicion always was that it had been made as a sort of tax dodge. It was the most ramshackle production. No one seemed to know what they were doing. Not only the cast but the crew as well. Not that I complained. It was a dream first job.'

If she wasn't on the verge of losing him as her special guest she would be enjoying hearing all this. Her curiosity got the better of her. 'How did you get the part?'

He seemed just as happy to talk, crossing his long legs in front of him. 'Three things, really. One, I was an unknown so I was cheap. Two, the way I looked. The director had a specific idea in his head and I happened to match it. And three, I was sharing a house with one of the producers. I've always had a sneaking suspicion that was the clincher.' A flash of that smile again. 'And TV back then was nothing like it is now. If anything, it was embarrassing to admit you'd done a TV show. The real actors stayed in repertory theatre.'

'That's why you went to America? To go back to stage acting?'

'No, I actually got a part in a very bad soap opera over there.'

'Really?'

'Really bad, do you mean? Oh yes, on every level. The writing, the sets, my acting.'

She was surprised again at how honest he was. Where was the big ego she'd been expecting? 'Would I have seen it?'

'I hope not, for your sake. I played the heir to a huge oil fortune who was making pornographic films to bring disgrace on his family. My name was Roger Hardwick. Imagine. I'm sure the scriptwriters thought it was hilarious.' He shook his head. 'I was thinking about it on the flight over. If I thought *Willoughby* was bad . . . Mind you, it made for some excellent dinner party stories over the years. All soft focus and cardboard sets. I also had to wear a large fake moustache.' He laughed again.

'So no one recognises you, at least?'

'No, luckily. That's being grateful for small mercies, isn't it?'

She was about to ask him another question when she remembered why they were both here. 'Mr Shawcross, perhaps we should get back down to business . . .'

'That actually sounds like a line from that very soap.'

'I'm sorry, but we really do need to sort this out. If I could just explain —'

He held up his hand to stop her. 'Please, Harriet, you don't need to. There's nothing to explain. It was a simple mix-up. I've had a nice flight over, a good night's sleep, a morning swim. It's been a pleasure to see St Ives again after all these years. So no harm done. I'm more than happy to refund you any of your expenses, and please, give my apologies to the tour group.'

An icy feeling shot down her spine. No. He had to stay. Harriet knew Mrs Lamerton was put out enough about James and Lara not turning up. She would *kill* her if there was no Patrick Shawcross. 'Please, Mr Shawcross, can't you give it some more thought? The group have all been looking forward to it so much. They've been doing nothing but watch *Willoughby* videos for weeks in preparation.'

'Really?'

She nodded.

'The poor things.'

She blinked.

'It really was a terrible program, you know,' he said. 'None of the plots ever made sense. There was one where the vicar's wife was murdered, and supposedly it was the jealous gardener who did it. Yet if you traced it chronologically there was no way possible it was him.'

She had watched that program the evening before. Series one, episode three: 'The Case of the Green-eyed Gardener'. 'That's what I thought. It all tied up too neatly in the end. It would have made far more sense if it was the visiting professor, the one who had rented the holiday cottage, who had been behind it.'

'Yes, exactly.' He smiled. 'That's funny. I haven't thought about that episode in years.'

She glanced at her watch. It was getting very late. There was no time for reminiscing. She had to plunge in again. 'Mr Shawcross, what would it take to convince you to stay? Because I'll do whatever I can.'

'Harriet, are you sure you didn't see that soap opera I was in? You seem to be quoting it back at me, line for line. I remember a casting couch scene just like that.'

'No, I didn't. And I didn't mean to sound —' she searched for the word and chose the first one that came to mind, 'racy.'

'Racy?' He laughed again, a deep, rich sound. 'What a wonderful word. And look, you're actually blushing. How lovely. I didn't think anyone blushed any more. Do you know, I was at an Actors' Equity dinner in Los Angeles last year and there wasn't a blush or a frown to be found in the entire room. They'd all had either plastic surgery or Botox injections. Women and men.'

'Really? You've had it yourself?'

'Good God, no. You know it's made out of a virus that causes paralysis? An actor friend of mine at home in Boston told me he is waiting for the day when all the side effects cut in and ninety-five per cent of the actors in America drop dead. "Think of the work we'll get then, Pat," he told me. "They'll come begging for us. The only standing actors in the world."'

'So you're not working as an actor much these days?'

'No, not much.'

He didn't seem worried about it. Her mobile phone beeped in her bag. Melissa checking up on her? The thought chilled her. She let it go to voicemail.

He stood up. 'I'd better not keep you. It's been a pleasure talking to you, Harriet, but as I said, I don't think —'

No. She couldn't let him go. She stood up too, glad her heels gave her some extra height. He was nearly a head taller than her as it was and she needed all the authority she could gather.

'Please, Mr Shawcross. Won't you at least come to the cocktail party tonight? I can't tell you how much it would mean to the group. It really wasn't their fault there was this mix-up and they'd be devastated if they didn't get to meet you.' She noticed something in his expression as he looked down at her. A wavering? She started talking at record speed. It seemed important to tell him everything. 'They've so many questions they want to ask you. And they're dying to show you their impersonations. Two of them want you to watch them act out their favourite bits from the series. And one of the ladies has even made you a jumper. With a little embroidered Patch on the bottom right-hand side.'

'Really?'

She nodded.

'Who was Patch again?'

'Your dog. The black and white dog.'

'The dog?' He frowned. 'So who was it I had the beer with at the end of each show?'

'That was George. The farmer from the adjoining property to your cottage.'

'Oh yes. *"That's people, isn't it, George?"*'

'*"Aye, Willoughby, so it is."*' Harriet answered without thinking. She rushed on. 'Could you see it as a challenge to you as an actor? I could help you. Feed you all your lines. I've got all the videos of the show here. You could watch them all, get a refresher course.' She gazed up at him, crossing her fingers behind her back, trying to stay calm, imagining a duck paddling madly under the water.

His next words gave her some hope. 'Tell me again how the tour was supposed to start?'

She knew the itinerary by heart. 'Tonight, officially. With a cocktail party here in the hotel so they could all meet you. Then we had trips planned for every day, to different locations from the program. The group helped us put the itinerary together. They even did a vote of which were their favourite locations.'

'Oh? Which one won?'

'It was a toss up between the smugglers' cottage in episode four and the historic hotel where you first met Lady Garvan and accused her of dealing in counterfeit artwork.'

Another puzzled look.

'When you kissed her, and she slapped you and said she didn't mess with commoners. And then you took her to bed.'

'Did I? Good Lord. Did I enjoy it?'

'I think so.' The program had been surprisingly sexy for its time. Lots of groans and flashes of bare skin in that scene, before it faded to out-of-focus and then came back to them both in bed, puffing away on cigarettes.

She had to make one more effort to convince him to stay. Her words came in a rush. 'Mr Douglas has even bought a digital camera to take photos of you. He's going to set up a *Willoughby* website for everyone when he gets home. And little Miss Talbot has hardly been able to sleep with the excitement. It's the trip of a lifetime for everyone. Please don't go. I'd hate to let them all down.'

'Harriet, that was so heartfelt. Have you ever thought of taking up acting yourself?'

She could see the amusement in his eyes. He wasn't only smiling at her, she realised. He was practically laughing. She couldn't bear it. If he'd had any idea how hard the past year had been, stuck behind her desk, doing nothing but filing, and computer work, feeling nothing but scared and a failure. This time tomorrow he'd be home in America, while she'd still be trying to explain to the tour group and James and Melissa why the trip was a disaster before it had begun. And that didn't even begin to take into account why Lara had decided not to show up.

She was suddenly furious. With him, with James for landing her in this mess, with Melissa for all her bullying, with Lara for disappearing, with Clive and his Big Bird remarks, all of them . . . 'No, I haven't. And never mind. I understand. I'm sorry to have brought you all the way here for nothing. If you can give me an hour or so I'll get on to the airline and organise your flight back home to London or Los Angeles or —' Oh, damn it, now she'd forgotten where he lived, 'Silicon Valley, wherever it is you want to go.'

'Silicon Valley? Because of the plastic surgery?' He laughed out loud. 'Very droll, Harriet. And please calm down. I'm not going anywhere.'

'You're not?'

'Apart from a strange ragbag of *Willoughby* locations, it seems.'

A tremor of hope. 'You'll do it?'

He put his fingers on his temples and shut his eyes.

'Mr Shawcross?'

He opened his eyes. Blue mischief looked at her. His voice was low, deep. It filled the room. ' "*There are some mornings when I wake up and see the blue of the sea and feel the freshness of the wind and I know I'm home.*" '

She knew the line by heart. It was from the beginning of episode one, 'The Case of the Prodigal Postman', setting the scene when Willoughby first returns to his home place. He had it word for word. And he'd spoken in a perfect Cornish accent.

She couldn't stop the big smile. 'Oh. Oh, thank you. You won't regret it, I promise. We'll spoil you rotten.' It was all she could do not to hug him.

Back in her room five minutes later, she had to stop herself somersaulting onto the bed. She'd managed it! She'd pulled the tour back from the brink! It was going to be okay! The sound of the mobile phone interrupted her victory lap of the room. She snatched it up.

'Harold? Is everything okay? I rang your mobile before and only got your voicemail.'

It was Austin. 'I was in doing a briefing with Mr Shawcross.' She loved how normal it sounded.

'Oh, right. And everything's fine with him?'

'Absolutely fine, yes.' She kept her voice even, but inside she wanted to shout the words. She wanted to leap in the air and click her heels together it was so fine.

'Harold, I've decided to come over to Bath as soon as I can, to have a word with Lara's flatmate. I've checked out the airports. I'm going to fly to Plymouth first, come and see you in St Ives and then drive up to Bath. Talk to Lara's flatmate, some people at her college, see if they've noticed anything out of the ordinary.'

'You're coming here?'

'It'll just be a quick visit.'

'You don't need to on my account. It'd be great to see you, but I'm fine.'

'It's no trouble. Besides, I need to pick your brains about Lara some more. She's obviously upset about something and between the two of us we might be able to figure it out. Work out where she's gone. Get her back on to the tour as soon as we can.'

She sat down abruptly. 'But what if she doesn't want us to find her?'

'What?'

The words felt like they were bursting their way out of her. 'What if she doesn't want us to know where she is?'

'What's got into you? She's our sister, Harriet. Aren't you worried about her too?'

'I suppose I'm playing devil's advocate,' she hedged. 'If she did want us to know, then wouldn't she have told us where she was going? Maybe she does just want some time on her own.'

'If that's what she'd wanted, if everything was all right, then you know as well as I do that Lara would have rung one of us, told us what arrangements she was making, kept us all up-to-date and then gone away. You know how organised she is. And she would never leave a tour group in the lurch like this. Or you, of all people. I think we need to find her, to make sure she's okay. Then if she wants to be left alone, we'll leave her alone.'

'You, of all people.' She had to tell him. She needed to explain to someone what had happened between her and Lara. She'd just begun to speak when she heard him have a brief conversation with someone near him.

He came back on. 'I have to go, Harriet. See you in a couple of days. I'll find her, don't worry.'

'Austin, wait, please . . .' She was too late. He'd already gone. Her words were left hanging in the air.

CHAPTER ELEVEN

Harriet was eight years old when Lara first came to stay with the Turners. James was sent out by his mother to round up her and Austin so they could hear the news. He found Austin in the back garden of the house and travel agency, lying reading in the hammock strung between the plum tree and the clothes-line post. He gave it a push, nearly toppling Austin out onto the ground. 'Mum wants to talk to us.'

'I'm busy.'

'She said it's important.'

'This is important. I'm sleeping. It's an important activity for fourteen-year-olds. We do most of our growing while we're sleeping, so if I interrupt the growth spurt now there's every chance I'll have halted it mid-cycle and I'll never grow another inch.'

'Austin, I don't give a rats myself but Mum wants to talk to you.'

Austin stood up and stretched. 'When I'm a parent I'm going to let kids do whatever they want.'

'And then you'll know the torment you've put me through.' Mrs Turner had come out and overheard. 'Where's Harriet?'

'In her room.' Austin said, yawning. 'Locked inside her jigsaw puzzle prison.'

'Go and get her, Austin, would you?'

He headed inside, picking a plum on the way and throwing it, with perfect aim, at James. He found Harriet in her room, bent over a card table their father had set up for her. A cardboard box with a picture of three kittens peering out of a wicker basket was propped up in front of her. She was frowning, her black hair in little tufts from where she'd been pulling at it as usual.

'Harold, Mum wants a meeting.'

'I'm nearly finished.'

'Now.'

'Help me find the middle one's tail first. I thought I had it but it was his ear.'

He found it within seconds, slotted it into place and she reluctantly followed him outside, bringing the lid of the puzzle with her.

Mrs Turner waited until they were sitting down, James at the top of the table, Austin on the bench against the wall and Harriet on the chair beside her mother. 'Thanks, Harriet. I promise you can get back to your kittens in a minute. I want to give you all some news first.'

Harriet put up her hand. 'Are we getting another kid?'

'Child, not kid, Harriet, please. And you're at home, darling. You don't need to put up your hand to speak. What made you think we're getting another child?'

'Bernie at school. She said that every time her mum and dad tell them they have some news they get a new baby.'

Mrs Turner bit back a smile. The Kellys were up to seven children already. She reached across and kissed Harriet's head, smoothing down her tufty hair at the same time. 'No, I'm not having a baby. But it's a bit like that. You're going to have a new sort of sister. An instant sister. Just for a little while.'

Three blank faces looked at her.

'Boys, do you remember Rose Robinson? My English friend from the ship? And in the hostel?'

'A bit,' James said. Austin thought he vaguely remembered her. Harriet wriggled. She didn't like it when they spoke about the days on the ship from England or in the migant hostel. She'd heard all the stories and almost convinced herself she could picture the early days in Australia, but they weren't her own memories. All she knew for sure was she had been born in one of the tin huts at the migrant hostel, eight and a half months after her parents and two brothers arrived in Australia. Her mum had told her there hadn't been time to go to the hospital. 'You were in such a hurry to arrive, Harriet.' 'You should have called me Hurriet, then,' she said. It was her first ever joke. She was really happy when everyone laughed and after that first time she said it as often as she could until Austin told her to put a sock in it. She had to ask him what 'put a sock in it' meant.

Mrs Turner was explaining. 'Rose was pregnant while she was on the ship too, and she had her own little girl just a few days before you were born, Harriet. You've even seen a photo of her.'

Harriet nearly remembered. There were lots of photos of the other families. Pale people blinking into the bright sunshine.

'She and her husband moved up to Queensland and we lost touch with each other,' she told them. She explained that Rose had since moved back to Melbourne to live, seen an ad for Turner Travel with a photo of Penny and Neil and got in contact again. She had been writing and telephoning often since then.

'That's who you've spent all those hours on the phone to lately?' James said.

'Things have been tough for her and she hasn't been well. She's needed someone to talk to.'

Austin rolled his eyes. 'So go tell it to the marines, Rose.'

'I beg your pardon, Austin?'

Austin looked embarrassed. 'Sorry. I'm not sure what I mean, to tell you the truth. I heard it on a film. As long as you don't neglect us for some troubled woman from your past.'

'I won't, I promise.' She told them the rest of it. Rose needed a break for a few weeks. She'd thought of the Turners, and remembered that their daughter was the same age as her own. She'd wondered if it would be possible for Lara to come and stay with them for a short while. Just until she was better.

'Where's her dad? Why can't he look after her?' James asked.

'Lara's mum and dad don't live together at the moment. Her dad still lives in Queensland, but Rose and I thought it might be better for Lara to come and live with a family like ours. So she can keep going to school.'

'Will she go to school with me?' Harriet asked.

'I think so. I'm talking to your principal about it tonight, and it looks that way.'

Harriet quite liked the sound of that. A brand-new friend to show around. 'But who do I say she is?'

'You tell the truth. Say she's Lara and she's come to stay with us for a while.'

'But she's not a relative, is she?'

'No, but that doesn't matter. You can tell your friends she's the daughter of a friend of mine. Which is what she is.'

'Where will she sleep?'

'In your room, with you, if that's okay with you?'

There was nowhere else, really. The house behind the travel agency was compact. Three bedrooms, one for her parents, one for James and Austin and now one for Lara and Harriet. She nodded. She didn't mind one bit.

'We'll move that spare bed out of the shed into your room, and hopefully you can make room in the chest of drawers for her clothes as well as yours. It's going to affect you more than anyone, Harriet, but I know you'll be able to rise to the occasion.'

That sounded so grown up. 'I'll be really kind to her.'

She forgot about the jigsaw puzzle for the rest of the day. It was much more interesting to help prepare a room for a motherless child. She said as much to Austin as she helped him and James move the bed in to her room.

'She's not motherless, Harold. She just can't live with her mother for a while.'

By the end of the afternoon she was ready. 'Mum, come and look.' She had piled all her toys on top of the spare bed. 'I thought Lara might like them.'

'That's very kind of you, Harriet, but I think she's bringing some of her own toys with her.'

'But I thought she could have a loan of these too. In case she's feeling homesick. And I've put some tissues beside the bed, in case she starts crying and missing her mum.'

She found herself bundled up in her mother's arms. A kiss was pressed firmly into the top of her head. 'You are a lovely little thing, Harriet Turner, and no mistake.'

Two nights later she was doing her homework at the kitchen table when the phone rang. She ran to answer it before James or Austin got there.

'The Turner house, hello.' That was what her mother said when she answered the phone.

'Is that Harriet?'

'Yes.'

'Harriet, this is Rose calling. Your mother's friend.'

'Hello, Rose.' She thought she should say something else. 'I hope you are feeling better.'

'Better?'

'Mum said you hadn't been well which was why you wanted us to look after your daughter for a while.'

'Oh. That's actually why I'm ringing. Is your mum there?'

'Yes, I'll get her.' She didn't want to get off the phone yet. 'I have the room all ready for her. I've got the bed by the window but if Lara really wants it she can have it. And I've put lots of toys and dolls out for her too. They're dirty but I said to Mum it wasn't worth washing all of them yet, that it was better to wait until Lara got here and then we can wash the ones she likes.'

'Thank you, Harriet. That's really kind and thoughtful of you.'

Harriet thought she sounded funny, like she had a cold or was trying not to cry or something. Her mother came in through the door then. Harriet put her hand over the mouthpiece as she had seen her mother do, as well. 'Mum, it's Lara's mum.'

Mrs Turner came over, her hand outstretched to take the phone. 'I didn't even hear the phone ring. Thanks, Harriet. Rose, how are you?' There was a pause as she listened for a minute or two. Sitting back at the kitchen table, ears straining, Harriet could hear the murmur of Lara's mum's voice. She sounded like her own mother, except she spoke much more quickly. Harriet concentrated fiercely on the page, wishing she had been able to keep talking to her herself.

'Has he? No, I understand. Of course. No, of course not,' her mother was saying down the phone now, her first words, apart from a few murmurs, in some time. 'Hold on, Rose, would you?' She put her hand over the mouthpiece. Harriet was pleased to see she'd had it right when she did it herself. 'Harriet, would you mind giving me some privacy for a little while? I need to have a quiet chat with Rose.'

Harriet got up happily enough. But an hour later her mum was still talking to Rose. She crept into the kitchen after a while to get her homework off the table. Her mother nodded, to let her know it was okay. She took as long as she could to gather her pencils and books. It sounded like Rose was doing all the talking and her mum was doing all the listening. She wanted to stay longer but she noticed her mum's hand going towards the mouthpiece and got out quickly before she was told to.

She was up in the lounge watching *Candid Camera* with her dad, Austin and James when her mum finally reappeared. Harriet had already filled them in on who was on the phone.

Her father looked up at her mother. 'Long session?'

Mrs Turner nodded, holding her hand to her ear. 'It's burning hot.'

'Can I feel it?' Harriet asked. Her mother leant down. She was right. Her ear was warm to touch.

'Everything okay?' her dad asked.

Harriet looked back and forth between her parents. Austin and James were oblivious, eyes glued to the man on the screen trying to prise off a fifty cent piece the *Candid Camera* people had glued to a footpath.

'She says so.' Her mother lowered her voice. 'He's come back. A new start and all of that. But I don't know. She sounded terrible, tears one minute, laughing the next, saying it was for keeps this time, that it was a fresh start, they mean the world to each other . . .'

Her father spoke as quietly. 'She said that the last time, didn't she?'

'And the time before.'

'She says he promised her it won't happen again . . .'

What wouldn't happen again, Harriet wondered. She knew not to ask. She lay quietly, pretending to watch TV but listening intently.

'So what about —?'

'No. Rose wants the three of them together.'

Harriet understood that. She kept quiet but had to pretend to be surprised when her mum told her, James and Austin in the next commercial break that there had been a change of plan and that Lara wouldn't be coming to stay after all.

Harriet was genuinely disappointed. 'Should I put all the toys back? And will the boys put the bed back in the shed?'

'We might leave it there for the time being. She might come. But I'll let you know.'

'Give me plenty of warning, won't you?' She'd heard Austin use the phrase and had liked it very much.

Her mother had given her another one of those nice smiles. 'I'll give you plenty of warning, Harriet, I promise.'

Two months passed. School was nearly over for another year. Six weeks of summer holidays would be theirs to play in. Soon it would be Christmas. The cards had already started arriving from their mum and dad's friends back in England. Harriet loved opening them, seeing the pictures of snow-covered fields, robins, mistletoe and fireplaces, presents and stockings bundled all around them. She and her mother had gone out shopping, trying to pick the best Australian Christmassy ones they could send in return. Oddly, all the Australian cards had the same northern hemisphere pictures, Santas in full regalia, plum puddings and winter scenes, even while the skies were blue and the sun beating down outside.

Harriet volunteered to make their Christmas cards instead. For two weeks she stayed inside, away from the beach, her fingers getting increasingly multicoloured from felt pens, as she drew Santas in shorts on the beach and drawings of her whole family with captions in her best handwriting underneath, 'Mum, Dad, Austin, James and Me', with a sun big and yellow over their shoulders, the rays nearly covering the page. She added a red starfish to every card. It was her favourite thing to draw. She liked the way starfish had five pointy arms, one for each member of her family.

Gloria loved her drawings. 'Will you come and do one on the blackboard for me, Harriet? Once a week?'

'On your special blackboard?' She looked at her mum.

She smiled. 'If Gloria says you can touch the special blackboard then you can.'

Each Monday she went in after Gloria arrived and drew a summery picture in the corner of the blackboard. Sometimes Gloria had already written her special travel fact by the time she got there, in which case she had to fit her drawing around it. Other times the blackboard was still bare, and Harriet had more freedom. Once she drew a picture so big – of a tropical island, with palm trees and coconuts and a trio of monkeys – there was no room for Gloria's fact.

Gloria was impressed. 'I love your drawing. We can give my fact a miss this week.'

'Oh no,' Harriet said, already rubbing it off. 'Mum says that you and your facts are the goo that holds this place together.'

'Did she really?' Gloria looked like she was trying not to laugh.

'Something like that.' Harriet had overheard it, and wasn't sure if she'd got it right.

'We'll compromise then. You do the same drawing, just smaller, and I'll think of the smallest fact I can.'

That morning she came out to the kitchen after helping Gloria to open up. Austin and James were silently eating their toast. Austin was reading a section of the newspaper. James was scribbling something in the notebook he always carried round with him. Her father was dressed for work, standing up, finishing a cup of tea. He seemed in a hurry.

'Where's Mum?' she asked, as she settled herself at the table and helped herself to a bowl of cornflakes.

'She got called away early this morning,' her father said, finishing his toast and quickly drinking his tea. Harriet thought she had heard the phone ringing during the night, but had gone back to sleep. 'She'll be back as soon as she can. Austin, James, look after Harriet, won't you? I've got to go into Geelong this morning for a meeting, so don't forget to eat something at lunchtime if I'm not back. And call in to Gloria if you need anything.' All of this was delivered as he shrugged into his suit jacket and collected his keys. 'I'll see you all later.' He paused long enough to plant a kiss on Harriet's forehead.

They called out after him.

'Thanks, Dad.'

'Okay, Dad.'

'Thanks, Daddy.'

'Thanks, Daddy,' Austin mimicked Harriet after their father had gone.

She looked up, stung at the teasing. 'He is my daddy.'

'Daddy-waddy.'

'Stop teasing me.'

'Austin, give it a rest.' James didn't look up from his notebook.

'What, Jamesy-wamesy-pamesy?'

'I'm ignoring you. But leave Harriet alone.'

'Oh, poor Harriet-larriet-carriet.'

'Shut up, Austin,' James said, still writing.

'Make me.'

Harriet dropped her spoon with a clatter. 'Stop it, both of you. Stop it.' She hated it when they fought. It made her stomach feel funny. She had to fix it, quickly. She took the notebook away from James, ignoring his protest. 'Come on. Take me to the beach. Or for a picnic.'

'Later, Harriet. Let me finish my breakfast first.'

She didn't care if they went to the beach or not. But it had worked. She'd stopped the tension. Austin gave a loud yawn and then started beating out a rhythm with his fingers on the edge of the table. He was always doing that. He'd told her once he heard music in his head all the time.

James had overheard. 'That's because you're mad, Austin.'

'Better to hear music than have moths flying around in a great blank emptiness, like in your head, James,' he had snapped back.

She pulled at Austin's sleeve, getting in before James said anything about his drumming. 'Come on. Let's go to the beach now. You said you'd teach me bodysurfing this holidays.'

'Harriet, you're eight years old. I'm too cool to be seen with someone like you.' Austin was now tapping away at the table with both hands, the way he did when he was especially bored.

'Can you stop that noise, please? It drives me mad.' James spoke again without looking up.

'You're just jealous.' Austin kept up the tapping, adding cymbal crash noises for good measure. 'No natural rhythm, that's your problem, James.'

'All rhythm, no brains, that's your problem, Austin.'

'Stop it, you two. Dad said you're not to fight.'

'We're not fighting. We're just bored. You really are a little anxiety bag of a child, Harriet, aren't you?'

'I am not a —' She'd forgotten the insult. 'What did you say I was?'

James and Austin both laughed.

'An anxiety bag of a child,' James said helpfully. 'It's all right, Harriet, relax. We're not going to kill each other. Not yet.'

'Mum's away,' Austin said, stopping his tapping. 'Dad's in Geelong. Gloria's busy. Don't you think it's time we played the game?'

Harriet looked up and felt the shiver of excitement. The Game? Austin's Game?

The three of them had been playing the game for two years now. Austin had first had the idea for it in winter, but the locals knew them too well and weren't so easily taken in. Summer, however, brought hundreds of families with children to the small seaside town. Plenty of potential victims. It wasn't something they could play every day, though. The conditions had to be right. In other words, both their parents had to be away.

Harriet loved Austin's game. It was so funny when it worked. 'Yes, please,' she said.

Austin stood up and stretched, lazily. 'James, you in?'

James pushed back his chair. 'Why not? Nothing better to do.' But Harriet knew he was as pleased as she was.

Austin got what he needed from the cupboard and then the three of them went outside. Weather-wise, things were perfect. Dry, hot, the sort of day that brought plenty of kids from the caravan park up the road past their house on the way to the beach.

Austin went to the shed and got his bike while James and Harriet took up position on the roof of the house, climbing first onto the low wall, then swinging up from the veranda railing, until they landed on the rainwater tank. From there it was just a step across the tank to the roof. It was the best place to get a view of any approaching kids. Down below they could see Austin getting ready.

'Three coming, from the caravan park end,' James called. 'Go, Austin, quick.'

Harriet didn't have to watch Austin to know what he'd be doing. She kept her eye on the road. The three kids – all boys, Harriet could see now – were coming closer. They looked older than her, ten, eleven maybe. She had to put her hand over her mouth to stop herself from making any sound as they came closer, noticed Austin lying in the middle of the road, his bike tipped on its side next to him. They started quickening their step. Austin was motionless, his arms and legs spreadeagled, pools of red all around him.

'Oh yuk, look, is that blood?' one of the boys said.

'He must have fallen off his bike.'

'Is he dead?'

James nodded at Harriet. From their position on the roof, they'd clearly heard the conversation. They sprang into action, leaping from the roof to the rainwater tank, then swinging down from the veranda railing. That was always Harriet's favourite bit.

'What's going on here?' James said in a gruff voice.

The boys looked horrified. 'We don't know,' the oldest one said. 'We found him like this.'

None of them heard the car coming up the road behind them.

Just then, Austin stirred. The three boys jumped. 'He's alive!' one of them shouted.

Austin made a gurgling sound. 'Barely. I don't know how much time I have left.' He reached out a hand to the three boys. 'You saw it. Will you tell the police when they start their investigation?'

'But we didn't see anything.' The older boy sounded panicked. 'Shouldn't we call for an ambulance?'

'I think it's too late for that,' Austin said, dramatically. 'The agony. A searing pain shoots through me.'

Harriet felt a shiver of delight. Austin was so good at this. He caught her eye, prompting her with an expression. Whoops. She'd nearly forgotten her line.

'Have you got a final message for all of us, Austin?' she said, as he had taught her.

Behind them, a car door shut. Then another.

Austin raised himself on one arm, addressing the three boys. 'I want to say to all of you, if I die here today, that knowing you, even for this brief time, has meant the world to me . . .'

'What's going on here? Austin? James? Harriet?'

They all spun around. Mrs Turner stood by her car, with a little girl beside her. Harriet noticed immediately they were holding hands.

The oldest of the three boys stuttered his answer. 'There's been a terrible accident. He fell off his bike . . .'

Mrs Turner walked over. The little girl came too. Harriet saw she was wearing a nice red dress and shoes that matched. Shoes with buckles. 'Yes, it looks fairly terrible,' Mrs Turner said. 'There's a lot of blood, anyway. Or a lot of tomato sauce, at least.'

The boys looked again. 'It's tomato sauce?'

'A whole bottle, by the looks of things.' Mrs Turner smiled at them, even while she glared at Austin, now sitting up and looking in much less pain. 'Get off the road, Austin Turner, and apologise to these poor boys immediately.'

'It's just a bit of fun, Mum. You know how the school holidays drag.'

'Do it now, Austin.'

'So it's a joke?' the oldest of them said, looking relieved.

'Yes, hilarious, isn't it? Austin, apologise please. James, you should know better. Harriet, stop snickering.'

Austin leapt up, wiping off the excess sauce on his shorts. He put out his hand. 'Thanks, kids, you were good sports.'

Mrs Turner apologised to them once more. 'I'm so sorry, I promise you it won't happen again. Don't let them put you off going to the beach, either.'

The older boy and his brothers took off. They didn't look convinced.

Mrs Turner looked down at the little girl standing beside her, still clutching her hand. She gave her a big smile. 'Not quite the introduction I'd have liked, but never mind. Austin, James, Harriet, let me introduce you. This is Lara.'

While Lara was unpacking her small brown suitcase – Harriet had seen she also had a plastic bag of toys with her – James, Austin and Harriet gathered around their mother in the kitchen.

'I'm sorry there wasn't much warning, but I wasn't sure until I got to Melbourne whether or not she'd be coming home with me. So please, the three of you, be kind to her. You know how we've talked about other people not being as lucky as we are? Well, Lara and her mum and dad have had some bad luck and that's why we're helping.'

Harriet liked the idea of that. It sounded mysterious. It made Lara even more interesting, she decided. She was going to be really, really kind to her.

In her bedroom soon after, Harriet was very interested in the way Lara had taken all her clothes out of her suitcase and refolded them into five neat piles. She had counted them. One for underwear, one for tops, one for shorts, one for dresses and one for jumpers. Lara was now neatly putting them away into the third and fourth drawers of Harriet's chest of drawers, as Mrs Turner had shown her. It had taken Harriet a while to decide whether to give her the top two or the bottom two drawers. In the end her mother had made the decision, hurriedly moving the contents to allow Lara the use of two spare drawers.

'Mum, they're all crumpled now,' she had protested.

'No more or less crumpled than they were to begin with. We'll tidy them up later. I'll give you a hand. You're a good, kind girl, Harriet, thank you.'

Now, Harriet perched on the end of her bed and watched Lara empty the contents of the plastic bag.

'How old are you?' she asked.

'Eight.'

'Me too.'

As she watched her unpack, Harriet decided it was as if one of the black babies she sponsored in Africa had come to live with them. Things took on a rosy glow. Lara could be her new project. Her 'be kind to less fortunate children' project, the way the teacher had said last year at school, when they were doing their fundraising. Harriet had loved it. They'd saved up their pocket money and sent it away in a small cardboard box to the missions and then a few weeks later they'd got a letter back with strange stamps and a polite note. 'Thank you for your kind and gracious generosity. We now have a new water tap in our village and we think of you every time we see the clean, fresh water.'

'Will you be coming to school with me?' Harriet asked her. 'And to swimming?'

Lara sat neatly on the side of the bed. 'I don't know. I suppose it will depend on how long I stay here.'

Harriet was a bit surprised by her. Lara didn't seem nervous at all. If Harriet had been a little kid arriving out of nowhere like this she would have felt really sick, she thought. Perhaps Lara felt bad inside but was good at hiding it. Harriet felt really sorry for her then and tried to think of the most kind thing she could do, like her mother would want. 'Which bed would you like? I always sleep by the window, but if you would like that one, I don't mind.' She had her fingers crossed as she said it. She did mind. She minded badly.

'I'd love to sleep by the window. Thank you.' Lara picked up her plastic bag and went to the bed by the window.

Harriet blinked and uncrossed her fingers. That hadn't gone how she'd expected. She tried again to be friendly. 'When's your birthday?'

'May 14.'

'Mine is May 17.'

'I was born early,' Lara said. 'My mother said that for a little while they worried that I wouldn't live.'

'Were you sick?'

'No, just really small.' She showed how small, holding her two hands about a foot apart.

'How do you know how small you were?'

'My dad did a drawing of me once.'

'Oh.' Harriet didn't know what to say about that. She knew her Dad sent lots of people away on holidays but she didn't think she'd ever seen him do a drawing.

There was a noise at the door. It was Harriet's mother. 'Hello, girls, are you getting on? Good. Now, how about something nice to drink? Lara, what's your favourite drink?'

'Chocolate milk,' she said.

How could Lara be so sure? Harriet never knew what her favourite of anything was, if anyone asked her. How could she choose between Coke and lemonade and orange juice?

'We'll have to take a walk down to the shop to get some, then. Harriet, would you like chocolate milk too?'

She was amazed. Not only was Lara going to get chocolate milk – even though there wasn't any in the house – her mother was going to take them to the shop to buy it. This never happened. It wasn't a matter of being asked what would you like either. There were the options – lemonade or water. Quick, make up your mind.

'It's nice here,' Lara said as they walked along the beach path. The sea looked very blue. There were people on the beach, paddling, building sandcastles, setting up umbrellas.

'The sea air is good for you too,' Harriet said. She'd heard her dad say that the week before.

Lara looked up at Mrs Turner. 'Mum says she always thought that until she had a month of it on her way here to Australia.'

Mrs Turner laughed. 'Your mother didn't like that ship much, did she?'

Harriet started feeling even more bewildered. This girl had arrived out of nowhere and yet she and her mother were talking about things she had never heard of. And how did her mum know whether Lara's mum had liked it or not? 'Where is your mum?' she asked Lara, wanting to make her look at her for a change, instead of her mother all the time.

'At home.'

'Is she sick again?'

'No.'

Harriet knew her mother was giving her The Look. She deliberately glanced down so she was out of its firing range.

'Where is home?'

'Melbourne.'

Harriet nodded. She knew where Melbourne was at least. 'We lived there when we first got to Australia. Before I was born.'

'I know. My mum and dad and your mum and dad lived in the same place. We've got photos in our kitchen.'

That was too much. 'Mum, how come we don't have photos?'

'We do. Lara's mum and dad came out from England on the same ship as us.'

'The *Plymouth Wanderer*.'

'That's right, Lara. The *Plymouth Wanderer*.'

'Were you named after the captain too?' Harriet asked.

Lara didn't smile. 'The captain was a man.'

'I know. But I was named after him.'

'Harriet's a funny name for a man.'

'No, not Harriet. His name was Harold. But Mum thought I was a man, I mean a boy, so she promised she'd call me after him because that's where I was made, on the ship, wasn't I, Mum?' It seemed urgent to be the one doing the talking, the one having the proper conversation with her mother. 'That's why Austin calls me Harold sometimes.'

'Which one is Austin?' The question was directed at Mrs Turner, not Harriet.

'The middle one. The naughtiest one. Here we are.' They'd reached the milk bar. 'So, chocolate milk for you, Lara. And what about you, Harriet?'

'Chocolate milk,' she said firmly. Even though she hated it.

Later that afternoon Mr and Mrs Turner were in the garden. While Mr Turner weeded the edge of the path leading to the corrugated iron shed, Mrs Turner spoke to him in an urgent whisper.

'Of course some warning would have been better, Neil. But what could I do? She was begging me. Tears one minute, shouts the next. She was in a complete state. Her husband rang while I was there and you should have heard the screaming match. And the house was a mess. Chaos. It was no place for a child.'

Inside, at the window of the laundry, Harriet stood still, listening to everything.

'The whole place in a mess, except for Lara's little room. She had it as neat as can be. And her bag all packed in minutes. She nearly broke my heart.'

'She didn't mind going? Leaving her mother?'

'She seemed to understand. I asked her about it on the trip back and she said her mum had told her she needed to go and get her dad. And that it would be easier if she could travel on her own.'

Harriet strained to hear. Luckily her father's voice was louder than her mother's. She heard him clearly.

'I keep thinking of all the beers we had on the ship together. He seemed like the nicest of fellows. Not the type to do this.'

'That's what I thought. I asked Rose why she puts up with it and she started crying again and went on and on about how much she loves him, that he's the centre of her universe, that he can't really help himself, that he —' Her mother's voice was drowned out again by the sound of a passing car. When Harriet could hear again it was her father talking.

'So how long does she want us to keep the little one?'

'A week, two weeks perhaps. You don't mind, do you?'

'No, of course not. She'll be company for Harriet, anyway. Let me finish that up, if you want to go and make up the beds or get her settled.'

'Thanks, love.'

Harriet slipped away up the hallway as the back door opened and her mother came into the house.

Lara only stayed five days the first time. A phone call came after dinner one night. Mrs Turner had another conversation. Harriet came in at the end in time to hear the arrangements being made. 'Are you sure? I can run up with her. No, lunchtime is fine.'

She scooted back into the lounge room where they'd been watching TV so she'd be there for the announcement from her mother.

Mrs Turner came in and touched Lara gently on the head. 'That was your mum, Lara, love. They're coming to collect you tomorrow.'

Harriet glanced at her. Lara's expression didn't change. 'Thank you.'

That night in bed she had a feeling of excitement, as though they were her parents coming to get her. 'What's your mum like?'

She almost heard Lara's shrug in the darkness. 'She's shorter than your mum, and she's got brown curly hair.'

'And what about your dad?'

'He's taller.'

'And you really haven't got any brothers or sisters?'

'No.'

'Do you get lonely when you're home on your own?'

'No.'

'I would.'

'You get used to it.'

They arrived at the Turners' just after one o'clock. Harriet's mother and father were both there. The table had been set. There were sandwiches, egg and lettuce, ham and mustard, and cheese and pickle. There were two sorts of cakes. It was all under white netting cages, used as flyguards. It was Harriet's job to put them on and take them off. She knew it was important to make sure there were no flies trapped underneath when she put them on.

They were all in the kitchen as their mother got things ready. 'Wouldn't that be terrible, Mum?' Harriet said, trying to get her attention as Mrs Turner moved back and forth between the fridge and the sink. 'If you had put them on to stop the flies getting on the sandwiches and the whole time there was a fly trapped under there.'

'If I was a fly that's what I'd do,' Austin said. 'Sit there quietly, my wings whirring a little bit, while the sandwiches were being made. And then, in that split second, after the sandwiches had been made and the human was reaching for the —'

'Not a human. Me.'

'All right, Harold. When you were reaching for the flyguard, I'd set my wings whirring to five hundred miles per hour and just as the guard was about to go down, whiz in underneath and there my feast would be.'

'That wouldn't work,' Lara said.

Austin turned to her, an eyebrow raised. 'No? Why not?'

'The noise. Flies make a lot of noise. What I would do is sneak in under the plate. Flies can run really fast, as fast as they fly, but without the noise. They could go in under the plate and sit there. There would have been plenty of time too, while the sandwiches were still being made and the human was walking back and forth to the fridge.'

'You know, Lara, I think you're right.'

'So when the guard came down, even if the human —'

'Me,' Harriet said. 'I'm the one with the guard.'

Lara was still looking at Austin. 'Harriet wouldn't see us, because we'd be hidden under the plate. And we could wait until the coast was clear and then crawl out and eat everything we wanted.'

'Smear our germs all over the bread.'

'Climb inside the sandwich and have a sleep,' Lara said, grinning now.

'We could dance on the crusts.'

'No,' Harriet said too loudly. 'No, you couldn't. I'm in charge of keeping the flies out and I would kill you both.'

'You wouldn't,' Lara said. 'You wouldn't know we were there.'

'Lara's right,' Austin said. 'We tricked you, Harold.' He held out a hand and shook Lara's vigorously. 'Well done, team. The flies win.'

'The flies win,' Lara echoed.

After that, Harriet wasn't so keen to meet Lara's parents. She deliberately went into the lounge room and started watching television. She pretended she didn't hear the car arrive, or her mother calling out hello over the fence or her name being called.

James came up after a while. 'Harriet, lunch is on. Lara's mum and dad are here. Come on.'

'I don't want to meet them. I just want her to go.'

James shrugged. 'Mum wants someone to take off the flyguards. No problem, she'll ask Lara to do it instead.'

Harriet was up in a moment. 'That's my job.'

'Then come and do it, would you? I'm starving.'

She sidled into the kitchen, staying close to the wall. Her mother was saying something about the travel agency being busy but stopped as she noticed Harriet in the corner. She gestured to her.

'Here she is at last. Rose, Dennis, this is Harriet. Harriet, this is Lara's mum and dad, Mr and Mrs Robinson.'

She felt shy. She hated it when adults all stopped and looked at her like this. 'Hello.'

'Hello, Harriet. We spoke on the phone the other night, didn't we?'

She nodded. Lara's mother did have brown curly hair. She also had a bruise under her left eye. It was either coming or going. Lara's father had gone back to talking with Harriet's father. He was tall, smiley. He had something in his hair that made it shiny and wavy. Mr Perrotti at Mass had hair like that, Harriet remembered. She always wanted to touch it, or put a marble in one of the waves, to see if it would run down. If she and Lara made jokes with each other, she would have joked to her about that.

Lara was sitting beside Austin on the bench by the wall where Harriet usually sat. Since she had arrived she had been sitting in the guest's chair. Where she belonged. That side belonged to family.

'That's my chair, Lara.'

Mrs Turner's smile stiffened. 'Harriet, don't worry about that. Say hello to Mr Robinson.'

'But Lara is in my chair. I always sit next to Austin.'

'Today's different, because we've got guests so we are all sitting wherever we want to.'

That ripple of something hot and uncomfortable went through her again. Lara had gone back to talking to Austin. They were playing rock, scissors, paper. It was Harriet's favourite game. She knew it wasn't right, but she wanted to spoil it for everyone, the way it had been spoiled for her. She turned back to Mrs Robinson and thought of the rudest thing she could ask.

'Mrs Robinson, why have you got that bruise under your eye?'

'Harriet, please. Don't be nosy.'

Mrs Robinson gave a loud laugh and reached up and touched the mark. 'It doesn't matter. It's nice to meet a curious child. I was a silly-billy, Harriet. At our house in Melbourne we have a big apple tree and last week we were pruning it – do you know what pruning is?'

Harriet shook her head, hating that her question was now being answered, while beside her Lara and Austin kept playing their game. She didn't like Lara's mother's voice either. It was too high and she kept looking over at her husband when she was talking instead of looking at Harriet. She kept doing twitchy things with her fingers too. If Harriet had been at school doing that she would have been told off for wriggling.

'It means cutting back the branches and dead wood, so that all the new spring growth can come and there'll be plenty of apples. I pulled down a big branch and thought I had it and it went ping,' another laugh, 'well, not so much ping as splat. It hit me right in the eye and sent me flying.'

She was torn between her curiosity and wanting to join in with Lara and Austin. 'Is that why Lara came to stay with us? Because of the tree?'

'Harriet, please.' It was her mother.

'I couldn't see for a couple of days and I had to go to hospital,' Mrs Robinson explained. 'And my neighbours were away. Your mother was a wonder to step in when she did.' That smile again, directed right at Mrs Turner.

'Why didn't Lara's dad take care of her?'

'That is enough, Harriet.'

Mrs Robinson was now answering the questions directly. 'He wasn't there.'

'I work interstate.' It was the first time he'd spoken. He had an accent like her own father's.

'But you said *we* were pruning.'

'You've got a detective on your hands here,' Mr Robinson laughed.

'Or a lawyer.'

'We were. Me and Lara. Lara called the ambulance for me, didn't you, Lara?'

Lara nodded. 'Mrs Turner, can I please have a sandwich?'

'Of course you can. Dennis, Rose, you must be ravenous. Now, sit down everyone and help yourselves.'

The flyguards were whipped away without ceremony.

'Watch out for flies,' Harriet said to no one in particular.

CHAPTER TWELVE

Three months later, James, Austin and Harriet were in the living room watching *Gilligan's Island* on TV after school when their mother came to find them. Austin was stretched out on the sofa. He was getting so tall he hung over the end of the cushions. James was in the beanbag, also stretched out. Harriet was lying on her beach towel on the carpet. She'd got it for her eighth birthday and liked using it all the time. She loved the colours, the feel of the material and especially the fact that her mum had got someone to sew HARRIET'S TOWEL in curvy letters on the bottom.

'Harriet, boys, I need to talk to the three of you about something important. Can I turn the TV off?'

They sat up immediately.

'It's about Lara. You remember Lara?'

They all nodded. As Austin said afterwards when they were alone and talking about it, of course they remembered Lara. How often did their mother think strangers came to live with them out of the blue for a few days?

'And you remember her mum and dad?'

More nods.

'I don't know quite how to tell you this, but something terrible has happened.' She paused and took a breath. 'Lara's parents were killed yesterday. In a car accident in Ireland.'

Austin and James were straight in with the questions. How? Where? When? Harriet just sat there. There was shock but there was also a kind of excitement. She had met two people who had been killed in a car accident! It was only afterwards she thought how sad it must have been for her mother, that her friend Rose had been killed like that.

'What were they doing in Ireland?' James asked.

'Rose's mother was Irish. She died a month ago and Rose and her husband went back to Ireland to sort out her things.'

James wanted all the details of the crash. 'Was it night? Or was it bad conditions during the day?'

'I don't know, James. I don't know the whole story yet.'

'Were they killed instantly?' Austin wanted to know.

'I think so. I hope so, for their sakes.'

Harriet still couldn't speak, her mind filling with images of a car slipping and sliding on a road and then Lara's mother and father being dead, just like that.

'Is Lara all right?' Austin again. 'Has she been hurt?'

'She's fine. She wasn't with them. She's away on a school camp in Melbourne.'

That made it even sadder in Harriet's opinion. Would she have been killed if she had been with them? Austin got in first with the question. 'So does she know yet?'

Mrs Turner shook her head. 'I'm driving there this afternoon. The police contacted me. They want me to tell her.'

Austin frowned. 'The police in Ireland contacted you? How did they know where you were?'

'They got in touch with the Australian police who contacted me.'

'But how did they know to contact you?'

'Because Rose asked me if I would be the contact person while they were away. She didn't know many people in Australia, and she knew we'd be close by if anything happened.'

'It's as if she had a premonition,' Austin said.

'What's a premonition?' Harriet asked.

'A feeling that something bad was going to happen. Maybe even that the car was going to crash.'

Harriet knew from the tone in Austin's voice that he was feeling that same excitement. It was awful but it was also thrilling.

Mrs Turner stood up. 'We don't know all the details yet, but what it means for now is that Lara will be coming to stay with us again. And it could be for longer than a few days.'

Harriet felt a bit funny about that. She didn't remember every detail of Lara's brief visit those months ago, but she knew it hadn't all been good. That she had wanted to be kind but it had backfired on her.

'Your dad is driving up to Melbourne with me to get her. Gloria will be in soon, she'll stay here with the three of you while we're gone. Harriet, would it be all right if Lara stayed in your room again?'

'Yes, Mum.' She decided she did want to be kind again. She liked how it felt when she was. But this time she wasn't going to offer Lara the bed by the window. All her books were on the windowsill there and she liked the feel of a cool sea breeze on her face on hot nights. But maybe they could take turns. If Lara really wanted the bed by the window she could have it now and again . . .

'She's going to be very upset,' Mrs Turner said. 'So I need you all to be kind to her, all right?'

'Is she an orphan?' Harriet asked.

'Yes, Harriet, she is.'

Gloria arrived with an overnight bag. There were more whispered adult conversations in the kitchen, and then their parents drove away.

When Lara arrived with Harriet's mum it was immediately obvious she didn't care where she slept. Harriet, James and Austin stood back as she came in. She was pale, her eyes red-rimmed. She was clinging to Mrs Turner.

They had talked to Gloria about what they should say to her.

'Do we say "sorry about your parents"?'

'Or "we're sorry you're an orphan"?'

'Just say you're sorry. Leave it at that for the time being.'

Harriet tried when she arrived. 'I'm sorry, Lara.'

Lara turned and Harriet was frightened by the look in her eyes. She looked like she was a long way away, even though she was there in front of her. Harriet wanted to say more. She glanced at Gloria. Gloria gave a nod.

'About your mum and dad.'

That blank look again. She noticed Mrs Turner was holding her close. Even when Harriet came back into the room a few minutes later, after her father had asked her to get some milk from the kitchen, her mother and Lara were still holding hands. Harriet wondered if they had been like that for the whole drive. Would they have sat in the back of the car, side by side, or would her mum have sat in the front while her dad did the driving? If that's how it was, then Lara would have been in the back on her own. That wouldn't be fair. Not for hours in a car when your mum and dad have just been killed in a car crash.

She needed to find out. She went over to her dad, who was

sitting at the table. 'Did Lara sit in the front or in the back with Mum?' she whispered.

'What, love?'

'On the drive, who sat where?'

'Harriet, does it matter?'

'I just wondered.'

'Not now, Harriet.'

Lara slept in the bed by the door from the first night she arrived. Harriet was relieved. She had been prepared to let her have the window bed the first night, but she was glad it hadn't come up. Mrs Turner tucked both of them in, and then sat beside Lara on the bed stroking her head until she fell asleep. Harriet waited for her to come over to her next, but instead she blew a kiss from the doorway.

'You were nice and kind to Lara tonight, Harriet, thank you,' she whispered.

'But I didn't do anything.'

'I thought you did. You were very welcoming.'

She hadn't really been. She had got Lara a glass of cold milk but that was only because her dad had told her to. 'I feel sorry for her,' she said. It was the best she could do.

'It's going to be a difficult time for her, Harriet.' Mrs Turner came over then, even though the room was nearly in darkness. Only the light from the living room was spilling in, giving her a path to follow. She crouched beside the bed and Harriet waited for her forehead to be stroked too, but her mother's hands stayed on the edge of the bed, smoothing down the sheet. 'I know it will be tricky for you, too. But we'll all make it as easy for her as we can, won't we?'

She wasn't sure what her mother was talking about but nodded anyway.

'Good girl. Night night.'

'Night night.'

She got a kiss on the head. Not as good as the stroking on the forehead Lara had got but then her mum and dad hadn't just been killed in a car crash.

Lara stayed home for the first week. Harriet had to go to school, but she didn't mind because she got to tell all her friends about Lara, the orphan who was now living with them.

'What does she look like?' her friends asked.

'Like a normal person,' she admitted. Her friends seemed disappointed. Harriet was a bit, too. In her books orphans all wore rags and had black circles under their eyes.

'So if she lives with you forever, does that mean your mum and dad adopt her?'

She didn't know. She asked them one night. Lara had gone down to the beach with Austin. Harriet had been torn between spending time with them and having her parents to herself for a while.

'Are you going to adopt Lara?'

'We don't know yet.'

One afternoon she saw Lara go into the garden with her mother. They stayed there for a long time. Harriet wandered out after a while and tried as casually as she could to get close enough to hear.

'Harriet, love, what are you doing?'

'Having a look at the garden.' She leant down to touch one of the rose bushes to back up her story.

'Pet, can you leave me and Lara alone for a little while? We're having a talk about a few things.'

Harriet deliberately didn't look at Lara. 'Do you want to talk to me about it as well? I might have some good ideas.'

'In a while perhaps. But for now it's between Lara and me. So be a good girl, won't you, and go back inside?'

She stayed in the kitchen. There was a good view out to the garden from there. Her father came in.

'Harriet, come and help me wash the car?'

She couldn't say she had to stand at the window and keep watch. She turned away, reluctantly.

That night after tea her mother called Harriet, James and Austin together and told them the news. Lara was going to be living with them all the time from now on. 'Isn't that great?' their mother said.

Harriet nodded. Austin and James asked a few questions, but seemed relaxed about it. Afterwards they all went back into the living room where Lara was sitting watching TV with their father.

As Harriet came in she gave Lara the kindest smile she could produce. Unfortunately, Lara wasn't looking at her when she gave it.

Over the next few months it felt like there were many new layers to the household. Before it had been Harriet and James and Austin, and then her mum and dad. There was the travel agency, the main street, Gloria, school, the house and the beach. They roamed freely back and forth and everyone was where Harriet expected them to be. Now it was all different. Everywhere it had been only her it now seemed to be her and Lara.

People in the town knew all about them. 'Is this your new sister, Harriet?' they would ask when they saw them walking back from school together, or going down to the beach. Harriet wasn't sure what to call Lara. If she was asked that, she would nod and smile, to be polite, which was what her mum and dad said she had to be as much as she could.

'Do you want me to call you my sister?' she asked Lara once.

'I don't mind,' Lara said.

Lara called her mum and dad Penny and Neil, like Gloria and Kevin did. Harriet didn't feel good about that when she first heard it. She asked Austin what he thought.

'She has to call them something, doesn't she? And Penny and Neil are their names, after all. Would you rather she called them Mum and Dad?'

'No.' She was sure about that. They weren't Lara's mum and dad.

She heard the man in the shop next door ask her mum if she was going to adopt Lara. She heard bits of the conversation, words like guardian and legality, that she didn't understand. She went to Gloria again. 'If Mum and Dad adopt Lara, does that mean she can call them Mum and Dad too?'

'She could if she wanted to. But I think she likes calling them Penny and Neil.'

'Would I call her my real sister then?'

'I think legally you'd call her your stepsister. But you could call her your sister now, if you wanted to. I don't think they're going to formally adopt her, though, are they? Your mum said that they'd decided on a legal guardianship, which is almost the same thing.'

'I don't know. No one tells me anything around here.'

She nearly caught Gloria laughing. But then her face went serious again. 'Here, Harriet, help me put these brochures in these envelopes, would you?'

As they stuffed them – glossy pamphlets advertising the islands off Queensland and Fiji resort holidays – Gloria asked her about school. About her jigsaw puzzles. And about Lara.

'So how are you and Lara getting on, Harriet?'

'Fine.'

'Are you in the same class at school?'

'We were at the start but she's better than me at reading and maths, so they moved her into a different one.'

'And are you okay about that?'

'She is better. I don't like maths much.'

Lara also played with different girls at recess and lunch, but sometimes they all played in a big group. At home, they all did things together – ate their meals, watched TV, went to the beach. At least her mum and dad got Lara to do the dishes and sweep the floor, too. Harriet had been worried she would get out of it, but her mum and dad seemed to be treating her like another kid. Austin and James did too. Sometimes they teased Lara, sometimes they ignored her. Just like they did with Harriet. She wasn't sure how she felt about that.

Lara started having nightmares about six months after she arrived. Night after night, Harriet was woken up by Lara talking in her sleep. Once or twice she would scream or wake up crying. The first time Harriet tried to help her, but it scared her. She started running into her parents at the first noise.

'Ah, Lara, you poor little mite.' Her mother would cradle Lara, do that thing where she stroked her forehead until she fell asleep again. It lasted for more than a week sometimes, night after night. Harriet would hear the screaming and go and get her mother. Each time, her mother would come, hold Lara tight. Once she stayed for more than an hour, murmuring to Lara in a voice too soft for Harriet to hear.

There was a break of three nights and then it happened again. Harriet had had enough. She put her pillow over her head and tried to block out the crying. It wasn't until Lara was sobbing very loudly that her mother came in.

The next morning her mother sat down next to Harriet at the kitchen table while she was having breakfast. It was the weekend, so there was no school. Lara was outside with Austin, filling the bird feeder that hung on the plum tree. 'Harriet, why didn't you come and get me last night when Lara was crying?'

She kept eating her cornflakes. 'I didn't wake up.'

'You must have. Please, Harriet, come and get me if Lara's upset. You know we have to be kind to her.'

That was too much. She put down the spoon. 'I am being kind. But you and Dad love her more than you love me now.'

'Harriet, we don't.'

'Then you love her as much as you love me. And she just got here and I'm your real daughter and it's not fair.'

She got up and ran away. She only got as far as the beach path. The sea scared her in wintertime. The waves sounded too noisy and sometimes people would appear, just when you thought the beach was empty. Some of the kids at school said there were even people who lived on the beach. She stood for a while by the grass path, near the swings and the barbecues.

She waited for more than ten minutes but no one came to look for her. When she slowly made her way back she saw her mum was now out with Austin and Lara, moving the bird feeder to a new place.

They hadn't even noticed she was gone.

The first anniversary of Lara's arrival came around. Their mother made an announcement over lunch a few days before. 'I want Lara to have a special way of remembering her parents. So we're going to have a little ceremony.'

'At church?'

'No, not at church. Here, in the garden.'

She knew then that Lara and her mum had already talked about this. The decision had been made. 'What will we do?'

'Lara thought she'd like to say something, and then I will say something about her mum and dad, and so will your dad, and then we will think about them, and how sad we are that they're not with us, but how glad we are that Lara has been able to stay with us and become part of our family.'

'What date will it be?'

'We talked about that, too, didn't we, love?' Her mother smiled over at Lara, who was sitting quietly. 'And we thought maybe the day Lara came to live with us, rather than —' she hesitated, 'rather than her parents' anniversary. So we remember something good at the same time as we remember something sad.'

Harriet liked the sound of this. 'Can I do something?'

'I think this first one is for Lara, Harriet. We'll see how we go after that.'

'But I could do the flowers or help with the prayers. I'm good at prayers.' She'd got a star last week at school for the prayer she wrote about wanting the weather to be good for sports day. She had rhymed *keep the rain away* with *on our sports day*.

'Not this time, Harriet.'

Harriet got up and walked away then. It wasn't until ages after that her mother came out to find her. She'd had to start dropping plums from the tree she'd climbed up to draw attention to herself.

'Harriet, please don't be like this.'

'Lara gets to do everything.'

'Harriet, this isn't a treat. This is a way for Lara to remember her mum and dad, and for her to know we remember them too.'

'But it's not fair. You're always *asking* her to do things. You *tell* me.'

'What do you mean?'

'You say to her, "Lara, would you like to go into your room and finish your homework." And you say to me, "Harriet, go and do your homework."'

Her mother was silent for a few seconds and then nodded. 'You're right. I have done that. I'm sorry, Harriet, I didn't realise. We're trying to make it as easy for Lara as we can, to be as kind as we can to her. Do you remember, we talked about being kind to her?'

'But she's okay now. She hardly cries at all any more. She doesn't even have those nightmares.'

'That doesn't mean everything is okay, though. She's still very sad inside.'

'How do you know?'

'Because I know what it feels like when your mum and dad die.'

'That was different. You said your mum and dad were old when they died.'

'It's still sad, whenever it happens. Come down from there, Harriet, come and help me. And you'll have your own special days down the track, I promise you. This one is for Lara and her mum and dad memories.'

Harriet climbed down. She didn't really need her mum's help but it felt nice to take her hands and jump into her arms like she used to do when she was little. 'What's she calling it? It's not a birthday or Christmas Day, is it? What's the name of this day?'

'It's an anniversary, of when she came to stay with us, and a day to think about her parents.'

'Can she call it Memory Day?'

'You can ask her if you like.'

Harriet asked her as soon as they went inside. Lara thought about it and then shook her head. 'No, thanks anyway, Harriet.'

'But Memory Day is a good name. You can remember your mum and dad and remember when you first came to live with us.'

Mr Turner patted her on the head. 'Harriet, I don't think Lara wants to call it that.'

She couldn't do anything right. Anything. 'It's always about Lara in this house!' she shouted, as loudly as she could. She slammed the door after herself, ran into her room and threw herself onto her bed.

Her mum didn't come to find her that night. She eventually fell asleep. When she came out the next morning she was told off, by her mum and by her dad, for being so rude.

CHAPTER THIRTEEN

The St Ives hotel had set aside a corner of the bar area for the *Willoughby* cocktail party. Harriet checked with the manager that all the preparations were in place. They were. He told her Lara had faxed through a detailed running list and everything she'd asked for was organised. Harriet checked the date. Three days previously. It was so peculiar. If Lara had known she was going to leave them like this, would she still have been checking that the buffet and wine were going to be in place?

Harriet glanced at her watch. Twenty minutes to seven. She had promised Patrick Shawcross she would meet him in his room and escort him down to the cocktail party. It was a way of keeping things in control. It was also for his own safety, but she hadn't told him that. She didn't like to imagine what Mrs Lamerton might do if she happened upon Willoughby on his own in the hotel corridor.

She made one last check of her appearance. She'd washed and blowdried her hair and applied night-time make-up – darker eyeshadow and a bolder shade of the red lipstick she liked. It was how she looked from the neck down that was the problem. After spending the afternoon in normal clothes she was back in her now dry Turner Travel uniform. Another one of Melissa's rules – full uniform to be worn at all group functions, as well as during travelling days. It made the tour leaders easy to spot across rooms, as well as in airports. She had three attempts at tying the scarf before deciding it would have to do. Perhaps Miss Talbot would show her how to tie it again. She had seen her itching to get her fingers on it in Malaysia during the stopover and eventually given in. Those nimble knitter's fingers had proved equally skilled at twisting and tying a silk scarf. If she'd had time she would have called in to Miss Talbot's room and asked for her help. She suspected there would be a flurry of activity in all the rooms already though, especially those of the women. From what Harriet had seen so far, they all took a lot of trouble to dress up each evening.

As she put her key in her bag she realised she had run out of peppermints. She liked to have a supply with her on tour, more for her clients than herself. Gloria called them the tour guide's secret weapon. As they had all discovered over the years, there was nothing more upsetting for groups of people travelling in close quarters than someone with halitosis. She decided to nip out quickly to the chemist she'd seen down the road when they pulled in. She glanced out the window and saw dark grey clouds had covered the sky. There was even a smattering of rain on the window. She took her own, non-Turner Travel red macintosh off the hook and slipped it on over the uniform.

Ten minutes later she had a new supply of peppermints and a beating heart. There had been a queue in the chemist and she was late getting back to the hotel. There wasn't time to take her mac back to her room. She smiled at the receptionist and darted into the room where the cocktail party was being held. Everything was set up. The bar was open, its wooden shutters pulled aside. There were cocktail glasses and bowls of glacé cherries, pineapple chunks on sticks and a giddy arrangement of paper umbrellas and twirly straws. It looked like something from a cruise ship. Across the room two uniformed waitresses were arranging the buffet dinner. They had ordered a simple selection of poached salmon, cold ham and salads, with plenty of warm bread rolls and dishes of butter curls. Nothing too spicy, nothing too exotic. Elderly stomachs had a habit of 'playing up', as their clients often delicately put it, when on tour. Most of the group were already there, more than ten minutes early. Their faces lifted in expectation when she opened the frosted glass doors and then fell again when they realised she was on her own. She gave a big smile and promised to see them again shortly.

'With the guest of honour?' Mrs Lamerton said, sharply.

'The man himself,' Harriet said with a smile.

She went up the stairs to Patrick Shawcross's room, catching sight of herself in the mirror at the end of his corridor. A little wind-blown but not too bad. And at least the red of the macintosh suited her, which was more than could be said for the yellow uniform. She knocked on his door at ten to seven, as they'd agreed. There was no answer. Another knock.

'Mr Shawcross?'

Nothing.

'Mr Shawcross?'

She tried the door. It opened. She walked in, just in time to see him step in from the open balcony. 'I'm sorry to just come in like this. I knocked but . . .' She stopped. He looked terrible. Pale, with beads of sweat on his forehead. There was no sign of the amused, relaxed man she'd seen earlier.

'Harriet, hello.'

'Mr Shawcross, are you all right?'

'I think so. I will be.' He gave a weak smile. 'Just a bit queasy.'

What could it be, food poisoning? Or perhaps he had an allergy?

'I'm so sorry. I can call a doctor, we could maybe get you some emergency medication or —'

'I'll be fine. Well, not fine, but you don't need the doctor.'

'But if it's food poisoning —'

'It's not food poisoning. It's nerves.'

'Nerves?'

'Stage fright.'

'You mean about the cocktail party?'

He nodded.

'But you can't be nervous of them. It's twelve old people.'

'I'd be nervous if it was four toddlers.'

'But you've been working as an actor for years, haven't you?'

'Yes, and I've been sick with nerves beforehand for years too.' The colour was coming back into his face. 'I know it's ridiculous. And I know I'm hardly on the brink of stepping out into the Royal Albert Hall, but a performance is a performance.' He gave her a shadow of his usual smile.

'But you'll be great. You will be. They're all beside themselves at the idea of meeting you. They've been talking about it non-stop. Like teenagers . . .' She regretted her words immediately as she saw the blood rush out of his face again. But she couldn't pretend the group wasn't excited. She tried again. 'Once you get to know them you'll be all right, I promise you. And you will get to know them, over the next few days. They'll be like family by the end of it.' A particularly deranged family, but it wasn't the time to tell him that.

He still looked pale. 'I shouldn't have said yes to this.'

'Of course you should have.' There was no way she was letting him escape now. 'Please don't worry, Mr Shawcross. Really. I know you'll be terrific.'

'Harriet, I won't be, you know. I told you, I could have bluffed a magazine article, but this? I'm hardly the world's best actor, am I? Known for what? A long-forgotten role in a bad TV detective series?'

He was like a different man, not the confident, amused man she'd met earlier that day. He had seemed like something from a celebrity magazine then, all jokes and good looks and accents. Now he seemed like a normal human being. A nervous normal human being. The peculiar thing was that the more nervous he seemed, the more her own nerves were subsiding. She felt perfectly calm. It all seemed straightforward. 'But that's exactly who they want you to be. That's why they're here and why they wanted you to be here. It's not really Patrick Shawcross they're interested in. It's who they think Patrick Shawcross is. Which is Willoughby. So all you have to do is pretend to be Willoughby again. Or at least a sort of Willoughby.'

He stared at her.

She thought that might have been hurtful and stepped closer, hurrying to correct the impression. 'I mean, of course they'll be interested in you, Patrick Shawcross, your life and all of that, but I think deep down they just want you to be like Willoughby the detective.'

He came close and, to her astonishment, took her face in his hands and kissed her forehead. She got a faint scent of mint mouthwash and that nice aftershave again. 'You're a genius, Harriet. It's that simple, isn't it? It's got nothing to do with me at all. I just have to start acting from now on, don't I?' He sat down at the table. 'The only problem is I can't really remember much about Willoughby.'

Harriet could have done a PhD on Willoughby. 'He was moody.

Mysterious. Charming. Enigmatic. All those kinds of things.' He was sexy, too, but she didn't say that.

'Did he have any catchphrases?'

'Sorry?'

'Like Dirty Harry said "Go ahead, make my day" and Kojak had "Who loves ya, baby?"?'

'I don't think so. Only that line at the end of every program. *"That's people for you, George."*'

He answered her distractedly. '*"Aye, Willoughby, so it is."* That's right. But no, that wouldn't work in a crowd situation. We don't have time to watch the video now, do we? To refresh my memory?'

She checked the time. Five minutes to seven. They were already cutting it fine. She wouldn't have been surprised to hear slow hand-clapping coming up from the cocktail lounge. 'I'm sorry, no.'

'What did he wear?'

Harriet had a mental picture immediately. 'Thick sweaters. Dark blue shirts. I think that was supposed to be his postman's uniform. And in the opening credits, he wore a sort of baggy white shirt, with a dark duffle jacket over it.'

'That would help.' He went to the cupboard, unbuttoning the blue shirt he was wearing as he moved. 'A white shirt like this?'

She saw dark hair on his brown chest as he turned back from the wardrobe with the new shirt. She also noticed his toned body. A swimmer's body. 'Just like that,' she said.

He did up the shirt quickly, rolling the sleeves up over his elbows. He had well-shaped hands, too, with long fingers. He flicked through the cupboard again. 'No, nothing even close to a duffle coat. Would this do? It's not too casual, is it?'

She looked at the jacket he had taken out. It was a dark blue corduroy one. It felt strangely intimate, advising him on his appearance like this. 'No, that looks perfect.'

He tried it on and looked over at her again. 'It's okay?'

'You look great. You look like you should. Just like Willoughby.'
He did too.

'I don't suppose you could get me a black and white dog from somewhere? A stand-in Patch? To complete the look?' He shot her a grin. He was starting to relax again.

'I think the hotel has rules about dogs. Except guide dogs, but that might not be quite the right look,' she said, straightfaced.

'No, perhaps not. Another, smaller animal perhaps?'

'I did see a cat outside the kitchen earlier, if you want me to try and catch it for you?'

He pretended to consider it. 'What colour was it?'

'Ginger, I think.'

He shook his head. 'No, the colours would clash. But thank you anyway.'

'My pleasure.' Harriet bit back a smile. The mischief was back in his eyes again. She was surprised at how much she was enjoying this. And how relaxed she was feeling. As if this was a perfectly normal way of spending an evening, watching a stranger get dressed, talking about cats and dogs. She checked her watch. Nearly seven. They were cutting it fine. She stood up. 'I'm sorry to rush you, but I think we'd better get going.'

'Of course. I'm ready now. And thanks, Harriet. You've been very understanding.'

'I'm glad I could help.' She waited in the corridor as he closed the door. They walked side by side down the carpeted corridor to the lift. 'It really will be informal, I promise, but as I said, everyone is quite —' she stopped there, as the word hysterical came to mind.

She didn't want to make him feel nervous again '— excited about meeting you. If it gets too much, please just signal me to help out and I'll do what I can.'

'Signal? Wave wildly across the room at you, do you mean?'

She smiled. 'Well, that's one way.'

'Something more low-key, perhaps?' They were waiting for the lift. 'We need a code word. Something I can drop casually into the conversation that will let you know I need rescuing.'

'That's a good idea. What did you have in mind?'

'Armadillo,' he said, as they moved into the lift. 'If I happen to slip the word armadillo into a sentence, you'll know I need rescuing.'

'Armadillo? Won't that be a bit obvious? I don't think there's going to be much chance of you spotting one wandering across the room.'

'That's my challenge. So do you agree? Armadillo it is?'

'Armadillo it is.' He was quite mad, she decided.

The lift stopped at the ground floor and the door slowly opened. He held it open but didn't make any move to step out. 'Can I ask you one more thing before we go in?'

'Of course.' She had stepped forward and was standing closer than normal to him.

'Would you please call me Patrick? This Mr Shawcross business is really making me feel like a schoolteacher.'

'I'm not supposed to. It's one of our company rules, particularly with a special guest.'

'Even if I command you? In my best Willoughby voice?'

'Well, perhaps. But only in private.'

'Then I'll have to make sure we're in private together as much as possible.'

Was he flirting with her? She shot him a glance but he looked innocently back. 'I can probably make the occasional public exception, too.'

'Thank you, Harriet.'

'You're welcome, Patrick.' She stopped around the corner from the cocktail party. 'Here we are. They're all waiting. I'll introduce you and please feel free to say a few words too, if you want, but it might get a bit —' like a rugby scrum, she suspected, '— hectic, after that.'

'I'm ready for anything, I promise. Me and my armadillo.'

She realised she was still wearing her red macintosh. She quickly unbuttoned it and folded it over her arm as they came to the closed doors. Beside her, Patrick Shawcross came to an abrupt stop.

'Harriet, what on earth are you wearing?'

She turned back, puzzled. 'My company uniform.'

'You've started working for a banana exporter since I saw you this afternoon?'

First Big Bird, now this. She gave a weak smile. 'No, it's the Turner Travel uniform.'

'Your family did this to you?' That amused look in his eyes was well and truly back. 'That's grounds for legal action, surely?'

The clock in the hall chimed. Seven o'clock. She decided to ignore his comments. 'We'd better go in. You're sure you're all right?'

He chose to misunderstand her, touching her briefly on the back as she moved to open the door. 'I think so. But will you promise to stay out of any bright lights? I've left my sunglasses in my room.'

CHAPTER FOURTEEN

Harriet had once read an article in a wildlife magazine in which a safari guide described how it felt to be almost trampled by a herd of buffalo: 'They came rushing towards me, and for a minute I thought this is it, this is the end.'

As she escorted Patrick Shawcross into the cocktail room, she knew the sensation.

Ten minutes earlier, when she had called into the room to check all was fine and everyone had made it there safely, the tour group had been normal human beings. The women had been a little overdressed, perhaps, Mrs Lamerton like a peacock in full plume in a purple trouser suit, with a bright dragonfly brooch securing a mauve chiffon scarf around her neck. Beside her, Mrs Pollard, Mrs Hart and Mrs Pennefeather were in smart pastel twin-sets. She'd overheard them talking during the journey. Nylon was perfect for travelling, they'd all decided. It didn't crush and was so versatile. She'd noticed both Mr Douglas and Mr Fidock were wearing cravats. Their accents had changed too, she thought. Both of them had been living in Australia for many years, and while they hadn't lost their English accents entirely, there had certainly been nothing like the House of Lords plums they now seemed to be speaking with.

All their clothes and accents were virtually a blur, though, as they surged past her now towards Patrick. Harriet barely had time to say, 'Good evening, everyone, may I introduce our special guest, Patrick Shawcross,' before she had to step out of the way. She'd warned Patrick they were eager to meet him but she hadn't prepared him to be mobbed. About to rescue him, she watched as the crowd parted. Patrick appeared again. Harriet was reminded of Moses and the Red Sea.

'Ladies and gentlemen, thank you so much for that enthusiastic welcome.' His voice had a deep, rich tone, with just the right hint of soft Cornish accent. He glanced over at Harriet and she was sure he gave her the slightest of winks. 'Now, please, there's no rush. We have four days together and I know there is going to be an opportunity to talk to each of you and for all of us to get to know each other very well indeed.'

They were visibly calming. Mrs Lamerton still seemed to be trembling, but she was at least keeping a normal distance. The group had somehow arranged themselves in a circle around him, as though in some pagan ritual. Any trace of the nerves Patrick Shawcross had shown earlier had disappeared. They must have been part of his preparation, to get himself into the mood and get the adrenaline rushing, Harriet realised.

'Now, let me get myself a drink.' He had barely uttered the word and one was thrust at him. 'Oh, thank you, Mrs —'

'Lamerton, Dorothy Lamerton,' Mrs Lamerton said, her voice cracking. 'It's Guinness. I read that it's your favourite.'

'And it is. Thank you, Mrs Lamerton. Here's to your excellent research abilities.'

There were peals of laughter.

He held up his hand again and looked around at them. They fell silent. 'Let me say first and most importantly how delighted I was to be invited on this tour. My *Willoughby* years were among the happiest of my life and I'm truly touched,' he put his hand on his chest, Harriet observed with some amazement, 'that the program still means so much to all of you, despite the years that have passed. Since the invitation arrived from my friend Harriet over there . . .'

Harriet felt Mrs Lamerton bristle beside her. Uh oh. She should have filled him in on the whole story of the trip, and particularly Mrs Lamerton's role in it. There hadn't been time, though. She suspected he would be hearing it from the horse's mouth soon. She stared fixedly at Patrick, ignoring Mrs Lamerton's pursed lips beside her.

He was now completely relaxed, the pint of Guinness in one hand, the other hand leaning casually on the antique dresser beside him, the white shirt and dark curls painting the perfect Willoughby picture. ' . . . I've found so many memories have come rushing back. There's a lot to making a series like *Willoughby*. Not only the scripts, and the location hunts, but all the laughs, the dramas, the sheer bloody hard work,' (there was a ripple of oohs at the carefully placed swear word) 'as well. It will be my pleasure to go walking back down the *Willoughby* memory lane again with all of you.'

He smiled and threw out a hand. 'And that's it for the formalities. Please, enjoy yourselves and feel free to approach me at any time. I promise I won't bite.' There was more laughter. He held up his pint. 'Here's to wonderful times and travels ahead.'

There was a loud burst of applause, a raising of glasses and then another surge forward. Harriet was impressed. Who would have thought twelve elderly people could move so quickly, or make so much noise? Their comments were flying around the small room. Several of them were speaking loudly, as if Patrick Shawcross was still on television and not able to hear them.

'He's so charming, isn't he?'

'That voice of his nearly makes me melt.'

'His mother must be so proud of him.'

'I think he's even better-looking than he was on the TV. Do you think he's had plastic surgery?'

The final remark sailed through the room.

Patrick Shawcross gave a wry smile. 'Well, if there's something I've learned about Australian tour groups today, it's that there is no beating around the bush. So you deserve an honest answer. No, I promise I haven't had plastic surgery, lip implants or taken any performance enhancing drugs.' There was more laughter. 'But if any of you would like to come closer to check for scars, please feel free.' He caught Miss Talbot's eye. 'Perhaps I could ask you to check on behalf of everyone, Mrs —?'

'It's Miss,' she said in her high, bell-like voice. 'Miss Emily Talbot.'

'Would you like to check, Miss Talbot?'

To whoops from Mr Fidock and Clive, who had just sidled in from the front bar, a now pink-cheeked Miss Talbot marched up and took Patrick Shawcross's face firmly between her little hands. He had to lean down and she had to stand on tiptoes but she made a thorough inspection.

'No, all clear,' she said, stepping back and smoothing down her red velvet pantsuit. Harriet recognised it from the front window of Tina's Teen Wear in Merryn Bay. 'And I can also tell you he smells lovely!'

The room soon filled with questions, laughter and conversation. Harriet remembered as a child desperately trying to get Austin or James to include her in their ball games, jumping up and down, calling 'Kick it to me! Kick it to me!' The same urgent tones sounded all around her now. 'Mr Shawcross, come and have a drink over here!' 'Mr Shawcross, can I get you a drink?' 'Mr Shawcross, look at me! Talk to me!' She checked to see if he was all right. He was more than all right. He was in his element.

Two hours went past before Harriet felt a touch on her arm. After his speech she had started circulating around the room, making sure everyone had drinks, that there was plenty of food and no trouble with spillages or allergies. She kept a close eye on Patrick Shawcross. There had definitely been no mention of an armadillo, or any animal at all, when she had been near enough to listen in to the conversations he was having. She had spoken to every member of the tour group, but she realised they weren't at all interested in talking to her. Not tonight, anyway.

At one stage, she and Clive stood back from the group, watching it all. Clive had changed from his bus driver shirt and shorts into quite a natty suit. His manner was the same, though.

'He seems like a nice enough bloke,' he said, too loudly. 'But how come I've never heard of him since *Willoughby*? He's hardly set the world on fire with his acting, has he?'

Clive was jealous, Harriet realised. She felt a need to defend Patrick Shawcross. That protective instinct kicking in again, she realised. 'Actually, Clive,' she whispered, 'he's hugely famous in America. We had to ring ahead to check that there weren't any Americans staying in the hotel, or he wouldn't have got any peace at all.'

'Really?'

'Really.'

He still didn't look convinced.

Harriet had just fetched Miss Talbot another Fluffy Duck

cocktail from the bar ('Oh, would you, Harriet?' she had said. 'They're so pretty and they make me feel so nice inside.') when she felt the touch on her arm. 'Harriet, could I have a word?'

It was Patrick Shawcross. She hadn't noticed him escaping from the scrum. 'Of course.'

'That outfit of yours really does have its uses, doesn't it? I'd have spotted you a hundred miles away.'

'That's the idea. Is everything okay? No sign of any, um, armadillos?'

'An extremely large armadillo, unfortunately.'

She lowered her voice. 'You'd like to go?'

'As soon as you can manage it.'

'Of course. I wasn't sure if you were enjoying yourself or not.' Talking in whispers like this, standing close to each other, she had the strangest sensation that they were a long-married couple deciding whether it was time to go home.

'More than I'd thought possible. I'm not being sarcastic, I promise. I have enjoyed it. It's just been a little more . . .'

'Overwhelming?'

'Exactly.' He smiled. 'Overwhelming than I expected. Could we go? And could you come up to my room with me? I need to talk to you about something.'

She didn't like the sound of that. 'Of course. Let me just say goodnight to everyone.'

She clinked a glass to get their attention. 'Hello again, everyone. I'm sorry to interrupt your conversations. I wanted to let you know that Mr Shawcross needs to take his leave of us now.' Had she actually said 'take his leave'? Somehow it fitted. Everyone in the room seemed to be speaking in heightened English this evening. 'Thank you so much for making him so welcome. Please continue to enjoy yourselves and I'll be back down with you soon.' Not that they would miss her for a second.

Beside her, Patrick paused, waiting until he had everyone's full attention, not speaking over remnants of conversations and glass shifting as she had. All the stage tricks were obviously coming back to him. 'Thank you, Harriet, and thank you, everyone, for that warm welcome and all the fascinating conversations I've had with many of you already tonight. I'm looking forward immensely to the next few days together.'

They left the room surrounded by applause, walked down the corridor in silence and into the small lift. She waited for him to speak, but there was someone else in with them. He obviously wanted them to be alone. She dreaded what it was he needed to talk to her about. Please don't let him say it was all too much. Or that he'd changed his mind about staying on. It would be even worse now if he left, now that the group had had a glimpse of him, brushed against him. It would be like so much promise being snatched away.

She started talking as they left the lift and walked along the corridor but he touched her arm, nodding at a guest standing outside his door further down. He spoke in a low voice. 'Can we wait? Just until we get to my room?'

'Of course.'

They were barely inside when he turned to her. He was very serious.

'Harriet, they are all mad. To the last person, completely and utterly mad.'

Oh, thank God, she thought. That's all that was wrong. 'No, they're not. Not really. Not all of them, anyway.'

'Harriet, they are. They know more about me than I know

myself. I've heard of fan conventions but this lot are in a league of their own.'

'I'm sorry, I did want to warn you . . .'

'I need a crash course in not only *Willoughby* but in my own biography, fake or not. Why did I agree to do this again?'

'Because you didn't want to let everyone down.' She was struck again by the difference. He had been larger than life downstairs. Now he seemed . . . he seemed normal again. Worried, even. She rushed in to help. 'It's not an examination, I promise. It's pure enthusiasm. They just love the show so much. And when we knew we had you as our special guest, Mrs Lamerton started holding *Willoughby* information evenings. That's why it's all so fresh in their minds.'

He ran his hand through his dark curls. 'I'm going to have to do something about this.'

Did he mean make a complaint? About her? 'Oh, please, don't do that. It wasn't anyone's fault. I mean, it was more a chain of things, James falling off the ladder, and then Lara deciding to go away like that, and maybe faxing the magazine article didn't help in the first place, I can see how that might have been confusing, but —'

'Harriet, I'm sorry, but what are you talking about?'

'I'm trying to explain how it all went wrong. I can see how you might want to make a complaint, but it's just there is an explanation for everything —'

'I'm not going to make a complaint. I meant I'm going to have to do something about this, before I really do let everyone down. Did you say you had tapes of the *Willoughby* series?'

'Two series.'

'We made two series?' He shook his head. 'I'd forgotten that too. Of course we made two series.'

'Twenty episodes. Half an hour each.'

'Do you have the itinerary?'

She reached into her bag. She carried it with her everywhere. 'Right here.'

He took it from her and glanced through the pages. Harriet knew what he would be reading. The list of locations they'd be visiting and the episodes they had featured in. It was there, in great detail, with James's extra handwritten comments alongside.

He handed it back. 'Harriet, I'll need your help. Can you watch some of the *Willoughby* episodes with me? Two heads will be better than one. Then if I forget you could nudge my memory?'

'Now?'

'If that's all right?'

'Of course. I just need to say goodnight to everyone first.'

He checked his watch. 'It's nearly nine-thirty. That's not too late for you?'

That mixture again of actor confidence and regular courteous human being behaviour. 'No. Anything to make the tour go well is fine by me.'

'While you're doing that, I'll call the front desk to see about a video player.'

'I already have one. It's set up in my room.'

'You're a mind-reader as well? That's great. I'll come to you, then.' He glanced at his watch. 'Is fifteen minutes okay?'

'That's fine.' She gave him her room number, trying to remember how much mess she had left behind. She'd have to quickly tidy it before he got there.

Downstairs, the tour group had barely noticed she'd gone. Everyone was swapping stories on what they had said to Patrick Shawcross, what he had said to them, what they planned to say to him tomorrow. As expected, Mrs Lamerton was holding court.

'As I said to Mr Shawcross . . .'

Harriet coughed politely in a bid to get everyone's attention. It was difficult over the hubbub. A clink of a spoon on a glass again worked much better. 'Hello again, everyone, and thank you all for making Mr Shawcross so welcome.' At the mention of his name the room quietened completely. 'If you'll all excuse me, I need to say goodnight myself and go and check some of our arrangements for tomorrow. Please enjoy yourselves and I look forward to seeing you all at breakfast in the morning.'

Mrs Lamerton gave Harriet one of her imperious waves, spilling her bright pink drink as she did so. 'Harriet, I've ordered another round of cocktails for everyone. I assured the young lady behind the bar that was all right.'

Harriet decided not to worry. It was the first real night of the tour. They were excited. Turner Travel could wear the expense. 'That's no problem at all, Mrs Lamerton. Goodnight, everyone.'

But, just in case, she went to the bar manager on her way upstairs and asked her to close the tab.

She had time to hastily tidy her room before his knock came. The room was compact, and the addition of the TV and video player on their stand made it even more crowded. There was only one arm-chair, as well. He could have that. She would have to sit on the edge of the double bed.

As he came into the room, she saw he'd changed his clothes. He was now wearing a dark blue sweater and a pair of dark jeans.

He was very relaxed again. 'Thank you so much for this, Harriet.'

'It's no problem at all. You don't want to watch all of them tonight though?'

'No, it's an episode or two a day, in a way, isn't it? Taking in several locations, is that right?'

She nodded.

'I think the best thing is if we watch the right episodes the night before each trip. I can learn the lines again, refresh my memory, come up with a few anecdotes.' He shook his head again. 'Did you know those two men can do the dialogue from all the final summary scenes? Twenty programs' worth?'

She nodded. She'd heard them do it often enough.

'And that lady with the blue hair —'

'Mrs Lamerton.'

'She could describe every outfit every female character was wearing. Down to the jewellery. I heard her telling that tiny lady, the one with the white hair and the funky clothes —'

Harriet's lips twitched. 'Miss Talbot.'

'Miss Talbot. The pair of them were swapping facts about Willoughby's girlfriends and who was better suited to him. In all seriousness.'

Harriet wasn't at all surprised to hear it. She knew Miss Talbot had been keen on Willoughby ending up with Lady Garvan, whereas Mrs Lamerton felt she was nothing more than an upper class gadabout, to use her term. 'They have taken their research seriously.'

'They were like vultures, Harriet. I was a rotting set of bones in that cocktail room.' He looked at her and once again surprised her with a deep burst of laughter. 'I'm taking it a bit seriously, aren't I?'

She smiled. 'A little bit.'

'It's only a television show, isn't it?'

'A very popular TV show.'

'Then we'll just have to beat them at their own game.' He sat down on the end of the bed and patted the cover beside him. 'I'm ready when you are.'

She sat next to him, conscious that she was perched on the end of her bed in a tiny room next to their guest of honour. She pointed the remote control and sat back as the theme music started to play and the opening credits began.

Several times over the next hour she shot a glance at Patrick. Once she was sure she saw him wincing, at a particularly emotional moment between Willoughby and Lady Garvan. And he was definitely smiling – laughing softly even – at a scene involving Willoughby and one of the postmasters from a neighbouring village. She referred to the itinerary notes a couple of times, checking what had happened at each of the sights, a small fishing village, a police station, a cliff lookout point. Lara and James had really done their research. All sorts of locations had been picked out for the group to visit, from houses and churches to scenic lookouts and harbour pubs.

In the break between episodes she made him a cup of tea, boiling the plastic kettle on the cupboard. He took it with a smile and then they turned back to the TV. Towards the end of the second episode her phone beeped to alert her to the arrival of a text message. She checked it. It was from Austin. She quickly read it. Still no word on Lara. Flights booked. Arriving day after tomorrow. See you then. A x

Patrick Shawcross pressed pause on the remote control and stood up. 'I'm sorry, I'm probably keeping you from work business.'

'No, it's fine. It's a message from my brother.'

'That's probably enough for tonight in any case.' He seemed

distracted now. 'That's been very helpful. I'll cast my mind back and see what stories I can remember from those filming days.'

'I know they'll appreciate whatever you can tell them.' She turned to the video player, finding it disconcerting to be standing so close to him. It had to be the change from staring at him for so long on the screen to finding him standing beside her like this.

As he went to leave, she half-expected him to kiss her on the forehead again or give her a flamboyant actor hug. Instead, he gave a formal nod of his head. 'Thanks again, Harriet. I'll see you in the morning.' He looked down at the itinerary, then read aloud in an excitable voice that exactly matched James's tone and exclamation marks.

'*We'll be reliving Willoughby's dramatic altercation with Sergeant Kendall, the corrupt policeman, at the harbour in Boscastle, followed by lunch in the restaurant near the old mill!! Perhaps they'll even have those famous crab claws on the menu from the lunch scene in episode six, "The Case of the Crooked Chef"!! Yum!!*' He glanced at her. 'You're sure you didn't write this?'

'I promise you I didn't.'

A flash of that grin of his again. 'Thanks again. Goodnight.'

CHAPTER FIFTEEN

Molly Turner was outraged. 'Lara's gone missing? Why didn't you tell me?'

She had come in to the Turner Travel office after swimming training and overheard her mother on the phone to her father. Her mum hadn't realised she was there. Molly heard the whole thing. 'No, James, not a word yet. It's like she's disappeared into thin air. Austin's on the case with her flatmate. No, apparently Harriet's doing fine on her own. Well, no dramas yet but it's early days. I'm sick with worry about it. I don't think she's told them anything much, no. What's she going to say, in any case? "Sorry it's just me in charge, Lara's mysteriously gone missing"?'

Molly had barely let her mother hang up before she demanded an explanation.

Melissa turned around. 'Molly, calm down. She's not missing. We just don't know where she is.'

'That's missing, isn't it? Is she all right?'

'Of couse she is. She's probably just got some personal problems she wants to sort out on her own.'

'So why are you so worried?'

'We're not worried.'

'You are. I heard you talking to Dad.'

'Of course we're concerned. It's a lot to ask of Harriet, her first tour in months. We were expecting Lara to be there to help her.'

'Lara said she'd be back at the end of May. In six weeks.' Molly was counting down the days. She wanted Lara to be home in time to help her plan her sixteenth birthday party.

'And I'm sure she will.'

'Why don't you ring her and ask her what's wrong?'

'We did. She hasn't answered.'

'She'd answer me. We've been texting each other the whole time she's been away.'

'Have you heard from her in the past few days?'

'Well, no, but I thought she might have got busy.'

'Would you write her a quick text now?'

Molly nodded, reaching into her pocket for her mobile phone. She nimbly pressed buttons. Hi L. R u ok? Worried about u. L Mol xxx Send. Message sent. 'She'll text me back now. I know she will.'

'When she does, could you ask her to give us a call? As soon as she can.'

'Of course.' Molly hesitated. 'Are we still going shopping tomorrow, Mum? You and me? Even though Lara has —' What? Disappeared? Gone missing?

'Of course, Molly.' She leaned over and gave her a kiss. 'You know how much I like our trips. I wouldn't give it up for anything.'

Molly tried to smile. It sounded good, but it wasn't true. Her mum cancelled week after week. 'Sorry, Molly, I need to finish these bookings or poor old Mr and Mrs Jennings won't get to have their holiday and wouldn't that be terrible?' 'I'm sorry, Molly, but I completely forgot I'd agreed to help out at the golf club luncheon. Did you have to get anything urgent, or will it wait until next week?'

No, Mum, it won't. I need to talk to you. I want to talk about what feeling in love is, and check if that's what's happening to me. I need to talk to you about having sex or not. She loved her mum, she really did, but she made it hard sometimes. Come back, Lara, Molly said to herself as her mother turned back to her computer. Lara never cancelled on her. She always listened to her, too.

Once when Molly was about thirteen she'd had a crush on a boy at school. One of her friends had told him and it had been horrible, because the boy had wanted nothing to do with her. It had been so awful, she had felt like her heart was breaking in two, and she had felt so stupid as well, knowing that he and his friends were probably laughing at her. Lara had heard her crying in her bedroom and had come in and been so quiet and gentle about it that Molly had told her everything. She thought that Lara would probably have said, 'Oh, don't worry, Molly, you'll get over it,' but Lara hadn't. She had said that yes, of course it hurt. If you loved someone and they didn't love you back then that wasn't a nice feeling, but the thing to do was be patient and wait for the person who did feel the same way about you. And she'd told Molly that there were so many special things about her and it was a good thing to wait for the person who saw all those things. It had really helped.

Molly went back into the house and into her bedroom. She sat on the bed and took out her mobile phone again. It was getting urgent. Maybe she should send Lara a long text, spell it out, so Lara would know why it was important. She wrote it out in full, seeing the words appear on the tiny screen. She knew there was only enough space for 500 letters. She kept it as short as she could.

Drst Lara. Hav got sm big news. Am going out w my new swimng coach. Yes, ther is age difrence, but doesn't mattr, he loves me & I love him, 2. No, havn't had sex. But he wants to & so do I. He wants me to tell M&D I am at swimng camp for w-end but insted we going 2 motel 2gethr. Shld I?????? I think I want to do it. Am on pill, in case, but I'm just not sure. Help!!!!! Love Molly xxxxxoooo

She hesitated, her thumb poised over the Send button. It looked a bit funny written out like that, but she really needed to talk to someone about it. It had nearly come up at school today. Sitting around at lunchtime with her girlfriends, Hailey had been making a big deal about the fact she and her boyfriend Jake had been caught kissing on the sofa by his parents. 'I was mortified,' she said. Hailey was always mortified about something. That was her favourite word. The others had all shrieked about it for ages. Molly had got annoyed with them in the end. That was one of the problems. The other girls were all so immature, and hers was an adult problem.

She imagined if she had told them. 'Do you remember that trainee swimming coach I had?' She pictured them screwing their eyes up, trying to remember. 'The student teacher?' she'd prompt. 'Dean?'

'Oh, him. Yes. Why?'

'We've been going out for the past two months. He's invited me to go away for the weekend with him. Just him and I, in a motel.'

Would she say it as simply as that? And what would they say back?

'But he's a teacher!'

She had her arguments ready, even in pretend conversations. 'It would only matter if he was a teacher at my school. And school is only for a few hours each day. The rest of my life I'm me, and Dean is a man, not a teacher.'

'But he's so much older than you!'

'Not really. He's only just turned twenty-six, and I'm nearly sixteen, so it's only about ten years. That's nothing.'

'Just tell your parents it's a training camp, Molly,' he'd said last time they met. 'I'm going crazy not seeing you. Imagine what

it would be like. Just you and me, together. The whole weekend.'
He'd leaned down and kissed her lips, her neck. She'd got that
incredible feeling again, of being scared and excited and thrilled,
somewhere deep inside her body.

She knew he was talking about having sex. They'd had enough
lessons about it. There'd been one particularly embarrassing video
the previous term. Two actors pretending to be lovers, stopping and
starting at different points. Kissing. Touching. Him touching her
breasts. Every now and then words would flash up on the screen in
red letters. *Stop if you feel uncomfortable! It's your body! Say no
if you want to!*

Those videos always made it sound as though sex was like fighting
off an army or something. What they hadn't told them was how good
it felt to be kissed and cuddled and caressed the way Dean did it. It was
the same with the magazines. They warned you about diseases and
getting pregnant and being called a slut and all the reasons why you
shouldn't have sex until you were sixteen, or even older. But if it was
so wrong to do all those things, how come it felt so right with Dean?

Just thinking about him gave her that lurching, tumbling, breathless feeling again. It wasn't anything like the few times she'd kissed
any of the boys from school, not that she had done very much of it.
Or even the story Hailey had been telling, being caught kissing Jake
like that. It didn't feel bad, either. They'd all been warned about
chat rooms on the Internet. About being with strangers. The teachers carried on sometimes as if there was a whole tribe of perverts
lurking in a shadowy ring outside the school. That there were dirty
men out there waiting for them to let down their guard, to smile
too brightly, or offering them lollies or rides into town in exchange
for something dirty.

It just hadn't been like that with Dean. It had happened so

naturally, as if it was meant to be. That's what Dean always said, too. And her swimming had improved, as well. Because apart from the talking, and the drives they took together, and the kissing, he really had been helping her to swim better.

She reached up to the shelf above her bed and took down the photo. It had been taken at her last swimming carnival. Her mum and dad had wanted to come, but there had been an association of travel agents' dinner in Melbourne that weekend. To Molly's delight, Harriet and Lara both came along instead.

Lara had brought her camera, the one with the long lens, and had taken all sorts of action shots. One of Molly diving off the blocks, and one of her winning her race. She'd even taken one with a sort of slow exposure that had made the water look all silky, like it was carved marble. Molly had framed that one and put it up on her bedroom wall. There were the victory photos too. One of Molly standing up on the top step of the podium. Best of all was this one, the only photo she had of her and Dean together. It had been a natural one for Lara to take, too – the swimmer with her coach. Both Lara and Harriet had been so proud of her. 'Come on, arms around each other. The winning combination.'

Molly touched Dean's face in the photo. The cropped blond hair, that beautiful smile. He was all muscly, too, but in a nice way, not like a bodybuilder. She really liked his body. She felt different in her own body, too, since she and Dean had started seeing each other. He'd told her so many times how beautiful it was, and that he loved how she looked. He often whispered that he especially loved her breasts, that she shouldn't try and hide them like she used to do under baggy windcheaters and T-shirts. 'Not that I want you showing them to anyone else. You won't, will you?'

She'd shaken her head.

'And you haven't told anyone about us?'

'I won't.' She'd affected a casualness. 'What, and have you get into trouble for interfering with an underage girl?'

'I'm serious, Molly.'

'I'm joking.' She'd wanted to kiss him, kiss that line of worry away from his face. But they had made a rule that they never touched in front of other people. They had to be so careful. He'd told her it was enough to have him thrown out of teaching for ever. Maybe even a prison sentence.

'No one would understand the truth of us, Molly. They wouldn't believe that I tried to fight it. I did. But I knew that it was something special between us.'

She could replay all the things he had ever said to her. Sometimes in bed, when it had been a while since she had seen him – they tried not to make it longer than two weeks, but sometimes his training commitments made it hard – she made up plays in her head, reliving the whole thing.

It had been special from the start. She thought so, at least. Sometimes she wasn't sure if she had slightly rewritten his arrival in her life, made it more dramatic than it might have been, because of what had happened afterwards. But it didn't matter either way. It still felt the same now.

It had been a normal training session, straight after school. Her coach Mr Green was there. They called him Greenie. Beside him that day was a young man, dressed in a tracksuit. They were all quickly introduced. 'This is Dean, down from Melbourne. He's going to be my assistant coach for the term.' She shook hands with him, then went into the changing room. He told her afterwards, when they were together, that he had noticed her straightaway. 'How couldn't I, you were so beautiful.'

She had wrinkled her nose. 'I was in my training suit, in my cap and goggles. You couldn't tell what I looked like.'

'You're wrong. I saw what was important.'

It was just like Lara had said. She'd been patient and someone who loved her for herself had come along. It was terrible when he first had to go back to Melbourne after his work placement finished, but he kept texting her, telling her he loved her every single morning without fail, calling when he could. She hung out for the carnivals when she'd see him. He managed to come back once every fortnight or so for a training session and it was fun to pretend they were normal swimmer and coach. He'd stay back late those nights, and they'd go in his car to the lookout in the hills back behind the town or to one of the beaches further down the coast from Merryn Bay. They'd talk a bit, but mostly they'd kiss. A lot. He was always so patient and kind to her, telling her how pretty she was, and kissing her really slowly and checking each time that she was happy with what he was doing.

He had asked her the last night he was in Merryn Bay if she wanted to go in the back seat, where there was more room, but she had felt funny. He'd been so kind. 'That's okay, Molly. We'll only do what you want to do.'

She'd felt bad then, so she'd let him touch her a bit more than she wanted, and then she'd touched him as well. She'd felt really shy and inexperienced, but he had been so good then as well, showing her what to do, how to touch him. 'You're so beautiful, Molly. That's it, that's perfect, don't stop.' She replayed that over and over in her head as well.

He'd touched her again afterwards too, and she had felt incredible, all kind of full and open and hungry in a funny way, as if she really wanted something to eat or drink or have, in some way, but wasn't sure what it was. She'd tried to tell him that and he had given her another kiss and whispered in her ear. 'Just wait, Molly, if you thought that was good.'

It was Dean who'd suggested she go on the pill. 'I'm not putting any pressure on you, Molly. It's about being responsible. Looking out for you.'

'But wouldn't we use condoms?' She felt shy saying that, but all the classes insisted that they were the most important thing.

'For a start, if that's what you want. But condoms are only if you're not committed to the person you're sleeping with.'

'But what about AIDS? And other diseases?'

He kissed her again. 'I promise you, Molly, I don't have AIDS, or VD, or chickenpox, or even a hint of a cold. Will you do that for me? Will you go on the pill? Then when we're together, you and me, it'll be just us, skin on skin . . .'

Another long kiss. His voice whispering, 'You're so beautiful.'

'No, I'm not.'

'Yes, you are. You're like a colt.'

'A colt? A horse?'

'All long legs and silky.'

She was embarrassed about going to the doctor, but she did what her friends had done. Jenny had bragged how easy it was. It was better if you got the male doctor, she said. Tell him you are having problems with your period. Bad pains, irregular cycles, something like that. And make sure you have a cover story ready to tell your mum, in case someone tells her you were at the doctor's.

Molly told her mum she was having trouble with her ears, that she thought she might need them to be syringed on account of all the chlorinated pool water. She was worried her mother would suggest coming with her, but luckily she was busy organising the autumn brochures and was working long hours.

She made her own appointment, went confidently into the doctor and talked in detail about how bad her period pain was. After he had written the prescription for the pill, she casually asked him to check her ears, to see if they needed syringing. 'You're still swimming?' She nodded. There had been an article about her in the local paper the week before. It meant she didn't even have to lie when her mother asked her later how the visit to the doctor had gone. 'Fine, he said my ears were clear.' Once again, she'd called the question out across the office, not caring for one second about Molly's privacy.

Her mother had been the same three years before when the time came for Molly to be fitted for her first bra. Molly had nearly died with embarrassment. No one liked their private business to be broadcast like that.

'I'm going to Melbourne for the day with Molly tomorrow, Penny,' she'd called out to Molly's grandma. 'There's not a decent bra shop in this town.'

'Mum, *please*.'

'Well, there's not.'

Molly had gone out to the back of the house, very upset. Lara and Harriet were sitting there, having morning tea together.

As usual, Lara noticed something was up straightaway. 'What's up, Mollusc?'

'Mum,' she said, rolling her eyes. 'Why doesn't she take out an ad in the local paper that we're going to buy me my first bra? She shouted it to Grandma, right in front of Mr and Mrs Kingston.'

'Grandma won't tell. And Mr and Mrs Kingston are both deaf, don't worry. They wouldn't have heard.'

It helped to have two aunties. Lara and Harriet sat telling stories about their first bra-fittings. Harriet had got hers first, even though she and Lara were nearly the same age.

'I was flat-chested until I was seventeen,' Lara said matter-of-factly.

'Were you? Were you worried?'

'I don't think so.'

'You weren't,' Harriet said. 'I remember. You didn't mind one bit.'

Molly was fascinated with her aunts' relationship. She knew of course that they weren't real sisters, that Lara had come to live with the Turners when she was little. She asked them lots of times to tell her stories of things they'd done when they were kids, but usually the stories were about her uncle Austin, and all the naughty things he used to do. If Molly had had a sister, foster or real, she reckoned they would have got up to all sorts of things, tried on make-up together, put on concerts, been good friends as well as sisters, but it didn't seem like that with her two aunts. Molly secretly thought that she was closer to Lara than Harriet was.

A few nights before Lara went to England, she and Molly had sat talking for ages. For the first time, Lara talked about coming to live with the Turners. How she'd had to change schools, houses, her whole life, really. Molly had also heard about the memorial days her grandma had organised for Lara, as a way to remember her parents.

'Did it help?' Molly asked.

'Just a bit,' Lara said quietly.

'So you're not my real aunty, are you?'

'No, I'm not. Not really.'

'You feel like a real aunty.' She'd leaned over and hugged her.

Lara had hugged her back. 'You feel like a real niece.'

Molly had felt even closer to Lara since then. Which was why she really wanted to talk to her now. Of course, she was going to make her own decision, but it would be interesting to hear what Lara thought. And it wasn't as if Dean had been putting any serious pressure on her yet. He hadn't, not in any bad way at least. But she knew that if she didn't go to bed with him, he would go to someone else. 'You know I love you, Molly,' he'd said on the phone the day before, 'but I need to know you feel as strongly as me, otherwise . . .'

He hadn't had to finish his sentence. Otherwise it would be all over between them. She told him how much she loved him. Twice. 'I just need to think about it.' He understood. She'd had that beautiful l l u text from him again this morning. She'd been so relieved.

She glanced down again at the text she'd written. Would she send it to Lara? Or decide for herself? She shut her eyes and imagined Dean's face. It helped her make up her mind. She did love him and she did want to sleep with him. And, at the end of the day, it had to be her decision, not Lara's, didn't it?

She started deleting the text, letter by letter.

Kevin Hillman tapped three times on the kitchen table. 'Gloria? Gloria? Dearly beloved husband calling his suddenly deaf wife?'

Gloria turned away from the window and put down the cup of tea she'd been holding. It had gone cold without her realising. 'Sorry, Kev, were you talking to me?'

'Only for the past five minutes. That's all we need, me blind, you deaf. What's up, love? You've been distracted the past couple of days. Is it Lara or Harriet you're most worried about?'

It was Lara. But nothing about Lara that she could tell Kev about. Were promises between people still promises even after one of the parties had died? Because she was longing to talk to Kev about it. She hated being the secret keeper like this. While Penny was alive, she hadn't needed to think about it. If the subject had come up, it would have been up to Penny, not Gloria, to deal with the fallout. If there had been time, perhaps Penny would have even given her some advice on what to say. Or told her how much of the truth she had told Lara. That was the worst of it. Gloria didn't know how much Lara knew. It was like carrying something fragile, but not knowing if it was going to melt or explode in your hands.

She leaned over and touched Kevin's arm. She touched him a lot these days. That was how they communicated – physical smiles, she thought of them as. 'I'm worried about Lara. I hope she's okay.'

'She'll turn up, love. It might be her version of Harriet's break-down. Parents dying affects different kids in different ways. Being back in England might have brought back a lot of memories of them, of both sets of parents. She might just need some time out.'

'You're probably right.'

'Are you working late tonight?'

'I am. Is that okay? I'll be back at teatime though. Did you want me to do something?'

'No, you're okay, love.'

She stood up with a sigh. 'I'd better get going. The Cuthberts are coming in this morning. Off on their annual trip.'

'Where are they going this year?'

'Spain, Portugal and Italy.'

'Again? They're getting showy since they retired.'

'We can be as showy when we retire, if you like. We can be away the whole time too. I have contacts in the travel world, I reckon I could get us a few good deals.'

'No.'

'Why not?'

'Because you're too young to retire. Because you love your job.'

'You don't believe me, do you? I'd retire at the drop of a hat.'

He was serious. 'You'd go mad with boredom at home.'

'No, you'd be here to entertain me. It's you I worry about going mad with boredom at home.'

'I'm fine.'

'Are you?'

'Course I am. The blokes from the council depot are going to drop by this afternoon.'

She could picture it. They'd shuffle around, look and act uncomfortable and then leave, glad the visit to their old blind mate was out of the way for another few weeks. It struck her again how unfair it all was. All the plans they'd had. The two of them hoping to work until retirement, and then perhaps setting off with a caravan for a few months, heading up the east coast of Australia. They'd had bigger plans than that, too. Overseas trips. Gloria had even sent away for information on a get-over-your-fear-of-flying course. They'd talked about trying to get to New Zealand first. Then maybe Europe. Kevin had a longing to eat a real Italian meal in a real Italian village. They wanted to see so much. They were lucky, they had good health, enough money.

His loss of sight had been so rapid. It was as if the diagnosis had sped things up. It went from a gradual fuzzing of his vision, to complete loss of sight in one eye two months later. He could only see the barest outlines now. Legally, he was blind. It changed things, of course it did. Kevin had been so vital, so independent. It took all her acting skills to stop herself crying when he despaired at how weak he had become, how dependent on her he was. They had talked about him maybe getting a white stick, or even a guide dog, but Kevin had resisted all of it. 'I have to get used to the idea of being blind first.'

She'd found him in tears one night. She had come into the bedroom and discovered him sitting on the side of the bed, hands over his face, sobbing quietly. He had knocked something off the table and been unable to find it, even with all the lights in the room on. His sight had been practically gone by that stage. 'I'm useless, love.'

'No, you're not. You're just going blind.' She wouldn't let him feel sorry for himself.

'I'm blind and I'm useless.'

'Never useless.'

'It's too much to ask.'

'What is?'

'For you to help me. Lead me around like some invalid.'

She'd moved to him and held him close. 'I won't be leading you anywhere. You can walk beside me or in front of me if you like, but I'm not leading you. There was nothing about that in any marriage rulebook that I read. I'll sue you for false pretences if you start making those sort of demands on me.'

'You hard-hearted witch. No sympathy for a poor old fellow like me.' He'd held her tightly. 'A poor old blind fellow like me.'

'Try as hard as you like, that won't wash with me.' She had been smiling as she said it. 'Don't think about yourself like that, Kev. Because I won't be.'

'Gloria Hillman, I —'

'Oh, Mum, Dad, stop it. That's disgusting at your age. And it's not even night-time.' It had been David, their oldest son, calling in on an impromptu visit with his youngest child.

That was nearly two years ago. Kevin had left the house hardly a dozen times since, and each time had wanted to come home early.

There in the kitchen, the morning sun shining in on them both, it seemed obvious what she had to do. The feeling was getting stronger. Time was slipping past too quickly. She kept thinking that what had happened to Penny, with Neil dying so suddenly, would happen to her. She would regret all this time spent in the travel agency, getting mad at Melissa, worrying about Austin and Harriet and Lara, being tired and no company for Kev when she got home, all out of some probably misplaced loyalty to Penny and Neil. As she picked up her bag, she told him. 'When Harriet and Lara get back, I'm going to talk to them all about retiring.'

'Gloria —'

'It's simple, Kev. I want to spend more time with you.'

'You'll get bored.'

She wasn't imagining it. There wasn't the same vehemence in his voice. She leaned over and kissed his forehead. 'I can't leave you here on your own. Any fancy lady might walk past and see you.'

'That's good, because I won't see her.' It fell flat. He seemed to know it. 'Have a good day, love.'

'You too, Kev.'

CHAPTER SIXTEEN

It took Harriet three attempts to get the microphone on the bus to work the next morning. Clive finally leaned over and, with a sigh, jiggled the cord around, gave it a thump and then handed it back.

'Should be all right now, BB.'

'Thanks.' Monkey-face, she added to herself. Clive's BB jibes were wearing very thin. She picked up her script and started reading. '*Good morning, ladies and gentlemen. Now, we met each other informally and possibly a little drunkenly last night!* (James had inserted a handwritten question here: *Possible laugh??*) *But as today is really the first full day of our formal* Willoughby *tour, I wanted to say again, on behalf of everyone at Turner Travel, what a pleasure it is to have you all travelling on this tailor-made tour with us. If you're happy, we're happy, remember! And of course, I'd like to extend another special welcome to our guest of honour, Patrick Shawcross. (Gesture at guest of honour. Possible applause.)*'

Harriet refused to do the gesture. Patrick Shawcross was less than three feet away from her. She didn't need to point him out. In any case, the group members hadn't left his side since he came down and met them in the breakfast room that morning. James had been right about the applause though. There was an enthusiastic round of clapping, a whoop from Mr Fidock, a gallant bow from Patrick Shawcross and then Clive changed into gear and edged his way out onto the main road.

Harriet was in the guide's seat at the front of the bus. Patrick Shawcross was in the seat across from her, next to Miss Talbot. She was wearing a bright blue cotton jacket this morning. It went well with her spangly runners. Harriet had given her niece Molly a similar pair for her twelfth birthday a few years ago.

Mrs Lamerton was several rows back, looking unhappy. Her seating plans had gone awry when Patrick met Miss Talbot as they came out of the hotel, and escorted her, hand on elbow, on to the bus, taking the seat beside her. Harriet had half-expected an incident, or at the very least Mrs Lamerton insisting on taking the guide's seat. At the last moment, she had moved down the bus. She was making it clear with her dark glances at Harriet that she wasn't pleased.

Harriet did her best not to catch her eye in the rear-vision mirror and sat up as straight as she could. 'If you look in charge, they will think you're in charge,' James had reminded her during his hospital briefing. 'Be first on and last off, and you'll gain a natural authority over them.' He'd made it sound as if he was talking about lion-taming rather than tour guiding. Again, though, she had to admit he was right. She'd forgotten the nice feeling of being in the front of the bus, microphone in hand, clearly the one in control.

She knew Lara had done two familiarisation trips along this route since she'd been in Bath, checking everything she had organised from Australia, timing the journeys, discovering extra places of interest, passing on all the information to James to write up. Lara would have conveyed all the information from the script quite naturally, Harriet suspected. Pointed out this landmark and that fact as if it had just occurred to her. Harriet was conscious she was reading straight from the page.

'*We'll be making our first stop of the day at the picturesque village of Boscastle, known for its beautiful medieval harbour, its charming cottages and best of all for its use as the setting for the dramatic scenes in "The Case of the Crooked Chef". In the meantime, I'd like to take this opportunity to give you a few more details about the local area. The A30 trunk road we are travelling on is the backbone of Cornwall's road network and was constructed —'*

'Out of second-rate materials if you ask me.' Even without a microphone, Clive's voice was audible throughout the bus.

'*— as part of a streamlined approach to integrated traffic control following a Government review in the mid 1990s.*'

Harriet tried to ignore a gentle snoring sound coming from the driver's seat. Clive was right. Who wanted to hear about road networks? She turned the page and tried to find a more interesting topic. She picked one at random. It was a little early, but if the group squinted they might be able to see what she was talking about in the distance.

'*We'll also be passing one of Cornwall's wind farms later today, remarkable examples of man, and woman, learning how to harness nature's own energy.*' James was really losing it now. '*Wind farms may yet be the saviour of our environment and indeed the human race.*' He'd obviously copied this down word for word from a green information pack. She quickly read down the page. No, the group didn't need to hear about the ravages of the industrial revolution and the number of species of insects that had disappeared in the past ten years. She was almost relieved when Mrs Lamerton held up her hand.

'Yes, Mrs Lamerton?' Harriet hoped it wasn't a request to visit the wind farm. She needed to stick to their schedule.

'I'd like to ask Mr Shawcross when he first decided to be an actor.'

'Thank you, Mrs Lamerton. There'll be plenty of time to ask Mr Shawcross all the questions you like once we get to our first stop. *'As you all know, harnessing wind energy —'*

Mrs Lamerton was having none of it. Her voice rose a notch in volume. 'It's just this seems like a good opportunity to hear some of his stories. Certainly, much more interesting than hearing about wind farms and motorway construction.' It may have been meant as an aside, but her words came straight to Harriet's ears.

She glanced down. James's next set of notes involved the construction methods of traditional beehives. She gave in. James would never know, after all. She put her hand over the microphone and leaned across to Patrick Shawcross. 'Mr Shawcross, would you mind starting work a little earlier today?'

He whispered back. 'No problem at all. As long as you stop calling me Mr Shawcross.'

'Thank you, Patrick.'

'You're welcome, Harriet.'

As he and Harriet swapped places and she handed him the microphone, he touched Miss Talbot gently on the shoulder. 'It's been a pleasure talking to you, Miss Talbot,' he said. She turned bright pink again.

He chose to stand in the aisle beside the guide's seat, facing them all, his hand on the back of Harriet's seat. 'Good morning, everyone. I hope you can all hear me?' They sent a chorus of yeses to him. 'Thank you very much for your question, Mrs —?'

'Lamerton,' Harriet whispered.

'Mrs Lamerton. I'm more than happy to answer it, though I have to admit I was finding that motorway history fascinating. Perhaps you'll give me some private tuition later on, Harriet?'

There was a whoop from Mr Fidock.

Mrs Lamerton ignored him. 'Thank you, Mr Shawcross. I know I am speaking on behalf of all of us when I say we have so many questions that we would like to take every opportunity we can to ask them. So if I could begin. You said in an early article in a magazine I read, the article that sparked this tour, in fact, I don't know if you heard the whole story from Lara, or indeed James or Harriet – we seem to be going through the Turners at a rate of knots' – another titter – 'but to fill you in, I am proud to say it was me who mooted the idea of the *Willoughby* tour to Turner Travel.'

'Did you? Mrs Lamerton, I owe you.'

A scoff from Clive in the driver's seat.

Mrs Lamerton was now almost simpering. 'So could you tell us, Mr Shawcross, how did you first get into acting?'

For the rest of the day Patrick – he'd insisted they all call him Patrick, not Mr Shawcross – pulled anecdotes out of thin air. He answered questions for more than an hour on the bus, on everything from his early acting roles to his favourite food. He stood with the group in front of the old mill in the harbour village of Boscastle and talked about the sixteen takes – '*Sixteen*,' Mrs Pollard had breathed – required to film the scene when Willoughby confronted the restaurant owner about the black-market produce he was selling. The director had just called the final 'cut' when it had started snowing. Not only had they been unable to do any more outside filming for two days but the entire cast and crew had been snowed in together. All the filming had been moved inside. In his opinion, it had been a better episode because of it.

'You're right,' Mrs Lamerton said, nodding enthusiastically. 'There is such an air of claustrophobia, of hidden tension, in that scene.'

'All because of the snow,' Patrick said.

'Thanks so much, Patrick,' Harriet said as she walked with him back to the bus after lunch. It was the first time alone she'd had with him all day. He looked the part again, she thought. He was wearing a dark green jumper, made from what looked like handspun wool. The colour suited him. 'They're loving your behind-the-scenes tales.'

'I'm glad.' Then he lowered his voice. 'It's just a shame they're not true.'

'They're not?'

He shook his head. 'We made *Willoughby* on a shoestring. We had the luxury of two takes, if we were lucky. And if it snowed, it was too bad, we still had to film.'

'But what about that claustrophobic scene you mentioned? With those long close-ups?'

'The cameraman had a hangover and wouldn't get up. So they locked his camera into place in one corner of the room and switched it on.'

'Really?'

He nodded.

'So nothing you've said today has been true?'

'Can you remind me again what I've said?'

They were standing together near the bus. 'You told a story about Patch the dog finding that necklace under a hedge when you were filming one day and the scriptwriters deciding to write that into the "The Case of the Smuggler's Skiff".'

'No, not true.'

'You said the actress who played Lady Garvan was in real life descended from one of Bonnie Prince Charlie's mistresses. And you hinted that your romance had spilled over into real life.'

'No. I don't know anything about her past. And she was happily married to a stockbroker in Sussex back then. They had three or four children, I think. We used them as extras now and again.'

'The story about the post van getting stalled when you were filming on the railway line? And you only just getting away in time when a train appeared?'

'No.'

'The time the whole cast got the flu, but time was so tight you had to go ahead and film anyway, and dub your non-coldy voices in afterwards?'

He shook his head again.

She couldn't stop a smile. 'It's all been lies?'

'Not so much lies as fabrications. I swear, Harriet, if I told the truth they would all be snoring in their bus seats. Most days we just turned up, said our lines then went home. It was a completely uneventful program to work on. None of us ever took it that seriously, either. I think that's why it wasn't a big success.'

'It was in Australia.'

'I apologise. God bless Australia. Though now I think of it, not everything I said today was a lie.'

'No?'

'I really did enjoy those crab claws. They were delicious, just as I said.'

He smiled at her and she got a nice warm feeling. As if they were in on this together. They were interrupted by the group returning from souvenir shopping.

There was the usual scrum over who got to sit next to Patrick on the bus. Mr Douglas somehow managed it, with a bit of nifty footwork involving his wife as a decoy. Harriet realised she was going to have to think about a seating system before they came to blows. Or more to the point, before Mrs Lamerton came to blows with the rest of the group. She was now shooting serious daggers at Mr Douglas.

The question and answer session started as soon as they were back on the road. Harriet saw Mrs Pennefeather and Mrs Hart, the two sisters, nudging each other.

'Go on, ask him.'

'No, you ask him.'

'No, you.'

Mrs Hart finally convinced Mrs Pennefeather to stand up. 'Patrick, my sister and I were just wondering something. We all read in your biography that you've been married twice already —'

'Yes, in the late eighties,' Mrs Lamerton interrupted. 'Once to the Welsh actress Caitlin Moore and then to another actress called Alicia de Vries.'

'But what about now?' Mrs Pennefeather continued. 'Are you married at the moment?' She sat down with a bump, her cheeks flushed. She got a proud rub on the arm from her sister for being so brave. She stood up again. 'If you don't mind me asking,' she added.

'I don't mind at all, Mrs Pennefeather. And no, I'm not married at the moment.'

Miss Talbot stood up so she could see over the seat in front of her. 'What are those American women doing, Patrick, letting a catch like you run free?'

'I don't know, Miss Talbot. It's scandalous, isn't it?'

'Harriet's single too,' Miss Talbot said, standing on tiptoes so she could see Harriet as well. 'Aren't you, Harriet?'

In her guide's seat, Harriet decided it was time to study the itinerary.

Miss Talbot spoke louder. 'Harriet? You are single, aren't you? You broke up with that poor Simon you were living with in Merryn Bay, didn't you?'

'Yes, Miss Talbot, I did,' Harriet said, now extremely determined to look at the itinerary.

Miss Talbot sounded pleased. 'You should ask Harriet out, Patrick. She's lovely. And I've known her all her life, so I should know.'

'She certainly is lovely. Thank you for the idea, Miss Talbot.'

Harriet definitely didn't look up then.

An hour later, they were all standing by the waterside at the small Port Isaac harbour. They had slowly made their way down the narrow steep streets from a carpark above the village, past tiny shops and pretty whitewashed cottages crammed together. Clive had offered to piggyback several of the ladies down the steepest parts. They had all declined, taking their time instead, stopping to peek inside hotels and restaurants boasting freshly caught crab and lobster.

The harbour was peaceful, the water lapping against the stone walls, seagulls squawking, the sky above them a pale blue. Patrick was telling the group about the time the director got tangled in some fishing lines and nearly went over the edge of the lobster boat they were filming in.

'Did you catch him, Patrick?' Mrs Douglas asked. 'Was it you who saved his life?'

'I'm afraid I can't take the credit for that, Mrs Douglas. It was the soundman. He threw out the boom microphone just in the nick of time and the director managed to grab hold of it.'

He caught Harriet's eye and she knew from his expression that he had made all of that up too. She shook her head, pretending to despair. As they moved to the next spot on the itinerary – a pub a hundred yards up the road, also overlooking the harbour – he fell into step beside her.

'How am I going, Harriet? Staying within the boundaries of reality?'

'By the skin of your teeth, I think.'

'It could have been worse. I was going to say a shark leapt out of the water and carried the director away.'

'I'm not sure he's the one getting carried away.'

He smiled. 'It's your fault. You're the one who invited me on the tour.' They walked on. 'Poor Simon, by the way.'

She looked at him. 'I'm sorry?'

'I said, poor Simon. You broke up with him, I believe.'

'Yes. Yes, I did.' She shot him another glance. His face was expressionless. They kept walking. She couldn't resist it. 'And poor Alicia and Caitlin.'

'Alicia and Caitlin?'

'Your wives.'

'Oh, my wives. Yes, the poor things.'

'They recovered fully from the divorces?'

'Miraculously, I believe. You'd think the marriages had never happened.'

'Patrick? Patrick? Could we have you here for a photo?'

They both turned. Mr and Mrs Douglas were standing in front of a moored blue boat, smiling eagerly. 'We think this is the actual one from that episode, don't you?'

'I think you're right,' he called over. 'Excuse me, Harriet.'

'Of course. Mind the sharks.'

He laughed and walked over to them, just as Harriet felt her mobile phone vibrate to signify a new text message. Still smiling, she took it out. The message was from Austin.

Flights organsd. Wil b with u 2moro a.m. then onto Bath. Will find L, dn't worry. U could b off hook yet!! A x

She read it twice, feeling strange. She gazed around at the group. Several of them were chatting among themselves, pointing up at the old harbour building that had been in episodes six and seven. Miss Talbot, Mrs Lamerton and Mrs Kempton were involved in a lively discussion, seated beside one another on a bench near a pile of fishing nets and lobster pots. They made a real picture, with the grey of the stone wall and the orange and green of the nets and baskets vivid beside them. Snatches of their conversation floated across. They were still arguing about Lady Garvan and her suitability for Willoughby. Clive had left the bus and was lying stretched out on a bench, his newspaper under his head, soaking up a ray of afternoon sunshine, oblivious to a large black cat doing the same thing beside him. Mr and Mrs Douglas were moving Patrick back and forth in front of the boat, trying to get the best angle. He was laughing good-naturedly.

Harriet read the text once more. She couldn't deny it. She didn't want Austin to find Lara. Not yet. The reasons why were getting more complicated each day.

CHAPTER SEVENTEEN

By the time Harriet and Lara turned twelve, in some ways it was as if she had always lived with them. Three children had become four, which made games easier to play, although Harriet secretly wished she didn't have to end up partnering James all the time. Austin was always more fun.

Her parents were careful to make sure that what one of the girls got, the other did too. Two kittens. Two birds. Two goldfish. Their birthdays were both in May, yet there were always two separate parties.

Lara puzzled Harriet, though. She wasn't how she'd imagined a sister would be. She'd thought a sister would be another girl she would play with and laugh with, and be kind to and teach how to do things. It wasn't like that. Lara already seemed to know how to do most things – ride a bike, swim, do her homework. If she wanted to find things out, she asked Austin, or James, or her mum and dad, even Gloria, as often as she asked Harriet.

Sometimes it felt as though Lara was the one who had always been there, and Harriet was the one feeling her way. Lara seemed to be more confident. Harriet felt nervous about things, and often had to check with her parents or with Gloria if she had done something the right way or if she had said the right thing. Lara didn't seem to need that reassurance.

Harriet tried to put herself in Lara's shoes, the way her mother had asked her to do. To understand how hard it must have been for Lara, her own parents being killed, having to come and live with a whole new family. Harriet gave it a lot of thought. She would have felt scared, she decided. And she would have done her best to make everyone like her, and been really well-behaved and done lots of housework and not sworn and tried to be kind. In her mind, it started getting a bit confused with the Cinderella story, that she would become the unpaid slave, but it was the truth. She would have felt uncertain, that she had to behave really well so that she didn't stand out and so her new family didn't ask her to leave.

Lara didn't behave anything like that, though. She had grown-up conversations with Harriet's mother and father, talking to them in a serious way that Harriet herself had never done. Lara got on well with James too, watching cricket with him and saying quite sensible things when Harriet couldn't make head or tail of the game and found it too slow, anyway. Lara and Austin got on especially well. They did a lot of laughing.

Harriet and Lara were still sharing a bedroom. That caused more problems. Lara was extremely tidy. Harriet was the opposite. She would come back from school and throw her belongings around, while Lara would fold hers neatly. It wasn't Lara who complained, but Harriet's mother.

'It's not fair on Lara,' she said one afternoon. 'Your mess is all over the whole room, Harriet. You have to try and be tidier.'

'I try, I really do. But something happens.'

'Your clothes grow legs and run over to Lara's side of the room?'

Harriet nodded, smiling. 'It's nicer over there. It's tidier.'

Gloria came up with the solution. She'd done the same thing

with two of her sons. A line down the middle of the room. Harriet could be as messy as she liked but not on Lara's side. Lara had every right to push any of Harriet's mess over the line.

It summed up their whole relationship in a way. They got along perfectly well, as long as neither of them crossed the line. It worked well, most of the time. Then Harriet crossed it. Very publicly.

Her class was asked to write a true story from their family history as though they were an eyewitness. Her friend Emma wrote about the time her grandfather's house nearly burnt down in the 1945 bushfires. She described the smell of singed hair, the feeling of his eyeballs nearly bursting in the heat from the flames. Sitting beside her, Harriet did her best to make hers as thrilling as possible too. She started with the story of her mother and father and brothers coming out from England in the boat, as one of the 'Ten Pound Poms', and how they had lived in that hostel place for a year, but after a few paragraphs it all seemed a bit boring, especially compared to the burning trees and sirens Emma was writing about. Emma had the habit of reading aloud as she wrote, which was sometimes annoying, but often a help with school projects.

Harriet tried to think of an alternative event from her family history. She was about to settle for the time her mum had been bitten by a wasp at a family barbecue when she remembered the story of Lara's parents being killed in that car crash and how Lara came to live with them afterwards. Harriet didn't know all the details. They didn't speak about it much any more, but she knew enough to be able to write a 900-word essay. She knew Lara hadn't been there during the crash, but she decided that it would make it much more dramatic if she was. She also decided to make Lara into a baby in a car seat, rather than an eight-year-old. It didn't change it too much, after all. Lara would still come to live with them at the end.

Her story began as Lara and her parents were driving through the mountains somewhere in Ireland. Harriet wasn't sure where in Ireland the crash had happened or if there were many mountains in Ireland, but it painted a sort of scary picture, she thought. She described the noise of the engine, even the sound of the radio in the car. Their teacher had asked them to use all five senses to tell the story, so that was hearing covered, she thought. She was particularly proud of a description of the village they had driven through. There was a poster of an Irish village in the travel agency, showing lots of coloured doors and curvy lettered signs over pubs, and she'd sort of taken it from that.

Out of nowhere she had a flash of memory, overhearing a conversation between her parents about Lara's parents. About the two of them having a screaming match. Perfect. She wrote a sentence about Lara's parents shouting at each other, while little Lara slept in the back, luckily unable to hear. As she kept writing Harriet started to feel she was in the car herself. She leaned over the page, writing as quickly as she could. She imagined the squeal as the tyres hit an icy patch and Lara's dad shouted, 'It's out of control,' and Lara's mum said, 'Oh God,' turning around to look at Lara in her seat in the back. And then the car crashed through the white road barrier, skimming over rocks and gathering grass as it did so, the three of them being thrown around, the car turning once, twice, before coming to a stop in the river at the bottom of the valley. Somehow, miraculously, the seat Lara was sitting in, wedged in with extra pillows because she was so little, had been torn from its holdings and flung out of the (luckily open) window. Harriet hadn't been too sure if that was possible, but she hoped her teacher wouldn't pick her up on a detail like that. Lara's parents wouldn't have had a hope. But thank God – Harriet's hand was nearly a blur on the page by this stage – someone had driven by then and noticed the car. They'd run to a nearby phone box and called for an ambulance. It was the female ambulance driver who had found Lara, still strapped into her seat hours later, as the rescue party was about to leave the scene. 'We've got a survivor!' she shouted out into the night air, Harriet wrote. She had nearly been in tears.

Her story got the second highest mark, behind Tran Hien, the Vietnamese student whose parents had come to Australia in a terrifying trip in a flimsy boat, escaping from torture and imprisonment. Harriet was even more amazed when 'Lara's Rescue' appeared alongside 'The Boat Trip' in the annual school magazine. The teacher told her afterwards she'd wanted it to be a surprise for them both. The first she knew about it was when Lara came up to her at the end of year school assembly, looking shocked and angry. Harriet had never seen that expression on her face. It made her feel sick inside.

'Harriet, how could you do this? Why did you write it?'

She looked at the magazine in Lara's hand and blinked, in shock. Part of her was thrilled to see her name in print like that. She thought Lara would be happy for her. 'We had to write a story about something true that happened to our family.'

'But it isn't true. I wasn't in the car.'

Harriet was embarrassed. 'I know. But I didn't know how else to write it, because if I wrote it only from the point of view of your mother and father then they . . .' She stopped before she dug herself any deeper. She couldn't say because she wouldn't have been able to write about it if it was only them, because they weren't her family, only Lara was now, so Lara had to be in the car if she was to use them in the story. She'd started to explain, tried her best, but Lara interrupted her. Harriet got that frightening feeling again, that Lara was there, but a long way away, all at the same time.

'Don't ever do that again. It's my story, not your story.'

'But you're my family, aren't you. Aren't I allowed to write about you?' She was genuinely confused.

'Am I your family?'

'Aren't you?'

Lara didn't answer.

'I thought you were,' Harriet said in a small voice.

The rest of the family all read it. Mum, Dad, Austin, James. It was very dramatic, they all said. 'But Lara wasn't in the car, was she?' she heard James say. 'And she wasn't a baby at the time either, was she?'

It was talked about in the travel agency. Many of their customers had children at Harriet and Lara's school. The school magazine was read by everyone. Folding brochures one afternoon, Harriet overheard a conversation between Gloria and one of the clients.

'I didn't realise it had been so traumatic for Lara. I knew her parents had died, but I didn't realise she'd been in the crash with them.'

Gloria lowered her voice. 'No, actually, she wasn't.'

'But Harriet's story in the school magazine . . .'

'A little artistic licence.'

'But her parents did die in a car crash?'

'Yes, but Lara wasn't with them.'

Others were even blunter, and talked about it to Lara herself. 'I hadn't realised you were adopted, Lara. And under such tragic circumstances.'

Harriet felt sick. Her parents told her off, for not thinking about Lara, not thinking through the consequences of her actions. Even Gloria told her she should have thought more before she wrote it.

She'd gone to Gloria, the way she always did when her own family didn't make sense.

'I didn't mean to hurt her.'

'Are you sure?'

'Why would I?'

Gloria was serious. 'Look, I know it isn't easy sometimes for you, Harriet.'

'I've been really kind to her. I've always been kind to her.'

'Maybe she doesn't always want your kindness. Maybe sometimes she just wants to feel normal.'

It changed things between her and Lara for a while. Until Harriet went into their bedroom one night, with a carrot cake she had made herself. She knew Lara loved her cake. She had written *Sorry Lara* in icing on the top.

'I didn't mean to hurt you. I'm so sorry.'

'It's okay.'

'I didn't think.'

'It's okay, Harriet.'

Not long after that, Harriet kept coming across Lara and her parents, especially her mother, having the secret conversations again. Sometimes they were out in the garden, sitting together on the bench near the plum tree, talking quietly together. They stopped talking when Harriet came out with a basket of washing. Another time she came into the travel agency after hours to get some paper from the stationery cupboard. She surprised them, sitting close together in the waiting area. Her mother was holding Lara's hands. One afternoon she came home from a swim at the beach and walked into the living room, to see Lara sitting on the couch, crying, with her mother on one side and her father on the other.

'What's wrong? What's happened?'

Her mother's expression was obvious. 'Harriet, please, Lara needs to talk about a few things.'

In other words, Harriet, go away. It made her feel she was eight, all over again.

'Do you want to talk to me, Lara?'

'No thanks.'

'It's not because of the story, is it? I promise I won't tell anyone ever again.'

'It's okay, Harriet.'

She went back to Gloria again. 'They won't tell me what's going on. They're shutting me out.' She was going through a dramatic phase.

'There are things she wants to know about her own parents.'

'Why?'

'Because she can't remember them very well. And she wants to.'

'But she's got my parents now.'

'She still misses her own parents.'

'I suppose.' She thought about it. 'And it's not like she's adopted, is it? She can't go and find her parents. Get to know them at all, can she?'

Gloria looked at her for a long moment. 'No, Harriet, she can't.'

James started going out with Melissa the year Lara and Harriet turned sixteen. Melissa and her family had moved to Merryn Bay at the end of summer and she and James were an item within a month. As Melissa said at the first family barbecue she attended, 'I took one look at James in the main street and knew he was the one for me.'

'He didn't stand a chance,' Harriet heard Gloria say to her mother one night. She didn't think she was supposed to have heard it. But she knew what Gloria meant. Melissa frightened Harriet a bit. She was small but bossy and James seemed to almost hide behind her. He also made a big deal to Austin about the fact he had a girlfriend and Austin didn't. Harriet heard them have a horrible fight about it.

'Melissa's your girlfriend? Yes, James, that's one word for her, I suppose.'

'Meaning what?'

'Well, it's a funny thing. I often wondered what a female Rottweiler would look like in human form, and now I know. Blonde hair, tanned skin, remarkably like someone you know well, actually.'

'Fuck off, Austin,' James had said. Harriet had put her hands over her ears. She still hated it when they fought.

Austin was right in a way, but it wasn't a nice thing to say about James's girlfriend. Lara, however, didn't seem scared of Melissa at all. She talked to her, quite nicely, answered her questions and somehow didn't let her boss her around, the way Melissa was able to do to Harriet. Harriet was always surprised to find herself in the shop down the road, having been sent – ordered – by Melissa to go and buy some drinks, or a newspaper, or some chocolate. Gloria had said to her quietly one day that she should remember she was James's younger sister, not Melissa's slave.

'But she's his girlfriend. I'm being polite.'

'You don't have to let her walk all over you, Harriet. Some people like to do that to others.'

'I'll try not to let her do it any more. Anyway, they might split up soon, mightn't they?' she asked hopefully.

She'd been wrong. James and Melissa got engaged six months later, on Melissa's twenty-fifth birthday. Melissa asked Lara to be her third bridesmaid and Harriet to be one of the ushers. She'd explained to Harriet that she thought Lara's blonde hair, almost the same shade as hers, would look a bit better in the photographs. Harriet didn't think she minded, though she felt a bit strange on the day of the wedding. She'd overheard her parents saying how kind it had been of Melissa and James to ask Lara to be in the wedding party. 'It must have really made her feel one of the family.' It felt wrong to feel a bit jealous, so she did her best to hide it.

Harriet was eighteen and in her bedroom studying for her final year exams when her mum and dad came in. They both sat on the bed and formally invited her to come and work for Turner Travel.

'We'd love it if you would.' Her mother was all smiles.

'But only if you want to,' her father added. 'We want you here, but not under pressure.'

She had accepted straightaway, and not just because she wanted to make her parents happy. She'd never thought about working anywhere else. She'd always hoped that's what would happen, but she was very touched they'd asked her like that. After Austin's decision to go to music college rather than follow James and work in the agency, Harriet knew it was important to them.

It was a special moment for Harriet. Sitting in her room with her parents, hearing them say so casually that they loved the way she already helped in the travel agency, all the after-school hours she did, the way she made people feel so looked after when they called in or phoned about any of the tours.

'That's a real gift, Harriet,' her mother said. 'You make me very proud when I see you with our customers. We'd have loved you to work for us even if you weren't our daughter.'

They spoke about the sorts of things she would be doing, and asked her whether she wanted to work as a guide down the track, or stay in the office. She felt the ideas bubbling up inside her. She made suggestions there and then. What about guided tour groups to sporting events? Themed tours based around different sorts of restaurants? Historical tours, visiting towns connected with the colonial history of Australia? Her teacher at school had been brilliant the way he'd made it all come alive. Maybe he could come as a special guest speaker? Or geological tours? She'd seen a documentary and it was incredible when the history of a mountain or a bay was explained, all the things you looked at every day without ever really seeing them. Lots of people might be interested in that, mightn't they? She'd felt as though someone had thrown open a window, showing her all sorts of possibilities.

Her father had sat back and given her a beautiful smile. 'I don't think coming up with ideas is going to be a problem for you, Harriet.'

Her mother had been as happy. 'We'll have to take on extra staff to cope with all the business you're going to bring in, by the sound of things.'

'You have asked Lara to come and work with us as well, haven't you? I don't want her to feel left out.' Even as she asked, even as she genuinely hoped they had, she'd felt a stirring of her eight-year-old self. Please don't let them have asked her first.

'Not yet. We're asking her next. And we hope she'll say yes too.'

They'd asked her that same night. Harriet had been in the next room and had overheard. She'd made sure she could overhear, in fact. Lara hadn't said much. She had just gone to Mrs Turner and then to Mr Turner and held them in a very tight hug. 'I'd love to. Thank you.'

After James and Austin moved out of home, their bedroom became the Turner Travel storeroom. Harriet and Lara continued to share a bedroom, until Lara moved out of home the year they both turned twenty. She'd saved enough for a deposit on her own flat, on the first floor of one of the oldest stone buildings in the town, beyond the main street shops. They all knew, but didn't say, that there had also been a legacy from her parents.

Lara announced her plans quietly over breakfast one morning. It had come up for sale, she had been to see it, fallen in love with it.

Penny had been alarmed. 'Are you unhappy here, Lara? Oh, darling, you should have said something. We could have talked about it.'

'No, I'm not unhappy at all. It just felt like the right time.'

'You're not thinking of leaving the business, are you? Because we think the world of you, you know that, don't you?'

'No, I love working here. I'd just like to live on my own.'

They were all invited to a house-warming drinks party. It was the first time any of them had seen the flat since she'd moved in. She had kept them away, gently but firmly. 'No, not until it's perfect.'

Harriet hadn't been pleased. 'Come on, Lara. We want to see the before and after.'

'No, I'd rather you only saw the after.'

Even Mr and Mrs Turner hadn't seen it. Harriet had a feeling they were hurt by it. She'd heard her mum talking about it with Gloria one night.

'It's her first place, her first real independence,' Gloria tried to explain to Penny. Harriet had been in the staffroom, able to clearly hear their conversation, even though she wasn't sure if she should be listening. 'The first time since she came to live with you. She must have always felt like she was taking part of Harriet's bedroom. This is the first time she's really had something of her own. I think you need to respect that. Give her time.'

Whatever the flat had looked like when Lara first moved in, they didn't know. But she'd made it lovely. It was three large rooms at the front of the big stone building, which had previously been a bank. On top was a roof garden. It was one of the few two-storey buildings in the town, with a view over the pine trees lining the caravan park at the seafront. It was almost total sea view, if you ignored the car park and the kiosk, and the children's playground.

The rooms were simply but beautifully decorated. There wasn't a lot of furniture: a low sofa and two matching armchairs in soft white leather; a rectangular dining table in pale wood, with six wooden chairs, their padded seats matching the leather of the sofa. One wall was bookshelves, the books arranged neatly, art books and non-fiction on one row of shelves, hardbacks on another, paperbacks on another.

They peeked into the bedroom. It was decorated in the same pale colours, off-white walls, a cream quilt cover on the bed, a pile of soft pillows and cushions in shades of pink, light blue and pale yellow adding gentle colour. It was a very peaceful room. Even the kitchen was uncluttered, white cupboards and a stainless steel oven, with the cheery addition of a row of bright green cups and a thriving spider plant on the deep windowsill.

There were no heavy curtains over any of the large windows, just light gauze material in a soft turquoise that framed the view perfectly. A large painting hung on the main wall in the living room, an abstract seascape in different soft shades of blue and greens. It was very beautiful, the renovations thoughtfully done, the decoration stylish and feminine.

In a corner, pouring drinks, was Lara's boyfriend of six months, Tom. They had heard about Tom, but this was the first time they had seen him. Lara had met him at a travel agents' dinner in Melbourne. A pilot with one of the new airlines, he'd been one of the guest speakers.

'He's gorgeous,' Gloria said to Lara in a whisper. Not only physically, though the combination of fine Asian features inherited from his mother and height from his Australian father was striking. Later, emboldened and made giddy by too many champagnes, Harriet said to him that if she was ever destined to be in a plane crash, she hoped he was at the helm.

She realised too late what she had said. Her hand went to her mouth. Everyone looked at her, then Lara. 'Oh Lara, I'm so sorry.' No one needed to say it aloud, but they'd all been thinking of Lara's parents dying in a crash.

Lara fixed it, smoothly, gracefully. She went to Tom's side, kissed his cheek and said, 'It's fine, Harriet. Tom wouldn't crash. He's too good a pilot, aren't you?' She somehow stitched the tear in the conversation without fuss. The music was turned up, the conversation continued, the evening went on.

They'd all liked him very much, they told her at work the next week. She seemed pleased but didn't say much. Several months later she casually remarked that she wasn't seeing Tom any more. Harriet had wanted all the reasons why not, but Lara wouldn't be drawn. 'It wasn't working out between us,' she said. It was the explanation she used from then on, whenever she ended it with one of her boyfriends.

Harriet met Simon when she was twenty-six. It hadn't been an instant attraction, but she grew to like lots of things about him. How sure he was of everything. How definite he was about what he wanted to do with his life. He was nice-looking, solid, with sandy hair and an open, smiling face. Sometimes they ran out of conversation, and didn't always laugh at the same things, and she often wished he wasn't quite so quick with his lovemaking, but she reasoned with herself that she couldn't have everything. His good points easily outweighed the bad.

Austin was appalled at the news. 'A policeman? You're going out with a policeman? Oh bloody hell, Harriet. Talk about put a halt to all our gallops.'

'He's not *square*, if that's what you're getting at,' she said, stung. 'Anyway, you shouldn't be smoking drugs, if that's what you're getting at.'

'I don't smoke drugs. I inject them. Or freebase them. Sometimes I even take a bath in them.'

Lara was laughing. 'Don't mind him, Harriet, he's teasing you.'

'I know he is.' Of course she knew that. 'Don't worry, Austin, I've asked him to let you off lightly if he ever picks you up.'

'I don't know if I want to meet him. What if he starts lecturing me? Wants to teach me the right way to cross the road? "Look left, then right, no, no, Austin, not three rights and then a left. Look, if you kill yourself it's not my responsibility." '

Harriet wasn't enjoying this any more. She'd been dying to tell Austin about Simon, had saved it up for his visit home, and now he and Lara were making a joke of it. Austin had changed since he'd started touring with the orchestra, she decided. He only visited now and again, breezing in for a night here or there, sometimes midweek, sometimes on a Saturday. This visit – home for three nights – was a rarity. Harriet had pictured how it would be, Simon arriving for a barbecue, he and Austin hitting it off immediately – with a bit of teasing about Simon being a policeman of course, but then they'd find all sorts of things in common.

She made one last effort. 'Mum and Dad really like him, don't they, Lara?'

Lara nodded. 'He's very likeable.'

Harriet should have been pleased that Lara had said that. It was true. It was a statement of fact. But it felt condescending. 'Please don't talk about him like that.'

Lara frowned. 'Like what, Harriet? I meant it. He is very likeable.'

'You make him sound dull. It was like a put-down.'

Lara seemed genuinely confused. 'I didn't mean it to.' She turned to Austin. 'He is a nice man. And Harriet's right, he gets on really well with your dad too.'

That was even worse. She couldn't put her finger on it though. She could see Austin was puzzled by her reaction. On the surface everything Lara was saying was perfectly acceptable. Simon was very likeable, he did get on well with her father and, yes, he was a nice man. But it was the way she said it. Harriet rubbed her wrist, the way she had started doing when she felt under siege.

Austin came over, disarming her with a big hug, the sort of hugs he used to give her when she was small. 'Harriet, relax, would you? You're a little tense, and it's perfectly understandable. Your boyfriend is meeting your big scary internationally successful percussionist brother for the first time and you are hoping he comes up to scratch. That's your boyfriend, not your brother. But don't worry. I will sniff around him in the manner of all good dogs, and if I decide that, yes, he is good enough for my dearest baby sister, then I promise you he will see nothing but the most angelic and adorable side of my many faceted personality, okay?'

'Okay.'

'And Harriet, I'm sorry too if what I said came out wrong,' Lara said. 'I like Simon.'

There it was again. The words were perfect but Harriet couldn't stop herself from wanting to pick them up, shake them around, find out what Lara really thought about Simon. But they were both looking at her, with concern and, yes, with affection. She took a breath. Perhaps they were right. She probably was just nervous about Austin meeting Simon for the first time.

'Thanks.' She glanced at her watch. 'He'll be here in a minute.'

As she went outside she heard Lara say to Austin. 'It must be his police training, but it's amazing, he is never, ever late. You can set your watch by him.'

Harriet had never noticed it, but Lara was right. She glanced at her watch as Simon pulled up in his blue Mazda. It was exactly seven o'clock.

Their father managed the barbecue. It was nothing formal, chops, burgers, vegetarian sausages for Lara, salads, some of their mother's homemade patties, her special recipe of mincemeat, vegetables and what she said was her secret ingredient. Harriet knew it was soy sauce. Simon loved them and complimented her on them. He helped himself to several more, as well as another chop and a sausage, after offering the tray to everyone else first. They all accepted except Lara.

'You a vegetarian, Lara?'

'I am, yes.'

'Moral grounds or taste grounds?'

'Moral, I suppose.'

He bit into a chop. 'Don't think I'd last a week if I was a veggo.'

He'd announced when he arrived that he could only stay until ten o'clock as he had an early start the next day. Harriet tried not to, but as the time moved closer to ten, she noticed Austin and Lara glancing at their watches, exchanging knowing grins. She knew what they were up to. They were laughing at him.

At ten to ten she went over to where Simon was sitting talking to her father. They had discovered early in their relationship a shared passion for cricket. Simon barracked for Australia and Mr Turner supported England, despite his many years in Australia, so there was always plenty of scope for arguments and, this season in particular, even some gloating on Simon's part. The current English team was one of the weakest in memory.

'It's your batting that lets you down,' Simon was saying now, as she came up behind him and put her arms around his waist. She loved the solid feel of him. He lifted up one of her hands, squeezed it then kept talking. 'Too much focus on the opening batsmen, and the middle order are too unreliable.'

'I'd agree with you there, but the coach has to take some of the blame. They're prepared for a completely different sort of bowling style, not to mention the conditions. Harriet love, get me a beer, would you?'

'Sure Dad. Simon, you too?' She hoped he'd say yes. It would take him at least ten minutes to drink it, which would delay his departure and take those grins off Austin and Lara's faces.

He lifted up his wrist and checked the time. 'I'd better not, Harriet. I've got an early start tomorrow and I said I'd be gone by ten. I'll go and say goodnight to Penny now.' He leaned over and vigorously shook Mr Turner's hand. 'Pleasure talking to you again, Neil. And my commiserations again on your decision to back the English team.'

Neil laughed loudly. 'You young buck. We'll have the last laugh yet.'

Harriet followed Simon into the kitchen to get a beer for her dad. Mrs Turner was at the sink, rinsing out the dessert dishes.

'Thanks for a great night, Penny.'

'You're welcome, Simon. Off already? Don't tell me, early start?'

'Six o'clock.'

'Well, you don't want to be late.' She accepted his kiss on the cheek. 'See you next time. Thanks again for the flowers.'

Not her mother making digs about his timekeeping too? Harriet felt under siege from all sides. How dare they all laugh at Simon? It was all she could do to keep her temper as she walked to the car with him. He kissed her on the cheek, told her she had looked very pretty that night and that he'd enjoyed meeting Austin. 'A bit of a character, by the looks of things.'

'Yes, he is.'

She thought at first she was imagining it but then Austin's voice became louder, floating over the fence. She wasn't imagining it. He was doing a countdown to ten o'clock.

She didn't know whether Simon could hear or not. He got into his car and started the engine.

'Ten, nine, eight, seven . . .'

Simon put on his indicator.

'Six, five, four . . .'

Changed into first gear . . .

'Three, two . . .'

And drove away.

'One!' Austin poked his head over the fence. 'Ten o'clock, on the dot.'

'You're pathetic.'

In the background she saw her parents and Lara. All of them with big smiles on their faces. Austin had been playing to the gallery.

'Just helping him out, Harold. In case he lost track of the time in your fragrant company.'

'You're more than pathetic. You're pitiful.'

Austin was laughing. 'He's nice, Harriet.'

'I really like him. How dare you be so rude.'

'I wasn't rude. I talked to him. We had a long talk about sport and politics, man to man. Didn't we, Lara? You heard us.'

Harriet wouldn't look at Lara. 'I saw you laughing at him, Austin. How would you like it if you called the police in an emergency and they weren't there because they had slept in? He has to be punctual.'

Now not only Austin and Lara but her mum and dad were laughing.

'Harriet, that was the best defence of timekeeping I have ever heard,' her dad said. 'Now what about that beer, love?'

'Stuff your beer, Dad.'

When she came back from her floods of tears on the beach, it was to find her parents and Austin and Lara sitting around the back veranda. She went to her father, embarrassed but still prickly. 'I'm sorry.'

He took her hand and gave it a squeeze. 'I'm sorry too, love. I didn't mean to tease you.'

'That time of the month, Harriet?'

'Austin, stop it, would you?' The anger was still fizzing inside her. She wanted to shout at all of them – well, no, not at her parents. She wanted to shout at Austin and Lara. It was their fault. Sitting there, all cool and collected and supercilious. She liked Simon. She possibly even loved Simon. And she didn't want them to ruin it for her. It seemed important to say that. 'He means a lot to me. I didn't like that you were poking fun at him.'

Austin leaned back in his chair. 'Harriet, it's a good sign that I'm teasing him. It means he's one of the family. You'd have more reason to be worried if I was nice to him.'

Her mother patted her arm. 'He's right, Harriet. Don't be so sensitive about him.'

She wavered.

'Anyway, Harold, wouldn't it be creepier if I was really, really nice to him?' Austin stood up and made an elaborate bow. ' "Really, Simon, do tell me more about your recent law-defending antics. You caught a joy-rider? My word, what an adventure. Tell me every bit of it, from the start, now. You set the alarm for six a.m. . ." '

She couldn't help herself. She started to laugh. 'You are a bastard, Austin Turner.'

Austin kept going, even as a piece of bread left over from the barbecue went whizzing past his ear. ' "And tell me, Simon, how do you make those uniforms fit so snugly? Do you have any leather pants? Could I see them some time?" '

She went over and punched him on the arm. 'Bastard, bastard, bastard.'

He grabbed her. 'But lovable.'

She swiped him and went inside to help her mum make coffee.

CHAPTER EIGHTEEN

Harriet looked around her hotel room. Everything was organised. She'd asked the porter for another armchair and both were now arranged in front of the TV. It made the room even more cramped, but never mind. She had also asked for a teapot and two nice cups. The two videos they'd be watching tonight were also ready to go, one of them already in the video player.

She knew all her clients were happy. Tired, full and happy. Most had gone straight up to their rooms after dinner. 'Very nice meal, thank you, Harriet,' Miss Talbot said as she walked past. Mrs Randall just gave her a big smile and said nothing.

The hotel's menu was as old-fashioned as the decor, Harriet thought, but her clients were delighted with it. Good old English comfort food, one of them called it. Soup or pâté for starters. Pork chop, grilled sole or lamb cutlets with mint sauce for mains. Ordinary vegetables like mashed potato, carrots and peas. Desserts like treacle tart, trifle or apple pie, all served with large quantities of the local clotted cream.

Even Mrs Lamerton had pronounced herself pleased. 'Thank you, Harriet,' she had said regally as she sailed past on her way to the bar for an after-dinner port. 'I do like a nice pork chop.' Harriet knew all Mrs Lamerton cared about was being seated next to Patrick Shawcross. She would have been happy eating fried ants as long as she was beside him. She had definitely made up for all the lost opportunities on the bus. No one else had got a word in with him until after dessert. The poor man would be covered in bruises too, from all the arm clasping Mrs Lamerton had been doing. If he wasn't already covered in bruises from being thrown against the seats on the bus twice that day. Clive's fault, each time.

Patrick's arrival had definitely upset him. Clive had obviously enjoyed being the alpha male or whatever position he imagined being bus driver afforded him. Now Patrick was getting all the attention and Clive wasn't happy. He had started to subtly sabotage things. The microphone had inexplicably gone off twice when Patrick was talking as they drove along the coast road earlier that day.

Clive had called out loudly, not turning around. 'Sorry about that, folks, this is an old bus. They must have given the proper bus to the *All Creatures Great and Small* tour group. That's the really popular one.'

As Patrick was standing up answering questions there had also been unexplained sudden braking when there had been no traffic or obstacles in front of the bus. Each time Patrick had been jolted up against the seat beside him. If he hadn't been hanging on to the back of Harriet's seat he'd have gone flying down the aisle.

She would have to keep an eye on Clive. But at least her clients were happy and they were her priority. Their question and answer sessions with Patrick were getting more enthusiastic each day. At lunch that afternoon he had fielded them from all sides.

'Patrick, was it just one dog playing Patch or were there several of them?' Mrs Kempton had wanted to know.

'Just the one, but he did go missing one day. After that we tried to make sure we always had a double on standby.'

Mr Fidock was leaning over the table. 'A crossbreed, wasn't he? Part sheepdog and part something else?'

Harriet had taken the opportunity to make a quick call back to Australia. She'd been about to dial the Turner Travel office when she'd changed her mind, dialing the number of James's hospital instead. She hadn't spoken to anyone at home since the night she'd rung Austin. Another of the new Turner Travel rules. Melissa had declared no news was good news. 'Let us know if something is wrong, otherwise we will assume all is going perfectly, as it should. It's what our clients expect.'

Harriet was put straight through to James. He sounded very pleased to hear from her. She ran through the tour so far. 'No problems yet, either. I think they're having a really good time.'

'It sounds like it. Well done, Harriet. I know you must have got a shock about Lara, but it sounds like you're doing a great job on your own.'

'Still no word from her?'

'Nothing. You know Austin's on his way to Bath? And to you, of course.' He didn't wait for her answer. 'Melissa thinks there might be a man involved, but I don't know about that. I think Lara will tell us in her own good time what's up. She left enough information with her flatmate so we wouldn't worry, so I'm not worrying.'

Every now and then James surprised Harriet with a dash of good sense. It was often too easy to take Austin's side and dismiss James as Melissa's lapdog. 'You think that?'

'I do. That's what Lara is like. Something's up with her, but she's obviously taken herself off to sort it out. These weren't exactly the ideal circumstances, but then it's not a perfect world. And I had full faith in you, Harriet. Sounds like you're doing beautifully. Are they laughing at my jokes in the script, by the way?'

She had just reported that yes, they were (the ones she was reading aloud, in any case) and was about to finish up when she heard a loud voice in the background. She heard James speak to the new arrival. 'It's Harriet from St Ives.'

The phone was snatched. 'Harriet, hello. Everything's all right?'

Harriet felt the tension inside. 'It's going really well, Melissa, thanks.'

'Really?'

Why did she have to sound so disappointed? 'Yes. The group are all very happy.'

'And Mr Shawcross?'

'He's happy too, I promise.'

'Is he nearby? Can I have a word with him?'

'He's busy with the clients at the moment.' Harriet realised then that she was actually handling Melissa. Old Harriet would have run and got Mr Shawcross. Old Harriet would have stammered and said, actually there's a bit of a problem with the bus driver, and I think Mrs Lamerton is upset she isn't getting to sit next to Patrick Shawcross often enough, and Mrs Kempton keeps losing things. But she was coping with it all, she realised. It was going fine. And that was all Melissa needed to know. She decided to get away while the going was good. Just in case her new confidence had a time limit. 'Can I talk to James again?'

'He's with a nurse.'

'Never mind. Would you tell him I said goodbye? And give Molly my love? I'll call if anything comes up.'

'Thanks, Harriet.' A slightly too long pause. 'And well done.'

'Thanks, Melissa.'

'And we'll let you know as soon as we track Lara down. There might still be time to get her to give you a hand.'

Several replies came to mind. Harriet pushed them all down. 'Thanks, Melissa,' she said again. 'Goodbye.'

Patrick's knock came at ten o'clock, as they'd arranged. Harriet had made sure she was changed out of the Turner Travel uniform and dressed in her own clothes, a cotton skirt that felt light and summery, her favourite red T-shirt and espadrilles. The yellow outfit was pushed right to the back of her cupboard.

'I feel like I'm cramming for exams,' he said as he came in.

'You're passing with flying colours, then,' she said with a smile. 'They'd never guess you couldn't remember the first thing about *Willoughby* twenty-four hours ago.'

'Not strictly fair, Harriet. I had blocked it out. Buried it deep in my psyche somewhere.'

'You're not unleashing too many demons, excavating it like this?'

'If I feel a psychological breakdown coming on, you'll be the first to know.'

'Can I get you a cup of tea before we start?'

'That awful tea you served me last night?' He laughed at the expression on her face. 'Harriet, it's all right. You didn't make the teabags. You take things very personally, don't you? You reacted the same way when one of the women complained about the cloudy morning. It's called nature. Weather. You can't be held responsible.'

'No. Sorry. It's just this is important to me.'

'And me too.'

'You don't have to pretend, really. Not with me.'

'I'm not pretending. I'm having a great time. If I was home, I'd be living quite a different life. Not being feted at every turn and having people howl with laughter at everything I say. Do you suppose this is what life is like for celebrities all the time?'

'Don't you know? As an actor?'

'I was never truly successful, though. I usually felt too self-conscious and, as you saw yourself, too nervous. Let's forget the tea. Will you have some wine with me instead?'

She saw then he had a bottle with him, tucked in behind the itinerary he was carrying. 'It's a good one.' He glanced at the label. 'Italian.'

'Oh, yes, thanks very much. I'd love a glass of wine.'

'Excellent. We're having a party.' He sat on the end of the bed and pulled out the cork. She looked for glasses. There were only the tooth mugs.

'I'm sorry, they're not exactly fine crystal.'

'They'll do perfectly.' He poured two mugs and handed hers across. 'You have been given the servant's quarters, haven't you? We can switch our viewing sessions to my room if you're feeling too crowded?'

'No, this is fine.' It was, too. They were more relaxed with each other tonight.

He took a sip of his wine. 'So what do we have for our viewing pleasure this evening?'

'Episode five to begin with, "The Case of the Smuggler's Skiff". It begins with a big fight between you and Lady Garvan. And then episode fifteen, "The Case of the Leaning Lighthouse".'

'Those two were even worse than the rest, if my memory serves me right. We might need to fast-forward both of them. And we're visiting where tomorrow?'

'Patrick, are you looking at the itinerary at all?'

'No, I don't need to. I'm in such good hands with you. You seem to cater to my every need and guess my every want, before it's even a half-formed notion in my head.'

'You just can't cope with my brother's writing style, can you?'

'It was your brother who wrote it?' He laughed. 'No, I'm sorry, I can't. And I'm actually using all my free time to try and remember *Willoughby* stories.'

'They're loving everything you're telling them. Even if the stories aren't strictly true.'

'They could be, you know. I might be dredging up old memories. I'm very glad they're enjoying it. They're nice people.'

'Do you mean that?' The night before he'd thought they were all mad.

'Yes, I really do.' He stretched out his long legs. 'I'm also glad it's now, not fifteen years ago. Back then I might have laughed at them for being so interested in something as flimsy as a TV program. But I had an interesting discussion with Mr Fidock today.'

Harriet had seen the pair of them talking as they walked back to the bus in Port Isaac.

'He was embarrassed at first about why he was here,' Patrick said. 'He thought he shouldn't be interested in something so silly as a long-gone TV program. But he confessed to me that it was his link with home. That he didn't want to come back and wander about looking for something in his home town that he wouldn't find, or see school friends that he no longer had anything in common with. He decided this was a safe way, a fun way, to be nostalgic. And I thought, he's right, that's what it is. This is like a public service, not an ordinary tour.' He held up his mug in a toast. 'So well done to you and all at Turner Travel, Harriet Turner.'

He took charge of the remote control. They sat silently as he fast-forwarded through the opening credits, pausing before the end, for the aerial shot of himself and the dog walking across a windswept headland. They took a sip of wine at the same time.

Harriet had watched this episode during her *Willoughby*-athon the first night she arrived. Well, fast-forward-watched it, at least. It involved a missing watch, stolen from the jewellery store in the centre of St Ives. Called to investigate it, Willoughby uncovers a chain of counterfeit jewellery smuggling. The jeweller, new to the town, is in fact a prison escapee. There is nearly a shoot-out, before Willoughby sneaks up behind and disarms the jeweller. The gun goes off and Willoughby falls to the ground. A tense moment – the ad break would have come in when it was screened on TV – before they discover the jeweller has shot himself in the foot.

Patrick pressed pause just as Lady Garvan ran towards him on screen, her face anguished. 'I remember doing that scene. They were going to have a stunt double for me. But there was a problem with the budget so I had to do it myself. The man playing the jeweller kept joking that he was going to bring in a real gun, to add realism. I remember being worried he'd done just that.'

'You were supposed to be worried, though. So it looked like good acting.'

'It wasn't. Not really. I don't think I ever got the part right. Even though it wasn't a success, I'd like to be able to look back and think I'd done my best. But never mind.'

She turned to him. 'Why are you so relaxed about it?'

'Because it was years ago. I've already had my dark nights about it.'

'I thought actors were supposed to be insecure.'

'Oh, I can be. I'm just not in the mood for it right now.'

They watched the second episode in silence. As the end credits started to roll, Harriet stood up, about to pack away the video cases, when he surprised her.

'Enough work.' He reached across and poured some more wine into her mug. 'Tell me about you, Harriet.'

'There's nothing much to tell.'

'Let me ask you some questions then. I can decide whether there's much to tell after that. I'll start with an easy one. Favourite colour?'

She smiled. 'Definitely not yellow. Purple, I think.'

'Favourite animal.'

'Hyena.'

He smiled. 'An unusual choice.'

'I thought you were doing one of those psychological tests. Where your choice of colour and favourite animal gives away your inner secrets.'

'So a hyena isn't your favourite animal? What would it have meant if it was? That you were attracted to howling men with stripes on their backs?'

'Exactly.'

'Just as well you didn't say mouse, then. I'd have been disappointed in you.'

The wine was relaxing her. 'We used to play that game all the time as teenagers. You'd give someone four things to describe and it would instantly give you an insight into all their deepest, darkest feelings.'

'That must be an Australian game. Tell me about it.'

'No, it takes a while. You must be tired.' And she wasn't sure how she'd feel hearing what his attitudes to sex, death, himself, and his ideal partner were.

'Not too tired to play an authentic Australian game. I don't have to run around in shorts or kick a ball?'

'No.'

'Well, then. Play it with me now.'

She had that feeling again that he was amused by her. She hoped it wasn't only a way of filling in time. Though of course that's what he was doing. In his normal life he wouldn't be sitting in a hotel room watching videos and playing games with a tour guide. She had that rush of curiosity again to ask him about his life, his work in America, but he was waiting for her to explain the game. 'I give you four topics and you have to tell me in four words, off the top of your head, how they make you feel.'

'Right. I'm ready when you are.'

Still a little unsure, she reached for her bag and took out pen and paper. He did seem genuinely keen to play the game. 'First of all, imagine yourself in a white room and tell me how you would feel.'

'A completely white room? White floors, white walls . . .?'

She nodded. 'White ceiling. Completely white. The first thoughts that come to mind.'

He didn't hesitate. 'Calm. Clean. Peaceful. But I'd feel a bit wary in case I left marks all over it. Perhaps I'd take my shoes off before I went in there.'

She wrote it all down. When she looked up he was watching her, with that half-smile again.

'So Professor Turner, what have I revealed about myself?'

'It's supposed to represent your attitude to death. Some people say they'd be terrified in a white room, scared, trying to get out.' She checked her notes. 'Whereas you seem to be well-adjusted about the whole idea. You'd feel calm, clean, peaceful, but worried about leaving marks. That's probably guilt.' She kept a straight face.

'Probably? Definitely. All the sins of my past coming back to haunt me. So, next question.'

She was embarrassed now. 'Patrick, really, it's just a teenage thing. You don't need to do it.'

'Seriously, Harriet. I'm intrigued now. Ask me another.'

'The next one is about your favourite colour.'

'That's an easy one. Red. The exact colour of your T-shirt, in fact.'

'You're sure about that?'

He nodded. 'It's always been my favourite colour. So now what? I give you four words to describe how I feel about the colour red?' At her nod, he shut his eyes as if to concentrate.

Sitting opposite him, Harriet studied his face. She liked the character in it, the liveliness. In *Willoughby* he had been all moody and mysterious, and his dark looks suited that. In real life he was much lighter of spirit. Carefree, somehow. He opened his eyes. She noticed the dark blue again. 'Right. I have my answer. Cheerful. Vibrant. Deep. Sexy.'

She wrote them down. It was just as she would have described him herself.

'Don't tell me, I've revealed my ideal partner is a rooster?'

She smiled. 'No, that one's about you. It's how you'd like other people to see you, or how you see yourself.'

'What did I say again?'

She had a feeling he knew exactly what he had said. 'You are cheerful, vibrant, deep and sexy.'

'How extraordinary. That's right. I am all those things. To think you Australians have been keeping this incredibly accurate psychological testing to yourself all this time. Next one?'

'This one's about water.' Which was really about sex. She felt that odd tingle again, as though she was swimming and getting out of her depth. Another reference to water, she realised. So was she thinking about sex? With Patrick? She stared at him, taking in the expectant expression on his face, the relaxed body, the long fingers holding the glass of wine. 'Again, you need to tell me —'

She jumped as a mobile phone sounded. His, not hers.

'Excuse me, Harriet.' He glanced at the number and smiled before he answered it. 'Hello there.' His voice was warm.

Harriet tried not to eavesdrop, though it was difficult enough not to in the small room. He was obviously happy to hear from the caller. She could hear the voice faintly. It sounded like a woman. She couldn't help listening. 'I'll need to check my diary,' he was saying. 'I'm not in my room just now, can I call you back? Great. Give me a few minutes. Okay, thanks.' He turned to her. 'Harriet, will you excuse me? I need to make some calls home.'

'Of course. I think we're done for tonight anyway.'

'I think so too.' This time he did kiss her. Quickly, on the forehead. 'Thank you. I'm enjoying this very much.'

'You're welcome. So am I.'

When she went to bed an hour later, she could still get the scent of his aftershave on her skin.

In her bedroom in Merryn Bay, Molly Turner was sitting looking at herself in her dressing-table mirror. She'd hardly slept all night. It was still too early to go to swimming training but there was no way she could go back to bed. There was too much to think about. The house was quiet. She imagined she could hear her own heart beating. She tried to keep her expression serious as she stared at her reflection, but a smile kept breaking through.

It was finally going to happen. She'd made her decision.

Dean had been so proud of her. 'That's fantastic, gorgeous.' She loved it when he called her gorgeous. 'See, didn't I tell you it would be easy?'

Their plans had all come together when her mother had reminded her she'd be going to Melbourne for the night later that week 'You're still okay to go and stay with Hailey?'

In that instant she'd decided. It had all fallen into place in her mind, just like that. She had calmly said, as if it were true, that she had a swimming carnival that night, didn't her mum remember? She'd told her about it the week before? She'd be staying overnight in a billet because it was so far away? So she wouldn't need to go and stay with Hailey after all. And her mum had hesitated only for a minute and then said, of course, that's right, she must have forgotten about it, how was Molly going to get there, though? And as calmly, Molly had said that Dean, her new coach, was going to come and pick them up and drive them there. That was only the tiniest of lies, saying 'them' when it would only be her, but she didn't want her mum to get too worried.

She'd rung him straightaway. He'd been taken aback at first, she could hear it in his voice, but then he sounded really pleased. He would come and get her himself. He knew which motel they'd go to, as well. 'We'll have the whole night together, gorgeous. You won't regret it, I promise you.'

She leaned forward to the mirror. Would she look different when she got back? Would it show that she had had sex? Would other people be able to tell? She folded her arms around herself. It was the right thing to do, she was sure of it. She loved Dean and he loved her, and as he said, it was time they took their relationship to the next stage.

She glanced at her mobile phone. There had been no text from Lara. She decided to take it as a sign. She had to trust her own instincts. And she did. It was what she wanted to do. She was nearly one hundred per cent sure of it.

CHAPTER NINETEEN

Austin rang Harriet mid-morning the next day to say he'd be with her within the hour. He'd flown into Plymouth airport that morning and hired a car. He'd decided he would be able to stay for an hour at the most. 'I've only got three days off, Harold. I'll have to start looking for Lara as soon as I can.'

Harriet had imagined him having lunch with them, meeting Patrick Shawcross and all the clients. Maybe even coming on the tour of Bodmin Moor that afternoon. She couldn't admit it to him, but she wanted Austin to see how well she was coping. She still hated remembering the state she'd been in when he came to her rescue in the Flinders Ranges. He had told her many times since that he had practically forgotten it, but she hadn't.

The tour group were spending the morning sightseeing around St Ives on their own, visiting galleries and tracking down extra *Willoughby* landmarks. Mrs Lamerton had loudly announced her intention to be photographed standing in front of the lighthouse seen in many of the episodes. Clive had meanly, and too loudly, remarked that she'd better be careful she didn't block out the light. They were all meeting for lunch in one of the beachfront cafes. The afternoon would be spent on the Moor, looking for moorland ponies to photograph and taking a short walk to the tor that had been the backdrop for the confrontation scene in 'The Case of the Jilted Jockey'.

Harriet had taken the opportunity of having some free time to send a postcard home to Molly and to buy some creamy toffee for Gloria and Kevin. Back in her room, she had just finished checking the itinerary for the next day when the receptionist called to tell her Austin was downstairs. She'd contemplated wearing something different from the hideous yellow outfit, but she was meeting the group at the harbour at twelve-thirty and it made more sense to be already dressed in uniform.

Austin was waiting at the foot of the stairs and slowly shook his head as she came towards him. He looked as stylish as ever, his dark hair shiny and fashionably long, his linen shirt and dark trousers hanging perfectly on his lean frame. There was also the usual spark of mischief in his eyes.

'I see that outfit hasn't got any more attractive. Melissa's on the other side of the world and you're still obeying her?'

'It's very handy. My group don't have the best eyesight.'

'They won't if they keep looking at you in that get-up.' He hugged her. 'How are you, Harold?'

'I'm great. It's brilliant to see you, Austie.'

'You too. I'm sorry I can't stay long. I want to get across to Bath as soon as I can and talk to her flatmate. I was thinking about it the whole way here. It has to be something about her parents, don't you think?'

Harriet blinked. She knew he was here to talk about Lara, but she hadn't expected it to be so immediate. She was about to answer when she heard a voice.

'Hello again, Harriet.'

Harriet turned. It was Patrick. She was very pleased to see him. She could introduce Austin to her star guest, even if they didn't get to spend any more time with him.

'Patrick, hello.' She noticed him looking at Austin and made the introduction. 'This is my brother, Austin Turner. Austin, this is Willoughby himself, Patrick Shawcross.'

They shook hands. Harriet watched as Austin turned on the charm. 'You're having a good time, I hope. My sister's not working you too hard?'

'Oh no. Your sister is a gem. She's got all of us under her thumb. Especially me, isn't that right, Harriet?'

'I don't know about that,' she said. She liked that he was laying it on so thick.

'So you're enjoying your trip down memory lane?' Austin asked.

Patrick nodded. 'Even more than I expected. I may have to make an annual thing of it. What do you say, Harriet? Could you bear me once a year?'

'Of course. I just need you to survive this one first,' she said.

There was a noise at the front door of the hotel. They looked over. Miss Talbot and three of the other women were knocking on the glass and waving. Patrick smiled and waved across. 'Will you excuse me? I'm showing Miss Talbot and some of the others the way to the art gallery. A pleasure to meet you, Austin.'

They shook hands again. 'You too,' Austin said.

'I'll see you later, Harriet.' He touched her back lightly as he spoke.

'See you, Patrick,' she said.

She took Austin for a coffee at the cafe on Porthminster Beach, down from the hotel. It was a blustery day. The sand was whipping along the beach, red and white striped canvas deckchairs flapping, bright-coloured towels gusting, children running in and out of the water, squealing and chasing spatters of foam.

Austin gazed around. 'It's a beautiful place. Incredible light.'

'Gorgeous. Everyone loves it here.'

'So what do you think? Any more ideas?'

'Well, no, not really. I'm sticking to the itinerary pretty much. That's what everyone's expecting.'

'Sorry, Harriet, I meant about Lara. I tell you, it's times like this I wish Mum and Dad were here.'

She kept her face expressionless. 'Just times like this?'

'Well, no, lots of times, of course. But we could have asked them for help now. Asked them more about Rose, and her husband. Are you like me? A bit shocked about how little we know about where Lara came from, who her parents were?'

'We knew a fair bit, didn't we? Remember the memorial days? They were all about her parents.'

'I know that. But it's the facts we don't know. A little girl came to us out of the blue, and the more I think about it, the more I realise we hardly asked a question about it or did anything special for her. We went on as if it was a normal thing, that a stranger arrived to live with us.'

'No, we didn't. Everything changed when she arrived.'

'No, it didn't. We still went to school, to the beach, helped in the office. It's just there were four of us kids, not three.'

They were interrupted by the arrival of their coffee. The wind threatened to take the foamy tops off their cappuccinos. Across from her, Austin was checking his mobile phone. 'Sorry about this, Harriet. Want to double check I've got a signal here. I was thinking about calling Lara's flatmate first, but I think I might turn up unannounced. I'm going to call into her college too, see if I can have a word with one of her lecturers or any of the others in her class. They might have noticed something.'

'Thanks for taking the time to drop by and say hello.'

He picked up her tone. 'Harriet, I'm sorry.' He leaned over and tweaked her nose. He'd been doing that since she was little and she had always hated it.

She was cross enough now to say it. 'Please don't do that. I'm not a child any more.'

'You on your cranky pills, Harold? With me, your dearest brother, here on the other side of the world with you? And you not treating me with respect and adoration? Aren't you finding your heart beating faster with the excitement of being in close proximity to me?'

She couldn't help it. She started to smile.

'That's better. You looked like you'd been drinking sour milk. Harold, I'm sorry to talk about Lara and not shower you with praise about how well you're coping on this tour. I'm not surprised, that's all. I knew you could do it. I told Lara that as well.'

'Told her what?'

'That I had complete faith in you.'

She sat up straighter. 'When did you talk to her about me?'

'The day James had his accident. She rang to see whether I thought you were up to it.'

She could feel the colour in her cheeks. 'Why did she have to check with you whether I was up to it?'

'What else could she have done? Rung you, in the middle of the night? When she knew you'd be flat out getting ready? Calm down, would you? Think about it from her point of view. She'd spent months setting up this tour and then James pulls out the day before. She was concerned and reasonably so. Don't overreact.'

'I'm not overreacting. But it's a pretty funny way of showing how much you care about something, not showing up like this.

Leaving all of us in the lurch.' She felt a hot, prickly sensation inside. She knew she was being bitchy but she couldn't seem to stop herself.

'Which brings us right back to square one. Why I'm here. To find her.'

'But what if she doesn't want to be found? What if she wants to be left alone?'

'I told you before. I'll leave her alone as soon as I know she's okay.'

'I still think if she's decided she wants some space we should give her some space.'

Austin gave her a strange look. 'Harriet, this is Lara. Lara whose parents were killed when she was eight years old. Lara who had to go and live with a whole new family. Don't you think this is out of character for her? That something's up and she might be needing some support right now? What's got into you? I thought you and Lara were close.'

The feeling again. The uncomfortable ripple of hurt and confusion. 'Things change in a family, Austin. Relationships change, people behave differently. Lara might not want you chasing after her.'

'Lara's heart would skip a beat if she saw me appear out of nowhere, just as yours did. My two little acolytes, that's how I've always seen you. My little elfin-faced Harold, and ice queen Lara. Not so much sisters as followers, I always liked to think. Such sport too, playing you off against each other, making you do my bidding. I suspect I'm part wizard, actually. What do you think, Harold?'

She stood up. 'I have to go, Austin. I'm meeting the tour group.'

'Not until lunchtime, you told me.'

'I've got work to do.'

Austin didn't move. 'Don't be like this.'

'Like what?'

'Prickly. Pretending to be tough. It doesn't suit you.'

She lost her temper. 'What am I supposed to be like then, Austin? Answer me that? Because I don't seem to be able to win in this family. I'm either too weak, falling apart, the basket-case or it's "Don't get tough, Harriet, it doesn't suit you." Which one am I?'

'You're my dear little sister Harold, that's who you are. My little anxiety bag of a sister. Come on, Harriet, sit down and calm down, would you?'

He disarmed her, as he always could. Her temper flickered and then went out. But he was wrong. She wasn't just his little sister, the anxiety bag of a child. Not any more. But he kept choosing not to see it. They fell quiet again. She made a point of slowly stirring sugar into her coffee. The mood had changed and she didn't know whether she wanted to fix it or not.

Austin broke the silence. 'I thought he was supposed to be an old man.'

She looked up. 'Who?'

'That Patrick Shawcross. He's not old at all. In fact, he's a hunk.'

'A hunk? When did you ever use a word like hunk?'

'Don't you think it suits him? He's like one of those old-fashioned matinee idols. "Hunky actor Patrick Shawcross, pictured today in St Ives",' he spoke in a bad American accent. 'If I had known my little sister was travelling around the wilds of Cornwall with a sex symbol . . .'

'Yes, a sex symbol and twelve old-aged pensioners.'

'So he hasn't tried anything on you?'

'Tried what?'

'You know. These actor-types, no morals . . .'

She knew he was trying to joke with her, but she didn't like it. 'Austin, what's got into you? You never did this big brother act when we were at home, so why now?'

He shrugged. 'Because you had Simon guarding you back then. I might be your brother but I can see these things. He's an attractive man. You're a single, good-looking woman. I know from the orchestra that you put those things together on tour and boom. I saw the two of you, getting on so well, that touch on your back . . .'

'Of course we get on well. And he's an actor. Everyone knows actors are tactile.'

'Is he married?'

'Yes, with eleven children, but he told me this morning he loves me and wants to leave them for me. Austin, listen to yourself.' She was laughing now, but she was also serious.

'Just worrying about my little sister. Protecting her, as I always have.'

She poked out her tongue at him.

' "Please don't do that," ' he mimicked her. ' "I'm not a child any more." '

She couldn't help herself. She did it again.

After waving goodbye to Austin as he drove off in his hire car, she went for a walk along the beach on her own. He had given her a nice hug, and told her he thought she was great, and the tour was obviously going well, but he'd been distracted when he said it. It was obvious he wanted to get on the road.

She walked down the beach, taking in deep breaths of the fresh air, trying to focus on the peaks of white on the water. The seagulls were loud. The weather was changing. The blue in the sky was being taken over by large dark clouds, and the wind was picking up, getting colder and gustier. The buildings and streets of St Ives were to her right, just out of her line of vision. She tried to concentrate on the fishing boats out on the water, real, solid things, not the uncomfortable thoughts pushing their way into her mind.

She'd had the dream again the night before. Reliving the phone calls that her parents were dying and she was rushing to get to them, feeling the panic in her chest that she wasn't getting closer even though she was running as fast as she could. Getting to the hospital and racing to the door, only to find it locked. To find Lara standing there behind the glass, staring at her without expression. Hearing herself call out, 'Lara, let me in.' Not being able to get her to understand, or to hear. She'd woken up then, her heart racing. It had taken her a long time to get to sleep again. If she had the dream, the bad memories always followed. Memories of the terrible conversation with Lara three months ago, the night before she left for her course in England. Like a video in her mind she couldn't erase.

She should have told Austin about it. Explained why she felt so strange about finding Lara. Told him what she had learned, from Lara herself.

One of the nurses from the hospital had set it in motion, unwittingly, at Lara's farewell party. It was the first time Harriet had seen her since the day her mother died. The young woman had put her hand on Harriet's arm and expressed her sympathies again about Mr and Mrs Turner, asking how she was getting on, in a tone of voice that gave away she knew about Harriet's breakdown.

Harriet had answered as brightly as she could. She'd told the truth. She missed her parents very badly. 'I just keep wishing I could have one last conversation with them.'

'It must have been some consolation to Lara, I suppose. Nothing takes the sadness away, but perhaps it would have helped.'

Harriet didn't understand. 'I'm sorry, I'm not sure what you mean.'

'It might have helped Lara, that she was able to speak to your mother before she died. Before she had the second stroke.'

'But Mum wasn't conscious after the first stroke. She was in a coma when she had the second one, wasn't she?'

The nurse had looked uncomfortable. 'I'm sorry. I thought you —'

'No, it's fine. Really. Will you excuse me?'

She'd gone directly to James, who was in mid-conversation with several clients. She'd pulled him to one side. 'James, did you know Mum was conscious before she died?'

'What, Harriet?' He'd looked unhappy to be interrupted.

She repeated the question.

'Harriet, why are you asking this now? What will it change?'

He didn't understand. She went to Austin, on the other side of the room, and asked him the same question.

'Harriet, don't do this to yourself.'

'I'm not doing anything. But did you know?'

'Harriet . . .'

He didn't understand either. Lara was in the far corner of the room, talking to several clients. Harriet could hear her explaining what the course in Bath was about. She knew it was rude to interrupt but she couldn't stop herself.

'Lara, can I talk to you. In private?'

They went outside to the garden. Harriet blurted it out. All the nurse had said. 'Is it true? Were you talking to Mum? Before she died?'

Harriet didn't know what she'd expected from Lara. A denial perhaps. An explanation that the nurse had got it wrong. What she hadn't expected was what Lara did.

She nodded. After only a moment's hesitation.

Harriet was shocked. 'But when? I thought she was in a coma. Why didn't any of you tell me she'd been conscious?'

'Harriet, it wasn't for long. We'd just got to the hospital and James went outside to ring Austin and Melissa and he asked me to ring you and . . .' Lara stopped there.

Harriet stared at her, trying to make sense of what she was saying. 'James asked you to ring me? To tell me Mum was in hospital? That she'd had a stroke?'

Lara nodded.

'But you didn't ring me. James rang me.' Even as she said it, a sharp memory of James's call that day seemed to echo in her mind. '*Harriet, thank God I got you.*'

Harriet saw something in Lara's expression. She knew what it was immediately. It was guilt. 'Lara, did he ask you to ring me? And you didn't?'

Lara didn't answer that time. She just kept looking at Harriet.

Harriet had to know. She had to know for sure. 'Lara? Is that true? I have to know, can't you see that? Did James ask you to ring me and you didn't?'

'Harriet . . .'

'Is that what happened?' She knew the answer from Lara's face. 'But Lara, if you had rung me, I could have got there earlier. I might have been with Mum when . . .' Back it came, the panic and the hurt and the desperation of not being with her father or her mother when they died. She could hardly look at Lara, unable to believe what she had just learned. 'I can't understand. How could you have done it?' Still no answer. 'Lara, please, you have to tell me. How could you have done it? Don't you see what you have taken from me?'

There had been no response from Lara. Nothing. That's what had stunned her. No tears, no apologies. They had just stared at each other, and then Lara had turned and gone inside.

The next day Lara had left for England. They hadn't spoken of it – spoken of anything – in the months since. Harriet hadn't known where to start. How did she begin to ask about something that she knew would hurt so badly to hear? How did she get past the fact that Lara had done something so terrible?

Should she have told Austin about it? She couldn't have, she realised. Something inside, some instinct, had stopped her. The uneasy feeling that he wasn't automatically on her side any more. Because like it or not, she knew there had always been rivalry between her and Lara over Austin. Over who spoke to him the most. Who made him laugh the most. Who he liked the most.

Austin had looked at her as if she was crazy when she dared to suggest it hadn't all been smooth sailing when Lara arrived. For once, she had heard herself voicing something close to the truth, but it had been dismissed. Austin was in his rescuer mode, and nothing was going to get in his way. He'd always been like that. Playing the older brother card, but only when it suited him.

For the hundredth time since her parents died, Harriet wished they were there, so she could ask for help and advice. She thought about what Austin had said about wanting to ask about Lara, her parents, what had happened to them.

The questions she wanted to ask them came straight into her mind. 'Did you know how much I loved you? Did you love me?

Did you love me as much as you loved Lara?' She knew what they would have said. 'Of course we did, Harriet. We had enough love for all of you.' She'd never been able to hear it enough times. And what questions would they ask her, she wondered.

Perhaps they knew all about her already. If, as she hoped, they were up in some sort of heaven somewhere, she liked to think of them keeping an occasional eye on her, or at least getting regular reports, like dossiers. She liked to imagine the two of them, sipping cocktails on some big cruise ship in the sky, a tuxedo-wearing waiter swishing up to them with a tray. 'Here's this week's report on your children, Mr and Mrs Turner.'

It had disturbed Harriet recently to discover that her memories of her parents were fading. When she tried to picture them sometimes, the edges were hazy, as though she was looking at them through frosted glass. She could remember minor details, but not the whole. The way her father walked, an upright, brisk movement. The way her mother laughed, with one hand covering her mouth, so ladylike. She could still imagine their voices, though. They'd always kept their English accents, even after so many years in Australia. Sometimes just a touch of another similar accent was enough to hear them in her head.

Harriet came to a boat pulled up on the sand. She leaned down to touch it, running her hand along the wood, the solid feel of the paint layers. *Will o' the Wisp* was written in curvy letters on its side, a bright starfish painted beside it. She traced it with her finger, counting the five points. A childhood memory came back to her. A conversation she'd had with Gloria about six months after Lara had come to live with them. Harriet had just finished her regular drawing on the travel agency blackboard. Gloria had come over to look.

'That's lovely, Harriet. But you've forgotten your starfish.'

Since doing her Christmas cards, Harriet had started putting a small starfish in a corner of all of her drawings, as a little symbol of her family. She hadn't forgotten it this time. She'd been thinking about it, picturing the five pointed arms, trying to decide what colour she would do it, when she had realised it didn't work now. 'No, I haven't. I can't do it any more.'

'Why not?' Gloria asked.

'Because there are six of us in my family now, not five.'

'You can get six-pointed starfish. Twenty-pointed starfish, even. Starfish come in all shapes and sizes.'

'I've never seen them.'

'You'll just have to search harder, then. And in the meantime, the five-pointed one can still be your family. You'll just have to look at it differently.' Gloria had drawn a five-pointed starfish on the blackboard then and there. 'See? One of you can go in the middle of the starfish – you for now, as a special treat, but you can take turns.' She'd written Harriet's initial in the centre of her drawing. 'And the other five, your mum, your dad, James, Austin and Lara, can surround you,' she'd been writing their names as she spoke, 'standing in a circle with their funny pointy heads, looking after you.'

The memory made Harriet smile and made her sad, all at once. She ran her hands along the wood of the boat again, picturing it out on the water, riding waves. As children they had built rafts and swum in the sea, but she had never spent much time sailing or boating, preferring to swim. She imagined climbing in, setting sail, going across the water for miles, until she arrived at a whole new place. Is that what Lara was trying to do, make a fresh start somewhere? Leaving the Turners, and that whole life, behind her? Reclaiming the life that would have been hers if her parents hadn't died?

Harriet suddenly had the same urge. To go somewhere, start all over again. Leave pain and sadness behind. Be happy, laugh. Out of the blue she thought of Patrick Shawcross. That lightness of spirit he had. Was it a choice he had made or was it luck that he had got through life unscathed, unshaken by grief or jealousy? She wanted to ask him. She had a hundred questions she wanted to ask him. Why he had stopped acting. What he did now. Why he was still single . . .

She thought of Austin's description of him as a hunk, a sex symbol. 'Has he tried anything on, Harriet?' What if she'd yes? What would Austin have done? Gone and punched him on the nose? Or if she had said to Austin, 'Actually, yes, we've been lovers since the first night we met. It was an instant and incredible attraction.' What would Austin have done then? He'd be shocked at her, she knew. He thought of her as a child, not an adult. No matter what she did.

As for Melissa's reaction if something were to happen between her and Patrick Shawcross . . . Harriet pictured it. The two of them, her and Patrick, spending hours of long, lazy lovemaking in her bed – no, his, it had more room, and a much better view – and finally deciding a choice had to be made. She imagined herself stretching across to the phone, dialing the international number while Patrick ran a gentle finger down her bare back, following with his lips, soft, warm kisses. 'Melissa, hello, it's Harriet. I'm ringing to let you know I've called off the tour because I'm having an affair with Patrick Shawcross and, unfortunately, the clients are getting in the way.' She would lie in his arms, still talking, while he stroked her body some more. Her voice would go husky, as Melissa shouted down the line. Finally she would simply hang up and turn to . . .

'Hello, Harriet.'

She spun around. 'Patrick!'

'Are you all right? You look quite flushed.'

She put her hands to her cheeks. Flushed? Of course she was. 'No, just windburn, I think. I'm not running late, am I?'

'No, I'm early. I saw you from the harbour steps and thought, that's either Harriet off for a walk or a yellow duck has been blown onto the beach.'

She took refuge from her embarrassment by pretending to be insulted. 'The uniform's really not that bad. Anyone would think you and Clive had never seen the colour yellow before.'

'That's right,' he said, as they started walking back to the steps together. 'He calls you Big Bird, doesn't he? Very clever. Perhaps we could hold a contest to see what names the others can come up with.' He laughed at her reaction. 'Harriet, you really do have the most expressive face. I'd call that one mutinous. Can you do heartbroken for me? Or exultant, perhaps?'

She shook her head. 'No. I specialise in worried or anxious.'

'Worried? What do you have to be worried about?'

She told the truth. 'The tour. Something going wrong. Making sure everyone is having a good time.'

He put his arm around her shoulder and hugged her against him as they walked. 'They are. I am. We all are. You're doing a great job. I meant what I said to your brother. I'd happily come back every year and do this. I'm being treated like a king. I have twelve people who seem to think I am the funniest, wittiest person they have ever met in their lives and a lovely woman minding me every step of the way.'

Her senses had sprung into life. She kept waiting for him to drop his arm, but if anything he was holding her closer against him as they walked. She was the right height to be leaning against his shoulder. She could smell his aftershave again. She tried to stay relaxed, as if walking along a windy beach with his arm around her was nothing out of the ordinary. She tried to give a normal-sounding answer. 'As long as you're enjoying it, that's the main thing.'

'I certainly am. And I know the group is, too.' They walked in silence for a while, Harriet was conscious of their closeness, the way their steps were matching. How would they look to anyone watching? Like lovers? Yes, if you ignored the fact one of them was dressed like a duck.

The weather was changing dramatically around them. There was now little blue in the sky and the wind was getting gustier. He had to raise his voice to be heard, leaning down to her height again. 'So is your brother in the travel business, too?'

She shook her head. 'He's a percussionist, touring Germany with an opera company.'

'And he came all this way to say hello to you?'

No, he'd come all this way to find Lara. But she wasn't going to go into that at the moment. She hesitated, noticing again the darker flecks in his eyes, and how good his arm felt. 'Yes, he did.'

'You're lucky to have a close family like that.'

'Yes. Yes, I am.'

They reached the steps to the beach cafe as the first spatters of rain started. Only then did he take his arm away from her.

CHAPTER TWENTY

Austin drove along the fast lane of the motorway towards Bath, tapping his fingers on the wheel in time to the windscreen wipers. The rain had started as he left St Ives an hour before and hadn't stopped since. The sky ahead was black with clouds. He'd listened to the weather forecast. The bad weather was expected to continue for the next few days. On the seat beside him was a street directory and the scribbled directions he'd made for finding Lara's address. In the back seat was his rucksack, filled with enough clothes for three days.

The orchestra manager had been surprisingly understanding when he'd explained about Lara going missing, though only able to spare him for a short time. Austin was glad he'd been able to drop in and see Harriet, brief and all as it was. Even though she was a grown woman, he still had that urge to look after her, to make sure she was okay. He felt differently about Lara, he realised. He'd given it a lot of thought on the plane on the way over. Some of it had to be because Lara wasn't his natural sister, of course. He'd met her when she was eight, whereas Harriet had arrived as a screaming bundle. He could still hear his mother saying, 'Keep an eye out for your little sister, Austin, won't you?' Had she said the same thing about Lara? Austin couldn't remember. Lara was so different to Harriet, in any case. So much more self-sufficient.

Good fun still – he and Lara had always got on well, right from the start – but she had never needed him the way Harriet always had.

He'd liked getting another, instant sister. He knew Gloria had been all for it, too. She'd thought it would do Harriet good to have someone to play with. Not that Gloria knew he'd heard her say it. He'd overheard her talking to her husband when he had been doing some gardening for them. Nothing like open windows to keep a kid up-to-date. Back then adults seemed to be under the impression that if you couldn't see a child, then they couldn't hear you. Austin had heard more dirt by sitting still than he ever would have by asking.

Where could Lara have gone, he wondered. Was she somewhere nearby, right now, upset about something or having the time of her life, off on holiday with a new boyfriend? She hadn't given anything away last time they talked. She'd sounded fine. Normal. He was convinced of it. Would he have noticed if she had been distressed, though? Possibly not. He'd been calling in between rehearsals, with a lot of noise in the background, not really the circumstances for a heart-to-heart discussion.

He'd thought Harriet would have had more of an idea how Lara had been lately, given him some clues, but she hadn't been helpful at all that morning. She'd been odd about Lara, if anything. Women could be so weird. Best friends one minute, all moody and prickly the next. He wondered if Harriet was jealous that Lara had got to go to the tourism college. Perhaps that was it.

He tried to recall more from his last conversation with Lara. They'd had a joke about something, hadn't they? His social life again, probably. He'd always thought it funny the way she was at him to settle down, when she'd shown no inclination to do the same thing herself. He'd teased her about it often enough. 'Time's running out, Blister. Biological clocks ticking, nuclear war clocks ticking. I want to hold another niece or nephew in my arms while I still have the strength.'

'It's your fault I can't settle on any one man, Austin. You've shown me such a bad example.'

'No, I've been helpful. Showing you how not to do it. Therefore, you should want to go off and do it properly. Get yourself married, a nice little home somewhere, two and a half children. Don't ask me to babysit, though, will you? I like full children but I can't bear half-children. I never know what to say to them.'

He'd made a joke of it, as he always did. He'd had enough practice over the years, with the endless comments from Harriet, Lara, even Gloria, about his social life, asking when was he going to settle down, stop playing the field.

He wondered how they'd react if he actually answered them truthfully for once. If he told them that in fact there was nothing he wanted more than to meet a woman he wanted to settle down with. A woman he wanted to have children with. Of course that was what he wanted. He'd loved his own childhood, the fun, the freedom, living by the sea, especially. He loved the idea of giving all that to his own son or daughter. Perhaps even several of them.

He'd seen his own parents together, the respect they had for one another, the affection. The partnership and love. He wanted that as well. But it wasn't that simple, was it? Just because it was what he knew he needed didn't mean the right woman for the job was going to turn up saying, 'Here I am, Austin. Ready when you are.' A woman he enjoyed being with, enjoyed looking at, who challenged him, enjoyed the same sorts of things. Who liked him and liked being with him. It wasn't that simple. It was very difficult, in fact.

All the travelling he did didn't help, he knew that. Twice in the past five years he had been involved with women he had really started to like. Things had been going well between them – not that he'd told any of his family, in case they had started booking churches and printing wedding invitations. But both relationships had ended badly. The first woman, a teacher he'd met at one of the school workshops in Melbourne, had insisted he give up the travelling. She had started leaving newspaper advertisements around for cover bands advertising for drummers or teaching posts in suburban schools. He'd thought it was a joke and then realised she was serious. 'But I love the touring,' he'd tried to explain. 'It's not good for our relationship,' she'd said. 'I need you to be here, close by.' They had split up soon after, on the eve of a month-long tour of Asia. She had told him he would have to choose and he had realised at that moment life with her would always be too hard. He'd chosen touring.

The second woman hadn't minded his absences. She was an artist who worked part-time in a gallery in the city centre. She liked the fact he was a musician and she told him she liked the freedom his coming and going gave her. The truth was she had found someone else to fill the space whenever he was gone. Austin had discovered them together when he had arrived home from tour a day early. It had been like a scene from a film. Hurried dressing, embarrassed faces. He had been surprised how much it had hurt him. And how it had affected him afterwards. He'd become wary, he realised. Since then he had made a conscious effort to keep all relationships light, to keep any bonds flexible. He knew he was taking the easy way out but he was only thirty-eight, after all. Picasso was in his seventies when he was having children. There was no hurry, was there? Sometimes he nearly convinced himself.

He stopped at a red light and checked the map again. He decided to go off the motorway for a short while, take in the more scenic back roads. With luck the rain would clear and he'd manage to see something other than grey skies and drenched fields. He was in no hurry. Her flatmate probably worked. She might not be back until after six at the earliest. He could have stayed longer with Harriet, perhaps, but he needed to keep on the move. He needed to feel he was doing something, not just talking about doing something.

He looked out across the fields, at a village backing onto the motorway. He'd been to England several times before, twice with the orchestra, once on a quick trip to visit his birthplace. It hadn't been an emotional homecoming for him, in any way. He had hardly any memories of England. He'd left when he was six. He liked the fact being born here had given him an English passport, and he sometimes felt torn between supporting England or Australia when watching cricket or rugby, but otherwise he didn't feel any great pull either way. He had reverted to an English accent for a while in his teens, when he'd gone through his Goth and new wave stage, but that too had faded away.

He pressed the radio button to change stations. Classical music filled the car. He quickly switched to a pop station. The hire car smelt new, and felt new. Everything from the seats to the steering wheel was smooth and spotless. He liked driving. He liked any kind of travel. Just as well, considering all the time he spent on the road, in cars, buses and planes, these days.

He heard the sound of a text message arriving and swiftly checked it, taking his eyes off the road for a second. Not from Harriet, or Lara, but one of the female members of the orchestra. She'd been sending him flirty texts now for a few weeks. He liked her well enough. She was pretty, certainly. And he knew that if he wanted to take it further it would be simple, as it often seemed to be. 'Too good-looking for your own good,' Gloria had said to him once. Perhaps it was true. Perhaps that was the problem. He didn't have to try hard to attract women. But lately the heart had gone out of it for him. The term 'the thrill of the chase' came to mind. Apt, if not politically correct. The thrill had gone out of all the flirting and chasing and catching. Was it old age setting in? No, he knew it wasn't.

He had really started feeling differently about that side of his life after his parents died. He'd felt his behaviour was – he searched for the word – too frivolous. Life had become serious. Grief hurt, he'd discovered. Some friends had asked him if he thought his mother had died of a broken heart, that she had simply decided life wasn't worth living after his father died. There was no way of knowing. When it first happened, it had been too shocking to be able to analyse the reasons why. And was such a thing possible, in any case? He knew his parents had loved each other, and had had a particularly good marriage. But was it something his mother could have chosen? To die, rather than go on living without his father? He tried again to imagine feeling so strongly about a woman. Loving her on every level – physically, mentally, spiritually. Some of his girlfriends had been model-beautiful and, shallow as it sounded, that was all he had wanted from them for a while. He had other female friends who challenged him intellectually, made him defend his politics, his religious beliefs, even his sporting allegiances, but he had never been physically attracted to them. Perhaps that's what real maturity would bring, he decided. A realisation that he couldn't have everything. That he'd have to choose between beauty and brains. Sex or intellectual stimulation. Or continue along as he had been doing, picking and choosing as it suited him, ignoring the empty feeling inside himself . . .

An image of James and Melissa came to mind. No, he couldn't settle for that kind of relationship, either. Imagine wanting to live with someone like Melissa for the rest of your life. Not only the bossiness, but the noise of her. It was Molly who Austin felt most sorry for. He was very fond of his niece. James had voluntarily chosen to be with Melissa. Poor Molly hadn't been given a choice. With any luck her swimming career would take off and she could start travelling the world, participating in competitions, and get away as early as possible. If she could. He presumed she was already under pressure to stay in the family business. Melissa was making it clear she was building a family empire. He felt his temper simmer at the thought of how she had ingratiated herself into Turner Travel, starting with helping out now and again, insisting Penny and Neil take some time off. Pretending to be amazed when they offered her part-time work after she and James got engaged. She'd turned it into a full-time position within six months and had been slowly taking over ever since. He'd watched her after his parents died. It was as if she had been waiting to seize her chance. Waiting until they were all vulnerable. She had swooped in with her changes, the new uniform, the new logo, the new tours. She had no right, but no one had stood up to her. Harriet hadn't been strong enough. Lara had seemed to agree, to Austin's amazement. James, of course, had gone along with everything she suggested.

He had been joking to Harriet that he paid Gloria to spy for him, but in truth he did get regular updates from her. Just because he didn't work in the agency didn't mean he didn't want to know what was going on. Gloria had tried to be fair. 'Yes, Austin, Melissa can be a bit annoying . . .'

'It's me you're talking to, Glorious. You don't have to be reasonable. You and I are the only ones who have seen through her clever human disguise. She is the Anti-Christ. Say it after me. "Melissa is Evil. She must be destroyed."'

Gloria laughed. 'I will not say that. You say after me, "Melissa has some good ideas."'

'So why doesn't she go and start her own travel agency then? And leave us alone.'

'Because we need her. Because she is married to James, your brother. Remember him, that man with the red hair you've been picking on for the past thirty-eight years?'

'He's my brother? I thought he was some stray a visiting circus left behind.'

'One day, Austin, you will wake up and be mature and it will be a day of great celebration for all who know you.'

He was smiling at the memory as a sign for Bath appeared in front of him.

It was nearly dark by the time he found Lara's suburb. He was cursing his earlier sightseeing. He'd got stuck in a tailback when he got back on the motorway and then hit the rush-hour traffic on the outskirts of the city as well. It was now past seven o'clock. Lara was renting a room in a share house in the northern part of the city. He finally found it after getting two different sets of directions from passersby and getting lost in the busy Bath streets, distracted by the elegantly restored buildings, crowded cafes and restaurants.

He parked the car opposite Lara's house and gazed around him. Once the terrace of two-storey buildings would have been quite grand, but they were now shabby. The row of buttons beside each front door was the giveaway. Each had been divided into separate apartments. Harder to be house proud in those circumstances, he supposed, as he got out of the car.

He checked the address on the piece of paper he was carrying. Number fifty-three, flat two. He pressed the button. A buzz sounded somewhere. He waited for a voice from the intercom. Nothing. Another buzz. He was about to try again when he heard the noise of a window being opened above him.

A young woman poked her head out. 'Sorry, were you trying the door?'

He stepped back. She had short hair, dripping wet. Her shoulders were bare. He could see the top of a towel. 'Yes, hello there,' he called up. 'My name's Austin Turner. I'm Lara's stepbrother.' Brother, stepbrother, foster-brother. He'd never made the distinction, switching back and forth between the terms. 'Could I talk to you about her?'

'Oh, hi. Of course you can. Hold on, I'll be right down.' She was there at the door in a minute, her hair still wet. She was about his age, barely five foot, in cut-off jeans and an orange T-shirt. He couldn't help noticing she wasn't wearing a bra. 'I'm Nina. Sorry to keep you waiting.' She had a slight accent, not quite English, something else. 'Come in. We're on the first floor.'

He followed her up the wide staircase and onto the landing. The door opened onto a colourful living room, with a large bay window overlooking the street. The curtains were orange. There was a blue patterned rug on the floor. One corner was a riot of spider plants, rubber plants and even a palm. Someone here had a green thumb. She gestured towards a sofa covered in a bright red throw. 'Take a seat, I'll be right back.'

He looked around. He doubted Lara had had much to do with the decoration. It wasn't her style at all. He thought of her apartment in Merryn Bay, all white walls and pastel colors. This was like living in a kaleidoscope. Maybe that's why she'd disappeared. She couldn't bear to live in this mass of colour another day.

Nina came back in. Her hair was drier. He could see different colours in it now. Bright red streaks here and there among the dark brown, even some golden strands as well. She'd also put on a bra, he noticed.

'Sorry about that,' she said. 'I promise I haven't just got up and that wasn't my first shower of the day. I've been for a run.'

'It's no problem.' She had very bright eyes, he noticed. Full of life.

'So, how can I help? It's about Lara going off like that, I suppose?'

He nodded. 'Do you mind if I ask you a few questions?'

'Of course not. I'm as puzzled as you are, to tell you the truth. I thought she was in fine form. And then she announced she was going away for a few weeks, asked me not to rent out her room. It wasn't until I got all those messages on the answering machine from your sister at the airport, and then her call, that I realised something more might be up.'

'So how did she seem before she left?'

'Physically? As groomed as ever. You know Lara. She'd come out of a hurricane with her hair in place.' She smiled. 'We've had a few nights out on the tear and I don't know how she did it but she would look as bandbox fresh at the end of the night as she did at the start. I'd have mascara under my eyes, wine spilt on myself. I've never been able to wear white clothes. But she was always spotless. The brat never had hangovers, either.'

'She's never drunk much.'

'No. Imagine saying you didn't like the taste of alcohol? Chance would be a fine thing with me. But was she distressed at all, do you mean?'

Austin nodded.

She gave it some thought. 'I really don't think she was. She was focused, if you know what I mean. Pre-occupied, I suppose, but she often was, especially when one of her assignments was due. She was into her course, doing lots of extra hours. But it wasn't all slog. She said she was getting a lot out of it.'

Austin knew that already. 'So she's been living here with you since she arrived?'

Nina nodded. 'I've got an arrangement with the tourism college. I do a lot of short-term lets, students or visitors. I had a good chat with Lara the first day she came to have a look at the room. I thought at first sight she might be a bit reserved, but she's not underneath, is she? And it suited her here as well, of course, with the college down the road.'

'You're a student there too?'

'No. I'm working as a temp. I took a career break and went travelling last year. And I can't decide what to do next, so I'm doing casual work. I'm actually a scientist.' She smiled at the expression on his face. 'I know, I should be wearing a white coat. I'm a biologist, to be exact. I do lab work, research. But I got tired of being so clean all the time. And peering into microscopes. I had a permanent red mark around my eye. Terribly hard to conceal. I was going through pots of make-up.'

Austin was finding her very entertaining, but also distracting. He was here about Lara, after all. 'Would it be all right if I had a quick look in her room?'

'Of course it would. It's this way, here.'

He followed her out of the living room, past a small, equally bright kitchen and down a narrow hallway. Black and white photographs lined the walls, details of buildings, rooftops, stonework. 'They're mine,' she said. 'I'm trying to be arty. Here's Lara's room.

What we charmingly call the box room.' She opened the door and turned on the light.

It looked like Lara's type of room. A white quilt cover lay on the three-quarter size bed, heaped with pale blue and white velvet and silk cushions. Muslin hung on the window. A pile of books stood on the shelf. He glanced at them. A mixture of travel books, some fiction. A poetry book. He hadn't known Lara read poetry.

He felt uneasy, as though he was snooping. And what was he looking for anyway? A note on the pillow? *I have run away. Don't try to find me.*

'Thanks,' he said, not sure what to do next. He didn't want to start sorting through her belongings, going through her cupboards.

Nina was watching him closely. 'If you don't mind me asking, why are you all so worried about her? She's over thirty, isn't she? A grown-up? Or are you a particularly close family?'

It was hard to explain. 'It's just that it's so out of character. She's so reliable. And she was due to help out on this tour. And then she didn't turn up, or let us know there was any problem. That's not like her.'

'Tour? Oh, that TV series one? I did wonder about that, when she said she was heading away. She'd been talking about it quite a lot. And you're right, she is reliable. I think she's the only flatmate I've ever had who's always paid her rent on time.' She stepped out into the hall again. 'What about a coffee?'

'That would be great, thanks.' He followed her into the kitchen, taking a seat at the wooden table, watching as she took down cups and a silver espresso maker and prepared coffee.

'You should think about becoming a drummer,' she said.

'Sorry?'

She gestured towards his hands, tapping a rhythm on the side of the table. He hadn't realised he'd been doing it.

'Oh. Sorry about that. Actually, I am a drummer. A percussion-ist, at least.'

'In a band? What are you called?'

'The Southern Cross Orchestra.'

'That's catchy. Hard for some of your fans to spell though.'

'Most of the fans are over sixty, so their spelling's pretty good.'

'So you're a classical musician? Wow. I thought they were only old people too.'

'No, we're all in our thirties. It's just the formal clothes make us look grown-up.'

She smiled. 'Milk? Sugar?' As she fetched both, she looked over her shoulder. 'Can I ask you something else? Did you call yourself Lara's stepbrother?'

Austin nodded.

'I hadn't realised it was a blended family. Your father married her mother, something like that?'

'Not so much a blended family. She's my foster-sister really. Lara came to live with us after her parents were killed.'

'Killed?' She turned completely. 'Oh God, I'm sorry. She men-tioned that they had both died a year ago, but she didn't say they were killed. What happened?'

'Not a year ago. More than twenty years ago. It's a bit compli-cated. Her real parents were killed in a car crash in Ireland. When Lara was little. That's when she came to live with us. My parents, Lara's foster-parents I suppose you'd call them, died within a few months of each other, just over a year ago.' He noticed Nina's con-fusion. 'She didn't tell you about it?'

'No. I mean, I don't know when it would come up in normal con-versation, but when we talked about our families she said she had a sister and two brothers, and that her parents had died recently.'

'Well, that's true. She does have a sister and two brothers. Just not biological. My parents were her guardians, rather than adopted parents. So she had two sets of parents, I suppose.' He was uncomfortable talking about this so soon, but in a way that was what he was there to talk about, wasn't it? He stirred his coffee. 'So she didn't seem upset about anything lately, then? Study? Home life? Being away from home?'

'Not that she said. Nothing I can put my finger on, anyway. Look, let's go into the living room and talk, it's nicer in there.'

He picked up his cup and saucer and followed her. He'd heard that trace of accent again. A lilt, as though English was her second language. It reminded him of the waitresses in the Italian coffee shop near their rehearsal rooms in Melbourne, the daughters of immigrants, their accents a musical mixture of Australian and Italian. He should be talking about Lara, but he had to ask. 'Are you English? I'm trying to place your accent . . .'

She smiled. 'I knew I shouldn't have skipped those elocution lessons. I'm Italian. I was born there, but I've lived here since I was a teenager. My parents moved over to run a restaurant here in Bath.'

'So you went from cooking to lab work?'

'Is it any wonder I gave it up? I can't eat the results of my experiments. I think my parents had a much better idea.' She went to the bay window, pushed it up as far as it would go, then perched on the sill and lit a cigarette. It was only after she'd blown out the first plume of smoke that she asked him. 'Do you mind? I'm trying to give up, but I like it too much.'

'No, not at all. It's your house.'

'I kid myself it helps me think. I know it's not fair for a non-smoker like Lara, so I sit here, like a pigeon. Half in, half out.' She squinted. 'If I disappeared suddenly, it would be because I was having a mad love affair and my lover wanted to spirit me away.'

'You think Lara was having a love affair?'

She shook her head. 'No, I don't actually. I think there were a few guys interested in her, and she went out to see films and bands with people from her course, but no one special. Unless she'd met someone else recently that I didn't know about. And she might have. I mean, we got on well, and we'd go out together now and then, but we were both busy. Sometimes days would go by without us having a proper conversation. So she might have met someone.' She went quiet, drawing on the cigarette again, then sending another plume of smoke out through the open window. 'It would have to have been a bolt from the blue. Love at first sight, wouldn't it? I can't really picture that happening to Lara.'

'Why not?'

'Because she seems too organised. Controlled, almost. Though they say still waters run deep. That's the saying, isn't it?' She laughed. 'I used to say too many cooks spoil the bread until someone kindly pointed my error out. I thought it made perfect sense – how could a whole lot of cooks knead the bread at the same time?'

She hopped off the windowsill and started pacing the room, still with the cigarette in her hand. This time the smoke went into the room. She had a real restless energy, Austin noticed. But she was graceful with it. Like a dancer. It was very attractive.

'Have you been to her college yet? Someone there might know more.'

He shook his head. 'No, I came straight here. Via Cornwall at least. I called in on my other sister Harriet in St Ives this morning.'

'After you'd flown in from Australia? It must be a close family.'

'No, from Berlin.' He filled her in briefly on the orchestra's tour.

Again the conversation veered away from Lara, as she fired questions at him. Which cities had he been to? Which operas were they doing? She'd seen a few, but wasn't an expert. The problem with being Italian, she told him, was that people always assumed she'd spent her childhood singing *Tosca* and *Rigoletto*. In her opinion opera was an acquired taste. She frowned. 'There's not a lot for a drummer to do in opera, though, is there? Don't you just have to hit the cymbals now and again?'

'That's about it.'

'So what do you do the rest of the time? Look around the theatre a lot?'

'A fair bit.'

'That would be good fun. Because everyone in the audience would be staring at the singers, so you'd have a real chance to stare at them.'

'I do, yes.' He was about to try to bring the subject back to Lara when she stubbed out the cigarette, took a peppermint from a bowl beside her and checked her watch.

'Come on,' she said. 'We might as well go down to Lara's college now. They have classes on Wednesday and Thursday nights, so there might be someone there you can talk to. One of her classmates or one of the lecturers.'

'I can go on my own if you point me in the right direction.'

'No, I'm as puzzled as you. I want to know where she is too. Let's go.'

In her St Ives hotel room, Harriet answered the phone for the third time in five minutes. The tour group was travelling to the nearby harbour town of Padstow for a special dinner tonight and the preparations had sent most of the ladies in the group into a spin. She'd already had Miss Boyd wondering if Harriet had seen her handbag anywhere. Yes, Harriet assured her. She'd had it when they got off the bus that afternoon. 'Oh, yes, here it is. Thank you, Harriet.' Mrs Kempton had rung to ask if Harriet could loan her an umbrella as unfortunately she seemed to have lost hers. Harriet said that of course she could and she would bring it down to the foyer with her. The latest call was from Miss Talbot.

'Harriet, could you please give me some fashion advice? Would a silver halter top go better with pink trousers or a blue skirt?'

'There's a bit of a wind outside tonight, Miss Talbot. You might be happier in something warmer, perhaps?'

'Do you think?' Harriet heard a rustling of coathangers. 'That's a good idea, Harriet. I have just the thing. Thank you!'

'You're welcome.'

Harriet had barely hung up when the phone rang again. It was Mrs Kempton again. 'Harriet, I was sure I took out my favourite scarf but now I can't find it. Would you have a minute to pop down?'

'Of course. I'll be right there.'

She quickly finished her own make-up and collected her bag and wrap from the foot of the bed. En route to Mrs Kempton's room she took a quick detour and ran downstairs to check on the men. They were already changed into sports jackets and smart slacks, perfectly happy in the seaview bar with pints of beer in front of them. They didn't notice her, engrossed in the racing results on the TV. There was no sign of Patrick. He was in his room getting ready, too, she assumed. She smiled at the thought of him ringing her, too. Asking her advice about his clothes as he had that first night. 'Harriet, should I wear the white shirt or the blue shirt?' She had a memory flash of his toned brown body and had to blink it away.

As she made her way to Mrs Kempton's room she found her mind filling with more thoughts about Patrick. He had been great company again all day. He had such a nice way with the group, able to put them at ease and make them laugh. Make her laugh, particularly. Or perhaps they just had very similar senses of humour.

Clive had also finally decided he liked him. At least, he'd stopped doing the sudden braking when Patrick was standing talking to the group. She had been watching for it that afternoon, keeping a close eye on Patrick as he was answering their questions. Out of the corner of her eye she had seen Clive lean forward to the brake pedal. She'd leapt up and grasped Patrick around the waist, convinced he was about to go flying down the aisle.

Patrick had looked startled and then amused. 'Harriet, what a lovely surprise.'

She'd let go immediately. 'I'm so sorry, I thought you were going to go flying.'

'Not without special effects wires, I promise. But thank you very much anyway.'

Harriet had gone red and hurriedly sat down. Mr Fidock had given another whoop. Mrs Lamerton had just looked annoyed that she hadn't thought of doing the same thing.

On the way home from Bodmin Moor, they'd travelled to a coastal lookout near Newquay, the location for a dramatic scene in episode nine, 'The Case of the Rogues' Reunion'. They asked Patrick for memories of the punch-up on the cliff top between Willoughby and Jonas Herron, the crooked abattoir owner who featured in a number of episodes. It had been a two-part storyline, the first episode ending on a – literally – cliffhanging sequence featuring Willoughby hanging by his fingertips from the cliff edge, having been pushed over by Herron. They were enthralled as he described how he nearly fell in real life and had to be winched to safety by a crane.

Mr Douglas managed to secure the seat next to Patrick for the trip back. Harriet overheard him telling the actor about the searing heat of an Australian summer and how he'd had to have a skin cancer removed from his nose only a week before he'd left for this trip. 'It went well, I think. I'm just waiting for the autopsy results.'

'Autopsy?' Patrick said.

Mr Douglas nodded. 'I'm not that worried. I'm sure it's nothing serious.'

She and Patrick had exchanged a glance. Faces solemn, eyes laughing.

All day she'd found herself watching him, enjoying his ready humour, noticing the small courtesies, his good manners with everyone in the group. He watched out for her just as much, opening doors for her, making sure she was fine, that she was happy with how it was all going. The two of them also managed to have lots of snatched conversations, quick exchanges about the tour, or Patrick asking about previous trips she'd worked on, Harriet asking about his pre-*Willoughby* days, about America, and Boston. She'd been surprised again how relaxed he was about his acting career. He didn't seem to do much work these days, yet he didn't appear anxious about it. He was more interested in talking about books he'd read, wondering if she had read them too, or wanting to talk about changes he'd noticed in England since his last visit. The more they talked, brief as the conversations were, the more it was changing from her being the guide and him being the special guest. It wasn't just the feeling that the two of them worked very well together. Something else was happening as well. She'd become acutely aware of him. She knew if he was nearby, if he had left a room, if he had come back into a room. Not in a protective 'looking after the special guest' way. It was something different.

Harriet came up the stairs again and knocked on Mrs Kempton's door. It was opened immediately. The room was almost full. Mrs Kempton had been joined by Miss Talbot, Mrs Randall and Miss Boyd. It was like a senior citizens' sleepover. They gave her an enthusiastic welcome.

'Oh Harriet, you look beautiful,' Miss Talbot exclaimed. 'Like a sea creature.'

'Really? Not a jellyfish, I hope?'

'Oh no, like a nymph. Something glorious like that.'

Harriet had changed out of the yellow uniform into a special dress she had brought with her. She had tried it on in a boutique in Melbourne several months earlier and known immediately it was something out of the ordinary. It was made of dark green silk, and both the colour and the material seemed to catch the light in an unusual way, glistening almost. The design left her arms bare, while the scooped neckline showed off her skin and skimmed the tops of her breasts. It fitted her body, ending just below her knees. She had felt different as soon as she tried it on. Beautiful, confident, adventurous, as though she was in costume for an acting role, or an actress preparing to step onto the red carpet for a premiere. The boutique assistant had got into the spirit, bringing over pieces of expensive jewellery for Harriet to try on, making suggestions for make-up and matching glamorous hairstyles. She had also produced the perfect matching shoes. The toes were pointed, the heels high. Harriet had ignored the price and bought them immediately. She didn't regret it. She felt different when she was wearing them, too. Elegant and feminine. She carried a silk wrap with her, in a darker green than her dress. While she'd been getting ready in her room she'd tried to remember the jewellery and make-up suggestions the boutique assistant had given her. 'Go dramatic,' the woman had said. 'The dress deserves it.' She was right. The ornate earrings, smoky eyeshadow, carefully applied eyeliner and darker shade of red lipstick did suit the dress.

'I love your make-up.' Miss Boyd said, inspecting her closely. 'Have you had professional training?'

'No,' Harriet said, surprised. 'I taught myself really.'

'It's beautiful, Harriet. Could you make my eyes look like yours?'

'And do you think I would look better with a darker lipstick?' Mrs Kempton said. 'Mine's a bit too pink, don't you think?'

'Could you do us too, Harriet?' Miss Talbot asked.

Harriet checked her watch. There was plenty of time. Clive wasn't due for another twenty minutes or so. 'I'd love to,' she said. She went back to her room and fetched her make-up bag. By the time she came back, the four ladies were lined up on the bed, side by side, towels around their necks protecting their outfits.

She started with Miss Talbot. First she helped her fasten the clasp of her bright pink resin necklace, and do up the button at the back of her satin flares. Together they found a shade of lipstick and blush that matched both the necklace and the flares.

Miss Talbot lifted her face, sighing in pleasure as Harriet gently applied the make-up. 'We'll have to take a photo so I can remember this. But you have to be in it too, Harriet. I know, I'll get Patrick to take it. He'll know all about cameras and he can teach us how to pose properly too.'

Before Harriet could stop her, Miss Talbot had leaned across to the phone, rung reception and asked to be put through to Patrick Shawcross's room.

'Patrick, it's Emily. No, you don't need to call me Miss Talbot, I told you that. Would you please be able to come and take our photo? Harriet's making us beautiful and we want to treasure the moment. Oh, thank you. We're in room twenty-three, second floor.' She hung up, very pleased with herself. 'He'll be here in a minute.'

Harriet finished Miss Talbot's make-up and was just applying a soft mauve to Miss Boyd's eyelids when there was a knock at the door.

Miss Talbot answered it. 'Patrick, hello. Look, aren't I a picture?' She did a little spin. 'I feel like a girl again.'

Harriet watched her with great amusement, then glanced over her shoulder at him. 'Thanks, Patrick. We're nearly ready. I just have two more sets of eyes, three lips and a necklace to do.'

'And my belt again,' Miss Talbot said, twisting around and refastening the buckle on her silver chainlink belt. 'They don't make clothes the way they used to. Patrick, do you want to come back in a minute? When we'll be really perfect?'

'I'm happy to wait, Emily.'

There wasn't room for him to come in. He leaned against the doorway. He had changed his clothes too, Harriet noticed. He was wearing a light grey suit, beautifully cut, over a white shirt. He'd either showered or been outside for a walk. She could see drops of water in his dark curls. He was talking very seriously to Miss Talbot, who was explaining in detail how her camera worked. He glanced up at her and she had to look away. She had that unsettling feeling again. That the room was full of people, but she was conscious only of him.

Harriet added a little more blush to Miss Boyd's cheeks and a dusting of powder. She had to concentrate. Her hands seemed to be shaking slightly. She moved to Mrs Kempton, choosing a pale brown eyeshadow, and just a touch of lipgloss. Mrs Randall only needed foundation, a light grey eyeshadow and mascara. All three women were like purring cats, their faces turned up to her, as she went back and forth doing the final touches, smoothing eyeshadow here, a little bit more lipstick there, some light finishing powder on each of them.

'I'm really not an expert,' she said. 'I hope you'll like it.'

'I don't mind what I look like. It feels so nice having it put on,' Miss Boyd said. 'You've got such a gentle touch, Harriet.'

They were finally done. She stood back and watched as they took turns looking into the mirror, delighted with themselves.

Miss Boyd nearly cried. 'I love it. You've made me look years younger.'

Mrs Kempton put her hands to her cheeks. 'Oh, thank you, Harriet, I love it too.'

Mrs Randall didn't say anything, just gave Harriet a warm, happy smile.

'Photo time, everyone,' Miss Talbot declared, clapping her hands. She was getting quite giddy. 'And quickly. We may never look this good again.'

Harriet insisted on taking the first photo: Patrick with the four women. Their fingers brushed briefly as he passed her the camera. She was aware of not just him, but of herself now, too. Of how she felt when he was near her.

Miss Talbot took over then, wanting different combinations, moving them all back and forth. 'I've brought twenty films with me,' she declared. 'I don't care if I use them all up tonight. Harriet, Patrick, I want one of the two of you together.'

She moved them until they were side by side. 'Put your arm

around her, Patrick, that's it,' she called. 'Perfect. Nice and close, now.'

Harriet felt his arm touch her back, his fingers against her bare skin. A combination of hot and cold sensation shot right through her. She didn't dare look at him. She also didn't tell Miss Talbot that her thumb was over the lens. She was worried her voice would sound strange.

Miss Boyd pointed it out instead.

'Never mind,' Miss Talbot said. 'I'll take a few more. Back together again, Patrick and Harriet. Closer, that's it.'

The merest touch of his fingers on her skin felt like a caress. Harriet could barely breathe. She felt like closing her eyes in pleasure, not smiling at a camera.

There was time for one more. 'Patrick, with all of you,' Harriet said, moving away from him, needing to take back a bit of control. She arranged them all, Patrick in the centre, Miss Talbot and Miss Boyd on one side, Mrs Kempton and Mrs Randall on the other. Another brief touch, her hand on his sleeve as she moved him into place, and that sensation again, as if electricity was zipping back and forth between them. She arranged Mrs Kempton's scarf and fixed the collar of Miss Talbot's fluffy cardigan. The simple actions calmed her. She was imagining this, she told herself.

'Now we're ready,' she said, taking a step back, smiling at the looks on their faces. 'What do you think, Patrick? Aren't they gorgeous?'

'Beautiful,' he said.

He was looking at her when he said it.

CHAPTER TWENTY-ONE

Austin and Nina parked the car in a side street down the road from the tourism college. It was part of a modern campus in the middle of Bath, the sleek concrete lines of the building incongruous after the tall elegant terraces and wide streets they had passed on the way. Nina had directed him in the same way she spoke, quickly, stopping and starting.

'That's the tourism section over there,' she said, pointing to a wing of a four-storey building. 'You could come back tomorrow, of course, when all the staff will probably be here. But as I said, you might see a few of her class and a couple of her lecturers tonight. Where are you staying by the way? Have you booked anywhere? Is that all your luggage?'

'I haven't booked anywhere yet. And yes, that's all.'

'A man who travels light. I used to know a quote about that too, but I forget it. Stay with me. We have a sofa bed in the living room.'

'I'll be fine in a guesthouse.'

'No, don't be mad. I insist. Lara would insist too.'

She would, too. She had already invited him to stay, when they had spoken the previous week. When she had seemed fine. No inkling of this at all. 'If you're sure.'

'I'm sure.'

He followed Nina across the open square. 'I met Lara here one night, last month,' she said. 'We were going to see a film, she came out of the classroom over this way.' She stopped a passing student and confirmed it. 'This way, Austin.' He had to walk quickly to keep up.

Half an hour later, Austin had spoken to two of Lara's classmates and her lecturer. They seemed puzzled at his concern. No, they hadn't been surprised when she wasn't in class the past couple of days. She was expected to be away on the *Willoughby* tour after all. And no, they hadn't noticed anything out of the ordinary with her behaviour before then, either.

Austin sat down at one of the desks. Nina and the lecturer, Brendan, sat opposite. He was in his late thirties, tall, lean, with glasses and tousled brown hair.

'Why do you think something is wrong?' Brendan asked.

Austin tried to explain it again. 'It's not like her. She doesn't do things like this, just disappear.'

'Maybe she felt it was time she did? I know I've wanted to make a run for it now and then.'

'Maybe.' Austin was starting to feel embarrassed. It had felt like the right thing to do when he was in Berlin, to drop everything and rush over here, like a man with a mission, the heroic rescuer. But now he was actually here, he wasn't so sure.

'You could talk to a couple more of her fellow students, if you like,' Brendan said. 'She might have mentioned something to them. They'll be back tomorrow. Or you can have a look at her computer. There might be a few clues there.'

'Clues?' Nina's eyes were bright. 'This is feeling like a detective program now. What sort of clues?'

Brendan shrugged. 'Maybe she had written a letter, or looked up some websites or something. That would give you an idea of where she might have gone.'

Austin and Nina followed Brendan over to a desk in the corner. 'The students move around a bit, but Lara generally worked on this one. I don't think any of the students keep much on the desktop, though. They save their work to disk usually. They use the computer more for research purposes, web surfing, that sort of thing.'

'We've been getting emails from her. Would this be where she sent them from?'

'Probably. Either from here, or one of the Internet cafes in town. But she'd have a password for that. You don't know it, I suppose? Or know who her server is?'

Austin shook his head. It would have felt wrong reading her emails, in any case. As it was it felt again like he was prying, looking at her computer like this. As it booted up, he saw neatly arranged folders with Lara's name on them appear on the screen. He hesitated and then clicked on one. The documents inside were also neatly labelled. Week 1, Week 2, all the way through to what must have been last week, Week 12. He clicked on one, but it was blank. That's right, the lecturer had said they saved everything on disk. So no clues there.

'She was doing well,' Brendan said. 'Some great ideas. Really dedicated, too.'

'She was looking forward to this,' Austin said. He remembered getting the call from her, when she found out she'd got the industry scholarship for the three month course. 'It's the best one in the whole world, Austie!' He hadn't heard her so happy in a long time.

Nina pulled up a chair beside the computer. 'If she packed a suitcase, she must have been going somewhere some distance away,' she said. 'So she'd had to have booked, wouldn't she? Maybe she'd have booked on the Internet?'

'Not necessarily,' Brendan said. 'She could have caught a train. Picked up a flight at the airport on stand-by. Hired a car. She could be anywhere.'

'I suppose there's no way of checking what sites she'd been looking at anyway, is there?' Nina asked.

The lecturer nodded. 'There is, actually. It's simple.' He leaned across and moved the mouse on Lara's computer. 'You go to Internet Explorer, then View, then Explorer Bar and then History. And there it is.' A long list of sites appeared on the screen.

Nina whistled. 'Everything you look at on the web gets recorded? I didn't know that.'

'Nothing ever leaves a computer,' Brendan said. 'Even if you delete it, it's still there on the hard drive somewhere.'

Austin's hopes rose. 'If she has gone somewhere, she might have been looking up info about it, mightn't she? We just need to see what travel sites she's been looking at . . .' He scanned the long list of sites Lara had accessed. There was address after address of tourism sites, airline booking sites, information for travellers. He hit his palm against his forehead in a gesture of stupidity. 'Sorry, I've just remembered where we are. A tourism college.'

The lecturer gave a wry laugh. 'Well, yes, I'd be more surprised if she hadn't been looking up travel websites. Most of the travel business is computerised these days.'

'And I couldn't know which of these Lara had looked at most recently anyway, or for how long, could I?'

'A technician might be able to tell you. There's probably a way of checking dates and times, how long they'd been looked at, but I'm sorry, I don't know how to do it.'

Nina picked up the mouse and scrolled through more of the history. 'There's some news sites, too. Telephone directories. Search engines, info on some cruise ships . . .'

The lecturer nodded. 'That was last week's project. We asked the students to put together some themed fantasy cruises.'

'That explains that one then.' She kept scrolling, reading aloud as she went. 'The Met Office, a book review site, more cruise ships, and then a whole bunch of Irish sites. One, two, three . . .' she stopped counting aloud. 'About ten of them. See, Irish newspapers. Maps. Would that have been for her course, too?' she asked the lecturer.

'Perhaps, though not necessarily. Our focus this semester was themed travel. That's why Lara applied to come here. It was in line with what she was doing at home in Australia.'

Austin moved his chair closer. 'She had a few links with Ireland herself, though. Her mother was Irish, at least she was born in Ireland, but she grew up in England. Before she and Lara's father emigrated to Australia.'

'Didn't you say her mum and dad were killed in Ireland?' Nina asked. 'Were they back there on holiday?'

'Her parents were killed there?' Brendan said. 'When? Recently?'

Austin shook his head. 'About twenty-four years ago.'

'When she was only a child? Oh, how sad.'

Nina was looking at the screen again. 'Maybe that's what's happened. She's on the other side of the world, feeling a long way from home and what family she has got, so she's gone looking for some connections. Her dad was English, did you say? Did he have family left here in England?'

Austin shook his head. He knew that much.

Nina was undeterred. 'All right, so she decides to track down some of her mother's Irish relatives. She might have found instant cousins or great uncles that she didn't know she had.' She glanced at the screen. 'Maybe she put an ad in the —' she squinted to read the name on the screen, 'the *Irish Times*, asking for information. Where was her mother from?'

'I don't know. I don't know much about her mother or her father, to tell you the truth.'

'There's no one at home you can ask?' the lecturer asked.

Austin shook his head. 'My own parents died a year ago, and it was my mother who knew Lara's mother. We have a family friend who's worked with us for years. Mum might have told her something. It's worth asking, I guess.'

Brendan turned as several students walked in. 'I'd better get back to work. I'm sorry I couldn't be more help. If I think of anything else, is there any way I can contact you?'

Austin scribbled his mobile number. Ten minutes later, he and Nina were back in the car.

Nina took Austin to her parents' restaurant in the centre of Bath. It was large, but with plenty of atmosphere: paintings of Tuscan landscapes on the wall, Italian pop songs playing in the background, and red tablecloths on each of the twenty or more tables. Most of them were full. Nina spoke briefly to her parents, her father in the kitchen and her mother looking after a large party of diners. She introduced Austin as Lara's brother, without going into detail about why he was there. He noticed Nina had inherited her mother's bright eyes and her father's big smile. They were too busy to talk long, waving Nina across to a spare table in the back section of the restaurant.

Over a pizza and a glass of red wine he filled her in on all he knew about Lara's early years.

Nina listened intently. 'I'm sorry I didn't ask her more questions when she was leaving, Austin,' she said when he'd finished. 'She seemed so matter of fact about it. Packed her suitcase. Said something about family business and off she went. And you know, with flat-mates, you have to keep some distance, respect each other's privacy.'

'We might be onto something with the Irish sites. I'll know more after I've phoned Gloria tonight.'

'But just because she was looking at Irish sites doesn't mean that's where she's gone, does it?' Nina asked.

'I don't know. I'm probably jumping to conclusions . . .' He tailed off. It had seemed much more certain in the college than it was now. And Nina was right. There were lots of places Lara could have gone. And lots of reasons why.

'So is Ireland where her parents are buried? If they were killed there? Or were their bodies flown home to Australia?'

'I don't know. I don't think so.' Surely he would have remembered if Lara's parents' bodies had been flown home to Australia? Wouldn't there have been talk about it? And they would all have gone to the funerals, wouldn't they? The difficulty was there had never been much talk at home about Lara's parents, except on the memorial days his mother had instigated.

'Was Lara in the car with them when they had that crash in Ireland? Would she have memories of it? Maybe that's what's happened, it's brought back some trauma. What's it called – post traumatic stress disorder? That might be why she disappeared like that. I thought she seemed focused, but perhaps it was shock.'

Austin shook his head. 'No, she wasn't even in Ireland when it happened. Her parents were over fixing up something about a fam-ily estate, I think. Lara's grandmother had died a few weeks earlier. I don't really know all the details.' He couldn't remember why Lara hadn't gone with them. He only remembered people saying it was lucky that she hadn't, or she probably would have been killed too.

'Don't you know anything about where Lara came from? She arrived to live with you and none of you asked *anything* about it?'

He wished Nina would stop asking him such awkward questions. 'We weren't that sort of family. My mother, especially. She thought it was best not to dwell on any of it too much, in case it upset Lara. We had to be as kind as we could to her.' He could hear his mother saying it.

'So she was a charity case?'

'No. Not for a minute. We never treated her like that.' Even as he said it, he had a memory of Harriet wanting to treat Lara like that. Like one of her school 'be kind' projects. But that had passed, surely? And he and James had always thought of Lara as an extra little sister. It hadn't been a big deal at all.

'No need to be defensive, Austin. I'm sorry, I touched a raw nerve.'

He calmed. 'No, you didn't. It's a fair enough question. I suppose it must look unusual from the outside, but really, she just became part of the family.'

Nina reached over and refilled their glasses. 'Maybe that's it. She didn't want to be a part of your family any more. She wanted her own family.'

'I don't think it's that. She would have said something, to Harriet, or to me. One of us anyway.'

Nina shrugged. 'Then maybe she just wanted to go away for a while. Have some time to herself. Maybe it's as simple as that.'

Austin found himself fighting an urge to start tapping. 'Maybe it is,' he said.

CHAPTER TWENTY-TWO

The *Willoughby* group was on board the bus, en route to Padstow, a forty-mile journey from St Ives. Willoughby himself hadn't actually set foot in the town during the series, but Mrs Lamerton had seen the harbour village featured on TV and insisted a trip to a celebrity chef's restaurant be included in the itinerary.

James had suggested in his notes that Harriet lead the group in a fish-themed bus-trip singalong but Harriet had tucked that suggestion away at the back of the folder. As they came into the harbour town, Harriet glanced at his script again – *Once one of Cornwall's principal fishing ports, Padstow is now famous for its gourmet restaurants and sandy beaches* – and put it away too. There was so much chatter and laughter in the bus she wouldn't have been able to make herself heard, microphone or not. Mrs Lamerton's laugh was loudest of all. She had managed to get the seat next to Patrick again. Harriet was reminded of the bellowing sounds of a water buffalo, happily splashing in mud.

Her mobile beeped twice just as Clive pulled into the car park beside the Padstow harbour. A text message had arrived. She didn't check it immediately, first opening the door and as usual helping her group down onto the ground. They were all in high spirits. Mr Fidock practically leapt off the step. Mrs Lamerton ignored Harriet standing at the foot of the stairs, putting on a girlish voice and asking Patrick to help her.

'Of course, Mrs Lamerton.' He smiled at Harriet as he came down the step.

Mrs Lamerton alighted, taking Patrick's hand. She didn't let go once she reached the ground, holding his hand high as though they were about to do a stately dance. Patrick had no choice, unless he was going to shake her away. Harriet did her best not to smile as the pair of them went hand in hand across the car park towards the restaurant. It looked like Mrs Lamerton would be sitting next to him at dinner, too.

As she watched, he stopped and turned. 'Harriet, will we wait for you?'

Harriet could tell Mrs Lamerton wasn't pleased. 'No thanks, Patrick. You go ahead. I'll be right there.'

Once everyone was off the bus, she took out her phone and read the text message. It was from Austin. Am with Lara's flatmate. On her trail. All for 2nite. Will keep you posted. A x

She turned off the mobile and put it back in her bag. The feeling of confusion returned. Wanting to know about Lara, but not wanting to know. Wanting to stay in the cocoon of the tour, not having to think about her real life, enjoying all of this so much, the travelling, the group, Patrick . . .

'Harriet?'

It was Miss Talbot. She'd come back for her. 'Is everything all right? You look like you're miles away.'

'I'm sorry, Miss Talbot. I was just daydreaming.'

'Oh, don't be sorry. I love daydreams myself. I go to all sorts of places in my daydreams. It's good for the soul.' She lowered her voice. 'Were you daydreaming about Patrick?'

'Miss Talbot!'

'Well, I would, if I were you. Who else is there? Clive? Mr

Fidock? Mr Douglas?' She made a disgusted face. 'Perhaps that could be Turner Travel's next theme tour, Harriet? A cruise for elderly singles like myself. We could call it the Old Love Boat.'

'That's an excellent idea.' It was, too. Melissa would jump at it. 'Will we do it together? I could be your chaperone.'

Miss Talbot nodded eagerly. 'Yes please.'

Harriet took Miss Talbot's arm as they made their way to the restaurant. The group had gathered outside, already studying the menu in a glass frame on the wall. The restaurant was in a two-storey corner building, looking out onto the harbour crammed with commercial fishing boats and smaller, colourful craft. Inside the tables were wooden, the ceilings high, the atmosphere welcoming, the walls and table decorations coordinated in blue and white. There was no formal seating arrangement at their long table. They took seats as they came in. Harriet had Miss Talbot on one side and Mr Douglas on the other. At the other end of the table she saw Mrs Lamerton take a seat next to Patrick. Harriet turned away, making a point of settling Miss Talbot into her chair, helping to stow her silver handbag on the back of her chair and then reading the menu to her. She couldn't help herself, though. She looked over in Patrick's direction. He was looking at her too.

Once they finished their main courses, everyone in the tour group started moving around the table. It seemed perfectly natural for Harriet to go to Patrick's end of the table and check that everything was fine with him. It made perfect sense, too, when he very nicely asked Mrs Lamerton if she could move up a little so he could put a chair for Harriet there beside him. It was quite crammed so it also felt right for him to casually place his arm around the back of her chair as they talked. It also seemed natural that he should later visit

Harriet's end of the table to talk to the people seated near her. He stood behind her, with his arm resting against the back of her chair, close enough so her head was touching his arm. The chair beside her became free. He sat down and it also felt right that her leg was touching his, and that his arm was along the back of her chair again. Once or twice she reached for her wine glass at the same time he reached for his. Their hands touched. A glance.

'After you, Harriet.'

'No, you first.'

'Please, I insist.'

As he had a lively conversation with Mr and Mrs Douglas across the table, she couldn't stop noticing more details about him. The way he used his hands to express himself. The long fingers and square-cut nails. The silver watch on his wrist. The sprinkling of dark hair on his arms. The tanned skin on his chest, where the top button of his pale blue shirt was undone. The dark hair there, too.

She was very conscious of her body next to his. The feel of the silk material of her dress against her skin. Even the feel of her fingers against the stem of the glass. Every movement seemed charged with something. Anticipation.

They returned to the bus, everyone in great spirits. They had drunk a lot of wine. Mr Fidock insisted on taking the microphone and performing an Elvis-style version of 'I do like to be beside the seaside' as they left Padstow. Harriet expected half the group to go straight to their rooms when they returned to St Ives, but she was wrong. The hotel boasted an old-fashioned disco once a week. The receptionist had promised it was perfect for the age group. More Tom Jones than they'll be able to shake a hip replacement to, she'd laughed. All of them, Clive included, came into the function room. It had been transformed with flashing lights and clusters of armchairs, overseen by a man with an obvious toupee behind a DJ desk.

Harriet danced with Mr Fidock, Mr Douglas and even Clive. She waltzed with Miss Talbot who was feather-light on her feet. She danced with everyone except Patrick Shawcross. She knew it didn't matter whether she danced with him, or whether they talked to each other some more that night or not. It had gone beyond that. Somehow, at some stage during the night, something unspoken had been agreed between them. He hadn't said anything. Neither had she. It was the strangest sensation, as though the entire time they were talking to other people, involved in other conversations, standing at other sides of the room, they were somehow connected, as if by invisible wires. She was intensely and completely aware of him, and knew that he was aware of her. Even when she was talking to Mrs Kempton, or dancing with Mr Fidock (and having to first laughingly and then firmly ask him to keep his hands to himself) she knew if she looked up Patrick would be watching her.

It felt so good. Exciting. Exhilarating. And something deeper, sexier than that. One part of her brain was clear, telling her all the reasons why it wasn't making sense. He was thirteen years older than her. He was the special guest on their tour. Melissa would surely have something to say about fraternisation between guides and tour guests. But obstacles like that seemed a long way away, connected to the side of herself she was trying to leave behind. This new, exciting feeling belonged with the freedom she'd been sensing as her confidence had grown the past few days, as she discovered she was able to cope, make decisions, take care of a group of people. She wanted something to happen between them. It was almost a need inside her.

Just before midnight she was helping a tipsy Miss Talbot out of the disco and up to her room when she heard her name being called. She turned. It was him.

'Harriet, are you leaving?'

Miss Talbot spoke before Harriet had a chance. 'She's helping me to bed, Patrick. I've had one too many Fluffy Ducks. I'm a disgrace.'

'You're not a disgrace,' Harriet laughed, holding Miss Talbot's arm firmly. 'You're just exhausted from all that dancing.'

'Can I help?' Patrick said.

'No, thanks anyway.' She smiled at him. 'We'll be fine.'

'Could I speak to you before you go up?'

'Talk away, Harriet,' Miss Talbot said, sinking into the armchair beside them. 'I'll just sit here for a while. It will do me good. That carpet is making me dizzy.'

They moved towards the door. His voice was quiet. 'I know it's too late to look at the videos tonight —' She felt a faint shimmer of disappointment. '— but there is something I need to talk to you about. Would you be able to call to my room instead, do you think?'

'Tonight?'

'If that's all right? If it's not too late?'

'No. Of course it's not. In half an hour?'

'Good. Yes. That's good.' He smiled at her. That was all. But it felt like a promise.

Forty minutes passed before she was able to go to him. Most of the group had started going to their rooms. As Harriet was helping Miss Talbot to bed, Mrs Kempton poked her head out of her door, just down the corridor.

'Harriet, I'm sorry to bother you but I don't seem to be able to find my reading glasses. Would you be able to come and help me look?'

'Of course, Mrs Kempton. I'll just settle Miss Talbot.'

Miss Talbot took less than five minutes to settle. She tipped into the bed and was snoring gently in the time it took Harriet to take off her shoes.

Mrs Kempton was waiting at her door. 'I am a silly sausage, aren't I? I can't find them anywhere.'

The glasses were on the bedside table, in full view of the door. 'Here they are, Mrs Kempton.'

'Oh Harriet, you're an angel. While you're here, would you be able to undo the buttons at my neck for me? I'm having such trouble with them.'

Harriet undid the row of tiny buttons. Mrs Kempton favoured old-fashioned clothing and this blouse wouldn't have looked out of place in a period drama, with its high neck and puffy sleeves.

'Thank you, Harriet. And not just for this. You're looking after us so well. We were all talking about it and we all think you're lovely.'

She felt her cheeks go warm. 'Thank you, Mrs Kempton. I'm glad you're enjoying it.'

She was almost at her door when she was summoned by Mrs Lamerton from her doorway further down the same corridor, needing help with the lock on her case. That was a first. Mrs Lamerton was normally the most independent of them.

Harriet didn't have any trouble with the lock. It snapped open immediately.

'Thank you, Harriet. You must have a knack.'

'Years of practice, Mrs Lamerton. I hope you enjoyed today?'

'Yes, thank you. It's all coming together well, isn't it? All the hard work Lara and I put into it in the planning stages, I suppose.'

'I'm sure that's it. I'm really pleased you're happy.'

'Well, goodnight, Harriet. Still no chance of Lara turning up?'

'I'm afraid not, Mrs Lamerton. I understand her other commitments got very demanding. Goodnight. See you in the morning.' She was at the door when the older woman spoke again.

'So what will you do now?'

'I beg your pardon?'

'What will you do now?'

'It's after midnight. I'll probably go to bed.'

Mrs Lamerton nodded. 'Goodnight then.'

Harriet went to her room, checked her make-up, her hair, realising her hands were shaking. She took a moment to breathe slowly, to calm herself, as she stood in front of the mirror. Her eyes looked very bright. She wasn't nervous. It was anticipation. Excitement. And a feeling that this was meant to be. As if everything had been meant to happen. James's accident. This tour. Even the dinner tonight. All the tiny details coming together to this point so she would feel like this, look like this, want what she knew was going to happen with Patrick. What she wanted to happen. She stepped out into the corridor.

She didn't see Mrs Lamerton's door open or see her peer out and watch her leave.

Harriet only had to knock twice, softly, before he opened the door. He smiled. 'Harriet, come in.'

He had taken off his jacket and rolled up the sleeves of his shirt. His room looked inviting. The bed through the doorway, the table and chairs in the centre, the door to the balcony open a little way.

He had turned on all the lamps in the room and switched off the main light.

'Can I get you a drink? Some wine? A coffee? A brandy?'

'A brandy would be lovely, thank you.'

She walked out onto the small balcony and put her hands on the rail, looking out over the beach and the dark sea. The sky was thick with clouds, only a few stars visible.

She could hear him fixing the drinks. Another time she would have felt the need to talk, to make conversation. Not now. There was the sound of the waves hitting the sand, traffic noise, tyres on the wet roads behind the hotel, a car horn. Murmured voices from the cafe on the beach below them, staff tidying up, bottles being taken outside. As she stood there, it started to rain again, a faint drizzle. She felt it against her face, the water swirling into the wind. There was water everywhere she looked. Sea, rain. Water equalled sex. She stepped inside the room again as he came towards her. He wasn't carrying any drinks.

She felt nervous, but she also felt good. Sure. 'You wanted to talk to me about something.'

He nodded. 'I wanted you to know that I told the truth all day today, Harriet. All of those *Willoughby* stories actually happened.'

'Did they?' She looked up at him and smiled. 'Well done.'

'I also meant it when I said you are beautiful.'

She went still.

He came closer, gazing down at her face, her bare shoulders, the curve of her neckline. She felt it like a caress. He was serious, his look intense. 'Harriet, I think something's happening. Something with us.'

She nodded. She couldn't pretend anything else. 'I think so too.'

'I can't even get you that drink. All I want to do is kiss you.'

She caught her breath as he brushed her cheekbone with his thumb. A charge of desire went through her as she felt his hands at her waist. He kissed her, a brief, beautiful kiss.

He lifted his head and she saw his eyes had darkened. 'I've wanted to do that all day.'

He kissed her again, her lips, her neck, then her lips again. She kissed him back. It was different this time, more intense. She arched her neck at the feel of his lips, closing her eyes. There were waves of intense feeling building deep inside her. She hadn't touched a man since Simon. It was as if all the passion and longing had been saving itself for now. She could feel it with each kiss, each touch. Her body was responding instantly to every caress he gave her, on her lips, her face, her neck, lower. She could feel his body under her fingers, the heat of his lips, as they moved closer against each other, tighter, harder. She felt his hand cup her breast, felt herself swell and push against him, as her hand found his skin under his shirt, as she moulded her body against his, the kisses getting hotter and deeper —

A noise filled the room. A banging noise.

'Harriet? Harriet? Are you in there? I need your help. Now.'

Harriet pulled away. There was no mistaking the voice.

'Harriet? Are you in there?'

It was Mrs Lamerton.

It was past one o'clock before Harriet got back to her own room.

The minute before she opened the door to Mrs Lamerton had almost been funny. She had smoothed her hair, checked her clothes were in place, trying not to look as if she'd been doing what she had been doing. Patrick had done the same thing. There hadn't even been time to say anything to each other. Harriet opened the door to find Mrs Lamerton standing outside, dramatically clutching her stomach. 'Harriet, I think I have food poisoning.'

Amid loud groaning, she insisted Harriet bring a first aid kit to her room and sit with her, until she felt better. She also insisted she didn't need a doctor.

Harriet quickly went up to her room, snatching up the first aid kit, catching sight of herself in the mirror, conscious of her flushed face, her too bright eyes. When she got back to Mrs Lamerton's room, Patrick was there.

'Do you want me to do anything?' he said. 'Call anyone?'

Mrs Lamerton groaned again. 'Harriet . . .'

'I don't think so. But I'd better stay with her,' she whispered. He nodded. He didn't touch her, but it felt like he had.

When she said goodnight to Mrs Lamerton an hour later, the older woman was sitting up in bed, in a quilted bedjacket. The groaning had stopped, even though she'd refused to take any of the array of tablets Harriet had been able to produce from the first aid kit. Harriet wasn't convinced any of it had been genuine. But she couldn't have abandoned her, much as she had wanted to. And she had wanted to, very much.

'Are you sure you're feeling better, Mrs Lamerton? You'll be all right if I leave you?'

'I hope so. But if I need to ring you again, Harriet, where will you be?'

'I'm sorry?'

'Where will you be?'

It was like being back at school. 'In my room. Just ring the number and I'll come down again if you need me.'

'I didn't interrupt anything, did I? With you and Patrick Shawcross?' The tone was accusing, triumphant even.

'No, Mrs Lamerton.'

It wasn't until she was back in her own room that she wondered why Mrs Lamerton had come to Patrick's room, not hers. Had she been following her? Watching her and Patrick together? Not just tonight but the last few nights? If she had been, she would have seen Patrick come to her room every night, once with a bottle of wine, stay for an hour and then leave. Oh God. She could only imagine what the older woman had been thinking.

Outside Mrs Lamerton's door, she had stopped. Down the corridor was her own room. Upstairs was Patrick's room. She was torn, but finally she had decided not to go back there. Not yet. Not tonight. She needed to think about this.

She went into the bathroom and looked at herself in the mirror. She felt different. Patrick had looked at her tonight, kissed her tonight, caressed her, as though she was the most beautiful, desirable woman he had ever seen. It gave her a breathless feeling, like the earth was slipping away, things were out of control. It was how the panic attacks had felt, she realised. Yet this felt good. Better than good.

Wonderful.

CHAPTER TWENTY-THREE

'Thanks, Molly, you've done a great job.'

Molly picked up the last box of envelopes and added them to the pile she and Gloria had been stuffing with tour brochures all morning. She had the day off school and had been in the office helping.

Gloria enjoyed her company. Molly had somehow escaped the worst of Melissa's genes, and inherited James's calm temperament. She was in fact very restful to be around. A good worker, too. A bit distracted today, though. Gloria noticed her checking her mobile phone again. She'd been doing it all morning.

'Waiting on an urgent message, Moll?'

'I still haven't heard from her.'

'From Lara?'

Molly nodded. 'Do you think she's all right, Gloria?'

'Of course she is, lovie,' Gloria said as brightly as she could. 'I'd say she just needs some time out.'

'But not from me. Not usually, anyway. She's always answered me. Especially when I told her it was urgent.'

'Is something up?'

'No, no, it's fine. Just a school thing she was helping me with.' She bit her lip. For a moment she looked like a little girl, not a fifteen-year-old.

'Can I help?'

'No.' She answered quickly. 'Thanks anyway, Gloria.'

'Well, just ask if I can.' She looked at the airplane clock. 'I'd better head out for lunch. Thanks again, Moll.' She picked up her bag and called over to the glass office. 'I'm off to lunch, Melissa.'

Melissa didn't turn around, just lifted her hand to say she'd heard.

Gloria hated the way she did that. She refused to let it bother her this time. She pulled the door shut behind her and stood there, in the shade of the veranda. She waved over at Reg from the deli, outside sweeping the footpath.

'Beautiful day,' she called over.

'Beautiful,' Reg called back. 'You're looking well, too. Everything good with Kev?'

'No worries at all.'

So she looked normal. No one was picking up anything different about her. It was only inside she was feeling sick. She had felt sick since Austin had rung and told her about Lara and the Irish websites.

He'd rung early that morning. It had been after midnight in Bath. She'd just unlocked the front door and walked into the Turner Travel office when the call came. 'Austin! What time is it there? Hold on, let me get my cup of tea. Of course, please fill me in.'

As he related the story so far, she found herself scribbling notes, out of habit when she was on the phone. *Flatmate Nina. College. Lecturer. Ireland???*

Ireland. She felt it in the pit of her stomach. The feeling of dread. 'Where are you now?'

'In Lara's flat. Nina's next door in the kitchen. She's as puzzled as we are. Said she wished she'd thought to ask Lara more questions.

She's been very helpful, actually. I think she feels like she's in the middle of a detective film.'

'Have you been to see Harriet yet?'

'This morning, briefly. She was in good form, I thought. She's got her hands full with that Willoughby, too. There's a thought. He's a detective, isn't he? We can get him onto Lara's case.' His joke fell flat. 'Maybe you were right about this having something to do with Lara's parents, Gloria. The way she said she had to go off and do some family business.' He laughed awkwardly. 'Sorry, listen to me, Austin the amateur psychologist. But Nina and I were talking about it. Maybe Lara went to Ireland without mentioning it to any of us, and it's sparked all sorts of horrible memories for her, from when her parents had that crash.'

Gloria was silent.

'Gloria? Are you there?'

'I'm here,' she said. 'Sorry, I was just thinking.'

'I realised when we were talking about it that there were all these things I didn't know about Lara's parents. Where they came from, who they were even. I don't even know where they are buried. Was it in Ireland, or in Australia?'

'They were cremated, as far as I know,' Gloria said. She knew for sure. There had been a lot of contact between the Australian police and the Irish police. The embassies had been involved as well. It was Penny again who had made the decision. She had requested the ashes be scattered somewhere in Ireland. 'I know you'll think I'm wrong, Gloria, you don't even have to say it. I'm doing it to protect Lara. It's what Rose would have wanted.' Gloria could remember her voice as clearly as if it was yesterday.

'So do you know the whole story from that time?' Austin asked.

'Not all of it,' Gloria said hesitantly.

'Has Lara asked you about any of this? I mean, she might have asked Mum and Dad about it, but we'll never know now.'

'I know they spoke about it with her a lot, around the time she turned eighteen especially.' Penny had come to Gloria, asking for advice. It had been one of the few times since that first terrible night that she and Penny had spoken about it. Lara had started asking lots of questions again about her parents and Penny hadn't known what to tell her. Didn't I tell you this would happen, Gloria had wanted to say to her. Didn't I tell you that it would all come back to bite you? They had nearly fought about it, Gloria remembered. But in the end Penny had stuck to her original story and, as far as Gloria ever found out from Penny, Lara had accepted it.

'Why wasn't Lara with her parents in Ireland that time, Gloria? Her flatmate asked me tonight and I couldn't remember.'

'I think her parents had been having problems,' she said, choosing her words with care. 'Lara had a school camp that week. Your mother told me they'd decided it was a good opportunity to go away on their own, to try and sort out a few things.'

'That's right. Mrs Robinson was always ringing Mum for help, wasn't she? For hours on end, now I think of it. So where did the crash happen in Ireland? Was it near where her mother's house was? Or somewhere else?'

'I'm not sure,' Gloria said. That wasn't true, either. She knew exactly where it had happened. Just outside a town called Clonakilty, near the city of Cork. The name had always stuck in her head. She was hating this, hating being put on the spot, having to think before she answered him. *Help me, Penny*, she implored silently. At least it was only a phone conversation. She would have found it harder to lie face to face. She tried to change the subject, to buy herself some thinking time. 'Look, Austin, you're not getting carried away with this possibility, are you? You don't think that maybe we should leave her be, wait until she decides to contact us again?'

'I can't, Gloria. Not now. It's like I said to Harriet, if we find her and she's all right, then we'll leave her alone. If she's not all right, then we'll be glad we went looking. But something's obviously wrong. She's upset about something and maybe it's got something to do with her parents and what happened in Ireland. Nina's convinced that's what it is. She's going to come and help me look for her, too.'

'Go with you? Where, to Ireland?'

'Yes. She's very fond of Lara. And she's worried now, too.'

'Have you got time to do this? What about the orchestra?'

'It'll be fine. I've still got two days off and I'll do what I can in that time. What do you reckon? It's worth a try, isn't it?'

'Yes, it is.' What else could she have said to him?

Gloria started to take her usual route home for lunch, along the beach path, but as she reached the end of the curved bay she turned right, instead of her usual left. She leaned down and took off her sandals and picked her way through the sand to the tree trunk. Bleached from the sun and the water, it had been there for as long as she could remember. She had played on it as a child. She had sat on it with Kevin when they were first dating, with their three boys over the years, and even with her grandkids. She'd sat there with Penny many times too, watching their kids swim, shriek and bodysurf for hours on summer days.

The sun was high. The water was the glowing blue she loved. There were a few people swimming, a couple under an umbrella far to her right, a mother and her two daughters trying to fly a kite. Her imagination turned the woman into Penny, and the two daughters into Harriet and Lara.

Gloria had come to this spot the night she had that awful, difficult conversation with Penny, the night they heard the news about Lara's parents. The night she'd made that promise. Gloria had regretted making it then and she regretted it now, twenty-four years later.

Gloria was in the back room of the agency, unpacking new stationery, when she heard the phone ring. She heard Penny answer it. The two of them were alone. Neil had left early to drop some tickets to one of their older customers.

Gloria finished the unpacking and was about to put on her coat to go home when Penny came in. Her face was white. Gloria's immediate thought was someone had died. Neil. Or Kevin. One of the kids. 'Penny, what is it?'

Penny told her. Gloria sat down, shocked. She was right. Someone had died. Two people. Lara's parents. Little Lara, who had stayed with the family just a few months before. Her hand went to her mouth as Penny shut the door, sat down at the table and told her the details. 'Oh God. Oh my God. That poor little girl.'

'I can't believe it, Gloria. How could something like that happen?'

Gloria shook her head, put her hand on Penny's arm. 'Did you have any inkling things were so terrible? How long was it since you spoke to Rose?'

'Just last week. Before she left. She asked me to be Lara's guardian while they were away. In case something happened. That's how the police in Ireland tracked me down. My details were in the back of her passport.'

'You think she knew? Had a feeling . . .?'

'I didn't notice anything. It was hard to tell with Rose. You know what she was like.'

Gloria knew well. She had answered the phone many times to Rose over the past few months. Rose had taken to ringing Penny during work hours, always with that edge of tears to her voice. Penny tried to be understanding about it, even while she was obviously getting impatient with the long, too regular and often increasingly drunken calls. Rose and her husband were always breaking up and getting back together. He'd moved to Queensland to live with another woman at one stage, Gloria recalled. That had sparked twice daily phone calls to Penny. Rose had nearly been hysterical, Penny had told Gloria. She would say over and over how much she loved Dennis, how she couldn't bear it if he left her again. Rose had eventually gone up there with Lara and pleaded with him to come back.

'I can't believe it, Gloria,' Penny said again. 'I just can't.'

'Who's told Lara? One of her teachers?'

'No one yet. The teachers don't know. That's why the police rang me. They want me to go and tell her.'

'Oh Penny, no! That's very hard on you.'

'It's worse than hard. It's impossible. What do I tell her?'

Gloria thought about it. 'As much as you think she can stand. Not all the details yet, but the basic facts.'

'Tell her the truth, you mean? Gloria, of course I can't. She's eight years old. What would news like that do to a child of that age? She wouldn't be able to take it in, let alone cope with it.'

'But you have to. What else can you tell her? Penny, her parents are dead. Nothing you say is going to change that. What could you say to soften it? Tell her they died in a car crash?'

'A car crash?' Penny was thoughtful. 'Do you know, I think you're right. I think that could be the best solution.'

'Penny, I didn't mean it. I was speaking hypothetically.'

'But I think you're right. What difference will it make to her if she thinks that's what happened? It won't bring her parents back if she knows the truth, will it? It might make it easier for her.'

'Stop it. You can't do this.'

'I can, Gloria. I have to. Can't you see it makes sense? I can't tell a little girl the truth. You met Lara, you saw how fragile she was. How damaging would this be for her, the rest of her life? You know how people talk. She'd never be treated normally.'

'But you can't make up a lie like that. What about her family? Uncles, aunts? Grandparents?'

'There aren't any. Rose was an only child, and Dennis's parents died before he emigrated. Her mother died a month ago, and she never knew her father. That's why Rose went over there, to finalise her mother's estate. There was no one else.'

'Penny, you can't be serious about this. You have to tell her the truth.'

'I don't. And I need you to promise that you won't tell her. I'm not going to tell Neil or the children, either. They don't need to know.'

Gloria had never seen Penny like this. 'You can't just invent a car crash.'

'I'm not inventing it.' Penny spoke in a firm voice. 'It happened. They were driving through the mountains outside Cork and bad weather came in. There are mountains outside Cork, aren't there? Perhaps I'd better just say Ireland for the time being. The road was winding. They must have lost control of the car and tipped over the cliff edge.'

Glora could hardly believe she was having this conversation. 'You can't just make something up like that, Penny. You can't. It won't change anything, anyway. They're still dead, aren't they? How can you think this will make it easier for her to cope?'

'It'll be easier than the truth at least. Can you think of another possibility? A plane crash? A train accident? No, I think you're right. A car crash. It's ordinary enough.'

'What do you mean I'm right? No, Penny, you can't make this my idea. You need to hold off. Think about it some more.'

'There's no time. What I tell her when I pick her up from the school camp tonight is how it will be. I know it's the right decision, Gloria. I really do. I feel it in my heart.'

'But what if she comes to you when she's older and says she needs to know more about her parents? What will you tell her then?'

'That they loved her. I'll talk about what they were like, the sort of people they were. That's what she'll want to hear. What she'll need to hear.'

'I think you're making a big mistake.'

'I know I'm not. And I need you to promise me you won't tell her, Gloria. That you won't tell anyone.'

'She'll find out some other way. You can't keep something like this a secret.'

'How will she find out? It happened on the other side of the world. I told you, there isn't a big family waiting for her to join them and wanting to tell her the truth. Gloria, that's why Rose asked me to be Lara's guardian. She didn't know other people here and there wasn't other family who could take her. She always said how lucky she thought I was. And how lucky it was that we were on the same ship to Australia. That it was meant to be that we were friends. And she was right. We are lucky. We should share that luck.'

Gloria couldn't think of anything to say to that. Since she had known her, Penny had always had the belief that things were destined, meant to happen.

'I'm telling you, Gloria, because I need to, tonight at least. But I want you to promise me that you'll always keep it to yourself. You mustn't even tell Kevin.'

'I can't make a promise like that.'

'You have to. If we're to keep working together, to be friends, I need to know I can trust you. It'll be too difficult for Lara otherwise, not to mention the rest of the family. I don't know for sure, but my feeling is that Lara will be living with us from now on. It's the only possible outcome. I want her to feel welcome. And loved. And secure. I need to know that you won't do anything to endanger that.'

Gloria felt she was seeing Penny for the first time. She was like a different woman. Driven. A thought flashed into Gloria's head. From one of their conversations, during the long, quiet times in the travel agency's earliest days. Penny had confessed she'd longed to have another child, two boys and two girls, but it had never happened. 'You're glad about this, Penny, aren't you? Glad to get Lara? Your second daughter?'

Gloria saw a flicker of something in her friend's eyes, but then Penny's chin rose. 'Of course I'm not glad. How could I be glad that something so terrible happened? What I'm trying to do is make the best of it. The best for Lara and what I know Rose would have wanted to happen. Please, Gloria. I'm asking for a promise.'

Gloria hesitated, then nodded. 'I promise. I think it's wrong, but I promise.'

She'd known for twenty-four years and kept her promise. As

she watched Lara settle in to the family, go to the local schools and start working for Turner Travel, she'd reluctantly admitted to herself that Penny had been right. It had made it easier for Lara. Gloria and Penny had rarely spoken about it. One of the few times they did was at a school play, sitting in the audience, watching Harriet and Lara on stage. Lara was considered one of the Turners now. A woman went past. 'You must be so proud of your girls, Penny.'

'Oh, I am.' Penny exchanged pleasantries and then turned to Gloria and spoke in a quiet voice. 'You see? It's made her ordinary, Gloria. One of us. If people had known the truth, she would never have been able to fit in. People would always have talked about her in a terrible way.'

'It was still wrong. You were changing her history.'

'No, I was protecting a little girl.'

'You can't protect her forever. She'll find out.'

'How? You promised me you wouldn't say anything.'

'She'll go looking one day.'

'She won't, Gloria. I just know she won't. She won't need to.'

'You were wrong, Penny.' Gloria said the words aloud, staring out across the water. 'I wish you had been right, but I think you were wrong. She has gone looking.'

Her heart went out to Lara. Please, God, let her not have found out, not like this, alone on the other side of the world. There was nothing she could have done to stop her though, she realised. She had to let it happen. Let it unfold, whether she liked it or not.

She got up and wrapped her arms around herself, cold despite the sunshine. Slowly, she walked up the beach and headed for home.

CHAPTER TWENTY-FOUR

Nina called out into the hallway. 'Austin, do you want more coffee?'

'More?' he called back from the bathroom. 'Have you got shares in a coffee bean plantation?'

'No, just an addictive personality. Caffeine, nicotine, and don't start me on Ovaltine.'

'Don't you have to go into work today?' Austin said, as he came into the room, freshly showered. He felt good, ready for action, optimistic, even. He'd expected to sleep badly on the sofa bed, or at least lie awake for hours. But he'd fallen asleep immediately.

'Not today. Not unless I get an emergency call that some filing needs doing somewhere.'

He and Nina fell into easy conversation again. Lara was still their main topic, but they kept veering off into side routes. What it was like living in Bath. How long he'd been a drummer. Some of the temping jobs she'd done. Whether he felt more at home in England or Australia.

She laughed easily. He found himself telling orchestra tales, spurred on by her questions.

'You can't all be well-behaved all the time, surely?' she'd asked.

He'd confessed that, no, they weren't. Musicians were terrible practical jokers. He told her about the time the cornet player discovered someone had put water into his instrument. When he picked it up and played, water sprayed out left, right and centre. Or the time the women in the first violin section turned the page on their score mid-opera to reveal some extremely explicit gay porn. The whole wind section had cracked up laughing. Only one had continued playing, to the conductor's disgust.

As she laughed, he saw again how sparkly her brown eyes were. Like a child's, he thought. He'd always noticed that with his niece Molly, how clear her eyes were. Innocent, he supposed. Untouched by life's hard knocks yet.

'So, Austin, do you have a girlfriend?'

Her sudden change of subject threw him, but he didn't show it. 'No, I don't.'

'A good-looking man like you? I'm not trying to flatter you, I'm stating a fact. I like your hair long like that, by the way. It suits you. But still no girlfriend?'

'No.'

'Surely someone fancies you or you fancy someone?'

'You sound like my sisters. They're constantly trying to marry me off.'

'You don't want to settle down?'

'I just haven't found the right girl.'

'I would have thought you'd come up with something more original than that.'

'I'm too young to settle down.'

'You're not too young. What are you? My age? Thirty-five?'

'Thirty-eight.'

'See, not too young at all. Better excuse, please.'

'Too many fish in the sea?'

'Oh, I see,' she grinned. 'You're a field player. A Don Juan.'

'A what?'

'A ladies' man. Of course you are, with those looks. And do you have much success?'

'I have my moments.'

'And is it enough?'

'What do you mean?'

'If you can play the field like that, is it enough for you mentally? Emotionally? Because you strike me as a clever man underneath all the front. Thoughtful, too. You wouldn't be here looking for Lara if you weren't a caring person.'

He was enjoying this and not enjoying it, all at once. 'You don't mince your words, do you?'

She smiled. 'I'm sorry, I actually meant it as a compliment. And yes, before you say it, I am far too nosy. I always have been, especially about people's love lives. It's the Italian in me. And I suppose I always wondered what it would be like to play the field.'

'You're good-looking yourself. You could try it. Have you got a boyfriend?'

'Alas, no, I haven't.'

They were flirting, he realised. He also realised he liked it. 'Oh, poor Nina. Do you want me to give you some tips?'

'Would you? Really? Oh yes please, great master.'

He had just started, in a mock-serious voice – 'First, identify your prey' – when the phone rang. It was Brendan, Lara's lecturer from the tourism college. He'd found something he wanted to show them.

They met him in the same classroom they'd visited the night before. He'd asked them to come as quickly as possible, before the morning classes started. He looked like an absent-minded scientist, Austin thought. His hair was even more tousled than before. His glasses kept slipping, too.

'I hope you don't think I was being nosy,' Brendan said, 'but I was mulling it over last night. I tried that Internet history search on my own computer at home, and I discovered it saves everything you've looked at, every word you've searched for on a search engine, not only the website addresses.'

They sat around Lara's computer with him. He clicked, and then moved the mouse again until the Internet Explorer page was open on the screen. 'You see, here's the history that we looked at last night, the Irish sites, the cruise ship info pages, all of that. But here's what I found on Lara's search engine this morning. I don't know, it might be helpful.'

He clicked on the search engine web address, and then clicked again. A long list appeared on the screen of every word Lara had typed into the search engine. Amidst ones they expected to see – Willoughby, Patrick Shawcross, airlines, weather bureau, airport information – was a list of more disturbing words.

Rose Dennis Robinson
Car crash
Ireland
Australian
British
Police
Two killed

There was no mistaking it. She had been looking for information about her parents.

'Did she find anything?' Austin asked.

'I don't know. I thought I'd wait until you got here before I tried searching the same words again. The history shows the terms entered, but not what results came up. It didn't feel right for me to look them up if you weren't here.'

Austin was grateful for his understanding. 'Could you try now?'

More clicks. He tried all the different combinations. Lots of random web pages came up, but nothing with any more information on Lara's parents.

'Of course, it was more than twenty years ago,' Brendan said. 'If it had been reported in any of the newspapers, and it probably was, it mightn't show up here. They wouldn't have had electronic editions back then. So if she was trying to find out more, she'd probably need to go to the offices themselves and check their archives.'

Austin sat back in the chair. It was a help, but it didn't narrow the search for her any more. 'She could be anywhere, couldn't she? Visiting every newspaper office in Ireland, asking to go through their back editions.'

'She might have phoned around first.' He pointed at the screen again. 'See, she'd done a search on all the police stations in Ireland too. They'd have the information as well.'

Nina was disappointed. 'It's like looking for a needle in a haystack, isn't it? She could be anywhere in Ireland, staying in any hotel or B&B, walking miles and miles of roads trying to find the exact spot where her parents were killed.' She sighed. 'Then again, she could be sitting in a spa, having a facial at this moment, unaware of all this fuss.'

'Not Lara. It's more than that. It has to be something to do with her parents. If we could just figure out where she was, here or in

Ireland, the next step would be easier. One island to search instead of two.'

Brendan glanced at his watch. 'I'm sorry to rush you, but I've got a class coming in a minute. You're welcome to come back if you like.'

Austin stood up, feeling flat, and pushed his chair back under the desk. 'Thanks again, Brendan. You've been really helpful.'

'Let me know if there's anything else I can do, won't you?'

'You couldn't run a check on her name on every airline leaving the UK for Ireland by any chance?' Austin said, only half-joking. 'See if we could track her down that way?'

Brendan gave a wry smile. 'No, I couldn't, sorry.'

Austin was about to turn away when Brendan spoke again, in a low voice. 'But a friend of mine could.'

In St Ives, Harriet was getting ready to go down to breakfast. She wasn't sure if she was feeling nervous or just confused. It was as if a spell had been cast over all of them the night before, she decided. The make-up and hair session with Miss Talbot and the others, the bus trip, the restaurant, the disco – the combination had acted like a potion. If Mrs Lamerton hadn't knocked on the door when she did, Harriet didn't know what would have happened. She corrected herself. Yes, she did actually. She would have kissed Patrick Shawcross for a lot longer and if those kisses had been as good as the first kiss, then she would have gone to bed with him. She would probably still be in bed with him now.

Perhaps it was as well she hadn't gone back to his room after leaving Mrs Lamerton. This morning she would see him, and it would be businesslike again and they would continue on the tour as if nothing had happened.

It was an easy day today, driving from St Ives to Land's End and then on to the Minack Theatre overlooking Porthcurno Bay. They were all dining in town together and then the rest of the evening was scheduled as free time for everyone. The group had been talking the night before about what they would do. Mr Fidock and Mr and Mrs Douglas had been investigating local pubs and had found a nautically themed one they wanted to try. Harriet was going to take the opportunity to make calls to confirm the next part of their tour. Go for a long walk. Do some reading, perhaps.

Her phone rang. It was Austin, calling from Bath.

'She's definitely gone to Ireland, Harriet. She flew there three days ago. To Cork, in the south. She left Bristol on a nine p.m. flight, the same day she was supposed to meet you. On a one-way ticket and so far she hasn't returned. Not that they've been able to tell by the bookings, anyway.'

Harriet listened as Austin explained about Lara's lecturer and his industry contacts. Lara had been cutting it fine. If their flight had been on time, they would have been arriving at nine-thirty. 'But why would she go to Cork?'

'It's got to be about her parents. Why else would she go there?'

'Has she found out where the crash was? I only remember Mum and Dad saying it was in Ireland, but I never knew where.'

'Nor did I. Maybe they knew, and maybe they told Lara years ago. Or she might have contacted the Irish police. I've checked the flights. There's one leaving Bristol for Cork later today, we might be able to catch it.'

'We?'

'Nina's as worried as we are. She's coming with me. Harriet, I'd better go. I'll ring you as soon as I have any more news.'

Harriet finished getting ready. Austin's call had brought her back to reality. That was her real life, the real world. Her family, Lara, Austin. Not what she had imagined was happening with Patrick. She had blown everything out of proportion.

On her way downstairs she stopped at the landing and looked out through the big windows onto the beach. There was only one person out there, in a billowing raincoat, walking a dog. It was still drizzling and the waves were high, but not as rough as the previous day.

The front door of the hotel opened. She knew it was him even before he appeared.

He saw her immediately. His face broke into a smile. 'Harriet.'

She walked down the final few stairs. Her legs were suddenly unsteady. 'Hello, Patrick.'

'Did you manage to sort things out for Mrs Lamerton last night?'

'I did.' She swallowed. 'Patrick, I'm sorry about —'

'I'm not.'

She fell quiet.

'Harriet, I meant it last night. I mean it this morning. Something is happening. We both feel it.' His face was serious. 'Are you sorry about last night?'

'No, I'm not. No.'

'Are you sure?'

'I'm sure.'

'Can I see you this evening? After the group dinner in town?'

'You've looked at the itinerary?'

'I have, yes.' A glint came to his eye. 'You see? If I'd known you would kiss me so beautifully, I'd have been checking it long before now.'

He hadn't even lowered his voice. The feeling came rushing

back. That warmth, the sharing, but now with something much deeper underneath it.

'Hello, Harriet. Hello, Patrick.' They both turned. It was Miss Talbot. She looked pale. 'Patrick, would you please come and peel my orange for me again this morning?'

'Of course, Miss Talbot,' he said. 'How are you this morning?'

'Not very well, I'm ashamed to confess. I think there might be alcohol in those Fluffy Ducks.'

Harriet was smiling as she followed them into the breakfast room.

They were all on the bus by ten o'clock. Harriet noticed a different mood among the group. She also knew what had caused it.

After breakfast, she had gone to her room to collect the day's tour notes when she was waylaid by Mrs Lamerton. She'd seen her in the dining room but they hadn't spoken. The older woman had been tucking heartily into kippers. It was a remarkable recovery from food poisoning.

'I need to have a word, please, Harriet. A private word.'

'Of course, Mrs Lamerton.' She stepped into her room, inviting Mrs Lamerton to come in as well.

The older woman seemed agitated. 'I've been thinking about this all night. I really don't think it's appropriate behaviour and I think Melissa would agree, if she knew. Lara, too, if she was here.'

'I'm sorry, Mrs Lamerton, I'm not sure what you mean.'

'I'm talking about you and Patrick Shawcross. You were in his room very late last night. And I've seen him go into your room late at night as well. More than once.'

So she had been spying on them. Harriet knew she had to call her bluff. 'Oh, Mrs Lamerton, have you been imagining hijinks between myself and Patrick?'

'Yes. Yes, I have. But I haven't imagined it. I've seen it.'

'Mrs Lamerton, I think I need to let you in on a secret.' Harriet stepped back, so Mrs Lamerton could see the TV and video on its stand in the corner of the room. A stack of videos was on the table beside it. The *Willoughby* titles were clearly visible. 'That's what Patrick and I have been doing.'

'Watching television?'

'Not television. Videos. *Willoughby* videos. I was brought onto this trip at very short notice, as you know, so I've been watching the videos each night. Patrick has been watching them with me, helping me to get familiar with the episodes. I knew I'd never be as familiar with them as James or Lara, let alone you and the rest of the group, but I wanted to do the best I could.' It was all nearly true. It didn't explain what she was doing in Patrick's room the previous night, but she realised then that Mrs Lamerton no longer cared about that. She was looking at the videos like a sugarholic in a sweetshop.

'You've got all the *Willoughby* episodes here with you?'

'Yes.'

'All twenty of them?'

'That's right.'

'Could I borrow them?'

'Pardon me?'

'Visiting the locations has brought back so many memories. I'd like to watch a few of the videos again myself. Tonight, if I could borrow your video player. In fact, can I take the videos now?'

'Now? But we're about to go on the bus.'

'Just so I know I have them. In case you get busy later today when we get back.'

Harriet softened. Mrs Lamerton really was the High Queen of the *Willoughby* weirdos. 'Of course you can.'

Harriet could see her in the middle seat of the bus now, taking one of the videos out of her bag and letting her neighbour, Mrs Biggins, take a look at it. Mr Fidock was leaning across the aisle. 'All twenty of them? Are you sure?'

'Yes, I've checked the titles. All twenty, right here.'

Yes, Mrs Lamerton had definitely made a full recovery from last night's food poisoning. Harriet wondered what else had happened the previous evening. Clive and Mrs Randall had been the last to get on the bus that morning, coming out of the hotel together. It might have been a trick of the light, but she was nearly sure she'd seen Clive give Mrs Randall a little pinch on the bottom before she went to sit down. He was certainly in better humour. And they had been dancing together a lot the previous night. No, Harriet had to be imagining it . . .

She took out her folder. So far she'd also done a good job of pretending nothing had changed between her and Patrick. For the sake of everyone, she'd greeted him normally when he got on the bus. She hadn't spoken to him since.

As she looked up he caught her gaze. He stopped mid-conversation with his neighbour. 'Excuse me, Mrs Douglas. Harriet?'

'Yes, Patrick?'

'I wonder would you pass me that map there beside Clive?'

'The map? Of course.' She passed it over.

A few minutes later he called her name again, thanked her for the map and asked her to put it back. A few minutes later, just as politely, he asked her to pass him the torch from the dashboard beside Clive.

'The torch?'

'I like torches.'

In the next ten minutes he asked her to pass him the St Ives street directory and then the newspaper that Clive had pushed into the seat pocket beside him. When Mrs Douglas got up to fetch something from her husband, Harriet took the opportunity to lean across to him, speaking in a low tone. 'Patrick, what are you doing?'

'Asking you to pass me things.'

'Yes, I know. I've passed you everything in the front of the bus. I'm running out of things to pass you.'

'Stop ignoring me then.'

'I'm not ignoring you.'

'Aren't you? What are you doing then?'

She started to smile. 'I'm trying to maintain a dignified and professional distance.'

'So I can't kiss you now?' That sparkle was back in his eyes again.

'No, you can't.'

'I want to.'

'You can't.'

'I'll be thinking about it.'

'I won't look at you.'

'I'll ask you to pass me more things.'

'Patrick, please.'

'I'm sorry. I'll be on my best behaviour.'

'Thank you.'

'But if you hear me say the word raven today during the question and answer session, you'll know I'm thinking about kissing you.'

'Raven?'

'Raven,' he said.

She took the microphone as usual once they got out onto the

open road and started reading. James had been surprisingly low-key in his script today. '*Welcome aboard, everyone. Just two days to go. On behalf of everyone at Turner Travel, I hope you're all enjoying yourselves and the trip is meeting your expectations in every possible way. If there is anything I can do to make it more pleasurable, you only have to ask.*' She couldn't help herself. She glanced over at Patrick. He had a big smile on his face.

She quickly looked back at her script. '*This morning we'll be visiting Land's End, England's extreme western tip and of course the scene for episode fourteen's romantic reunion between Willoughby and Lady Garvan, following her release from prison on forgery charges. We'll also be visiting the awe-inspiring Minack Theatre, the Greek-style amphitheatre set into the cliff face overlooking the spectacular Porthcurno Bay. Built in the 1930s by Rowena Cade, the theatre has seen many open air productions of operas, musicals and Shakespeare plays, but is of course also known to the Willoughby afficionado as the setting for the dramatic conclusion to episode twelve, "The Case of the Vanishing Vicar".*'

She swapped seats and handed the microphone to Patrick for the usual on-the-road question and answer session. He stood next to her, his hand resting lightly on the backrest, close enough to touch.

Mrs Kempton put up her hand. 'Patrick, did you have much of a say in any of the actors who were cast in the show?'

'Not in the first series, Mrs Kempton, no. But in the second series I did. We were fortunate to hear about a talented family of actors called the Ravens. There were seven of them, all talented in different ways and, remarkably for one family, all quite different in appearance, so we used them as much as possible. There was Andrew Raven, who you might remember as the gardener in episode three. Carlos Raven, the chef in "The Case of the Crooked Chef". His sister Cassandra Raven played a waitress in that same episode. Isabella Raven, who was a maid in Lady Garvan's mansion in several episodes. Santana Raven – the family had Spanish blood, I believe – was one of the customers in the jewellery shop at the time of the siege. And of course not forgetting the twins, Delilah Raven and her sister Anastasia Raven, who played a set of twins in "The Case of the Stolen Kiss".'

Mrs Lamerton was frowning. 'I don't remember that episode. Which series was that in?'

'I do apologise, Mrs Lamerton. That was its working title. You might remember it as "The Case of the Mislaid Mail".'

'Oh yes,' Mrs Lamerton nodded. 'Now I remember it.'

'A wonderful family, the Ravens. I've been thinking about them a great deal the past few days. I'm hoping to get in contact with some of them. Tonight, possibly.' He looked at Harriet. There was laughter in his eyes, but there was that deeper, more intense look as well. He gave her the slightest of winks and then turned as another question was called. 'Yes, Mr Fidock?'

CHAPTER TWENTY-FIVE

In Merryn Bay, it was the end of a long day. Gloria was battling a headache. The phones had been ringing constantly. Each time she expected it to be Austin. It was making her jumpy. It didn't help that she was running the office on her own. Melissa had made a great show the afternoon before of saying she might stay an extra day in Melbourne, that it was time she did a thorough reconnoitre of the city travel agents. Gloria knew it was a lie. She had heard Melissa make the appointment in the day spa herself. This time tomorrow Melissa would be frown-free and three shades of brown darker.

'That's fine.' She'd enjoy the peace in fact. 'Are you expecting any calls? Anything I need to know?'

Melissa had been distracted, cleaning out her handbag as she often seemed to do in work hours, all the little pots of make-up lined in a row across her desk. 'Go ahead and handle them for me, would you? If anyone asks, I'm away on family business. Molly will be away too. She's got a swimming carnival in the north of the state. You'll have the place to yourself.'

Gloria had closed the office for lunch, deciding on the spur of the moment to pick up sandwiches and go home to Kevin. It was hard to leave him after the hour was up. They sat in the garden, talking, drinking tea, doing the newspaper crossword. He was better than her at the cryptic clues, but he didn't rub it in. He liked to joke that he wouldn't let a crossword come between them. When she had got back to the office at two o'clock, there had been fourteen messages waiting for her on the machine.

She went into the back room now to make a cup of tea. Just half an hour to closing time. She was counting the minutes. The phone was ringing as she came back. She had to lean over the desk to grab it in time. 'Turner Travel, Gloria speaking, can I help you?'

'Good afternoon, can I speak to Melissa Turner please?'

'I'm sorry, Melissa's not in the office at present. Can I take a message?'

'Will she be in later today?'

'I'm sorry. She's been called away on family business. Who's calling please?'

'I'm sorry, I should have introduced myself. This is Regina Lewis, calling from Matheson Travel.'

One of the largest of the national travel companies. 'I'm sure I can help you, this is Gloria Hillman speaking. Melissa's asked me to deal with any business that came in today.'

'Oh, thank you. I'm calling on behalf of Mr Alex Sakidis, our franchise and acquisitions manager. He's asked if it would be possible for him to change the date of his viewing to next Thursday, rather than Wednesday.'

'That should be fine,' Gloria said cautiously. She'd been expecting a question about one of their tours, or an exchange of information. That was common enough among travel agents, even if they were apparently in competition. 'Let me check Mrs Turner's diary.'

She opened the diary on Melissa's desk and flicked to the right date. Nothing there. Then she clicked on the computer screen to her electronic diary. Melissa was the only one who used it every day – Gloria, Harriet, James and Lara preferred the paper trail. There was something marked on that date: M.T. Matheson Travel?

'And you'd like to change that date to —?'

'The following day, if that's all right?'

'That should be fine.' Gloria put on her most casual voice. 'Could I just double-check Mr Sakidis's title?'

'Of course. He is our franchise and acquisitions manager.'

'Oh, yes.' Were they actually talking about what she thought they were talking about? 'And Mr Sakidis has the address?'

'Turner Travel, 143 Main Street, Merryn Bay?'

'That's right. And all the background information he needs?'

'Let me check.' The young woman returned after a moment. 'I'll put you through to Mr Sakidis, Mrs Hillman. It is Mrs?'

'Yes, thank you.'

A short burst of classical piano and then a smooth, deep voice. 'Mrs Hillman, Alex Sakidis speaking.'

'How are you, Mr Sakidis? Your assistant probably explained that Mrs Turner is unfortunately out of the office today, but please feel free to ask me if you need any more information.' She felt she was walking a tightrope, hoping she was saying the right things.

'We have all the figures we need, thanks, Mrs Hillman. They look very healthy. And we received the forecast material from your accountant on Monday, as agreed. I think once we see the property itself, that will help us get more of a feel for what sort of package we'd be offering. That date change isn't a problem for you, I hope? Another possible acquisition property has come up further down the peninsula, so I want to take in both.'

'No, that's fine. I hope that second property won't have any bearing on whether you will or won't buy us out?' She shut her eyes, hoping she was still on track.

'We're currently planning an exciting expansion program, so no, let me assure you, we are still extremely interested. You haven't changed your minds, I hope?'

'Oh, no. Not at all.'

'So will I be meeting you as well, Mrs Hillman, or will it just be Mrs Turner?'

'Both of us, I hope. Thanks so much for talking to me. Goodbye.'

The shop was quiet after she hung up, only the sound of passing cars filtering in from outside. She must be mistaken. They must have been at cross purposes. They hadn't been talking about selling out Turner Travel. They had been discussing some shared tours.

No, they hadn't. He had spoken of acquisitions, buy-outs, figures, future plans. She had to check. She moved to her own computer, not wanting to touch Melissa's again. On to the Internet, on to the Matheson Travel website, on to their corporate page. *Mission statement: Matheson Travel is committed to becoming a world leader in international travel package suppliers, with plans to establish shopfronts and a presence throughout Australia.* In smaller letters: *For franchise and sales opportunities please contact Alex Sakidis.* A Melbourne number followed.

She had to be sure. She rang the number. The same young woman answered. 'Oh Regina, hello, it's Gloria from Turner Travel in Merryn Bay calling back. Sorry to bother you again. We're preparing some new brochures here and I meant to check, would Mr Sakidis need a sample of more of our itineraries, to give him an idea of the sort of business he'd be buying?'

'Oh, we have all that, thanks, Mrs Hillman. Mrs Turner sent a big selection through last month. You do some great tours, don't you?'

'We sure do. That's fine, as long as you have all you need. Goodbye now.'

She hung up. A photo of Melissa in her yellow uniform was on the pinboard in front of her. Gloria stared up at it and shook her head in disbelief. 'You scheming yellow cow.'

It was pouring with rain in Bath. There had been a thunderstorm that morning. Austin and Nina had to run from the flat down to the hire car. He'd been surprised, but also glad, when Nina offered to come to Ireland with him. 'I have some time off and I've never been to Ireland. Would you mind if I came too? Between the two of us we might be able to track her down more quickly.'

They were both drenched by the time they put their bags in the boot and clambered inside. 'Not exactly ideal flying weather,' Nina said, shaking her head, sending drops of water flying around the car.

Austin glanced at her. 'You're not scared of flying, are you?'

'Not usually, no. During electrical storms, yes. That was impressive flight organisation by the way. Especially considering you're a long way from home.'

'I was reared on timetables and flight bookings, remember. Travel runs in the Turner blood.'

'But you didn't want to go into the family business?'

He pulled out into the traffic. 'I did at first. But I also wanted to play the drums and it was hard to fit the kit in the office. The others complained I made too much noise while they were on the phone.'

She didn't acknowledge the joke. 'Yours is a family company, isn't it? So there must have been some pressure to stay with them?' She caught his expression. 'My parents run a restaurant, remember. I know all there is to know about family pressure.'

'I might have thought about going into it when I got tired of touring. And if my parents were still alive. It was different when they were there. But unfortunately my older brother James made the decision to marry a woman called Melissa. A woman from the black lagoon who has been slowly taking over our family business since the day James had the misfortune to meet her.' He stopped at the traffic lights, and adjusted the wipers to a faster speed. The rain was getting heavier.

'Fantastic, Austin.'

'Fantastic?'

'I've heard of people disliking their in-laws but you take it to a whole new level. You're sure you're not secretly harbouring a passionate love for her?'

'What is it with you and my love life?' He moved forward into the traffic again.

'I like you. I think we're going to be friends. And I worry about my friends. So am I right? Do you secretly love – what's her name?'

'Melissa.'

'Melissa. Is it a case of being jealous of your brother? Of having to take yourself out of the office because it was too much for your heart and your nerves to work so closely with your brother's wife?'

'Nina, can you stop it?'

'Your nerves taut as piano wire as you brushed against each other by the photocopy machine.'

'I'm serious.'

'Eyes meeting eyes across the formica lunch table.'

'Shut up, Nina.'

Her smile disappeared. 'Don't you tell me to shut up.'

He stopped at another red light and looked over. 'I'm sorry. You hit a sore point. No, I don't secretly love Melissa. I openly loathe Melissa. And I hate what she's done to our family business.'

'But it's successful, isn't it?'

He nodded. 'Very, these days.'

'You hate that she's made it successful? I can see why you'd hate it if she ruined it, but isn't success a good thing?'

'It's complicated.'

'In what way?'

'It's the way she does things. She rides roughshod over everyone. Makes decisions without asking us. She's taken over.'

'So who works in the family business? You don't. Your parents have passed away . . .'

'My sister Harriet. My brother James. Melissa. Lara. And Gloria, an old family friend. She's been working with us for centuries. Mum and Dad left her shares in the company in their will.'

'So it's not completely a family business then? More half and half.' She counted names off on her fingers. 'In fact, the non-biological family are winning. You'll have to go back and work there so there's more of you than them.'

Nina had an annoying habit of getting right to the point. 'I don't want to. It's the last place I want to work.'

'Then you can't complain if they make decisions without you, can you?'

He opened his mouth and then shut it again. He'd liked her at the start. Now he wasn't sure at all.

He stayed quiet for the rest of the journey, telling himself he was concentrating on the road. These were difficult driving conditions, after all. She made one or two attempts to break into his silence, but he wouldn't bite. She was messing up his head, with all these opinions and nosy remarks about Melissa and the travel agency. He was regretting asking her to come with him to Ireland now. Come to think of it, had he asked her along? She'd invited herself, hadn't she?

The music from the radio filled the car. It suited him that way. He indicated as the sign for Bristol Airport came up. The rain was still beating down. They had just driven into the hire car area when she leaned over and switched off the radio.

'What's it like up there, Austin?'

He manoeuvred the car into a parking bay, not looking at her. 'Up where?'

'On your high horse.'

He stopped the car and turned to her. Enough was enough. 'Do you ever give up?'

'Nope. Are you going to sulk like this the whole way to Ireland, because it won't be much fun if you do.'

'I'm not sulking.' They were having to speak loudly over the sound of the rain hitting the roof of the car.

'Aren't you? You've just decided to have some quiet time while you're in a car with another human being? You don't like teasing much, do you? I can be respectful if that's what you'd prefer. But I thought there was more to you than a sulky boy, Austin. I thought you were more interesting than this. More fun.'

'This isn't supposed to be fun. We're trying to find Lara, remember. This is serious.'

'And life goes on while we try to find Lara. Conversation goes on, manners go on. As life has always gone on, no matter what else is happening around a person.'

She kept getting to him. It needled him again. 'Well, aren't you the philosopher. A graduate from the school of cheery optimism, I see.'

'Yes, I am. I have been ever since my husband died.'

'I beg your pardon?'

'I said, yes, I am optimistic. I have been ever since my husband died.'

He stared at her. 'Are you serious?'

'He died four years ago. We'd been married for three years. Something like that changes the way you look at life, Austin. It made me appreciate it. It's also made me impatient.'

'I'm so sorry.'

'Don't be. You didn't know.'

'What happened?' It was his turn to ask the blunt questions.

'It was an accident. A silly stupid accident. He was playing Sunday football with a gang of our friends, a social league, out in the park. And the goal net wasn't secured properly and someone knocked against it. The bars tipped over and hit him on the head. Trapped him.'

'You were there?'

She nodded. 'We got him to hospital but he never regained consciousness. He died two days later.'

He didn't know what to say. All he could do was apologise again. 'I'm so sorry, Nina. About your husband. And for sulking. You're right. I was.'

'I forgive you. You know what I mean, though, don't you? You know how it feels when someone you love dies. It makes you look at everything in a different way.'

He did know. 'But mine wasn't the same as your situation. My parents had a good life. And they died within weeks of each other. It almost felt like the right thing for them.' Not that he hadn't been devastated when they died. And he still missed them, badly. But slowly, he had recovered. He had got used to it, at least.

She put her hand on his arm. 'I'm sorry to talk about it like this, in a car park. But I wanted to explain why I am like I am. I haven't got time to hang around and wait to find things out, or to put up with people sulking. Especially when I like them so much when they're not sulking.'

Austin acknowledged the dig.

'And I'm sorry if it's hard to take sometimes. But I try to grasp life now, Austin. All and as much as I can, while I can. So please, if you get mad at me over the next few days, say you're mad, would you, and we'll try and sort it out there and then? We haven't got time to mess around.'

'I'm sorry.'

'And stop saying sorry.'

'Can I buy you a drink?'

'Now you're talking.'

They climbed out of the car, grabbed their bags from the boot and ran through the rain into the airport building.

Clive drove the bus out of the Land's End car park just as the rain started again. The group hadn't been that impressed with their time there. An amusement arcade had been built on the spot where Willoughby and Lady Garvan had run into each other's arms in episode fourteen, 'The Case of the Jilted Jockey'. Still, they all enjoyed a stroll along the coastal path, peered over the cliff at the sea churning and boiling against the rocks far below. They queued patiently to have their group photograph taken in front of the signpost showing the distances to New York, John O'Groats and the focus of all their pointing fingers – Merryn Bay – 11 897 miles away. Harriet did a headcount as they came onto the bus. So far so good, she still hadn't lost anyone. She was about to give Clive the nod to drive on when Mrs Lamerton stood up and coughed, self-importantly. Harriet's heart sank. She had seen them all whispering about something as they walked back. Please don't let her say they didn't want to go to the Minack Theatre. Harriet was longing to see it.

'Harriet, we've been talking amongst ourselves and we were wondering if that TV and video up there works.'

Harriet glanced up at the small TV built into the plastic casing behind Clive's seat. Clive had heard the question and leaned around. 'Of course it does, Mrs L. This is one of the best buses in our fleet. Not the biggest, but everything on it is in first-class working order. Including myself.'

Harriet saw Miss Talbot nudge Mrs Randall.

Mrs Lamerton reached into her bag. 'In that case, Harriet, would you mind if we watched "The Case of the Vanishing Vicar" as we make our way to the Minack Theatre? To familiarise ourselves?'

'Watch the whole episode? But it's only a few miles from here.'

'We could take the long way, couldn't we?' They'd obviously looked at the map. 'It would add to the whole experience to see it on video before we saw the real thing.'

Harriet couldn't say no.

It took Clive only a minute to get the video running. There was a cheer as the *Willoughby* theme tune started and the familiar sight of a man walking across the field appeared on screen.

'Patrick, it's you!' Mrs Kempton said happily.

'Can you turn it up, Clive?' Miss Boyd called out.

'Can we pull the curtains on the bus, Harriet?' Mr Fidock asked. 'It's a bit hard to see otherwise.'

Harriet knew from James's script that they were about to pass some of Cornwall's most beautiful coastline: coastal paths and towering cliffs, long sandy beaches and wind-ravaged trees. And they wanted to watch TV. 'Of course,' she said.

They drove into the car park of the Minack Theatre as the closing credits came up. No one had said a word for the past thirty minutes, gripped by the storyline. Clive had been driving at about five miles an hour. The volume had been turned up to maximum. Mrs Kempton grabbed Patrick's arm at several tense moments during the episode. It ended on another cliffhanger note – Willoughby looking down the barrel of a gun being held by the fugitive vicar, on the stage of the Minack Theatre. The scriptwriters had obviously specialised in cliffhanger endings. There were sighs as the credits started to roll.

'There's your name, Patrick!' Mrs Kempton said, pulling at his sleeve again.

Harriet leaned over and asked Clive to turn the video off. She reached for the microphone and started reading from James's script. '*Welcome to the Minack Theatre, everyone. As you're about to see, this outdoor theatre is truly one of the most beautiful theatre spaces in the world. Unfortunately we are here too early in the season to see any of the plays but come with me and stand among the carved stone seats, halt awhile and surely you will be able to hear the ghosts of actors past, calling out their lines, enchanting audiences old and young.*' Oh, shut up, James, Harriet thought crossly. She put down the script. 'If you'd all like to follow me, we'll begin our tour.'

Mrs Lamerton pulled back her curtain. 'But it's raining.'

'No, it's just a slight drizzle,' Harriet said.

Mrs Pollard was peering out of her window too. 'It's looks very windy. And we're on top of a cliff, aren't we? Isn't that dangerous?'

Harriet was surprised she'd noticed where they were. None of them had looked outside the bus for the past half hour. 'I promise you it's safe.'

'I think I'd feel safer in here,' Mrs Douglas said.

'Me too,' Mrs Kempton said. 'Clive, does the video work even if the bus isn't running?'

'It should do. What was happening at the end of that episode? All that shouting? I could hear it but not see it.'

'It was Reginald Camphor, the vanishing vicar. Willoughby tracked him down to the theatre, in the middle of one of the performances, and the vicar pulled out a gun. He's threatening to shoot Lady Garvan unless she tells him where she put the safe with all the diamonds.'

'Which one was Lady Garvan?'

'The aristocratic one,' Mrs Lamerton said.

'So who was the other female voice I heard?'

'That was Mrs Flanders, the elderly postmistress. Haven't you seen *Willoughby* before, Clive?' Mrs Lamerton took another cassette out of her large handbag. 'I've got the first episode here. "The Case of the Prodigal Postman". It's my favourite.' She put on a deep voice. '*There are some mornings when I wake up and see the blue of the sea and feel the freshness of the wind —*'

A chorus of voices joined in. '*And I know I'm home.*'

'Put that first episode on, Clive,' Mr Douglas called out.

'No, let's have part two of "The Case of the Vanishing Vicar",' his wife said. 'We can look at episode one on the way back to the hotel.'

'Yes, part two of the "Vanishing Vicar",' Mrs Lamerton said firmly. 'Hands up who agrees with that?'

Thirteen pairs of hands went up. Harriet was astonished. 'Does anyone want to come to the Minack Theatre?'

They all shook their heads.

'You seriously want to stay on the bus and watch videos?'

Mrs Lamerton had the grace to look a bit embarrassed. 'Would you mind, Harriet?'

Patrick stood up. 'Of course she wouldn't. Would any of you mind if Harriet and I went to look at the theatre while you were watching videos?'

Clive had already pressed play. Patch was barking in the background. Mrs Lamerton was looking at the screen as she answered. 'No. Take as long as you like.'

By the time Harriet and Patrick bought their tickets and walked down the steps to the amphitheatre, the light rain had stopped. There were three small tour groups roaming through it. Harriet stopped at the bottom of the steps. It was the most spectacular sight she'd seen on the trip.

It was a perfect amphitheatre, set into the side of a cliff, long rows of seats curving around a stone stage area. There was no backdrop, just the pure view of ocean and the coastline stretching for miles. The sky was dramatic, blue in parts, with huge billowing white and grey clouds darkening in the distance. Far below them was a curved beach, tucked into a cove. She could see a path winding down the cliffside to the sand.

Everything was in place for a theatre performance. A lighting area, a director's vantage point, even a separate higher stage for tower scenes. It was something from ancient Greece transported to modern Cornwall.

'Magnificent, isn't it?' Patrick said, beside her. He'd been watching her reaction.

'It's absolutely beautiful. Has it changed since you were here last?'

'All those centuries ago?' He smiled. 'No, except we almost have it to ourselves. It was overrun with crew and actors when we were here. It wasn't quite the same. It's better today.'

They made their way along one of the rows of seats, stopping in the centre. Celtic emblems were etched into the stone. Grass was growing on the footpaths between the seats. The sea was in front of them, blue and grey with flecks of white, reflecting the sky.

He took her hand as they sat down. It was a simple gesture but it sent a spark of desire through her.

'Talk to me, Harriet. If you won't let me kiss you in public, you have to talk to me instead. Tell me everything.'

She smiled at him. 'Where do I start?'

'With the bad news. How old are you?'

'I'm thirty-two.'

'And you're still single?'

She nodded.

'You're not pining for poor Simon?'

'No, I'm not.' She hesitated. Did she tell him all that had led to her splitting up with Simon? The anxiety attacks? The breakdown? She stayed with the simple truth. 'I broke it off with him. I realised I didn't love him enough.' She paused. 'And you, Patrick? Were you really married?'

'To poor Alicia and Caitlin, you mean?' A glimmer of a smile. 'No, Harriet, not to them. But I was married. For nine years. To an American woman. We were divorced nearly five years ago.'

'And do you have children?'

'One stepson. He lives in Boston. We see each other still. We're close. He's great.'

'And now? Are you with anyone now?' It felt important to ask all these questions.

He shook his head. 'I was seeing someone until about six months ago. But it wasn't working for either of us. It's been me and work since. Too much work, I think sometimes.'

'What do you do, Patrick? When you're not being Willoughby?'

'I haven't told you?'

She shook her head.

'No, you're right, I haven't. There always seemed to be better things to talk about. I run a casting agency. A different sort of actors' casting agency.'

'You're not an actor any more?'

'No, I haven't been for years. I was no good at it, and it was no good for me.'

'No good?'

'You saw it yourself. I had an attack of the nerves before every performance.'

She remembered the night of the cocktail party. She had thought the nerves he'd shown were just part of the process, a way of getting his adrenaline running. It had worked, too. He had been the perfect guest star that night.

'I decided it was my body telling me to give it up,' he said. 'That I wasn't good enough.'

'But you were good. I thought you were great in *Willoughby*. And you've been so good with all the group, too. They love you.'

He smiled. 'Thank you, Harriet. But it was more than being good or being bad. More than feeling nervous, too. It was a matter of choosing a different sort of life.'

'Tell me.'

'It's quite a long story.'

'I'd like to hear it. I'd love to hear it.'

'Really?' At her nod, he continued. He was still holding her hand. 'After *Willoughby* was axed, I went to America with an actor friend of mine. Two British actors planning to take over the world. I'd been offered that role in the terrible soap, the one I told you about, so I was set up immediately. I met my wife around that same time. She was a producer on the program. Then the show folded. She got another job very quickly, but I couldn't get any work for a long time. My father was a carpenter, and I'd helped him out when I was young, so I did that for a while, picking up work here and there. My friend got some acting roles, but things were fairly desperate for both of us career-wise. Then he saw an ad one day, for department store Santas. For a joke, he put both our names down. We got called in the next day and started there and then.'

'You were a Santa Claus? In one of those shop grottoes?'

He nodded, smiling. 'For one Christmas, at least. Or one holiday season, as we call it in America. The two of us, in our thirties, dressing up in full suits every day for eight hours. My friend thought it was ridiculous and gave it up after a month, but I needed the money. I wanted to be working, too. I found it fun, easy in fact, but the guy who replaced my friend didn't have a clue what to do. He asked me for tips. The manager of the chain of stores heard me passing on some actor's tricks – the simplest of things – but he asked me if I'd be interested in training some more of his Santas. I did that for the next two years, for three months of the year. Good money, great conditions. I didn't have to worry about getting nervous and I was still involved in acting, in an odd way. In a funny way.'

She could see from his expression that he still found it funny now. 'My friend said I'd taken the easy way out, that I'd given up on this quest the two of us had to break into America. That I obviously wasn't hungry enough for the good parts, that I should be more like him, suffering for my craft. My wife thought the same thing, I realised later. They were right. I didn't have that hunger. I did my Santa training and the carpentry for the rest of the year and earned enough money to keep things afloat. My friend went in the opposite direction. He took acting classes five days a week. He had his teeth done. He had an eye tuck. He worked out all the time. It became an obsession with him. All he wanted was to be a success.'

'But it didn't happen for him?'

'Oh yes, it did.' He named his friend.

Harriet's eyes opened wide. 'Him? But he's famous. Really famous.' She had seen two of his films in the past year. 'He won an Oscar, didn't he?'

'No, he was nominated, but he didn't win.'

'Were you jealous of him? Are you jealous now?'

'Never. Not for a minute.' He hesitated. 'It was my wife who was jealous. That's what she wanted for me. For us. But I couldn't hunger for something I didn't want. And I didn't want that life. I didn't want all the perfection and the pressure. I wanted to swim every day because I liked how it made me feel, not because it was good for muscle definition. And I liked acting when the roles were interesting or entertaining, or when the camaraderie was good, but I knew from my friend, from my own experience, that was rarely the case. My wife wanted me to push forward and I wanted to pull back. That's when it started to go bad between us. We separated at first and tried to work it out, but we couldn't. We got divorced a year later.'

'She didn't go on to marry your friend?'

He gave a soft laugh. 'Looking for a happy ending, Harriet? No. My friend is gay.'

'Gay? But I read about him in a magazine last month. He's seeing a French actress, isn't he?'

'No, he's not. You see, Harriet? See how seductive it is, how all pervasive it is? You, on the other side of the world, reading about a complete stranger, and all of it lies. I didn't want that kind of life. Not that there was ever any real possibility of me getting it, in any case. I kept doing what I was doing, the training, a bit of carpentry. And then I got asked to train extras for a family Christmas film that was being shot in Boston. The producer asked did I know of any more normal-looking people for some other crowd scenes he was doing. I asked around, put out the word and that's how it started. I decided to set up an agency for normal people who wanted to do some acting, not the ferocious Hollywood celebrity-style jobs or Shakespearian tragedies. Ordinary people who wanted some of the buzz, some of the fun.'

'What did you call it?'

'NPA. Eventually, anyway. My assistant thought up the name. She came to me about three years ago, wanting to be an extra. She said all her grandchildren said she looked like Whoopi Goldberg so she wanted all the roles Whoopi said no to. She gave that up when she realised it was more fun organising the extras than standing around being one all day. I'd called my business the North Pole Agency, when it was just the Santa training. She shortened it to NPA. The NP Agency. North Pole, Normal People.'

'That's very good.'

'She's full of ideas. We have two offices now. Things took off very quickly. I'm based in Boston. The other one's in California. We're small, but very busy.' He paused. 'And there it is, Harriet. My life.'

'And all true?'

'All true.' He smiled, looking almost shy. Something went straight to her heart. 'Your turn, Harriet. Tell me everything. I want to hear about your life in Australia. About your family. About everything you've ever done.'

'I've nothing to compare to that.'

'Start with the small things, then. Can you ride a bike? Have you ever surfed? What's your favourite meal? Do you speak any other languages? What book would you take to a desert island? Can you dance? Do you like horses? Can you recognise the flags of at least twenty countries?'

She was laughing.

'I'm serious, Harriet. I want to know all those things about you. At least throw me a scrap today to keep me happy.'

She thought of something. She reached into her bag and took out Gloria's list. She didn't say anything, just handed it to him.

He took the envelope and at her prompting, opened it and unfolded the piece of paper inside. He started reading it, softly. *'I have worked and supported myself for more than fifteen years. I am buying my own flat. I have travelled all around Australia. I have led hundreds of tour groups. I can touch type. I know how to cook Thai food, Italian food and Malaysian food, make jam, chutney, and tomato sauce. I have grown my own tomatoes, sweet corn, parsley, coriander and pumpkins. I once made dinner for ten people on a camp fire. I can drive a car and a tractor . . .'*

As he kept reading, she heard him laugh quietly once or twice. He came to the end and smiled at her. 'I thought you were one of the most organised people I'd ever met, but this takes the cake. You carry it around just in case someone asks you about yourself?'

'No.' Should she tell him why she had that list? She wanted to, she realised. 'I had a nervous breakdown last year. After my parents died, one after the other. A good friend of mine wrote that for me, to remind me of the things I could do before it happened.'

'Your parents died?'

'Within two months of each other.'

'Oh, Harriet. That must have been hard.'

'It was very hard.'

'Did that bracelet belong to your mother?'

She was startled. 'How did you know that?'

'You touch it whenever you seem worried about something, I've noticed in the past few days. I thought it was either a good luck charm or it meant a lot to you.'

'It means a lot to me. My father gave it to her when they first arrived in Australia, after they emigrated from England.'

'You're English?'

'My two brothers are. I was born in Australia.'

'You're close to them, by the sound of things. Has that helped?'

'In some ways.'

He took her hand again. He held it between both of his. 'Tell me about your breakdown.'

It felt easy to tell him. Straightforward. As they sat close beside one another in the open air, looking out over the cliffs and the sea, she told him what had happened, describing her parents' deaths, the anxiety attacks, the tour in the Flinders Ranges, Austin coming to get her, the three weeks in hospital afterwards. He listened, asked questions, taking it all in. When she finished, he lifted her hand and kissed her palm. He read the list again, in a different way this time. More seriously.

'What does it mean "you welcomed Lara into the family"? Is that the Lara who sent the fax to me?'

Harriet nodded. 'She came to live with us when she was eight. After her parents were killed in a car crash.'

'She's your foster-sister?'

She nodded.

'And you get on?'

She couldn't answer that. It was too complicated. She nodded instead. He read the list again, then folded it very carefully and gave it back to her.

'I'm sorry, Harriet. About your parents. About the break-down.'

She didn't want to talk about herself any more. Not yet. Not here. 'I'm getting better. I am better, I think.'

'I think you're better than better.'

She reached up and kissed him. A quick, deep kiss. She saw his eyes darken.

'You shouldn't do that to me in public. I'm having enough trouble staying away from you as it is.'

'I'm sorry.'

'So am I. It's very hard to steal a kiss when there are twelve pairs of seventy-year-old eyes watching my every move.'

She told him about her conversation with Mrs Lamerton that morning. The mood lightened again.

He laughed. 'Then it's time we brought it out into the open. I'll make an announcement. "Ladies and gentlemen, I'm sorry to call off the tour but I've fallen in love with Harriet and we want to be on our own, so if you could all make your own way home . . ."'

'You haven't fallen in love with me. Not in four days.'

She was expecting another joke, but his face was serious. 'Haven't I? What is it then? What do I call the feeling I get when I see you? The way you laugh so easily, the way you make me laugh?

The way I feel when I watch you with the group, the way you look after them? The way you look after me? The way I feel when I kiss you? You delight me, Harriet. I've fallen in delight with you.' He paused. 'But not your yellow suit. I still don't like that.'

She laughed.

'Finish that game you were playing the other night when my assistant rang, Harriet. The question and answer one.'

'No. It's for teenagers, really. It's a silly party game.'

'Please. Finish it. There were two more questions, weren't there?'

'Yes.'

'Ask me.'

She tried to sound casual. 'The third one is about water.'

'I need to tell you how I feel when I think of water?'

She nodded.

'Let me think.' He held her hand against his lips. His breath was warm against her skin. She felt a response deep inside her again. 'I feel overwhelmed. Out of my depth. Uncertain, but also excited. Thirsty. You make me think of water, Harriet. Why would that be? Why would I think of water whenever I see you?'

She felt her heart beating. 'I'm not sure.'

'And the final question?'

'Your favourite animal.' Your ideal partner.

'My favourite animal,' he repeated. 'It's yellow, though not always, fortunately. Beautiful. It likes to travel. I think it's from the southern hemisphere.'

She pulled her hand away. 'You know this game, don't you? You knew it the whole time?'

He smiled. 'Of course. Everyone knows that game. What was it I said about water? I've forgotten.'

'You said it overwhelmed you. Made you feel out of your depth. Excited. Thirsty. And you said that I make you think of water.'

'I'm sorry, Harriet. That's not true. You don't make me think of water. You make me think of something else.' He whispered in her ear. Desire rushed through her again.

He leaned back. His tone was light, but she knew he was serious. 'What would you say if I asked you those questions, Harriet?'

'I wouldn't answer them.'

'No?'

'I'd tell you in a different way.'

'What would you tell me?'

'The truth.' She felt certain of it. 'That I've never felt like this with someone before. That you delight me too. That I think I've fallen in delight with you too.'

A group of tourists came down the steps behind them. Patrick stood up, drawing her up beside him. 'There's a path down to the beach. Do you suppose we could leave them in that bus for longer?'

Harriet checked her watch. 'There's only ten minutes of that episode left to go.'

'Then we'll have to hurry.'

The path was long and steep. They had barely reached the sand when he took her in his arms and pulled her against him. The kiss was different than the night before. This was hard, passionate, urgent. She felt it. She wanted to make love to him right there, and she knew he wanted her, too.

They had the beach to themselves. There was an outcrop of rocks to one side, almost a cave. From above they were hidden from view. The only noise was the waves crashing against the sand, the shrill cries of seagulls. They didn't speak. He took her in his arms again when they reached the rocks. The kisses deepened. Her desire was overwhelming. She was nearly in ecstasy from the touch of his fingers under her shirt, on her skin, on her breast. Her eyes were shut, his lips on her neck. The feeling was building, wave after wave.

'Harriet, I won't be able to stop soon.' His voice was heavy with desire.

'I don't want you to.'

They were moments from taking the next step, from forgetting where they were, when she heard her name being called. She stepped back from him, feeling half-drugged.

She wasn't imagining it. Someone was calling her name. More than one person. From high above them.

'Harriet? Are you down there?'

She came out onto the sand, away from the rocks and looked up. It was Clive, Mrs Lamerton and a man who looked like Mr Douglas, but could have been Mr Fidock.

She only just made out their words. 'Harriet, we need your help.'

'What is it? What's wrong?'

Mrs Lamerton's voice floated down, very clearly. 'The tape's jammed.'

Back in St Ives later that night, the hotel was quiet. Mr Fidock and Mr Douglas were in the bar. Several of the ladies were in the lounge area, playing cards. Others had gone to their rooms.

The whole group had ended up spending the evening together again, visiting an Italian restaurant on the waterfront for dinner and then moving on to the nautical pub. There had been an impromptu *Willoughby* quiz. Mr Fidock and Mr Douglas put on a five minute mini-play, stringing all their favourite pieces of dialogue together. It hadn't mattered to Harriet and Patrick that they weren't on their own. Even across the crowded room, it was as though they were linked.

They'd had a drink in the hotel bar with everyone when they returned. More talking, laughing. Around eleven he glanced at her. A question in his eyes. She nodded, the faintest of gestures. He left first, saying goodnight to each of the group. Twenty minutes later, Harriet followed. Mrs Lamerton was in deep conversation with Miss Boyd about the episode they'd watched that day. She showed no interest in doing any following that night.

Harriet went via her room. She quickly checked her appearance. No sign of the yellow outfit tonight, either. Just a simple, wraparound dress, dark red, worn with a soft cardigan. Only the opal bracelet for jewellery. Several of the women in the group had complimented her.

'You look so pretty,' Mrs Kempton said. Mrs Randall had nodded her head in agreement.

'Those colours are lovely on you,' Miss Talbot added. 'It makes those beautiful dark eyes of yours look all sparkly. Or is that a make-up trick again? Would you show me?'

It wasn't the make-up making her eyes sparkle. She felt alive again, she realised. The desire for Patrick, to be with him, touch him, talk to him, was giving her a confidence and a kind of joy she hadn't felt for a long time.

She knocked gently at his door and he answered. Barely a word was spoken before she moved into his arms and felt his lips on hers. They weren't in public. There was no one hammering on the door. They had talked about things she needed to hear. It had only been a short time, but she knew this was what she wanted to do, where she wanted to be, how she wanted to feel, who she wanted to be with. After months of indecision and fear and nervousness, it was overwhelming to feel so sure of something.

He kissed her lips, her neck, lower. He slowly undressed her, caressing her body, gazing down at her. She undressed him. They didn't speak. The kisses became more urgent and passionate. They moved into the bedroom and lay entwined, skin against skin. She could feel the strength of his body against her, his fingers stroking her and then the feel of him inside her. She wrapped her legs around his body, arching herself against him. She felt him hard and fast, the movement so perfect, so close and so beautiful. She held him tight, as tight as she could against her and inside her, waves of intense pleasure rippling through both of them, together.

She lay in his arms afterwards, his fingers caressing her back. She turned and looked at his face on the pillow beside her. His eyes were closed. She traced his features, touched the dark curls, the grey at the temples. She moved her hand onto his shoulder, his chest, placed her palm on his skin. She moved closer and kissed him. His eyes opened. She saw the blue of them again. She put her finger on his lips then leaned forward again and kissed him once more.

'Thank you.'

His lips curved into a smile. 'You're very welcome. Thank you, too.'

She closed her eyes, feeling him breathing under her cheek, the beating of his heart.

He touched the side of her face and then leaned over and kissed her lips. She kissed him back. He spoke, his mouth close against her ear. 'Harriet, how many of your company rules have we broken tonight?'

'So far?'

She felt his smile. 'Yes, so far.'

'Two at least. But I think they only count if I'm wearing yellow.'

He kissed her again. 'So if you're not wearing yellow I can do this any time I like?'

She was all sensation again. 'Yes, you can.'

'Would you do something for me?' His lips moved to her neck, then up to her ear.

She waited.

He whispered the words. 'Could you burn every piece of yellow clothing you own?'

CHAPTER TWENTY-SIX

Austin and Nina had arrived at Cork Airport in the early afternoon. There was a lot of building work going on, cranes and bulldozers surrounding the small terminal. As the two of them climbed into a taxi outside, they could see half the sky was blue, but the half they were standing under was filled with heavy grey clouds, dumping sheets of rain on them. The weather was getting wild all over the UK and Ireland. It had been a turbulent flight. There had even been talk at Bristol Airport of flights being grounded until the storms passed.

'To the city centre, thanks,' Austin told the driver.

'Anywhere special?' the man asked. Austin noticed the sing-song accent, as he tried to decide. He and Nina had talked about it on the plane. Should they go straight to a police station? Or find a place to stay for the night and then start looking?

They decided to go to a hotel first. The taxi driver recommended one overlooking the river in the centre of town. He'd drop them right to it.

Nina was quiet on the journey in. Austin was glad of it, touched by her thoughtfulness. He had that feeling again, that he was rushing forward too quickly. These bold gestures were all very well, but why did he keep feeling foolish, out of his depth? He needed to stop, think it over again. What if they did find Lara in Cork? And what if she was in pieces? He had been able to handle Harriet on her Flinders Ranges tour, but would he cope with Lara in crisis?

They checked in to the hotel. It was clean, serviceable. All they needed for the reason they were here. Austin left his bag on the bed and returned to the foyer to wait for Nina. He stared out the window, at the river running through the city, the houses clustered on the hill above the city centre, out to green hills beyond. He felt a touch on his arm.

'Do you want to get a coffee first?' Nina asked. 'Before we get started?'

It was a good idea. They left the hotel, walked out along the river into the centre of the city and into a pub with a coloured stone front. Nina ordered two coffees. Austin caught himself looking at the crowds walking past the window.

'You're expecting to see her?'

He nodded, embarrassed. 'Mad, isn't it? Even if she did come here, she might have left already. She could have hired a car, driven anywhere.'

'She might have, but she might also be here still. Will we ring around to a few of the hotels and B&Bs? Ask if they've had a Lara Robinson staying? Someone might remember her.'

Austin had the weirdest feeling they were talking about her in the past tense. 'She's fine. I know she is.'

'Of course she is.'

They were both quiet, sipping their coffee. 'Austin, why didn't Lara ever change her surname to Turner?'

'Mum and Dad never officially adopted her. They were her legal guardians, but I think they thought it would be too traumatic if she had to go through the whole adoption process, talking about her parents. She called my mum and dad her guardian angels.'

'That's nice.'

'She loved them a lot.'

'Was it hard on Harriet, your other sister?'

'When Lara arrived? No, I think she thought it was great. Like getting an instant sister.'

'I'd find it hard.'

'Would you?'

'Well, if you'd been the littlest, the only girl, and suddenly you had to share the position with another girl.'

'I never thought about it like that.'

After coffee, they stopped at a shop to buy two umbrellas. The rain was coming down in sheets now, yet there was still a tantalising patch of blue on the horizon. Taunting them, Austin thought. He walked along a pedestrianised street, dodging tourists and shoppers, taking in the Irish names and lettering above the shops, pointing some out to Nina. He heard several different languages being spoken. A newspaper seller's cry kept echoing through the air. They had walked down two streets when she stopped him, putting her hand on his arm.

'Austin, we're not going to find her like this. We need to look properly. Have a plan. Let's go to the police.'

'They won't be interested. She left voluntarily. There's nothing they can do.'

'They'd have records of car crashes, though, wouldn't they? Maybe that's what Lara did, flew in here, found out from the police where her parents were killed and made her way there. So we have to copy her.'

'Follow in her footsteps?'

A glimmer of her smile. 'Like all good TV detectives. Come on.'

The main police station was easy to find, down from the city hall, away from the river. A modern building, the foyer was big and airy, an atrium filled with light and marble pillars. The policeman behind the desk was in his mid-twenties, red-cheeked, sweet-faced.

Austin introduced himself and Nina. 'We're looking for my sister. She flew to Cork four days ago and we're trying to find her.'

'You're reporting a missing person?'

'Not exactly. She left voluntarily. We don't know for sure where she is.' He explained about Lara's parents being killed in a car crash. 'We don't know where, but we think it might have been here in Cork somewhere. Would you have details of accidents going back more than twenty years?'

'We would, but you'd have to put in an application to get the files. That could take a week or more. Unless one of the people here remembered the case. I could ask if you like?'

'Would you? That would be a real help. We're short on time.'

'Can you give me more details? The names and the dates?'

'Their surname was Robinson. Rose and . . .' Austin stopped, thinking hard. 'Sorry, I can't remember her father's name. It was around the middle of March, twenty-four years ago.'

'They hit another car, or was it a single vehicle incident?'

Austin had a flash of their car hurtling off the road after hitting a patch of gravel, before realising he was thinking of the story Harriet had written for her school magazine. 'I'm sorry, I don't know.'

They waited as the young man made a phone call and repeated the details to someone. Austin had to stop himself from leaning over the counter and taking the phone himself. Nina put her hand on his arm. He relaxed.

The man hung up and shook his head. 'I'm sorry, it's not ringing bells with anyone. But that doesn't mean it didn't happen around here. Have you tried the newspaper office down the road? It would have made the news, especially the fact it was tourists. It's not far, if you want to give them a try.'

The rain had slowed to a light drizzle by the time they reached the newspaper office, a glass-fronted building, with a row of framed front pages along the outside wall. Austin pushed open the door, letting Nina go in first.

A middle-aged woman was dusting the counter as they came in. Austin explained what they were looking for.

'Oh, I'm sorry, I can't help you there,' she said. 'We only keep six months worth of back issues here. The city library has them all on microfilm and hard copy, though.'

'It's like a treasure hunt,' Nina said as they walked outside again.

Not quite, Austin thought.

The Cork City Library was on Grand Parade, two blocks away. Austin and Nina were directed upstairs to the local history section. The room was lit by fluorescent lights and lined with glass-fronted cabinets filled with old books. There were several wooden tables, chairs, and a photocopy machine. A doorway led to another room filled with racks of shelving, each shelf holding rows of black folders. The man behind the counter listened as Austin explained once more what they were looking for.

'We should be able to help you. There are two local papers, *The Examiner* and the *Southern Star*, which covers the Clonakilty and Skibbereen area, west of here. From twenty years ago, did you say? Can you be more exact with the date?'

'Middle of March, twenty-four years ago.'

The librarian was back five minutes later with a large black folder, holding the newspapers from March and April of that year. Austin and Nina followed him across the room to a table.

'Let me know if that's not the one you want. We've got decades worth you can look through.'

'Thanks,' Austin said. He and Nina pulled their chairs close to the table, turned the heavy cardboard cover and started leafing through the pages.

They found it in the sixth newspaper they opened. Austin knew it was Lara's parents as soon as he saw the headline on the top of page three. It was all there. The names. The right date. The right location.

'Oh my God,' Nina breathed.

Austin reached for her hand without thinking. He held it tightly as they both stared at the page.

Tourists found dead in family tragedy

An Australian couple was found dead in a holiday cottage outside Clonakilty yesterday in what gardai described as 'a terrible family tragedy'.

The bodies of Dennis Robinson (38) and his wife Rose (35) from Melbourne, Victoria, were discovered when the cottage owner called to the house shortly after 8.30 a.m. It is believed they may have been dead for up to two days.

Gardai said Mr Robinson had stab wounds to the chest and abdomen. The cause of his wife's death is not yet known, but foul play is not suspected.

Although still trying to establish what happened in the hours leading up to the deaths gardai have confirmed they are not seeking anyone else.

'At this stage it has the appearance of a terrible family tragedy,' a spokesman said.

The state pathologist carried out a preliminary examination at the scene yesterday morning. Later, the bodies were removed to Cork Regional Hospital where a further post-mortem examination is due to be carried out today.

The cottage owner, Mrs Flor O'Regan, who lives nearby, said she was 'completely shocked' by the discovery. She called to the house because she had not seen the couple for two days, she said.

'They booked the cottage for a week and arrived four days ago,' Mrs O'Regan added. 'They said they'd been in England before coming here.

'The woman mentioned she had Irish connections – her mother or grandmother, I think – but I don't know if she had any relatives still living in this country.

'It's hard to understand how something like this could happen. It's tragic.'

'Austin, it's a nightmare.' Nina was very shocked. 'Are you sure it's them?'

'It has to be. The same names. The right dates.' He read it again. 'It's them.'

'It's not an awful coincidence? Another couple with the same name?'

'It's them,' he repeated. He knew right then that Lara had discovered this too.

'But I don't understand it. Why would Lara have been told they'd died in a car crash?'

'I don't know.'

'And what does it mean foul play wasn't suspected? They were both found dead, weren't they? Doesn't that count as foul play?'

Austin shook his head, pointing at the page. 'He had stab wounds. The cause of her death was still to be confirmed, yet the police aren't looking for anyone else. It means . . .'

Nina stared at the newspaper. 'It means Lara's mother killed Lara's father and then she killed herself.'

Austin nodded. He read the article again. 'It doesn't say how, just that tests were being carried out. It must have been an overdose of something. Any other method would have been obvious.'

'Oh my God, Austin.' She turned away from the article. 'Do you think Lara has seen this too? That this is why she disappeared?'

'It must be.' Had she done just as they had? Come here, looked up the newspapers? Or rung the police? He had an awful image of her, innocently going into a police station or this room, wanting to know the location of her parents' car crash, doing it privately, without letting any of them know. And then discovering this, as they had. But on her own.

Nina turned to him. 'What do we do now?'

'We ring Gloria,' he said.

An hour later they were both in Austin's hotel room, sitting side by side on his bed, a copy of the newspaper article between them. Austin had started to dial Gloria's number before realising it was the middle of the night in Australia. This was urgent, but it would have to wait. He was counting down the minutes.

'Austin, shouldn't you ring the rest of your family?' Nina said. 'Your sister? Your brother?'

He knew he should, but he didn't want to. Not yet. He needed to talk to Gloria before any of them. She had been his mother's best friend. She might be able to shed even the smallest amount of light on all of this.

'I want to talk to Gloria first.' He checked the time again. Still too early. But only just. His mind was racing through all they had learned. He turned to Nina again. 'What would you do next if you were Lara, Nina? If you'd somehow found all this out?'

She thought about it. 'I'd go to the holiday cottage,' she said.

'To the house?' His horror must have shown on his face.

'You'd need to. It would be something you'd have to do. I would, anyway.'

It took just a few phone calls to find out where the house was. They started with *The Examiner* office. The reporter who had written the article had long retired. They were advised to ring the *Southern Star*, the local Clonakilty paper. The news editor at the *Southern Star* knew of the story, but hadn't been working there at the time. He suggested they ring the local gardai. The garda who answered said yes, he did know the house. Someone else had been in asking about it a few days before, in fact.

Austin went still. 'An Australian woman?'

'Yes.'

Austin took down the name of the house. It was now called Glen View. It had changed names, and owners, several times in the past twenty-four years. The garda said he thought a German couple owned it now. A local property company managed the holiday rentals.

Austin got the after-hours phone number of the property company from directory inquiries. He hesitated before dialling it. 'Lara might be gone already, mightn't she? She might have had a look at the house and driven away. She could be back in England by now. In Australia, even. Maybe it would be better if we just had a quick look ourselves and then went back to Bath, in case she —'

Nina interrupted. 'Austin, I need to say something to you. I don't think it should be me here. I think it should be you and your sister. You have to ring her. The two of you should be doing this together.'

He still didn't want to ring Harriet. Not yet. 'Let me ring this number first. See what I can find out.' He dialled the number. 'Oh, hello there.' He exaggerated his Australian accent, ignoring Nina's surprised look. 'I wonder if you can help me. My little sister's over here travelling around Ireland on holiday and I'm trying to track her down to give her a surprise. Has she been in to your office to enquire about holiday properties by any chance? Her name's Lara. Lara Robinson.'

He waited. Nina sat still beside him.

'Two days ago. Brilliant. Right. Yes please.' He grabbed a piece of paper and started scribbling down directions. 'Thanks for your help. No, it's a big surprise, so please don't tell her I'm coming if she happens to get in touch. Bye.'

The cheery tone disappeared as soon as he hung up. 'Lara's there. She's rented Glen View.'

Chapter Twenty-seven

In Merryn Bay, Gloria was lying in bed, wide awake, waiting for the alarm clock to go off. Kevin was snoring quietly beside her. She'd had barely any sleep. She'd been too shocked and too angry to sleep. But the decision had been made. She was resigning from Turner Travel. As soon as Melissa got back from Melbourne.

She and Kevin had spent the evening talking about it. After she had hung up from Matheson Travel for the second time, she had moved into action. She had closed Turner Travel early, putting on the answering machine, pulling down the blind and locking the door. She'd practically run home and bundled Kevin into the car before he had a chance to protest.

She'd driven to another seaside town further down the coast, to their favourite restaurant. It was a small Italian trattoria, with red and white checked tablecloths, straw-covered chianti bottles, and a simple menu of pasta and pizza. They loved it. They felt comfortable and the food was always delicious. It was where they had gone over the years whenever they had something to discuss or to celebrate, either themselves or with their three boys. They hadn't been there since Kevin had gone blind.

Gloria barely let him get a word in at first, veering between disbelief and anger, going over and over her conversation with the people from Matheson Travel.

'You're sure you're not mistaken,' Kevin asked. 'Would she actually do something like that?'

'Of course she'd do it. She'd sell Molly if she was offered a good price. Can you believe it, Kev? She must have thought all her Christmases had come at once when Harriet had to leave on the *Willoughby* tour. All the Turners out of the way.'

'You don't think James knows?

'I haven't a clue. She walks all over him. Perhaps he knows and she's sworn him to secrecy. She probably broke his leg for him, so he'd be out of the way as well.'

'You a little bit angry about this, love?'

'I'm furious, Kev. Years of service and this is how she repays me. Sneaking around behind my back.'

'Is that it really?'

She stopped, and took a breath. 'No, it's not. That's not what it is. You're right. I've been well-paid. It's a job. It's not about being repaid. It's about not being told beforehand. It's the final straw.'

'For who? You or the Turner kids?'

She gave a half-smile. 'That's it, isn't it? I'm angry but on whose behalf any more? Whether James knows yet or not is immaterial. He agrees with everything Melissa does anyway. Austin doesn't care about the business and I don't know if he ever really did. I don't know for sure if this is where Harriet wants to be or should be any more. I think Lara needs to spread her wings. Going to England was part of it, I'm sure.' She shook her head. 'Listen to me, Kev. I probably know more about the Turner children than I do about our own boys.'

'That's not true.'

'No, it isn't. But it nearly is. I'm going to resign.'

'You're over-reacting.'

'No, I'm not. I'm tired, Kev. I want to stay home with you.' She leaned across and tightly gripped his hand. She could feel all the years of physical work in the rough skin, the strength in his fingers. Just thinking of the idea of him being taken away from her, as Neil had been from Penny. All the regret she would feel, that they hadn't done the things they'd been planning and talking about for years. It was going to be up to her to make those things happen, she realised. She had forced Kev into coming to this restaurant tonight because she had been so angry she wouldn't take no for an answer. Look what had happened. He'd thoroughly enjoyed himself. No one had taken any notice of them. He had spilt only one thing, and so what? There were worse things in the world than a blind man spilling a bit of soup on a tablecloth. Tonight was the start of their new life, she decided. They were going to go and do whatever they wanted, whenever they wanted. The two of them.

'You've been too quiet for too long,' he said. 'I can hear your mind ticking from here. You know that makes me nervous.'

'I'm hatching a few plans, now you mention it.'

'Let me guess. You're going to stay at home and watch me for hours every day? Not let me out of your sight?'

'That's it.'

'Be a bit boring for you, won't it?'

'Yes. So you better start learning a few tricks.'

'I've always wanted to try juggling or fire-eating.'

'Perfect,' she said, knowing he would hear the smile in her voice. 'We'll sit around to begin with. Just so we get to know each other again. But it's time we starting doing more stuff together, too. Not just around the house, either. I think we should take a few trips. Just get in the car and head off somewhere.'

'Like where?'

'I don't know. Up the coast to Queensland. Take the ferry to

Tasmania, drive around there for a couple of weeks. We could even drive over to Perth if we wanted to.'

'That all sounds pretty good.'

'You think so? Good.'

'There's just one big problem, though.'

'What's that, love?'

'I'm not sure I can do my share of the driving.'

She was suddenly laughing and crying at the same time. 'I don't mind, Kev. I don't mind one bit.'

It had been after one by the time they got home. They had lain in bed talking for another hour. Gloria checked the time now. Nearly six. She might as well get up. She switched off the alarm before it sounded. She'd get ready for work and then make Kev's tea. She wished Melissa was going to be in the office today. She was in the mood for a showdown.

She had just filled the kettle when the sound of the phone ringing made her jump. She snatched it up quickly before the noise woke Kev.

'Gloria, it's Austin. How are things?'

He'd barely given her time to say hello. How were things? Where did she start? She had found out Melissa was selling the business from under them, she had decided to resign and she'd been up all night talking about it. 'There's been a fair bit going on over here, Austin, to tell you the truth.'

He wasn't listening. 'Gloria, I'm in Cork. We've been looking at the newspapers. We've found out what happened and it's terrible. Lara's parents weren't killed in a car crash. It was a murder–suicide. Lara's mother killed her father, and then killed herself.'

Gloria couldn't answer. She'd waited twenty-four years to hear someone else say it and now the day had come she felt no relief, no sadness. She just felt numb.

'Gloria? Did you hear what I said?'

'Yes, Austin, I did.'

'Aren't you shocked?'

'No, I'm not.' She had no reason to be shocked. She realised what she felt was complete and overwhelming exhaustion.

'You're not? Why not?'

'Because I already knew.'

'You *knew*? You knew the car crash never happened?'

At last she didn't have to pretend. 'Yes, I did. I've known for twenty-four years.' She waited for the flare of temper. He didn't disappoint her.

'I can't believe this. We've been looking for her, worrying about her and you knew the whole time? Knew Cork was probably where she was going? That this was what she was going to find out? And you said *nothing*?'

'I made a promise to your mother.'

He raised his voice. 'For Christ's sake, Gloria. My mother is dead. How could you do this to Lara?'

Twenty-four years of anger welled in Gloria. How dare he talk to her like that? How dare he sound so self-righteous? She'd had enough.

'How could I do this to Lara?' Her voice was as loud as his. 'How could your mother do this to me? Do you think I wanted to be the secret keeper? The one who knew? Of course I didn't. How do you think it has been for me, Austin? It was your family, your secret. I never wanted to know, back then, or even now. I loved your parents, and I love all of you children, but I didn't want this. I never wanted it. And don't you ever, *ever* talk to me like that again.'

'I'm sorry.'

She was beyond apologies. 'You need to be more than sorry. If you stopped thinking about yourself and your own selfish charmed life for one moment, and looked out into the world occasionally, Austin Turner, then you'd have the right to talk to me like this. But you don't. So you have no right to question my relationship with your mother and you have no right to tell me what I should or shouldn't have said to you, to Lara, or to anyone. It was your mother who made the decision, Austin. She decided to change the story that night. She did it to protect Lara. She thought she was too young to hear something so terrible. That it would change the way people would treat her in Merryn Bay. And perhaps she was right, perhaps she was wrong. I don't know. All I know is I have hated knowing all these years and I still hate it.'

There was a shocked silence. 'Gloria, are you all right?'

'No, Austin. I'm not all right.'

'I'm sorry, Gloria, I'm really sorry.' A long pause. 'I'm sorry.'

There was a long silence and then Gloria spoke again. 'Tell me. What did you find out? And how?'

He told her, in a subdued voice. Gloria didn't interrupt. There was nothing she hadn't already known, nothing Penny hadn't told her that night. She knew some extra details, in fact. She knew Lara's mother had lain down next to her husband's dead body after she had taken the pills. She had been found wrapped around him, holding on to him. There was a bottle of vodka beside them. Her blood alcohol level had been at a dangerous level. The police hadn't known whether she had drunk the vodka before she killed her husband or afterwards. Gloria kept those details to herself. Austin had no need to hear them now, if ever.

'Lara must have learnt all this too, mustn't she?' Austin said. 'If we found it, she must have too.'

'I think so, yes.'

'How would she have known where to look? Had Mum told her anything?'

'I know she told her the crash happened near Cork. That would have been enough to start with. Had she been at the library, too?'

'We asked the librarian. He hadn't seen her. She might have found out some other way. The police, perhaps. Gloria, it's horrible.'

'Yes, it is.'

'What will this have done to her?'

'I don't know.' She had calmed down a little. 'I hoped at first when she went missing that it was something else. Then when you rang and said you'd found out she'd gone to Ireland, I knew she must have discovered the truth.'

'She must be so angry. So hurt. She probably thinks we knew all this time and none of us ever told her. That's even worse. It would explain so much. Why she left so suddenly. Why she left the tour. Left Harriet like that. That's why I knew it had to be something bad. She wouldn't have done that to Harriet otherwise.'

Gloria felt the exhaustion again. 'Austin, did you know that Lara and Harriet have barely spoken in the past three months?'

'They haven't? But they're so close. They grew up together. Have they had a fight?'

'Are they close? I've never really known. But yes, I think they have had a fight.' Once upon a time she would have kept her observation to herself. Now she wanted to unload every Turner secret she had. 'Something happened with your mother's death. I don't know what. Something that upset Harriet terribly.'

'She wasn't there when Mum died, I know that. Or Dad. But she came to terms with it, didn't she? And is it important right now?'

'Yes, it is. It's another fact about your family. Or is this how it will always be with you all? Hiding things, not saying anything and then suffering the consequences after?'

'Gloria, I'm sorry, but I don't know what you're talking about.'

She felt the wave of tiredness again. 'It's all right, Austin. I don't know either.'

'What do I do about Lara, Gloria? Do I go to the house? To Glen View?'

Her head was hurting. She felt like she had spent more time over the years worrying about the Turners than about her own family. She massaged her temples, trying to concentrate. 'I don't know, Austin.'

'I think I should. And I think Harriet should be there too. That feels like the right thing to do. So Lara knows we care about her.'

'Then that's what you should do.'

'But what do I say to her, Gloria?'

It was simple, at last. 'You tell her the truth, Austin. You tell her that you love her. That we all love her. And that we're sorry. For everything.'

She said goodbye then. There was nothing else to say. She had just hung up and leaned back against the chair, shutting her eyes, when she heard a noise and felt a hand on her shoulder. She turned.

It was Kevin. 'You want to tell me what that was all about, love?'

In Cork, Nina was hearing no arguments. 'Now, Austin. You ring your sister now.'

'It's a bit late. I don't know if I should.'

'Austin, ring her. You can't keep something like this to yourself any longer. Your whole family has to know.'

He tried Harriet's mobile number. It was switched to voicemail. He was about to speak when he hung up. 'I can't leave a message.

It's going to be hard enough as it is telling her news like this over the phone.'

'Then leave a message asking her to ring you back.'

'I'll try her tomorrow.'

'Why not now?'

It was complicated. He was worried news like this might tip Harriet over the edge again. But Nina was right about the whole family needing to know. He already had the other number he needed from the time he'd rung the hospital the night Lara went missing. It was early, but hospitals started early. He dialled and was put straight through this time.

'James, it's Austin. I'm sorry if I woke you up.'

'Austin? You didn't, don't worry. Have you got news on Lara?'

'I have. It's not good news, either.' Austin told him everything.

James was silent for a time. Then he spoke. 'Shit, Austin. You don't think she's gone there to kill herself too, do you?'

James had said out loud what Austin was thinking. 'I don't know. Maybe. That's why I want to get there as soon as I can.'

'You're going on your own? What about Harriet? Wouldn't it be better if you were both there?'

'Of course it would. I've tried her phone but I just got voicemail. You don't know where she'd be at the moment, do you? Is there another number for her I could try?'

'Hold on, I've got the itinerary here.' Austin heard a rustling of paper. 'They've had a free evening. Tomorrow's the last day of the tour. They're doing a quick trip to Marazion to see St Michael's Mount, then it's their farewell lunch. Mrs Lamerton's organised a *Willoughby* quiz for that, I think. And Mrs Kempton's got a Patch jumper that she's going to give Patrick Shawcross.'

Austin shut his eyes. Spare me the details, James.

James was still reading. 'After lunch they go by bus to Bath to link up with the other tour company for the *All Creatures Great and Small* and *Monarch of the Glen* tours. Harriet drops Patrick Shawcross at Bristol Airport so he can fly back to Boston and then she'll be free for a week. She could get to you in the afternoon. Could it wait till then?'

Austin ran his fingers through his hair. How the hell did he know? Was Lara at this moment getting ready to kill herself? Had she already done it? 'I don't know. How would you react if you found out something like this, James? If it had been our parents?'

James fell quiet again. 'I'd be shocked. Horrified. Angry. But Austin, I can also see why Mum would have kept it secret. Do you remember it all happened so quickly? Mum told us about Mr and Mrs Robinson being killed and then Lara was living with us the next day. I can see why Mum might have said something like that to begin with. What I can't understand is why she didn't tell Lara the truth when she was older.' He answered his own query. 'Though where would you start? When would you decide it was the right age to tell someone something like that. The poor kid.'

Not kid. Lara was thirty-two. But then so was Harriet, and Austin still thought of her as a kid. He was still puzzling over what Gloria had said about the relationship being tricky between Harriet and Lara. He didn't think it was true. They had always been best of friends, hadn't they? There must have been a few spats – he remembered Harriet storming off once or twice, but she had gone through a storming off phase for a few years. Was it because of Lara, though? He needed to talk about it. 'James, what did you think when Lara came to live with us?'

'I liked her. I've always liked her. She's my sister as far as I'm concerned. She's a brilliant tour guide too.'

'She didn't change your life?'

'Change it? In what way?'

'Affect you? Bother you?'

'No, it was just good to have another sister. It made it easier to play some of those games, with four of us instead of three. I suppose if it affected anyone, it was Harriet. She bore the brunt of it.'

'Bore the brunt?'

'Well, Harriet had been Mum and Dad's number one girl for eight years. Ours too. So I'd say it was tough for her at first when Lara came along.'

'Maybe you're right.' Nina had said that too. So had Gloria. Why hadn't he seen any of this? What had he been doing the whole time they were growing up? 'Harriet's doing really well with that *Willoughby* tour, by the way. That actor was singing her praises.'

'I'm not surprised. She just lost her confidence there for a while.'

James was making too much sense. Being too knowledgeable. Austin was feeling more and more confused. 'I'd better go. Thanks for your help.' He was surprised how helpful James had been. He felt a shimmer of guilt. Just because he didn't like James's wife didn't mean he and James couldn't get on. He was his only brother, after all. Perhaps he should have kept in touch a bit more . . .

'So you'll ring Harriet now?' James said. 'Get her to come as soon as she can? I think you should. I think it would be better for Lara if there were two of you.'

'I'll call her right now.'

'Keep me up-to-date, will you?'

'Sure.' He forced himself to ask the question. 'And Melissa's okay?'

'Fine. In Melbourne for a couple of days.'

'And Molly? All fine with her?'

'No worries at all,' James said.

In Merryn Bay, Molly was curled up on top of the bedspread, her face pressed into the pillow, trying to muffle her tears. Nobody had ever told her it would hurt this much. She wanted her mum. She wanted her dad. She wanted Lara and Harriet and all her family around her. She didn't want to be a grown-up. She wanted to be a kid again.

CHAPTER TWENTY-EIGHT

An hour later Austin still hadn't managed to get Harriet on the phone. He was getting anxious. 'Her mobile keeps ringing out. And she's not in her room, either. She can't have gone far, can she?'

'Maybe she's with one of the guests,' Nina said. 'Can you ask to be put through to another room, in case she's there?'

'I don't know the name of any of the guests. I only know the actor's name. The special guest.'

'Try his room, then. He might know where she is.'

Austin dialled the number of the St Ives hotel again. 'Could you put me through to Patrick Shawcross's room please?'

Harriet was in Patrick's bed, being kissed slowly and beautifully, her body coming alive again under Patrick's fingers. She stroked his naked body, too, loving the feel of his skin, loving —

The noise of the phone on the bedside table was like an alarm, making them both jump. They ignored it at first. It kept going. They reluctantly separated. Patrick reached out a brown arm to the receiver.

'Hello?' He listened. 'She is, yes. Just a moment.' He turned to Harriet. 'It's for you. It's your brother.'

Five minutes later, Harriet was still in Patrick's bed, naked, the sheet wrapped around her. He was half-dressed, wearing jeans, sitting at the end of the bed, watching her, his expression concerned.

She still couldn't make sense of what Austin was saying to her. Since she'd taken the phone he hadn't stopped talking about flight schedules and Nina and Ireland and police and he still hadn't told her what he'd found out about Lara. All he had said was he knew where Lara was and he wanted Harriet to fly to Cork as soon as possible and go with him to see her.

She finally managed to interrupt him. 'Austin, please, slow down for a minute. I can't come just like that. I can't abandon the tour group.'

'You won't be abandoning them. I told you. Nina's offered to come over and take your place. I've checked out all the flights. She can fly in just before you fly out tomorrow. There'll be enough time for a handover. And don't worry, Nina will be great. She's worked in her parents' restaurant for years, she's good with people. She knows the area. She'll get them to the meeting place in Bath and she can make sure Patrick Shawcross gets his flight too.'

'Austin, I'm sorry, but I still don't understand. You ring out of the blue, you won't tell me anything, you say I have to get to Cork for Lara's sake . . .'

'It's not something I want to tell you over the phone. It's awful news. Really awful news.'

Her breath caught. 'She's not —?'

'No, she's not dead. I haven't seen her yet, but she's alive.' As far as he knew. 'It's about her parents.'

The relief made Harriet impatient with him again. 'Austin, we've talked about this. That's Lara's business, not ours. If she needs to visit where the crash happened, we have to respect that, don't we? Give her some space?'

'It's not that simple. There was more to it than that.'

'What do you mean more to it? Was it drunk-driving? Was someone else killed in the crash?'

He had no choice. 'Harriet, Lara's parents didn't die in a car crash. Lara's mother killed her father, then killed herself. In a holiday cottage outside Cork. That's where Lara is. She's staying in the cottage right now.'

'No.'

'Yes.'

'No, that can't be true. You must have confused them with someone else.'

'Harriet, it's them. It's their names. The right dates. It's them. I've read the newspaper report. Spoken to the local police.'

'You're sure that's what happened? It wasn't an accident?'

'It wasn't an accident. She stabbed him and then she took an overdose.'

Harriet felt a chill. 'But how could that have been hidden from us? Surely people would have known?'

'It happened on the other side of the world. It was more than twenty years ago. There was no Internet. I don't know how, Harriet, but it happened.'

'But why would the police lie about a thing like that?'

'It wasn't the police. It was Mum.'

'Mum?'

'Mum made up the story about the car crash and the only person she told the truth to was Gloria. I don't think it was deliberate lying. Gloria said it was to protect Lara.'

'Gloria knew too? All this time? And she didn't say anything?'

'She made a promise to Mum.'

'But you don't keep a promise in these circumstances.'

'Gloria did.' He told her everything Gloria had said to him.

They were both silent for a long time afterwards. Then Harriet spoke again. 'Would Lara think we all knew already? That we've always known and kept it from her?'

'Maybe. I think so. It would explain why she disappeared so suddenly. Why she hasn't been in contact with any of us. Harriet, I'm going to go to the house tomorrow. We need to talk to her. I need you to be there too.'

'Of course I should be there. I want to be there.' She didn't hesitate. 'But Austin, I'm worried about the group being on their own. They're old people.'

'I told you, Nina can take over. She'll be able to handle anything that comes up. I'll arrange what I can from here, get all your flights sorted out. There's only a couple during the day, we haven't got a lot of choice. And I think you should read the newspaper report before you get here, as well. Let it sink in. I don't want to shock you any more than I already have. That's why I didn't want to tell you over the phone. I know you're still fragile —'

'I'm all right, Austin. I've been all right for a while. I can handle more than any of you think I can. I just can't believe it. Any of it.'

'It's true. It's horrible but it's true. I'll fax the article to you now, Harriet. And I'll see you tomorrow.'

'See you, Austin.'

She hung up, and turned, ashen-faced, to Patrick.

Nina was waiting when Austin came back to his room after faxing the article to Harriet's hotel.

He started talking as soon as he came in. 'You're still sure you don't mind taking over the tour? It should be fairly simple. You'll be handing them on to another tour leader within a couple of hours. Think of them as a flock of sheep being moved from one field to another.'

'I'll be fine. Do you need to let anyone else know it'll be me? Or can you and Harriet just change things like this?'

Austin had thought about it. It was a Turner Travel tour and he and Harriet were Turners, weren't they? They were allowed to sort it out between themselves. 'No, it's fine. I'll take responsibility for it all. As I said, it's straightforward anyway. Meet them all at the airport, take the group to the other tour company meeting point and then make sure Patrick Shawcross gets his flight home.'

She nodded. 'What's he like? Not a prima donna or anything?'

'No. He seemed nice enough. Friendly.' He got a mental image of Harriet and Patrick Shawcross together. He realised something else. Harriet had been in Patrick's room when he rang. 'Nina, could you ever have a fling with a much older man?'

'I've heard of sudden subject changes —'

'I'm sorry. My mind's all over the place. It's something I thought I saw when I was in St Ives. And something I realised now.'

'About Patrick Shawcross and one of the tour group?'

'About Patrick Shawcross and my sister.'

'Did she say something to you?'

He shook his head. 'No. It was just a feeling when I met him. The way he looked at her, or she looked at him. Something, anyway.' He knew the look well, from his own experiences with women over the years. 'And she was in his room tonight. Now.'

'How much older is he than her?'

'Harriet's thirty-two. I'd say he's in his mid-forties.'

'That's nothing. You made it sound like he was in his eighties.

You're not suffering from protective older brother syndrome, are you?'

'I am her older brother.'

'And how old did you say your sister was? Thirteen or thirty-two?'

'It's just she's been shaky lately.'

'So maybe what she needs is a nice big affair to get her back on her feet. Nothing like it to soothe the spirit, so I hear.'

'You're supposed to be on my side.'

'No, I'm not. Leave her alone, Austin. She's a grown woman.' She seemed to realise it wasn't a laughing matter. She went across and pulled Austin into a hug. 'I'm sorry, she's your sister, but that's what I think.'

He hugged her back. She felt good. 'You're probably right. I forgive you.'

She looked up at him. 'You're sure? I'd hate to leave you on bad terms.'

'I'm sure,' he said. She didn't just feel good. She felt better than good. He leaned down and kissed her.

After Austin called, Harriet quickly dressed and collected his fax from reception. She stood in the foyer and read the newspaper article three times.

She returned to Patrick's room. He'd asked her to come back. He read the fax while she sat at the table opposite and watched his face. He looked up, serious. 'It's terrible. It's a terrible thing to find out.'

'I have to go there. We need to see her, to talk to her. My brother and I.'

'Of course. Do you want to go tonight?'

She shook her head. Austin had already told her there were no flights that night. 'Tomorrow.'

He offered to take charge of the group. She explained about Nina coming over. He asked more, about Lara, about her arrival in the Turner family. The stories spilled from Harriet. She spoke about it in a way she hadn't before with anyone. The entire time the fax lay on the table between them.

She didn't stay with him that night. She couldn't. Something had shifted inside her. It was as if her confidence had gone. That happiness. It didn't seem right to feel good, to want to be in Patrick's arms, in his bed, when Lara was alone in the house where her parents had died so violently. Harriet kept getting terrible images in her head, of Lara mimicking her mother, taking pills, bringing it all in some terrible full circle.

She told Patrick she was sorry. She told him the truth, that it didn't feel right. She said goodnight and went back to her own room. She undressed, brushed her teeth, tried to read. Nothing was calming her. She tried to picture Lara's parents as they had been, not in the way the article had described them. All she had was a child's eye view, from the time they came to collect Lara, a few months before they died. She tried to picture Lara's mother, summoning only a hazy image of dark hair and nervous laughter. Her voice on the phone all the times she would ring and Harriet would answer. It was so hard to reconcile those images with thoughts of a woman stabbing her husband, then killing herself, abandoning her only child.

She couldn't sleep. She couldn't stop thinking about Lara, what this all meant for her, what it meant for their whole family. She kept trying to understand why her mother would have invented the story of the car crash. Thinking again and again of the horror that had happened to Lara's parents. And thinking, more than anything, of how Lara must be feeling right now.

The handover took place in front of Bristol Airport in the early afternoon, exactly as Austin had arranged.

Harriet had explained the situation to the group at breakfast time. She kept it simple, mentioning sudden family business, hoping they'd understand if she didn't go into detail about it and promising they would all be in safe hands with Nina. Only Mrs Lamerton had muttered about a revolving-door system of tour guides.

The final outing of the tour had been a short journey along the coast to Marazion, and a boat trip over to the small island and dramatic castle of St Michael's Mount. Harriet only half heard Patrick's talk about the *Willoughby* filming that had taken place there. He didn't seem to be telling any unusual stories. He kept it short, in fact.

On the way back to St Ives for their farewell lunch she sat in the guide's seat, looking out the front window, intensely conscious that he was sitting behind her. She knew he was concerned. She knew they needed to talk more.

There wasn't the opportunity. They returned from the bus trip with just enough time to change before they were due in the dining room. It was a lively lunch. Mrs Lamerton called out *Willoughby* quiz questions and answered most of them herself. There was some shifting of seats around the dining table to get close to Patrick for the final time, but several women in the group were already looking to the next trip, talking aloud about their favourite scenes from *All Creatures Great and Small* and *Monarch of the Glen*. Harriet made a short speech, thanking them all and presenting a bottle of whisky to Clive. The group gave her a big box of chocolates and a card they'd all signed. Mrs Kempton presented Patrick with her handknitted jumper, with the little Patch embroidered on the bottom right-hand corner. He put it on. It was at least three sizes too big. There was a lot of laughter. Harriet felt as if she was a long way away, watching it all from a distance.

Patrick had come straight to her in the breakfast room that morning. Touched her arm. 'Harriet? Are you all right? Did you sleep? Can I do anything?'

'Thank you, but no, I don't think so.'

'We need to talk. Will you have time after breakfast? Can you come to my room?'

She nodded. Twenty minutes later she was on her way to him when Mrs Kempton called out to her in the corridor. She'd lost not only her glasses but also her passport. She also had a row of small buttons on her shirt that she needed help with. It set off a domino effect in the group. Mr and Mrs Douglas broke a zip on their suitcase. The lens fell out of Miss Boyd's reading glasses. Miss Talbot lost her macintosh. Harriet had to phone Patrick to say she couldn't come yet.

There was a moment after lunch when she and Patrick were alone, but then Mr and Mrs Douglas insisted on a group photo and urged everyone outside to the hotel steps. Then she needed to make sure all their luggage was out of their rooms and on the bus. There were more last-minute hitches. Miss Talbot lost her macintosh again. Mr Fidock couldn't remember the combination of his in-room safe. Mrs Lamerton decided she wanted to take the *Willoughby* videos on the next tour with her and needed another bag to carry them in.

Now they were at Bristol Airport and they still hadn't had a chance to talk.

Nina had arrived on the early flight from Cork. She was waiting in front of the airport when they drove up in the bus. Austin had described her as small and very pretty. Harriet liked her immediately. She introduced her to Patrick, and had a strong sensation Nina knew something about them or had picked up something. The way she looked at him and then her, as if she knew. Perhaps it was obvious. Nina told Patrick she would come back as soon as she had dropped off the group in Bath to make sure he made his Boston flight. He thanked her but said there was no need for her to come back, that he was happy to look after himself.

Harriet's flight to Cork was already boarding. There was just enough time for her and Patrick to say goodbye to the tour group. They lost three minutes when Mrs Kempton announced she couldn't find her glasses anywhere. Clive eventually found them under one of the seats.

Patrick climbed on to the bus first. All the women hugged him goodbye and more than half of them kissed him, too. Mr Douglas and Mr Fidock hugged him as well. Clive just shook his hand.

Harriet said goodbye to them one by one. It wasn't even a final farewell. She'd be meeting them again in Bath in a week or so and escorting them back to Australia. Not only that, many of them lived near Merryn Bay, so she would see them again. She was still sad.

Clive started up the bus. Nina climbed on board and belted herself into the tour guide seat. She looked at home and very capable, Harriet thought as she waved goodbye.

Patrick walked her to the departures gate. The boarding sign was flashing. The flight was about to close.

He didn't touch her. 'Harriet, will you be all right?'

She nodded. She tried to sound in control. 'I'm sorry to abandon you like this. It's not our usual way of doing business.'

'I don't think much of this past week has been usual, has it? For either of us?'

'No, it hasn't.' What could she say to him? Where did she start? Thank you for being our special guest? Thank you for making me laugh. Thank you for making me feel beautiful and sexy and looked after and . . . all those things. She decided to say it as it was. 'Thank you for everything. I'm sorry it's ending like this.'

'I am too.' He touched her on the cheek and it nearly finished her. She wanted to kiss him. She wanted to talk to him and hear him talk until they ran out of words and stories. She wanted him to say, stay, don't go. She wanted him to say, I'll be here when you get back. She wanted him to say, I want to see you again, this wasn't only a dalliance for me. He didn't.

'You'd better go.' She said it first, not him.

He kissed her lightly on the lips. Then he stepped back, or perhaps it was her.

'Thank you again.' She couldn't stop thanking him. It wasn't what she wanted to say, but it was all that was coming out.

'Goodbye, Harriet.'

She walked through the gate and had to force herself not to look back.

Austin stood at the arrivals gate at Cork Airport, waiting for Harriet to emerge. His thoughts were with Nina. It was ironic. It served him right. The first woman he'd seriously been interested in for years hadn't been interested in him.

Their kiss the day before had lasted only a few seconds. He'd felt the faintest of answering pressure from her, the start of a response and then she had pulled away, her face serious for once.

'That was a very nice kiss, Austin, thank you.'

'I could give you another one if you like.'

She'd smiled and shaken her head. 'I'm sorry. It's not you. I'm just not ready.'

'I like you very much, Nina.' He did. She had touched him in a way he hadn't expected. Not just her looks, but her intelligence, her sparkiness. She made him think about things and she challenged him, too. He liked the feeling.

'And I like you very much. And I very much want to be your friend —'

'But that's all?'

She nodded. 'For now, yes, Austin, I think so.'

'For now? So we could revisit the idea in a year's time?' He tried to make light of it but he was serious. It felt important to say it. To be honest with her. 'Sooner, even? Could we keep in touch with each other?'

She smiled. 'I'd like that. Now, will we get back to work?'

She'd handled it as nicely as that. That morning before leaving for Cork she had given him a tight hug goodbye. 'I'll see you again, I know. And give Lara my love. Lots of love. Tell her the room is hers whenever she wants it. For as long as she wants it.'

'Can I ring you later? Tell you what happens?'

'Please. As soon as you can. Ring me any time you need to.'

'Nina . . .'

She waited.

'If you did decide you were ready to see someone again, would there be a list of possible candidates?'

'There might be. A small list, perhaps.'

'Could I put my name on it?'

She smiled. 'I already have, Austin.'

'At the top?'

She'd laughed then. 'I'm not telling you.' They'd shared another hug goodbye.

Harriet emerged through the gates then. She was wearing the yellow uniform. Austin stepped forward. She started talking before he even said hello.

'How would she be feeling, Aust? I keep picturing her on her own in the house. You don't think she would have —'

'No.'

'How do you know?'

'I don't know for sure. I don't want her to have done that, so that's what I'm telling myself over and over. Will we go straight there?'

She nodded.

'We've got time for you to change if you like,' he said.

His attempt at a joke. She didn't laugh but she took him up on it.

As they drove out of the airport car park fifteen minutes later, Austin looked over at her. She was now wearing black cotton trousers and a white linen shirt. She was very pale. He saw dark shadows under her eyes. 'You okay, Harold?'

She shook her head then turned to him. 'Did you know the truth, Austin?'

'How could I have known?'

'You were older. You might have heard them talking. Mum and Gloria. Mum and Dad.'

'Do you think Dad knew?'

'I suppose so.'

'Maybe he didn't. I never heard them talking about it. Not once.'

'Why wouldn't Mum have told us the truth?'

'Gloria said she wanted to protect Lara.'

There was a long pause. 'What else don't we know about them, Austin? About our family?'

'A thousand things, probably.'

They were quiet as he drove west through the winding roads towards Clonakilty. They'd gone straight from the airport grounds into countryside, past a topiary airplane perched on a roundabout outside the airport, onto a busy road beside fields lush with growth. For a time their route followed the path of a slow-moving river, edged by woods. They passed stone bridges, road signs in Irish and English, B&Bs and country pubs. The fields and the countryside looked wilder than the scenery in Devon and Cornwall. Another time Harriet would have loved looking around. She had grown up seeing posters of Ireland on the walls of the travel agency. She barely saw it now. There was too much to think about.

Austin needed to talk. He didn't like the thoughts that were filling his head when it was quiet. He glanced over at Harriet. 'So how did the rest of the tour go?'

'Good, thanks.'

'Patrick Shawcross managed to keep his hands off you?'

'No, Austin, he didn't.'

'Sorry?'

Harriet wasn't looking at him. 'No, he didn't keep his hands off me. I didn't want him to.'

'Are you joking?'

'No, I'm not.'

'So what's happening?'

'What do you mean?'

'Are you going to see him again?'

'I don't know.'

'That's it? The cad.'

She turned to him then. 'He's not a cad, Austin. He's not a hunk or a cad.'

'If he's disappeared on you, he is a cad.'

'He didn't disappear. I disappeared.'

'You have to watch out for men like that, Harriet. Ones that take advantage of —'

'Shut up, Austin.'

'I beg your pardon?'

'I mean it. I love you but shut up and mind your own business.'

'You love me but you also want me to shut up. Sounds like mixed messages to me, Harold.'

She lost her temper. 'Can you please stop joking for one minute? You've always done that. Tried to turn serious things into a laughing matter and sometimes it's wrong, Austin. Sometimes serious things have to be serious.'

'I see.' There was a pause. He started tapping the steering wheel. What had happened the past few days? Gloria going for him. Nina turning him down. James surprising him. And now Harriet attacking him as well. He had an uneasy feeling all those people couldn't be wrong. 'I suppose I could try not to joke all the time.'

'And could you please stop tapping too. Your tapping drives me crazy sometimes. It drives all of us crazy.'

'You're certainly firing on all cylinders today, Harold.'

'I'm sorry. I needed to say it.'

'That's fine. It's no problem.' He paused. 'So I won't joke and I won't tap for a little while, either.'

They were quiet for a minute, then Harriet turned to him again. 'And if you ever tweak my nose again I swear I will punch you in the face.'

Austin nodded. 'Mental note. No tweaking of Harold's nose ever again, either.'

'And stop calling me Harold.'

'Talk about the mouse that roared.'

'I mean it, Austin.'

He glanced over. 'I can see that, Harriet.'

She said nothing.

He couldn't resist it. 'Harriet the Chariot.'

She ignored him.

At Bristol Airport, Patrick Shawcross was standing at the airline desk.

The middle-aged woman in front of him ran her fingers across the keyboard. As she waited for the information to come up on the screen, she glanced at him. Did she know him from somewhere? He looked vaguely familiar. She mentally noted how blue his eyes were. Contact lens? No, he didn't look the type. If he was that vain, he would have dyed some of the grey she could see in those black curls. And he'd probably cut those black curls shorter too.

She glanced at the screen as the flight details appeared. 'Yes, sir, there are seats available on that flight. Will I go ahead and make the booking?'

'Yes, thank you.'

'You're welcome, sir.' If only all her customers were so decisive.

CHAPTER TWENTY-NINE

It took Austin and Harriet just under an hour to reach Clonakilty. The house was outside the town. He had detailed directions from the property company. They took a road to the right before the town entrance, drove on for five miles, then took a left turn onto a long hilly lane. They were surrounded by green fields, bordered by overgrown hedges and gorse bushes, small buds of yellow flowers visible here and there. The roads were narrow. Austin had to pull over sharply twice when another car appeared. The land was lush, the trees covered in new spring growth. There were black-and-white cows in some of the fields.

The house was on its own, set back from the road. Compact, modern, painted yellow. Two half-barrels of flowers stood on either side of the front door. A carved wooden sign on the right-hand post said Glen View. A small silver car was in the driveway.

Austin pulled into the side of the road about twenty feet beyond the gate. They sat there.

'Are you ready?' he asked.

Harriet nodded. They didn't know what they would find. Lara, in floods of tears. Distraught. Or something worse.

They got out, closed their doors as quietly as possible. The gravel in the driveway sounded loud under their feet.

There was lavender among the flowers in the barrels by the front door. The scent was strong. Clean and sharp. Austin knocked once, twice, three times. Harriet stood back a little way. She realised she was holding her breath.

They could see Lara's silhouette through the glass panels. She opened the door and looked at them both. She didn't speak.

She looked immaculate. Her shoulder-length hair was tied back in a neat ponytail at the nape of her neck. She was wearing jeans and a pale blue T-shirt. Her feet were bare. Harriet remembered then, incongruously, that Lara often went barefoot. She always had painted toenails, too. She glanced down. Lara's toenails were bright red.

'Austin. Harriet.' She didn't smile, or sound surprised.

Austin spoke. 'Can we come in?'

She hesitated for only a second. 'Yes.'

They followed her into the living area. It was open plan, a bright lounge area leading onto a kitchen, large windows looking out into the green fields. A herd of cows was making its way back from milking in a long line, one after another like toy animals.

Harriet was uneasy. Lara hadn't expressed surprise to see them. She was almost too calm. Harriet wondered if she had taken tablets. Lara didn't seem to be sedated. Her eyes were clear. Harriet looked again. It wasn't calmness. Lara was icy, she realised. And angry. Very angry.

Lara turned, crossed her arms and leaned against the wall. 'You both suddenly felt like a trip to Ireland?'

Austin answered. 'We've been looking for you. We've been very worried.'

'Have you? I'm sorry about that. How did the *Willoughby* tour go, Harriet?'

She swallowed. 'Fine. It went fine.'

'That's good.'

Harriet and Austin exchanged a glance. In the kitchen behind her they could see she had been cooking. There was a chopping board, several large ripe tomatoes, and a strong smell of basil.

Austin spoke again. 'Lara, are you all right?'

'I'm fine, thank you.'

'Do you know where you are?'

'Yes, thank you, Austin. I'm in Cork. I also know I'm in the house where my mother killed my father and then killed herself, if that's what you were wondering.'

Harriet couldn't help herself. She took a step back.

Lara noticed. 'So if you've come to break some news to me, you're a bit late. I found out for myself.'

'We didn't know, Lara,' Austin said.

'No? No more lies, thanks, Austin.'

'We didn't. We didn't know until yesterday.'

Lara didn't say anything.

'He's telling the truth, Lara.' Harriet spoke then.

'Of course he is.'

Austin tried again. 'Lara, I swear. We didn't know.'

'I don't believe you. You must have known. There is no way you couldn't have known.'

'We didn't. Mum told us it was a car crash too. She came into the lounge. We were watching *Gilligan's Island* on the TV.' It seemed important to Harriet that she give all the detail.

Austin nodded. 'She said she had bad news, that your parents had been killed in a car crash in Ireland. That's all we ever knew.'

'Penny told you it was a car crash?'

Austin and Harriet nodded.

'But she knew it wasn't. I spoke to the sergeant at Clonakilty police station. The same man who rang the Australian police that night. He told them exactly what had happened. Every detail of it. He told me what he had told them. What they would have told Penny.'

'That might be true. But she didn't tell us.'

Lara's expression changed. The anger was giving way to something else. Uncertainty. She turned her gaze to Austin. 'Did Neil know the truth?'

'I don't know.'

'Harriet?'

'I'm sorry, Lara, I don't know either.'

Austin tried again. 'All we know is how hard it must have been for you to find out.'

Lara went icy again. 'Do you? How do you know that?'

'Because we've just found out too,' he said. 'Because we've had a shock too. Because you are my sister and when something bad happens to my sister, to either of my sisters, I feel it too. So I know, not as bad, I'll never know that, but I have an idea how it must feel for you.'

'And you, Harriet?'

'I'm just as shocked. It's terrible, Lara.'

'What's terrible, Harriet? The fact it happened or the fact I was lied to?'

'We were all lied to, Lara,' Austin said softly.

'But why? Why would your mother lie to me? To you as well? That's what I can't understand. I've spent the past five days trying to understand all the lies.'

'I think Gloria knows why.'

Lara turned to Austin. 'Gloria?

'She knew the truth as well. She told me yesterday. She said Mum had made her promise not to tell anyone.'

'She's known for twenty-four years?'

'She hated knowing, Lara. She didn't like being the secret keeper. She was angry about it. She thought Mum made a big mistake. Gloria said to say that to you. To say sorry. And to tell you we love you.'

Lara stayed still.

Harriet needed to help. 'Mum would have done it for good reasons, Lara. She loved you very much. So did Dad. I'm sure of that. I think she must have wanted to protect you. To make it easier for you.'

'Make what easier?'

'You joining our family. Coming to live with us. Coming to Merryn Bay.'

'Building it on lies? How would that make it easier?'

'It wasn't built on lies. It was built on love. She loved you, right from the start. I know she did.'

'How do you know?'

Harriet hesitated. 'Because I could see that she did. That they both did.'

Lara made a dismissive noise.

Harriet made herself say it. 'Because I remember feeling jealous of you.'

'Jealous of what?'

'Their love for you. The attention they gave you. And how sure you seemed of them, of yourself.' She felt a tightness around her chest. This was too big, too raw, happening too quickly. It wasn't what they were here to talk about. She could feel Austin staring at both of them, confused.

'Sure of myself?' Lara gave a short laugh. 'You have no idea, Harriet. I spent my entire childhood feeling completely terrified.'

'When you came to live with us?'

'To begin with, yes. But before then, too. When it was me and Mum and Dad.'

Austin spoke. 'Did your parents hurt you, Lara?'

'Physically? No.' Lara was quiet for a long time. 'My father used to say cruel things to my mother, and she'd get upset, throw things at him. She used to cry all the time, tell me how much she loved him, how he meant the world to her. That she couldn't live without him. She'd sleep for days or she'd start drinking, or we'd have to go in search of him. I always knew I was second best. She said she loved me. But she loved him more.'

Austin and Harriet stayed quiet. They had never heard Lara speak about her parents before. She was talking quickly, but she wasn't looking at either of them.

'I never knew what was happening. He kept leaving. I'd get taken out of school and we would pack up and try to find him. We always did and she would always beg him to come back. Plead with him or scream at him. Make me stand there and say he had to come back because of me. And sometimes he would but not straightaway. So we would live in some guesthouse until it suited him to come home with us.' She gave that laugh again. 'So was I sure of myself as a child? No, Harriet. I was never that. I was scared.'

Harriet needed to hear more. 'You weren't scared of us, though, were you? Scared of my mother and father?'

'I loved your mother and father. And that made it worse. I felt like a fraud. I felt like a fraud when I came to stay the first time and I felt like a fraud every year on those memorial days your mother wanted me to have. Because the truth was I didn't want to remember my parents. I was glad I was living with your family. I liked it much more than I had liked living with my own. I did love my mother, but I couldn't fix things for her. I knew she was unhappy but I didn't know what to do about it. When I came to stay with you that first time, and then Mum and Dad came and got me, do you remember? After a couple of days? Mum had a black eye.'

Harriet and Austin nodded.

Lara seemed deep in the memory. 'It wasn't an accident with a tree. They'd had a huge fight the week before and he had thrown something at her. A book, I think. Something that caught her eye, made it swell up. She'd thrown it straight back at him, thrown glasses and cups, a bottle of wine, anything she could get her hands on. They were always like that. I thought that's how things were for everyone and then I met your parents and they were nice to each other. And you were all nice to each other. There was no shouting or fighting. I remember thinking, stay as quiet as you can, Lara. Be as good as you can. If you stay still, don't make a fuss, you might be able to stay for longer.'

Harriet remembered. She had seen it as Lara being so self-contained. Distant.

'All I wanted to do was be as quiet and polite as I could be and then maybe I could stay with your family for a long time. All the sheets smelt so good, and you probably don't even remember this, Harriet, but you let me sleep by the window. And I knew that was your bed, and I knew I should have said no, but I loved the idea of being by the window like that, all fresh and clean, and with all the books on the windowsill. I pretended it was all mine, the bedroom, the books. I pretended that your mother was mine, and your father was mine, and that something had happened to my mum and dad, and that I had come to live with your family.' Tears were forming in Lara's eyes. 'And then three months later, I was back. Because something had happened to my mother and father. And I thought

I had made it happen. I thought I had killed them. That my wish had come true. I kept getting nightmares, that I had wished it on them, because I had admitted to myself that I didn't want to live with them any more.'

'But you didn't make it happen. It was a car cra—' Harriet stopped herself. It hadn't been a car crash.

'I thought I had. In my mind I made them have the car crash. Except now I know it wasn't that, either. My mother killed my father and then killed herself. She chose to do both those things. So now I can't take the blame, I suppose. Because they didn't want to be with me either.'

Harriet wanted to move to her, to hug her. But that wasn't how it was between her and Lara. She stayed still and kept listening. Austin was just as quiet beside her.

'I told Penny how I felt. How guilty I was. She told me again and again that they didn't die because of me. Yet all that time she must have known what had really happened.' A long pause. 'That's what I've been trying to reconcile in my head. I've been going over and over it. I can't understand why Penny said what she did, why she lied to me. All my life.'

Harriet had been trying to understand it herself. She had thought about it all night. About her mother. The way she liked everyone to be good and kind. The way she had never liked to face up to the bad things in life. She had overheard her and Gloria arguing good-naturedly about it over the years. It had been a laughing matter sometimes. But it had its serious side as well. She needed to try to explain.

She spoke softly. 'Lara, maybe Mum didn't know how to tell you, how to give you such terrible news. I don't know how it feels to be a mother. Maybe all you want to do is look after people, and protect them and love them and keep them from harm. And you keep everything bad away from them that you can. I think that's what Mum tried to do with you.'

'That's not true, Harriet. It can't be true. What about my mother? She didn't want to do any of those things for me, did she? She didn't care what happened to me. Not for a minute.'

Austin stepped closer. 'Lara, please . . .'

For a moment Harriet thought she'd made a terrible mistake saying what she'd said. But then something occurred to her. 'But she must have cared, Lara. She got in touch with my mum. She came to see us that day, when you first stayed with us. She spoke to Mum all the time, and she asked her to be your guardian when they went to Ireland. Wasn't that what she was doing? Making sure you would be all right while she was away? Caring about you? Wanting to make sure you would be looked after?'

Lara was staring at her.

Harriet was struggling, but she felt every word. 'I can't even start to think why she did it, Lara. But I believe she had thought of you. Perhaps she had us there ready as your family, just in case. She had been thinking about you.'

'But I wanted *her*, Harriet. My mother. Dad was different in a way. He came and went all the time, and he would do me drawings and we would have some fun but then he would go again. But I remember Mum. We did have some good times. She and I would go on walks or catch the tram down to the beach and pick out shells together. And she liked cooking. She would make special meals just for the two of us sometimes, with candles and cutlery and napkins, and three courses. And we would toast each other. And she would buy little chocolate mints for afterwards . . .' She stopped. 'But none of it meant anything to her, did it? She wouldn't have done this if it had.'

'She must have been so sick, Lara,' Austin said. 'I can't understand it all, but she must have been. They must have had a huge fight, maybe they'd both been drinking, she did something terrible and panicked. Maybe she couldn't see a way out. She realised what she'd done to your father and she couldn't face —'

Lara interrupted. 'I remember the night Penny told me. I was at a school camp. The teacher made me sit in a room until Penny came. No one would tell me what had happened, but I knew it had to be something to do with my parents. There was nothing else. And Penny came in, and she knelt down on the floor beside me and she said —'

Harriet held her breath.

'She said that something very sad had happened but before she told me what it was she wanted me to know that I would always be loved and looked after and I would always have a home with her. And then she told me what had happened. That there had been a crash. And that my parents —' The tears were flowing but Lara didn't blink them away.

Harriet wanted to move closer to her, but something still kept her back.

Lara kept talking. 'And I said to her, "Did I make it happen? So I could come and live with you again?" And that was so wrong. I should have been thinking of my mum and dad and been so sad about them. But I wasn't. Not until later. That's how bad I was.'

'Lara, you were eight years old,' Austin said. 'How could you have understood what it meant? It wasn't because of you. It wasn't your fault it happened.'

'That's what Penny would always say to me, when I thought I had killed them, that I'd made the car crash happen. She told me I was never to blame myself.'

'Then believe her,' Harriet said. 'Please, Lara.'

'I knew something, Harriet. I always knew there was something that Penny didn't tell me. She would tell me all these stories about my mother and father and try to make them sound all loving and happy but I knew it hadn't been like that. I could remember the fighting and the mess and the moving around. And Penny must have known I would remember that, but she always tried to paint the brightest picture of them she could. Yet I always knew that something about my parents made her uncomfortable. I thought at first that she didn't like them. But she told me she did. Then I thought about it some more, and I came up with something even better. I decided that I was your father's daughter. That he and my mother had had an affair on the ship. That I was his natural daughter.'

'Were you?' Austin asked the question.

'No.' She gave a faint smile. 'I asked him one day. I asked both of them. He said he would have been proud if I was, but I wasn't.'

Harriet had a clear memory of Lara talking to her parents in the garden, and feeling jealous. Feeling left out. She was ashamed of herself.

'You were his daughter, though,' Austin said. 'And you were Mum's daughter too. It didn't matter to them where you came from, they were just glad to have you. It's true.'

'I'll never know for sure. I can't ask them now. I can't ask Penny about any of this. I'll never know the whole story now.'

Austin noticed Harriet's eyes fill with tears, and also that she quickly brushed them away. He made a decision. 'Will you both excuse me for a minute?'

He went outside and took out his mobile phone. It was nearing twilight, the air filled with sounds of insects, birds in the hedges, the mooing cows in the distance. The light was hazy. He could see through the window into the living room. Harriet and Lara were visible. Neither of them was talking. He dialled the long-distance number. 'Gloria, I know it's very late. I'm so sorry. We're here with Lara.'

It was as if she had been waiting for his call. 'Is she all right?'

'She's fine.' That was the wrong word to describe Lara, he realised. 'No, she's not fine. She's angry, with all of us. Confused. She needs to know more.' He hesitated. 'I know you've had enough of us, and you have every right to feel that way, but please, Gloria, can you do one more thing for us as a family? Would you talk to Lara? Would you tell her anything you remember about that night? About why Mum did what she did?'

There was no hesitation from Gloria. 'Austin, I'll talk to Lara for as long as she needs. Tonight or any time she likes.'

Lara was on the phone to Gloria for nearly an hour. Harriet and Austin sat outside on a bench in the garden while she talked to her. They heard murmurs. When she came out, her eyes were red-rimmed but there were no tears. She didn't tell them what Gloria had said.

Lara didn't invite them back inside the house. The three of them went for a walk instead. Harriet wasn't sure who suggested it. They didn't go far, just to the end of the road. There was a farm, neatly painted, whitewashed buildings, a two-storey house. Harriet thought of the newpaper article, the fax folded in her bag. Was this the farm where the woman who found Lara's parents had lived?

None of them spoke much. Austin pointed out a glimpse of a lake visible between some low hills. They tried to think of the name of a bird that came flapping out of a tree beside them. Lara thought it was a rook. Harriet thought it was a jackdaw. Austin said he didn't know.

They reached the gate and the yard of the cottage again. Something stopped Harriet and Austin from going any further.

Lara spoke. 'This will sound rude, and I'm sorry, but I want you both to go now.'

Austin was surprised. 'To leave?'

Lara nodded. 'I don't want you to stay here. I need to be here on my own.'

'Lara, is that a good idea?'

The chill again. 'I'll decide that, thanks, Austin.'

'We want you to be all right. I don't like to think of you —'

'I'll be all right.'

Harriet searched Lara's face. This felt wrong. Lara shouldn't be here on her own. 'You're sure you don't want to come with us? The three of us. We could —'

'No thanks, Harriet.'

No discussion. 'Lara, what will you do?'

'I don't know.'

'Will you come back home? Back to Merryn Bay?'

'I don't know anything yet. I need to think about it. Stay here and think about it all. On my own.'

Austin said what they were both thinking. 'Lara, please promise us you won't —'

'Kill myself? No, Austin. I won't. I've got so much to live for. So many people who will miss me,' Lara said. Her tone was sarcastic.

'Lara, please —'

'I won't kill myself, Harriet.'

Austin put his hand on her arm. 'Lara, you still have us. This doesn't change anything for us.'

'It's already changed, Austin.'

'This is it? You don't want to see us again?'

'I don't know.'

Harriet needed to try again. 'Lara —'

As Lara turned to her, Harriet recognised the look in her eyes. She remembered it from when Lara came to live with them after her parents died, that faraway, scared look. It silenced her.

Austin spoke. 'We'll go if that's what you want us to do.'

'It's what I want.'

'Can we ring you?' he asked. 'Make sure you're okay?'

Lara didn't say yes or no.

They stood for a second and then Austin stepped forward and gave her the quickest of hugs. 'See you soon, blister.'

Lara didn't hug him back. 'Goodbye, bother.'

Harriet was next. It felt wrong. It felt bad to leave like this. But Lara was like a statue. She wanted them gone. She didn't want them anywhere near her. Harriet could feel the coldness coming off her in waves. 'Lara —'

'Goodbye, Harriet.'

She didn't hug Harriet back either. She stood there, still, while Harriet awkwardly put her arms around her.

There was nothing else to say. Harriet and Austin walked back to the car in silence. They didn't wave as they drove past the house again. There was no point. Lara had already gone inside.

CHAPTER THIRTY

Austin and Harriet were on the main road back to Cork before they could talk about it. It was a beautiful spring evening. There was little traffic. Austin turned on the radio, changing the station from pop music to current affairs. He found an Irish language station and left it on there. For a while the only sound in the car was bursts of traditional music, interspersed with the rolling and rhythmic sounds of spoken Irish.

Harriet was the first to reach over and turn it down. 'Aust? Are you all right?'

'No.'

'She doesn't want us in her life any more, does she?'

'I don't think so.'

'She said goodbye. We said "see you" and she said "goodbye".'

'I know.'

'What can we do? How can we help her?'

'I don't think there's anything we can do. I think we have to wait. Let her decide what she wants to do.'

They were silent for a few minutes.

'What are you going to do now?' she asked.

'Now tonight or now the rest of my life?'

'Both.'

'I need to get back to work. We've got a performance in Cologne tomorrow night. I'll try for a flight back tonight. Go straight to the airport now. Beyond that, I don't know. What are you going to do?'

'I don't know.' She hadn't thought beyond seeing Lara. She made herself remember the itinerary. She wouldn't let herself think about Patrick. 'I need to be back in Bristol in a week to take the group back to Australia.'

'We can get a flight together. You can come with me to Germany if you want. If you don't want to be here on your own. It might be better if you're not.'

The kindness in his voice nearly undid her. She didn't know where she wanted to be. Her head was too full of Lara, of what Lara had learnt, of the expression on her face. Her mobile phone rang, the sound very loud in the small car. They both hoped for the same thing.

'Is it her?' Austin said.

Harriet looked at the number. She didn't recognise it. 'I don't think so.' She pressed Connect. 'Hello?'

'Harriet? I hope this isn't a bad time?'

'Patrick?' Harriet had been imagining him on his flight to Boston. It would have left an hour before. 'Where are you? Has your flight been delayed?'

'No, I changed my ticket. I'm in Cork.'

'In Cork?'

'Is Lara all right? Are you all right?'

'Yes. No . . . I don't know yet. Why are you in Cork?'

'I had to see you again.' A pause. 'I didn't like the way we said goodbye.'

She hesitated. 'I didn't like it either.'

'Is there anything I can do? Do you need me to come and get you?'

'No, I'm with my brother. We're on our way back to Cork.'

'Would you come and see me? When you feel you can?'

'Yes.'

He gave her the name of his hotel and the room number. She said goodbye and hung up. She wasn't shocked or surprised. She was numb.

Austin was watching her. 'Did you say Patrick? Was that Patrick Shawcross?'

Harriet nodded.

'Where was he calling from?'

'Cork.'

'But he was due to fly back to Boston today, wasn't he? Wasn't Nina looking after him?'

'He changed his flight.'

'Why would he have done that?'

Harriet hesitated. 'He wanted to see me again.'

'So he's followed you? That puts a different slant on things. Cads don't usually do any following. If he's followed you then he must —' He stopped there, sensing Harriet's mood. 'You want me to mind my own business, don't you?'

'Yes, I do.'

There was silence for a minute. 'It's hard. I want to say things.'

'You can't.'

'Can I say good luck? That I thought he seemed —'

'You only met him for a minute, Austin. You don't know what he's like.'

'No, you're right.' There was a long pause. 'Do you like him?'

'Yes, I do.'

'Very much?'

'Very much.'

'That's all right then.'

They were quiet again for a minute and then she turned to him. 'I liked Nina, by the way.'

'Did you?'

'Yes. Did you like her?'

'Mind your own business, Harold.'

'Don't call me Harold.'

'Mind your own business, Harriet.'

She smiled a little as she turned and looked out the window.

They hugged goodbye at the airport. Austin had phoned ahead. There was a flight leaving within the hour. Harriet was keeping the hire car. It was a difficult farewell.

'We have to let her come to terms with it, Harriet. If she wants that space, we have to give it to her.'

'Even if we're not sure it's the best thing?'

'Yes. This is huge for her. We have to give her what she wants. And she wants to be on her own.'

Harriet wasn't sure he was right. There wasn't time to talk about it any more. She hugged him goodbye. 'See you, Austie.'

'See you, too. Ring me. Or text me. Whenever you need to. Keep talking to me. Let me know if you hear anything from her.'

'I will. And you too. If she rings you. Keep talking to me, too.'

'Of course.' He reached over and pretended to tweak her nose. 'Only joking. See you, Harriet.'

They hugged each other goodbye again.

Harriet drove into the centre of Cork and found Patrick's hotel. She parked the car, took her bag and walked down the street. She didn't know how she felt. So sad for Lara, glad he had come, both at once.

It was a modern hotel in an old stone building, decorated with plush blue carpet, red sofas and modern art on the walls. She took the lift to the third floor, walked along the quiet, carpeted corridor and knocked at the door.

She didn't run into his arms. He didn't pick her up and sweep her off her feet. He just said her name. 'Harriet. Please, come in.'

It was a large suite with a living area, separate bedroom, a large window looking out over the city, the river shining below. The day before it had been the two of them in St Ives, in another hotel room. Now they were in a different country, looking over a river not a sea. More than that had changed.

'How is she?' Patrick asked. 'How was it?'

'I don't know yet. She's very angry with us. She's hurt. She wants us to leave her alone.'

'What do you want to do?'

'For her? Whatever she wants. Whatever she needs us to do.'

'And you? What do you want to do?'

'I don't know, Patrick. Cry. Think. Sleep.'

He opened his arms. 'Come here to me, Harriet.'

She moved towards him, feeling his warm, solid body, feeling his arms come tightly around her. She stood like that for what felt like a long time, his fingers stroking her back and her hair, hearing him murmur her name. It overwhelmed her. She pressed her face against his chest and cried and cried.

She woke. It was dark outside. She didn't know if she had slept for hours or just a short time. She was in the bedroom on her own.

Patrick had put her to bed once the tears stopped. He had pulled back the bedclothes and the crisp white sheets and helped her in. She had taken only her shoes off. Then he had lain down on the bed beside her, put his arms around her and listened as she told him all that had happened with Lara. He had asked questions. He had let her cry again. Then he held her close against him until she fell asleep.

She got out of bed. He wasn't there. There was a note on the table. He'd written the time he'd left and one sentence, in strong handwriting: *Harriet, I'll be back very soon. Patrick*. She checked the time. It was six p.m. He had just gone.

She took a shower, standing under the hot water, thinking hard. There was something she needed to do. Something she had been thinking about while she was driving here, while she was talking to Patrick. As soon as she had woken she knew it was the right thing. She also knew it was urgent. If she didn't do it now, as soon as she could, it might never be possible again.

When she came out of the bathroom, fully dressed, Patrick was back. He was sitting at the table by the window, reading. The lights of Cork were visible outside the window. There was a bottle of wine and two glasses on the table beside him. He looked over and smiled.

'Hello again.'

She walked across to him and put her arms around his neck. He drew her close against him and kissed her. It was a soft, sweet, gentle kiss. She kissed him back, feeling his body hard against hers, the cotton of his shirt, then his skin, smooth, underneath it. She wanted to be with him. She wanted to feel every part of his body again. Lose herself in him, feel safe and sure. But she couldn't. She couldn't when she knew how Lara was feeling.

She drew away. 'Patrick, I need to go back to her. Back to Lara.'

'Now?'

She nodded.

'But didn't she ask you to leave her alone?'

'She did. But I think if I obey her now, we might never see her again. She might leave our family.'

'You don't want that to happen?'

'No, I don't.'

'Do you want me to drive you? Come with you?'

'I think I need to do it on my own. I'm sorry. It means so much to me that you came here, but . . .' She hesitated. It was too soon to be able to assume anything, even though what had happened with Lara had changed things between them. Moved what was happening between them to a different stage, more quickly than might have happened otherwise. They had talked about so much, but she still felt her way through the next sentence. 'If you want to leave, I'll understand. If you need to go —'

'I don't want to go.'

'I don't know how long I'll be with her.'

'I'll wait here. If you want me to wait.'

'I want you to. I really want you to.'

'Then I will,' he said.

CHAPTER THIRTY-ONE

Harriet got lost on her way back to the house. The roads were hard to find in the dark of the countryside. After taking the wrong turn and doubling back, she finally saw it ahead, the yellow house, the two barrels of flowers outside, Lara's car in the front. She felt nerves but wouldn't give in to them. She imagined her parents, Gloria, Austin, James and Molly willing her on.

Memories and thoughts of Lara kept her going, most of all. The truth had started dawning on her as she had been driving back with Austin. How little she had known about Lara. How little she had thought about how Lara must have been feeling. Not just with this devastating news, but all her life.

Something else had hit her, too. How she felt when her parents died was how Lara must have felt as an eight-year-old. Scared, alone, uncertain of the world. Yet Lara would have had none of the happy memories Harriet had to draw on to console her. Lara would have had only the terror and fear and loneliness of grief, layered over the loneliness and frightening feelings she'd had when her parents were alive.

The enormity of it shocked Harriet. It must have been so hard for Lara. She must have felt so scared as a child. And how had Harriet reacted to her arrival? Badly. She had been jealous of the attention her parents had paid her. She had been jealous of Austin getting on so well with her. Of Lara getting on with James and Melissa, too. Harriet felt sick as it all came back, how put out she had been by Lara. She was shocked at her own selfishness. And not just as a child. More recently . . .

The gravel underfoot was very loud. There was only one light on, sending a faint path out into the yard. She knocked at the door. She had to wait longer this time. At first she thought that Lara had gone out, and she wondered what to do. Then she heard a noise. Footsteps. Lara opened the door. Her eyes were red. She had been crying. She didn't say hello. Her voice was cold.

'I asked you to go.'

'I know. I came back.'

'Why?'

'Because you're my sister.'

'No, I'm not.'

'You are my sister. Something very sad has happened to you. I'm not leaving you alone until I know you're okay. Until I can tell everyone you're okay.'

'Everyone?'

'Austin. James. Your family.'

'Harriet, I don't have a family. I have no parents. I have no brothers and sisters.'

'You do. You have us.'

'No, Harriet. You're wrong. I've got nothing. I never did have anything. I always suspected it, and now I know it for sure.' She turned and went inside.

Harriet followed her. 'Lara, please, can't you see —'

Lara stopped. 'No, Harriet, can't *you* see? I have nowhere to go from here. I can't pretend things any more. I know the truth. From the police, from what Gloria told me. I can't pretend that my mother and father had sorted it all out between them. That their trip to Ireland made them realise how much they loved one another and how much they loved me. That I was the last thought on their minds when they had that terrible accident in the car.'

Harriet was shocked by how open Lara was being. 'That might have been what they were thinking. When it happened.'

'No, Harriet, it couldn't have been. I know that. Because that's what finding out what really happened to them has done. It's taken all that hope away. All the fantasy I had that my mother did love me, not as much, never as much, but perhaps nearly as much as she loved my father. But she didn't. If she had loved me she would never have done this terrible thing. She would never have killed my father and she would never have killed herself.'

'She was very sick, Lara.'

'Was she? Sick with love? Sick of me?

'Unwell. Unbalanced.'

'Just words. Different words for it. Do you see what it's taken from me, Harriet? Any life with my parents at all. I didn't get any of them. I didn't get a life with them as a child and now I am left with no happy memories, either.'

Harriet was in trouble. This was harder and darker than she knew how to deal with. 'I can't know how you feel. All I know is that it hurts me so much that my mum and dad have died, and it must be a hundred times worse for you. The way it happened. The way you found out.'

'Gloria said Penny wanted to make it easier for me. That she did it for all the right reasons. That it was a terrible thing for a child to hear. But it wouldn't have made any difference. I don't want to know it as a child or as an adult. I don't want it to have happened.'

Harriet wanted to go across and hold Lara, tell her it would be all right, somehow. That they would do all they could to make it all right for her. But there was still that distance between them. She could only listen for now.

'I don't want my mother to have killed my father, Harriet. I don't want to think that I wasn't worth living for. That he was all that mattered and that if he was gone she didn't want to live. I should have mattered to her. She should have thought of me as she lay there. I was eight. I wanted my mother and I wanted my father and she did that to me.'

'She didn't do it to you, Lara. She did it to herself. To your father.'

'But she left me behind. She left me on my own. Then and now.' Her eyes filled with tears. Harriet took a step forward, but Lara turned away.

Harriet kept trying. 'You're not on your own, Lara. You have us.'

'I don't. Not any more. It's different now, Harriet. You know yourself. Penny and Neil are gone. Who's left for me? They're the ones who made the decision to bring me into the family. You didn't have a choice.'

'It's not about having a choice. Lara, we are your family. It's true. Ask any of us. Ring Austin. Ring James. Ring Molly. You are our sister and you are Molly's aunt. You grew up with us. You're one of us. We're . . . we're part of each other. That's what a family is, isn't it?'

'I don't know.'

'It is. It must be. Because that's what we are.'

'But it's different now. It'll never be the same. After Penny and Neil died, everything changed for me. I couldn't stop thinking about my own parents again. All the things I should have asked about them. My head was filled with questions. Things I wanted to ask Penny and Neil about their lives as well.'

Harriet knew what she meant. She stayed silent.

'I couldn't tell anyone. It felt too disloyal, that we were all grieving for Penny and Neil yet I was trying to find out about my own parents. So I didn't say anything. I thought I would find out where the car crash happened. Make a visit. Leave some flowers or do something there that would make me feel close to them. Make me feel I hadn't forgotten them. I thought about it for weeks, and then the course was nearly over and I realised I had to do it now. I started making enquiries a few days before you got here. The day you were arriving I got a call back from the sergeant in the Clonakilty police station. He told me everything. And it was like . . .' She stopped for a moment.

Harriet pictured it. Imagined Lara, finding this out for herself. On her own.

'I couldn't see reason, Harriet. I thought you had all lied to me for years. I wanted nothing to do with you. I didn't care if the *Willoughby* tour was ruined. I just needed to run. I told Nina I had to go and I left. I came here. I came here where it happened, to see if I could make sense of it. If I could feel anything of them.'

'And could you?' Harriet's voice was soft.

'Nothing. I felt nothing. Just anger and sadness and . . . I just felt alone.' She was quiet for a time and then she looked at Harriet again, as if she had just realised something. 'How did you and Austin find me? How did you know I was here?'

'It was Austin. Austin and Nina, your flatmate.' She told Lara all she knew, about Austin coming over, talking to Lara's lecturer at the college, coming to Cork with Nina, going to the police, the newspaper, the library.

'Austin did all that?'

Harriet nodded.

'And you came back here, Harriet. Even after I told you to go away.'

'I had to, Lara. I wanted to.' She could only say it again. 'You're my sister.'

'Harriet, I should have rung you. From England. After the farewell party. I should have tried to explain why I did what I did.'

Harriet was caught off-guard. Lara suddenly wasn't talking about the past few days. She was talking about the day Harriet's mother had died. This was the conversation Harriet had thought about having for three months. The conversation she had dreaded. This wasn't the time. 'Lara, don't —'

'You need to know what happened. I need to tell you why.'

Harriet couldn't speak. She waited.

'It was all just chaos that day, Harriet.' Lara's voice was very quiet. 'The ambulance and nurses and doctors and moving Penny into a room and we didn't know what was happening. I was with her and then James ran in and asked me to ring you while he rang Austin and Melissa and Gloria. And I was about to, I was about to call you. But something stopped me. I needed her to myself. Just for a few minutes, before I rang you, before James came back. I sat with her, holding her hand and it was so quiet suddenly, just the two of us. I didn't say anything but inside I was willing her to get better, telling her how much I loved her, thanking her.

'And then I heard her speak. I heard her voice, Harriet. I realised she was conscious. She was talking to me.' Lara's eyes filled with tears. 'And I needed her so badly. I didn't know what she was going to say, or what I could ask her, but I needed that time with her like nothing I had needed before. And if I had gone away to ring you then I wouldn't have had that time with her. I couldn't leave her. Not even to ring you.'

Harriet had tears in her eyes now too. 'I couldn't understand how you could have done that to me. I couldn't believe it when I heard you admit it.'

'I knew it hurt you so badly, but I was hurting too, Harriet. I loved Penny and Neil so much. And it felt like Penny was my last link with my own parents. That if she died, they were gone forever. There'd be no one I could ask questions about them. No one else I knew who had known them. I panicked. I needed her to myself, even for just a minute, because I loved her, but also in case there was something else she could tell me about them.'

'Was there?'

'A little. Just a little.' She didn't say what it was. 'She talked just a bit. She said she loved us all. And I told her we loved her . . . and then just as James and the nurse came back in she had the second stroke and . . .' Lara's voice was barely audible. 'I'm sorry, Harriet. I know I can't ask you to forgive me, but I just need you to understand.'

'I do, Lara. I promise you I do.' She did. She understood now. She could imagine how Lara would have felt. The same need Harriet had felt. Wanting to be with her parents. Wanting the last minutes. Knowing this was it. But what Harriet had been through, the pain she had felt, was nothing compared to what Lara must be feeling about her own parents. Right then, right now, she would have given her mother's last week to Lara. Her father's last words. She had never imagined being able to think those thoughts. But she could. And she meant it. She took a step forward. 'Lara, how can we help you. Is there anything —'

'I don't know yet. I don't know how I feel about anything yet.'

'Will you let us help you?'

'Help me?'

'With whatever you decide to do. Whatever you need to do. If Mum and Dad were here, that's what they'd say, too. But they're not. So we have to start again. Have a different sort of family. And you are part of that. We need you.'

'You don't need me.'

'I do. We all do.'

'Why?'

'To think about. To worry about. To care about.' Harriet gestured. 'All the sister things. All the family things. Please, Lara. Let us be your family. Don't leave us.'

Lara's expression changed. She looked sad and lost. Fragile. 'I need help, Harriet. I need lots of help with this.'

'Then we'll help you, Lara. As much as we can. I promise.'

Lara started crying then. Harriet didn't hesitate. She went over and took her in her arms.

They stayed up late that night talking. Not just about their parents. Not just about their family. They spoke in a different way. Without guards. Lara talked more than she had ever talked. About what it had been like coming to live with the Turners. Of how nervous she had been of Harriet. Of not wanting to take her place or step on her toes. Of wanting to be as well behaved as she could so she wouldn't be sent away.

Harriet was overwhelmed by sadness. How must Lara have felt? Had she waited day after day for something to go wrong, to be sent away? 'They always wanted you, Lara. They did. Right from the start. I know they did. We all did.'

'It was hard on you. All of you, but you especially.'

'Lara —'

'I know it was, Harriet. Your mother knew too. She asked me to be understanding. She told me that you might find it hard, that you'd been the only girl and that I should be understanding if you got upset. Do you remember her talking to both of us about it one night? That time she came in to our room? She said she knew how hard it might be but that we both had to remember she had a very big heart, bigger than either of us could imagine and there was room for all of us in there. And you said, how come she was only a normal-sized person if she had such a big heart. And Penny said it was made out of special material that let it stretch as big as anything.'

'Did she?'

Lara was smiling. 'You don't remember? And then in science class about a month later, before you and I moved into different classes, the teacher was talking about anatomy, and she had that model of a human body and you stood up and said your mother was different from that, that her heart was made out of some stretchy type of plastic stuff, not muscle. And you refused to give in. You said you weren't sure how she did it, but all of us lived in her heart as well as out in the world. The teacher thought Penny had been teaching some strange alternative science, I'm sure of it.' She laughed softly.

Harriet felt the memory returning. Yes, her mother had come in to their bedroom and said that about her heart. And Harriet had said that in a class. She remembered Lara telling the story when they got home from school that night, and her mum and dad laughing about it. Her mum had given her that nice special smile.

'And that time with the tent-rooms, Harriet. Do you remember? Before Gloria came up with the idea to draw a line down the centre of our bedroom? Neil brought home those two tents and we slept out in the garden for a few nights. They said it was a test to see who really was the messy one. And yours was full of jigsaw puzzles and all the books and even both of our kittens within about an hour, do you remember? And then it turned out the real reason we were out in the tents was so Austin and James could paint our room for us? Remember? They'd asked us what our favourite colours were. And I said yellow and you said pink, so that's why it was half and half.'

Harriet was feeling strange. She had forgotten that too. But back came the memory now. Her parents had called it the Miss Messy of Merryn Bay competition. Harriet had won hands down. She could remember laughing about it. Her mum had even made a little paper sash.

Where had these good memories been? She could conjure up memories of being hurt when her mother went to Lara first. When her father gave Lara more attention. Dozens of times when she had been cross or hurt by things that had happened to Lara and not to her. But behind those hurts she realised were other memories that she didn't ever revisit. Of Lara shyly waking her up on her tenth birthday. Giving her a little shell-covered picture frame she had made herself, from shells found on the Merryn Bay beach. Of other birthdays. Coming out into the kitchen in the morning, still half-asleep, and Lara stopping her, saying, 'No, you're too early,' putting her hand over her eyes until she got the signal from Austin or James that the candles on her cake were lit. The whole family singing 'Happy Birthday' to her. Lara, as loudly as anyone.

Of being so sad as a twelve-year-old when her kitten was run over. Lara had come to her with a basket. 'Here, Harriet. I want you to have my kitten.'

Of Lara coming to her one afternoon after school, when Harriet was in tears because the boy she had a crush on had ignored her. 'He's not worth it, Harriet. You're much better than him. Just wait and see.'

Kindness after kindness from Lara. Had Harriet forgotten them all? Blocked them all out? She had. She had turned Lara into something she wasn't. Made her into someone who had come in and ruined her life. Lara wasn't that. Lara was someone very like her. Someone who felt as scared and frightened as she did. Someone who had lost her parents, not just once, but twice.

Lara was right. She could remember all of these things. It's just that those good memories, those funny memories, weren't the ones she kept taking out to look at again and again. She seemed to bring out the ones that made her feel sad, or scared, or lost. Or jealous.

'I do remember, Lara. Just not as easily as I remember other things.'

'You remember the sad things instead?'

Harriet nodded.

'I do, too,' Lara said. 'All the time. But I'm trying to tell myself not to.'

Harriet tried to take that in. How could Lara not think of all those sad things. Those tragic things . . . 'Is it something you can choose? Something you can decide?'

'I don't know yet.' Lara's voice was soft. 'I hope so. I have to try. I have to try to remember the good things that have happened. Try to understand the bad things, but not let them win. I've been thinking about it ever since I found out. Trying to work out what I can do. Life is all about choices, isn't it? On a physical level, what we do, where we live? Perhaps it's the same with your mind and your memory. Perhaps we can choose what we want to remember. We can choose what we think about. I hope so. I hope it's like that.'

'I'm so sorry, Lara. I should have been so much kinder to you. All the time. I should have understood. And I didn't.'

'Yes, you did. Harriet, you were allowed to be mad that I arrived to live with you. But you weren't mad all the time. Things aren't one way or the other, Harriet. You can feel lots of different things at once. That's normal. Why wouldn't it be normal?'

'Because I knew it was wrong. Because I didn't want to hurt your feelings.'

'It hurt me more when I could see you were pretending. You're allowed to have feelings, you know,' she said again.

'I have feelings. They just haven't always been the most grown-up ones.' So many memories needed sorting through. 'You've always been able to be so calm about things, Lara. How do you do that?'

'I don't know. That's just what I'm like.'

Harriet looked at her. That was it. Lara was one extreme, Harriet was the other. 'I wish I was more like you, Lara.'

'Do you?' Lara gave her a sweet smile. 'That's funny. I always wished I was more like you.'

Harriet was up first the next morning. She was filling the kettle when Lara came out of her bedroom. She was fully dressed, wearing jeans, the pale blue shirt and suede boots. She was carrying a suitcase.

Lara came straight over and gave her a hug. 'Thank you,' she said. 'For last night. For coming back.'

It felt right, natural, to hug her back, to thank her as well. Then she noticed the suitcase. 'You're leaving? Now?'

'Not yet. After breakfast.'

'You don't want to stay here any longer?'

She shook her head.

'Where will you go?'

'Back to Bath for now.'

'Do you want me to come with you? I can. Whatever you need.'

'Will it hurt you if I say no?'

'No. I want you to tell me the truth.'

'I need time, Harriet. I need to think all of this through. Let everything sink in. And I need to finish my course. And then I need to decide what to do next.'

Harriet nodded. She understood. 'Lara, will you keep in touch? Please?'

'Will you keep in touch with me?'

'I asked you first.'

'We sound like we're eight years old.'

'As a thirty-two-year-old, will you please keep in touch with me? With us all? Let us know what you decide to do? Where you'll be?'

'I will let you know, I promise, but not yet. It's too soon. When I feel ready.' Lara hesitated. 'Is that okay?'

'That's more than okay.'

They made coffee and toast. Normal day-to-day actions that changed the mood, lightened it. It allowed them to talk about different things. Ordinary things. Lara spoke about her course, about living in Bath. Then she changed the subject.

'Tell me more about the *Willoughby* tour, Harriet. Did it go well?'

Harriet had to gather her thoughts before she answered. The *Willoughby* tour felt like it had been years before. 'Yes, it did. It was good. They loved every minute of it, I think.'

'I'm sorry for leaving you in the lurch like that. Especially after you'd stepped in for James.'

'It's fine. It was probably the best thing for me.'

'Really?'

'Really.'

A shared look of understanding again. Lara smiled. 'And was Mrs Lamerton okay? Did her brooches make the trip?'

'Every one of them, I think.'

Lara's lips twitched. 'And my little Miss Talbot?'

'She loved it. She bought a new red velvet pantsuit especially.'

'Not that one from Tina's Teen Wear?'

Harriet smiled. 'The exact one.'

'And Mr Douglas?'

'I heard him say the bay reminded him of a milkpond. He also told Patrick Shawcross he's waiting on some autopsy results.'

Lara laughed out loud, properly, for the first time since Harriet had arrived. 'And what was Patrick Shawcross like? Was he difficult?'

'No. No, he wasn't. I was expecting some elderly man in a wheelchair, carrying his dentures. He wasn't like that at all.'

'No, he's hardly changed from the *Willoughby* days,' Lara said.

'You knew what he looked like?' Harriet said.

Lara nodded. 'I found quite a lot about him on the Internet a couple of weeks ago. It took a lot of tracking down but I found out he runs an actors agency in Boston now. There was a photo of him on the website. I was going to ask James to include all that in the *Willoughby* info, but it wasn't in his official biography, so I decided he didn't want it broadcast. I thought it was up to him what he told them about his life now. I had a feeling Mrs Lamerton wouldn't leave him alone if she knew how to get in contact with him.' She took a sip of her coffee. 'So you got on okay with him?'

'Yes, I did,' Harriet said. Was it too soon to talk about Patrick?

Perhaps. But Lara was her sister. And surely if you told anyone that you thought you were falling in love, you told your sister. 'Actually, better than okay.'

Lara picked up the tone. Her expression changed. A slow smile. 'Something happened between you?'

Harriet told her. Not every detail, but enough. It was the kind of conversation she had never had with Lara. She felt her way. She could see from Lara's expression that she was enjoying hearing it. Not just the story but the fact they were talking about something like this. She asked a few questions, not many, not too intrusive. Just the right amount.

'You think it might be serious between you?'

'I don't know. I hope so. I think so.' She hesitated. 'Lara, would you like to come and meet him? Before you go to the airport? I'll understand if you don't want to, but —'

'I'd love to meet him,' Lara said.

It was cosy inside the hotel bar. The chairs were made of a deep red material, soft to touch. There were lamps lit on each table, soft music playing in the background, a clink of glasses and light laughter from a small group of elderly women in the corner table.

Harriet, Patrick and Lara were at the window table, looking out over the river and Cork city. The rain had stopped. In its place was pale sunshine.

'Lara, can I get you another coffee?' Patrick asked. 'Anything else?'

She shook her head, glancing at her watch. 'Thanks, Patrick, but no. I'd better go. My flight leaves at four.' She stood up, picking up her coat and her bag.

Lara had driven back to Cork at the same time as Harriet,

following her car. For the past hour the three of them had been sitting together in the hotel bar. Harriet hadn't felt nervous. She was introducing her sister to someone she cared very much about. Lara had been reserved at first. Not shy or stand-offish, but cautious. Harriet watched her as Patrick drew her out. He asked questions about her course, about other tours she had done. He laughed at her stories. She asked him about his agency. About Boston. The three of them swapped Mrs Lamerton stories. It had been good. Gentle.

Lara smiled at Patrick now. 'Goodbye, Patrick. I'm glad the tour went so well. I'm glad we invited you.'

'I am too.' He hesitated. 'And Lara, I'm sorry, once again. For all you learned in the past few days.'

She looked at him in her serious way. 'Thank you.'

Patrick stayed in the bar. Harriet walked with Lara to the front of the hotel where her car was parked. Lara had insisted on driving to the airport on her own.

In the foyer she turned to Harriet. 'He's lovely,' she said.

'You approve?'

'Completely.'

'Are you sure you won't stay?' Harriet asked. 'For the night, or as long as you like?'

'And be the gooseberry?'

'You wouldn't be. I promise. You wouldn't be. If you need, if you want it to be the two of us, you and me, I'll explain to Patrick and —'

'Harriet, I'm teasing. No, I want to go home. Back to Bath, anyway.'

'Could we see each other next week? When I'm back to collect the group?'

Lara didn't answer for a moment. 'I don't think so. Not yet. I might go away again. I need to think about so much. I think if I saw you, if I saw the group, it would interrupt me. Do you know what I mean? I'm sorry if that sounds hurtful, I don't mean to be, I promise. I need to be away. For a while, at least.'

'But not forever.'

'Not forever.'

'Lara, would you do something for me?'

Lara waited.

Harriet took off her bracelet. Her mother's opal bracelet. 'Would you look after this until the next time we see each other?'

'Penny's bracelet?'

Harriet nodded.

'But it's so precious.'

'I know. That's why I want you to look after it.' She passed it to her.

Lara took it. She held it very carefully. 'Harriet —'

'Please, Lara.'

Lara put Penny's bracelet on her wrist. Then she hugged Harriet. Properly. For a long time.

Harriet stood on the footpath and waited as Lara got into the car, put on her seatbelt and started the engine. She was about to pull into the traffic when she stopped and wound down the window. She looked over at Harriet. 'Thank you, blister.'

Harriet smiled. 'You're welcome, blister.'

She stayed waving until Lara was out of sight.

CHAPTER THIRTY-TWO

Gloria was ready and waiting for Melissa the next day. She'd been in the office since seven-thirty. She wasn't going to pussyfoot around. If there was anything she'd learned in the past few days it was that there was a time for plain speaking.

Melissa bustled in, straight into her office, and turned on her computer. 'Morning, Gloria.'

'Good morning, Melissa.' She was right about the beautician's appointment in Melbourne. Melissa was a different colour. Gloria didn't give her a chance to get another word in. 'I spoke to Alex Sakidis yesterday, Melissa. Does the name ring a bell? Alex from Matheson Travel?'

Melissa's head shot up. 'He rang here? You spoke to him?'

'Yes. So you know who I mean?'

'He's —'

Gloria interrupted. 'Franchise and acquisitions manager. The man you were going to sell Turner Travel to. Secretly. Under all our noses. Or was James in on it too? Had you convinced him to be as sneaky, as underhand as you?'

'You've got it wrong. It's not —'

'No, I haven't got it wrong, Melissa. I spoke to him. He told me. He was coming down here to view the building. Discuss the value. Discuss a possible sale.'

'That's partly true. I did invite him down. I asked him to make me an offer. But not why you think.'

Gloria couldn't believe how calm Melissa was. How brazen could she be? 'No? It was just out of interest, was it? You were just suddenly curious how much the business might be worth? And what the largest travel company in the country might be interested in paying for it? Don't treat me like a fool, Melissa.'

'I wasn't suddenly curious. I've been curious – we've been curious, James and I – for nearly two years.'

'I beg your pardon?'

'Since before Penny and Neil died. But we didn't want to rush anyone into it, and then after they died, it was too soon. This seemed like the most businesslike way to find out.'

'Melissa, find out what? What are you talking about?'

'I'd have preferred to wait, but since you've brought it up, I owe you the truth. Please sit down.' Gloria took a seat. 'James and I want to buy you all out, Gloria. Run Turner Travel ourselves. We've been thinking about it for some time. But we wanted to be sure we were offering what the business was worth. This was the best way we could find out. It wasn't very fair to Matheson Travel, we knew that, to go on as if we really did mean to sell, but we knew it would give us the most accurate figure of what it was worth.'

'Worth to who? Who were you going to make the offer to?'

'All of you. You, Lara, Harriet, Austin.'

'Why?'

'Because it feels like time. Something has to change. All of us have started going in different directions over the past twelve months. No one seems happy. Austin has stopped coming to the meetings. I've always known he doesn't like me, in fact I don't like him either, but it was starting to impact on the business. He was

464

stalling on decisions when we needed to move quickly. I've also not been sure this is the right place for Lara any more, either. Or Harriet, for that matter.'

Gloria could hardly believe this. Melissa had been noticing other people? Was she actually having this conversation with her? She looked around the office. Yes, it looked the same. The desks, the computers, the travel posters, the racks of brochures. Even Melissa looked the same, all blonde hair and brown skin and high energy. But she was making sense. And it sounded as though she had given all of this a great deal of thought. Gloria was still suspicious though. 'And me, Melissa? What plans did you have for me?'

'I know you've been thinking about retiring. But I didn't think you would leave until you were pushed —'

'You were going to push me?'

'No. Never. You're the backbone of this company. But I've seen it in you, Gloria. Your heart's gone out of it. And I thought – James and I thought – that perhaps a big lump sum of money might make it easier for you and Kev to make some decisions.' She gestured to the phone. 'Ring James, Gloria, if you don't believe me.'

Gloria did, still in a state of amazement. James backed up everything Melissa said. He was also more apologetic about the way Gloria had found out.

'It shouldn't have happened like that. I'm very sorry. You must have been furious.'

'That's one word for it.'

'Gloria, that absolutely wasn't our intention. It wasn't a matter of going behind everyone's backs. We just felt it was better to produce the offer as a complete package, figures and all. So we had the answers to any questions anyone might ask.'

Gloria knew it was true. James didn't lie.

'What do you think?' he asked.

She told him the truth. 'I think it's a brilliant idea.'

After she hung up from James, she felt different. The anger and shock of Melissa being so upfront passed. She relaxed. So did Melissa. She made coffee. She left the answering machine on. And she talked to Gloria in a way she had never done before. Or perhaps Gloria had never listened to her in that way before.

She wanted to organise even more theme tours, she said. The *Willoughby* tour especially had put lots of ideas in her head. People loved to travel for a reason. She was thinking of exploring food and wine tourism. Literary tourism. Historical tourism. Working with the schools and universities, putting together special offers for students. She had some new ideas for marketing, as well. Joint promotions. A new website. More regular newsletters. Gloria was impressed. She told her she was.

'Yes, they are good ideas.' Melissa was matter-of-fact about it. 'And it will be easier to put them into place if it's our company. That's if the others agree.'

'I think they will.'

'Do you? That's a good sign. You'd know.' She took a sip of coffee. 'I feel a bit underhand, I suppose, the way we've gone about getting the valuation, but I'm sure Alex Sakidis will cope. Perhaps down the track we may think about doing some joint work with Matheson Travel. His journey won't be completely wasted. Mind you, I actually think he's only coming to see your suitcase stamps.'

'The stamps? On the staffroom wall?'

'He's dying to see them. I told him all about the idea behind them. He said we should let one of the travel magazines know about it. So I did. They're thinking about doing an article on us. Great publicity.

James and I were talking yesterday about taking it one step further, if all of you agree to the buy-out. Using the stamps as our next logo and on all the stationery. Maybe even getting new uniforms made, yellow background of course, but with all the different-coloured suitcases as the pattern.'

Gloria nearly choked on her coffee. That would definitely send Harriet into a new career.

Melissa didn't notice. 'I'm going to get a photographer to take pictures of all the walls as a starting point. I actually did a count of the stamps last week.'

'You counted them? Why?'

'I was curious. Do you remember Penny saying that she and Neil would call it quits when she got to ten thousand suitcase stamps?'

Gloria nodded.

'I'm not sentimental but I wondered if we were close. If it was a good time to change hands. And there nearly is. We're about a hundred off, but there will be ten thousand by the time the buy-out goes ahead, if it does. It's a shame Penny didn't see it. But I think she and Neil would be proud. And I don't think they'd mind, do you? It'll still be Turner Travel, after all.'

Gloria didn't know if Penny and Neil would mind. It wasn't her business any more.

'I'll see what the others want to do, and you too, Gloria, of course. There's no rush. We want you to stay on as long as you like. But if we set up on our own we'll take on other staff. Non-family staff. I think it will be easier to expand that way. So much less complicated. And I want to cut back our hours a bit, too. Molly is a teenager, she's going to need us around a bit more.'

Gloria blinked. Melissa was still making sense?

'What do you think, Gloria? About all of it? I know you'll need to think about it some more, your retirement especially, but in principle?'

'I think it all sounds excellent. And I wish you well.'

'Really? Do you mean that?'

Gloria thought about it. She thought about herself and Kevin, driving off somewhere. She nodded. 'Yes, I really do.'

Ten feet away, lying in her bedroom, Molly Turner pushed the mobile phone back under her pillow. She was sure she wouldn't hear back, but even sending the text to Lara had made her feel a little bit better. I wish you were here and I could talk to you. I miss you. Molly xxx

She looked at her bedside clock. She had slept for nearly thirteen hours, after crying for what felt as long as that too. It felt like she had done nothing but cry for days. Her whole body hurt from it. She had lain, curled in a ball, on top of the bedspread, as she'd always done when she was upset as a child. It hadn't made the hurt go away, though. She was all alone and it was her own fault.

Dean hadn't turned up to collect her. She had waited and waited, ringing his mobile number, but he hadn't answered. She'd sent a text, and then another. She had been worried sick he'd had an accident. She had been about to ring the police, the hospitals, even her coach Mr Green in case he'd heard something, when her mobile phone had finally beeped. A text. She'd snatched it up.

Molly, I'm sorry. I'm not coming. It wld be wrong. D

She had rung him. The first time it had gone to voicemail. And the second. She kept ringing until he finally answered. She was in tears by then.

'But why, Dean? I thought you loved me.'

She hardly heard his explanation. He should never have kept it from her, but the truth was he had another girlfriend in Melbourne. He'd met her at university and they'd lost contact but he'd run into her again six weeks ago and it had all started between them again. He thought Molly was beautiful, the time they'd had together would always be special to him, but he'd realised, especially in the last couple of days, that it would be better if they didn't see each other any more.

His words weren't making sense. 'But you promised. That it would be so special. I was ready.'

He kept saying the same things. She was beautiful but she was so young, she'd find someone her own age in a few years, and —

She hung up on him midway through the excuses. She was angry at first. He hadn't thought she was too young in the beginning. He hadn't thought she was too young when he'd first made her fall in love with him. But then the anger went and the hurt and the tears came flooding over her. She glanced up and saw his photograph, saw him with his arm around her, and her stomach started to hurt. She knew it was childish but she reached up and tore the photo out of the frame, ripping it into little pieces and putting them in the bin. She thought it would make her feel better but it only made her feel worse. It was the only photo she had of him.

She had been crying for nearly ten minutes, curled on her bed, clutching her pillow to her, when her phone rang again. Her heart leapt when she saw the name on the display. It was him. He'd changed his mind.

'Dean?'

He spoke quickly, in that same low tone, as though someone else was in the room or nearby. 'I know you're probably upset and you've got every right to be, Molly, and I'll never be able to say sorry enough, I know. But I need you to promise me you won't tell anyone about us, Molly. It wouldn't do either of us any good if you did.'

She hung up on him once more. He didn't call back again.

She'd stayed in her room since. She'd told her mother the swimming carnival had been cancelled. She hadn't asked any more questions about it. Molly had wanted to talk about it, wanted to tell her, but she hadn't known how to start. There was no one she could talk to about it. Not even Lara any more. She felt another wave of tears start to well inside her and bit her lip to try and stop them.

She had just turned out the light and climbed under the covers again when she heard a sound from under her pillow. Her phone. She lifted it to her ear and heard a strange echoing sound as though there was a time delay, or the call was coming from a long way away.

'Hello?' she said.

'Mollusc? What's up, sweetheart?'

It was Lara.

Harriet and Patrick ignored her mobile phone when it rang the first time, early the next morning. They had woken at dawn. She felt his arms come around her again, felt his lips on her forehead, her cheek, her lips. Their skin was warm, their bodies tangled. She felt his fingers caress her, the two of them skin against skin. It was different this time. It was gentle, deep lovemaking. There wasn't the urgency. There was something richer.

They had talked so much. They had walked around Cork together, up steep hills, along the river. They had found a small restaurant, tucked into the back streets, and talked over dinner, over a bottle of wine. About Lara. And about other things. He spoke more about his life. He answered all her questions, describing Boston, his work, his house, his favourite restaurant, where he swam. Then he asked to see her list again, Gloria's list. He went through it item by item, asking her questions. Making her laugh. Making her feel good. Cared for.

She didn't know exactly what was happening between them, or what might happen beyond now. It didn't seem to matter. She knew there would be time to talk about it.

Other things in her life felt different too, she realised. When she thought about her parents, about Lara, about the future, or the past, she didn't get the jagged uneasy feeling she normally did. She felt calmer.

Her phone on the bedside table rang again. She couldn't let it ring out a second time. She reached over to it, smiling at Patrick's murmured protest. She didn't recognise the number on the display. 'Hello, Harriet speaking.'

'Harriet, it's Nina. I'm sorry to disturb you so early.'

She sat up abruptly. 'Nina? Is everything all right?'

'It's fine. Well, nearly fine. I've just had a call from the *All Creatures Great and Small* people.'

'What is it? What's wrong?'

'Would you have any idea where they might find Mrs Kempton's glasses?'

CHAPTER THIRTY-THREE

Eight months later

Molly Turner smoothed down her black skirt and white shirt and looked around the Turner Travel office. It had been her idea to have the party here. She had blown up the balloons herself, and she and Harriet had moved all the desks back and decorated the staffroom so it looked all bright and cheery. About sixty people were there already and it was a bit crowded but it didn't matter. It made sense that the party was here, as her dad had said. Gloria had spent more than thirty years working in these rooms, after all.

Molly picked up the tray and started moving through the room collecting empty glasses. As she dodged her way through groups of people, she looked up and saw that the 'Good Luck in your Retirement, Gloria!' banner had started to peel off the wall. She put down the tray and went out to get some more sticky tape. She'd spent days doing that banner and she didn't want it to end up on the floor. It had already spent far too long in the cupboard as it was. She had almost been tempted to add the word 'Finally!' at the end when a confirmed date for the party was at last set. It must have been the longest run up to a retirement in history. Molly had worked it out that afternoon. It was almost eight months to the day since Gloria had said she was retiring.

Molly remembered the day clearly. It wasn't only the day she heard that her mum and dad were going to start running Turner

Travel on their own. It was also just after that awful time with Dean. Molly remembered feeling so sad, feeling so horrible and then, out of the blue, Lara had rung. Exactly when she'd needed her.

She had told Lara everything. Lara had been very, very upset. Not with Molly, but with Dean. Molly had been a bit shocked how mad she'd been, and how relieved Lara had been to hear that nothing too serious had happened between them, apart from the kissing in the car. 'What he did was very wrong, Molly, do you see that?' Lara had said. 'He was out of line, as a man and as a teacher.' She had listened to Molly saying that she had fallen in love with him, and that Dean had said he loved her, but she had stayed just as angry. 'You should have told someone, Molly. Even if I wasn't there. It felt wrong to you because it would have been wrong. If it ever happens again, anything like this, promise me you will tell someone.' Molly had promised. It had made her feel so much better. It hadn't been all her fault, after all.

Then Molly had asked Lara where she'd been the past week. They'd all been so worried, she told her. They had talked for a long time, Molly curled up on her bed, Lara in her flat in Bath. Lara had told Molly all she had found out, that horrible story about her parents. It had made Molly feel so sad and so strange. It had almost made her forget all the trouble with Dean. That hadn't seemed so important compared to what Lara had been through. She had asked Lara what she was going to do now. Lara told her that she had decided to stay on in Bath. She was going to finish the course first, maybe have a bit of time off. She was going to call James and talk about it with him in the next few days. She had other things to tell him, too. She was thinking about resigning from Turner Travel. Trying something new. Maybe even starting her own travel agency. In England, not Australia.

Molly didn't like hearing that. 'Is it because of Grandma not telling you the truth? Does it make you feel funny about being part of the family now?'

Lara had been quiet for a little while. 'It makes me think that perhaps I should try being on my own. Stay here. Be myself, Lara Robinson, not Lara, one of the Turner family, and see how that feels.'

It felt so good when Lara told her how she felt, and why. She always explained it really well. 'I'll really miss you.'

'I'll miss you too, Mollusc.'

'I wish you were here now.'

'I am there now. My voice is, anyway. You just can't see me.'

She'd needed to talk about Dean some more. Lara seemed to understand. Afterwards she'd been really kind. 'Just trust your instincts next time, Mollusc,' she'd said. 'You didn't have to ask me. You just wanted me to tell you not to do it, didn't you?'

She was right. 'But how will I know when I meet the right person, Lara?'

'I don't know. I'm not very good at relationships. I always seem to send all my boyfriends away.'

Molly had thought about it. 'That's probably because of your parents. Because you saw them fighting all the time. That would make you feel a bit nervous you were going to do the same thing.'

Lara had gone silent. 'You're probably right,' she'd said finally.

All sorts of things had changed on the surface since that day, but underneath none of it had, really. There had been a lot more talking lately. There'd even been a few family conferences about her mum and dad taking over the company and the amazing thing was she was invited in to listen. Everyone had thought it was a good idea. They would take it slowly, they decided. Everyone could stay on working there for as long or as short as they wanted. Lara hadn't come to the meetings of course, but she'd sent emails and once they'd had a conference call with the phone in the middle of the table and Lara's voice coming out of it. After she'd hung up, her dad and Austin and Harriet had all talked about Lara and her parents and they'd decided the real story was to stay within the family, that no one outside Gloria and Kevin needed to know.

Molly had felt a bit guilty admitting it to herself, and she hadn't said it out loud, but she didn't really see how knowing the truth changed anything much. As far as she could see, Lara had come to live with them because her parents had died, and that hadn't changed.

She emailed Lara all the time now. She knew that Harriet did too. Sometimes Lara copied them both in on articles she thought they'd like, or a joke or just a little story about her life in Bath. It was much better than texting. Lara had her own office in the middle of Bath. She even had a website. She'd gone into business with one of the lecturers from the tourism college she'd attended. Brendan. He sounded really nice, Molly thought. He had a nice voice, anyway. When Molly had called Lara at her new flat in the centre of Bath at Christmas time, she'd been a bit surprised when Brendan answered. She'd been expecting it to be Nina, Lara's old flatmate, if it was anyone. Molly had asked Lara in her next email if she was going out with Brendan but Lara had just written back to say he was there at the flat because she was having a Christmas party and he was her work colleague. But then a few weeks later Molly had rung again to say a quick hello and Brendan had answered again. She'd emailed Lara straightaway. Are you sure there's nothing going on with you and Brendan?

Lara had emailed her back the next day to ask her, very nicely, to mind her own business.

She'd emailed back quickly. But if he's going to be my uncle I should know.

Lara hadn't answered that one. Molly knew that was Lara's definite way of saying mind your own business.

Still, she had another new uncle to be going on with. Molly had tried to explain to her friends at school that Patrick used to be really famous but none of them had ever watched *Willoughby*. It was on at the same time as the Top 10 music videos show on another channel. Molly had watched one episode when Harriet first came back and told them all, just straight out, that something had happened between her and Patrick and she wanted them to hear it from her, not from anyone else who had been on the tour. Molly had found it hard not to laugh at the look on her mum and dad's faces.

Patrick had come to visit a few weeks after that and everyone had really liked him. She'd heard her mum talking about him to her dad. She'd been going on about how good-looking he was, until her dad had said yes, he had eyes, she didn't have to rub it in. And her mum had said, but he's not my type, you're my type. And they had actually kissed each other. Her parents! It was revolting.

Her mum was right, though. Patrick was old, sure, but he was good-looking. Molly had actually enjoyed *Willoughby* too. It was a bit old-fashioned and she thought it looked like the actors were having trouble trying not to laugh, but she thought Cornwall looked beautiful, with all the cliffs and the little harbour towns. She and Harriet had sat in the living room watching it together, a week before Patrick's first visit. Mrs Lamerton had returned the videos that day and Molly had asked if she could take a look.

'If he's going to be my new uncle, I'd better be able to recognise him, don't you think?'

Harriet had just laughed at her. They had watched from the very first episode, a dog and some cliffs, Patrick turning up in a small car, barely unpacking before he started solving crimes. Molly had paused the action so she could have a good look at him.

'Does he still look like that now?'

'No, he's old with white hair.'

'Really?'

'No, Moll, I'm joking. He still looks just like that.'

He did, too. He was pretty yummy for an old guy. And he was mad about Harriet, anyone could see that. In the past eight months he'd been out to visit Harriet twice and she had spent a month in Boston. They talked on the phone all the time in between. Molly wondered how they found so much to talk about. Whatever it was, it must be funny. She always heard Harriet laughing on the phone whenever he rang. The latest bombshell was they were getting married and Harriet was going to go and live with him in Boston full-time. Harriet had come to Molly and told her, woman to woman. She'd wanted her to know that if she had been organising a big wedding, then Molly would have been her bridesmaid, but she and Patrick had decided that they didn't want a big wedding. Molly hadn't minded at all, really. They were going to get married in Merryn Bay, on the beach. Secretly. And then when they got back from their honeymoon, they were inviting everyone over to Boston for a holiday. The whole family, Gloria and Kevin too.

Molly was really looking forward to it. Not just because Boston sounded great and Harriet had said she could spend a few days working with her in Patrick's agency if she wanted, but because she figured it was the only way she was going to be able to get to know her new uncle. Each time he had come over to Australia and Merryn Bay to see Harriet, none of them had been able to get anywhere near him. They still didn't know how word got around so quickly that he was in town.

It was happening again tonight, Molly could see. If Mrs Lamerton and Miss Talbot stood any closer to poor Patrick they'd knock him to the ground. Mrs Lamerton hadn't let go of his arm since she'd come in and spotted him across the room. Miss Talbot was trying to get a word in, but she was having trouble.

Molly always had to stop herself from laughing every time she looked at Miss Talbot. She wore the funniest clothes. Tonight she was wearing a short tartan skirt she'd bought when she was in Scotland on that *Monarch of the Glen* tour. She also had a matching vest, apparently, but it was a bit warm tonight for that. Molly had heard her dad whisper something about Miss Talbot looking like an escapee from a Bay City Rollers convention, but Molly wasn't too sure what that meant. Some band from the olden days, by the sound of things.

She checked the time. Ten to eight. Her dad had said he'd start the speeches at eight. Molly heard the door open and spun around. No, false alarm. It was only Austin and Nina. She had been out to Australia on holiday a few months before and had come down to Merryn Bay with him for a few days. This was her second visit and she was staying longer this time. Molly really liked Nina. She was like a kid in an adult's body, always ready for fun.

Molly had decided to be daring. If adults could tell teenagers what to do, then she could tell adults what to do occasionally, she'd decided. She badgered Austin to give her a driving lesson – she'd got her learner's permit three days after she'd turned sixteen – and cornered him on the subject while they were driving up and down the back roads behind the town. She casually said she thought Nina was really lovely and she thought that her and Austin made a good match. To her surprise, Austin had nodded.

'I do too, Moll. But unfortunately Nina isn't quite as perceptive as you. She's playing with my emotions. Keeping me dangling.'

'Are you in love with her?'

'I think I am, yes.'

'And she's not in love with you?'

'She nearly is. But not yet. I'm still working on her.'

'Do you want me to have a word with her? As your concerned niece? Press your case?' She'd heard the phrase on an American law program the night before and decided it was very apt here.

'No thanks, Molly.'

She'd done it anyway. The night before, when Nina arrived she had just happened to say that she thought Austin was really nice and it certainly seemed that he was very keen on her. 'I think you'd only need to say the word.'

Nina had winked. 'Thanks, Molly.'

She looked over now. Yep, Austin was definitely smitten. She could see the way he looked at Nina all the time. She saw them both talking to Gloria. Gloria was all smiles, too. Molly knew she also really liked Nina. Gloria had told Molly that. It was just as well. Molly had a feeling it was very important to Austin that Gloria liked anyone he ended up with.

Her mum went past carrying a tray of drinks. She whispered, just that bit too loudly as usual, 'Molly, would you please check if Kevin needs anything?'

Whoops. Molly had forgotten she was supposed to be keeping an eye on Kevin. She went straight over to him. He was sitting on a chair at the edge of the room talking to Mr Fidock. Molly crouched beside him. 'Sorry, Kev, I should have asked you before. Do you want me to get you another drink or anything else to eat?'

'No thanks, Molly love.' He patted the chair beside him. 'Sit here for a second and tell me what it all looks like.'

She sat down, a bit amazed that he had known the chair was empty. 'It's getting really crowded. About eighty people now, I'd say, but there's still more coming in. Gloria is in the corner talking to Austin and Nina. She's been talking to heaps of people all night. She looks really happy. She's wearing a sort of blue dress, by the way. She looks very nice.' Molly liked giving Kev these reports. It made her feel like a football commentator. 'Not long now till you're off on your driving trip,' she said. 'Are you looking forward to it?'

He gave her a big smile. 'Can't wait, Miss Molly, by golly.'

Kev had become her sort of surrogate grandfather the past few months. She'd walked home with Gloria one night, helping her to carry some files back that she was going to sort through over the weekend. She'd been amazed to come in and find Kev cooking. She'd just blurted it out. 'How can you cook? You can't see anything.'

He'd explained that he still had four other senses and that he could cook simple things, as long as everything was where he could get his hands on it easily. And he said he cooked a lot with herbs because it was easy to tell from the smell how much he was using. She'd tasted the tomato casserole he was making and it was delicious. After that she hadn't been so amazed to see him doing things like gardening, even a sort of Braille jigsaw puzzle. She dropped in and out on the way back from swimming training these days, even if Gloria wasn't there. Sometimes she helped him do his cooking, or helped out in the garden, but lots of times they just talked away to each other.

Molly felt the mobile in her pocket vibrate. At last. She read the text. Am outside.

She did it as they'd discussed. She went to Harriet first and whispered. Harriet gave her a big smile then whispered something to Patrick. Molly saw Patrick smile and look pleased too. Next she went up to her dad and whispered in his ear. He looked really surprised and then gave her a big grin. 'No worries, Moll.' Then she went over to her uncle Austin. 'Are you serious?' he said. He was really happy too. He agreed to do what she asked. She saw him tell Nina. She looked surprised and then really happy as well.

Molly looked over at Harriet again and nodded, as quickly as she could so no one would see. They had hatched this up between the two of them. It had been good fun keeping it a secret from everyone. Now it was all about to be revealed.

Harriet went close to the microphone and stood there, waiting for the right moment.

Molly ran outside. There she was, leaning against her hire car just down the main street. She was smiling. Really smiling. Molly felt a big smile come over her own face.

'Hi, Mollusc.'

Molly didn't bother with hellos. She just gave Lara a great big hug. 'You're only just in time.'

'I like a dramatic ending. Are you ready for me?'

'I've been waiting for you to come home for nearly a year. Of course I'm ready.'

As Molly took her by the hand, she noticed Lara's bracelet. A really pretty one, made from opals. Molly thought it looked familiar. Then she remembered. Harriet used to have one just like it. She led Lara back towards Turner Travel. 'Wait here,' she said.

She peeked in through the door first to check it was all ready. It was. Austin and James were on either side of Gloria with their hands over her eyes. Molly gave Harriet the thumbs up. As she and

Lara came in, Harriet leaned in to the microphone and told Gloria to turn around and say hello to a special surprise guest here all the way from England.

Molly couldn't believe it. First Gloria started crying and then so did Harriet. Even her mum and dad and Austin looked like they had tears in their eyes. Molly looked up at Lara. She was crying too. What had got into everyone?

Molly didn't think it was sad. She thought it was brilliant. The whole family was together again. Now they could really have a party.

ACKNOWLEDGEMENTS

My love and thanks to my (baggage-free) families in two hemispheres – the McInerneys, Lemms, Johnsons, Gallifords and Meaneys in Australia and the Drislanes in Ireland and Germany. A special thank you to my sister Maura for her help just when I needed it.

Thank you to Angela Harman, Max and Jean Fatchen, Hugh Ponnuthurai, Aoife and Imacus Ling, Maeve O'Meara, John Allen, Jill Kirby, Danny Coholan, Karen O'Connor, Bart Meldau, Eveleen Coyle, Helen Peakin, Jean Grimes, Kristin Gill, Noelle Harrison, Melanie Scaife, Simon Lawlor, Laura Cochrane, Karen Wilson, Kylie Tyack, Ben Redden, Kathryn Black and Nicola Black. A big thank you to Col Cooley and Greg Cooley for the Mr Douglas-isms. My special thanks to Eileen in Dublin for sharing her insights and memories.

Thanks to my publishers: everyone at Penguin Australia, especially Clare Forster, Ali Watts, Anne Rogan, Cathy Larsen, Bridie Riordan, Sally Bateman and Daniel Ruffino; Imogen Taylor, Trisha Jackson, Daniel Watts and all at Pan Macmillan in the UK, and Alison Walsh, Michael Gill and the Tivoli team in Ireland. Thank you to my agents: Fiona Inglis and everyone at Curtis Brown Australia, Jonathan Lloyd and Kate Cooper at Curtis Brown in London, Christy Fletcher in New York and Anoukh Foerg in Munich.

And, once more, all my love and thanks to my husband John.

MONICA McINERNEY

The Alphabet Sisters

PAN BOOKS

A witty, wise family saga set in Ireland, London and Australia, full of warmth and humour, from the bestselling author of *A Taste for It, Upside Down Inside Out* and *Spin the Bottle*

Sisters are always there for each other . . . aren't they?

Anna, Bett and Carrie Quinlan were childhood singing stars – the Alphabet Sisters. As adults they haven't spoken in years. Not since Bett's fiancé left her for another sister . . .

Now Lola, their larger-than-life grandmother, summons them home for a birthday extravaganza and a surprise announcement. But just as the rifts begin to close, the Alphabet Sisters face a test none of them ever imagined.

An unforgettable story of three women who learn that being true to themselves means being true to each other.

Praise for Monica McInerney's bestsellers

'Sparkling . . . A long, glorious romp'
Australian Women's Weekly

'Resonates with a Maeve Binchy kind of generosity of spirit . . . Compassionate, clever and sometimes poignant'
***The Age*, Melbourne**

LOUISE HARWOOD

Lucy Blue, Where Are You?

PAN BOOKS

**A deliciously funny and utterly compelling novel
from the bestselling author of *Six Reasons to Stay a Virgin***

They were never meant to meet again . . .

Lucy Blue is not the sort of girl to pick up a stranger in a snowbound
airport and she's certainly not the sort then to leap into bed with him
in a motorway motel . . . Yet this is a strange, once-in-a-lifetime day,
and in any case nobody will know and they'll never meet again.

But actions can catch up with you and secrets have a way of being
told, and a spectacular gesture means that this time Lucy just can't
walk away.

Praise for *Six Reasons to Stay a Virgin*

'Refreshing, light-hearted and emotionally intelligent,
Six Reasons says that it's more than OK to stand apart from
the crowd and follow your heart'
The Times

LIANE MORIARTY

Three Wishes

PAN BOOKS

It happens sometimes that you accidentally star in a little public performance, your very own comedy, tragedy or melodrama

The three Kettle sisters have been accidentally starring in public performances all their lives, affecting their audiences in more ways than they'll ever know. This time, however, they give a particularly spectacular show when a raucous, champagne-soaked birthday dinner ends in a violent argument and an emergency dash to the hospital.

So who started it this time? Was it Cat: full of angry, hurt passion dating back to the 'Night of the Spaghetti'? Was it Lyn: serenely successful, at least on the outside? Or was it Gemma: quirky, dreamy and unable to keep a secret, except for the most important one of all? Whoever the culprit, their lives will have all changed dramatically before the next inevitable clash of shared genes and shared childhoods.

TARA HEAVEY

Eating Peaches

PAN BOOKS

There is nothing wild about Elena – every inch of her shiny blonde hair and tailored suit screams modern working woman. But all that is about to change, thanks to a man called Tyrone Power. He's her boss and is about to offer her the promotion she's always wanted, but there's a catch: she has to set up a new office for him in his sleepy home town of Ballyknock. City girl Elena is horrified – a full nine months in the back of beyond! Her Audi convertible will never take the wear and tear.

With her career in the doldrums and her love life with boyfriend Paul heading nowhere, will she stick it out? After all, there are compensations – the picturesque scenery, the relaxed pace of life and the local landlord's seven handsome sons . . .

ANITA DIAMANT

Good Harbor

PAN BOOKS

From the bestselling author of *The Red Tent* comes a rich and moving novel about the tragedy of loss, the insidious nature of family secrets and the redemptive power of friendship

When Kathleen meets Joyce, each has come to a turning point in her life. Kathleen, whose sister died of breast cancer fifteen years earlier, has just been diagnosed herself and finds her world abruptly thrown into terrifying turmoil. At the same time, Joyce is struggling to cope with her awkward adolescent daughter and burgeoning career as a writer, and is growing increasingly distant from her husband. Neither woman realizes that their chance meeting will result in a life-altering friendship.

With her trademark wisdom and humour, Anita Diamant explores the lives of modern women, who manage the precarious balance of marriage, career, motherhood and companionship. *Good Harbor* is at once a poignant and refreshingly honest novel.

'Immensely moving and delicately told. Anita Diamant's second novel fulfils every iota of the promise of the first . . . I was entranced by every word of it'
Daily Mail